In Dhar

*A pilgrim's Spiritual Journey
into destiny*

D Walkaboutdude Moss

Dedicated to all spirits waking from their sleep and seek that which is here, but invisible. May they have the courage to see themselves in this grand play called Life and dance to their own music without fear.

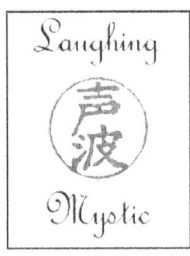

Published by Laughing Mystic
50 SE Hillcrest St
Madras, OR 97741 USA
laughingmsytic@outlook.com

I would like to hear from readers. Please contact me at:
laughingmsytic@outlook.com

The Purge.

When it began the Beast spoke a cautious whisper buried beneath the glitter of media.

We ignored it.

The Beast spoke a little louder but is was an insignificant voice of reason.

We ignored again.

The Beast then shouted and the people closest heard it.

But we still chose to ignore it.

But when the Beast awoke in his desert glass tower and roared like a gale then the entire world could no longer ignore it.

Heralding his intent for all to hear the angry and vengeful Beast spread across humanity like a firestorm, devouring everything with its fiery eyes, gnashing teeth and hunger. Its appetite did not cease until last humanity's wail faded and it consumed everything.

The Beast took everything, our past, present and our future, leaving only crumbling moments to our collective madness.

From the heavens the sun shone upon our silent, ashen world once green with songs of Life.

Eventually we woke from this nightmare. For the first we time saw what our world had become and remembered who we are and understood our rebirth.

A woman came from the East. She was the Taleju Mother and following her she took to the mountain. Stretching froth our arms we pledged the Beast will never walk among us again.

We are the Children of the Purge, the survivors of our ancestor's folly . . .and Humanity's hope.

Kathmandu, Nepal Commonwealth

The Three Thousand Four hundred and Ninety Second Kumari paused on steep steps leading to the red and yellow temple in the twisted pines above. She leaned against a stone rail and unceremoniously hiked up her long, blue and white skirt hiding her silk, saffron colored trousers. Undoing a green sash securing the cloth blue and gold boot to her slender ankle she removed and shook it. A small pebble fell out, bounced on the worn steps and continued its journey down the steep path to the village below.

"My big toe's going to feel that for a week," she grumbled, resuming her climb.

At the temple, sandalwood smoke curled from large, ornate bronze burners. Bells and flags fluttered on the cold wind. Excited voices danced on the air, reminding her that her audience waited since dawn to for her to formally announce the commencement of the Conformation 1262CE Pilgrimage.

Nearing the top, she turned and followed a narrow path to a moon gate. There, a servant bowed as she entered an empty courtyard. She eyed the strands of prayer flags and thangka hanging in neat rows in tall windows. She instantly recognized the Kumari Mother, Taleju, but drew a blank when she tried to recall the names of the Kumarisattvas who preceded her. She was alive and they were not, so to her it didn't matter.

She rested her gaze on the one who mattered most: herself. She paused beneath it, head craned up, eyes intent. The artist portrayed her sitting serenely cross-legged on the slain Purge Beast with its bulging, red eyes and fangs. A solar eclipse, representing Rebirth was behind her. In her right hand she held Taleju's eight pointed star and in her left a mirror with flames. She wore the same clothing she spent twenty years hiking up and down this mountain to speak to her followers.

Well, at least the artist did not update her image by adding white streaked hair and a head scar she acquired several years ago when she tumbled down the steps in a fit of bravado.

You look so young, Ku," she muttered lightly, covering the final steps into the building. As she headed down the narrow, green hall her generally delicate footsteps fell loudly on the ancient wood floor, reminding her of a cow. A servant standing in front of a door opened it and she quickly entered the preparation chamber. She flopped into the wood chair while people in yellow and red tunics descended upon her. She waited patiently as they applied red and yellow paint to her forehead and created a flaming crescent moon. A jewel was attached between her brows then her eyes were outlined in heavy kohl. She held a mirror and commented her eyes were hard to see. The liner was replaced with a lighter shade, this time accenting her black eyes. Then the red and gold ornate crown with ornate flames presenting Taleju's Eight Flames of Life was secured to her thick, black hair with a silver pin. She puckered her lips, smiled and sets the mirror down.

Sometimes I feel like I'm a performer on a stage," she remarked to herself more than her staff. "Is the audience ready?"

"The Satori Council asks to see you before, Kumarisattva."

She rolled her eyes impatiently and uttered a deep sigh. "Very well, send them in."

She hated waiting. It seemed like she spent half her life like a stage hand waiting for the play to start or end. She fidgeted and coughed in the heavily scented room. She wrinkled her nose. The sandalwood was particularly irritating today. They must have gotten a bad batch.

Taking a silver scepter with the eight pointed star at the end she tossed it up and down as though she was at a carnival game. The assistant watched in dismay.

"Does our Kumari Mother teach that a light heart is the dance of life?" the Kumarisattva stated with a tinge of humor.

The girl quickly recovered and smiled, "Yes, Kumarisattva."

Two men in green and black robes entered. The Kumari stopped her activity and waved away her attendants.

"You both look like you just been bucked off a disgruntle water buffalo," she commented.

The man with the white sash bowed. "Apologies, Kumarisattva. The child did not pass the test. "

She raised a brow. "Well, that's fifty four candidates. Seem our search for my Spiritual Successor is slim this season."

She surveyed the chamber with its ancient wood shelves, thangkas and lamps. She shuddered. She never liked this windowless room with its musty smells and gloomy memories spending too many days cooped up during her childhood. "I think it's time we get windows in here. Maybe that will change our luck."

The two men exchanged curious glances.

"The Conformation begins in three months; our brave travelers expect my replacement. I hope we don't disappoint them again."

"And if not, Kumarisattva?"

The Kumari offered a weak smile. "Then this old Sattva gets older."

She waved them away. Sighing she took the scepter and mirror, pulled herself from the chair and paused by a simple, wood door. She glanced at the large thangka of the Kumari Mother above the door. Taking calming, deep breaths an attendant slid it back and the Kumari stepped into the white and green hall and the waiting crowd bathed in steely sunlight.

Kumargi Mandala

Part One: The Seeker

Kumargi flag

Contents

Italia Commonwealth

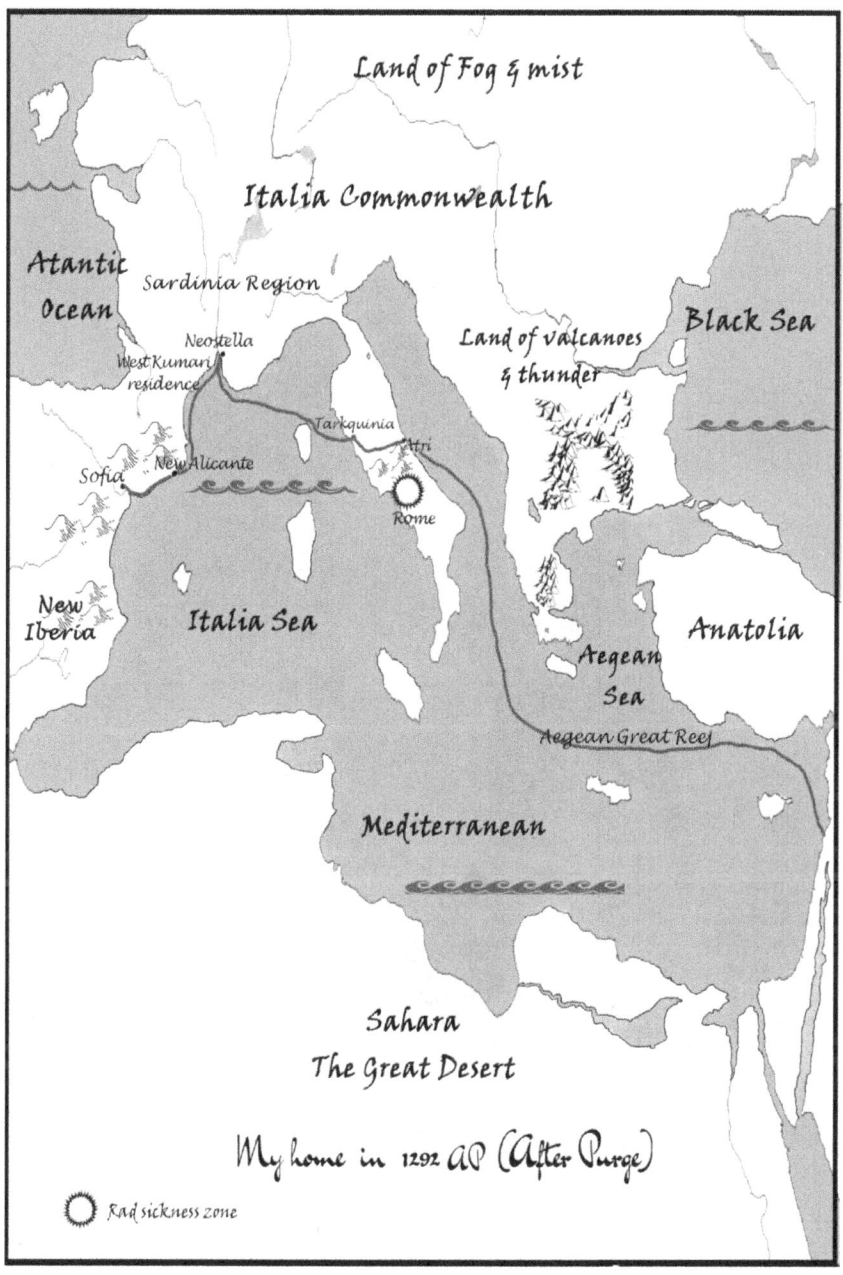

Land of Fog & mist

Italia Commonwealth

Atantic Ocean

Sardinia Region

Black Sea

Neostella

West Kumari residence

Land of valcanoes & thunder

Sofia

New Alicante

Tarkquinia

Atri

Rome

New Iberia

Italia Sea

Anatolia

Aegean Sea

Aegean Great Reef

Mediterranean

Sahara
The Great Desert

My home in 1292 AP (After Purge)

⊙ Rad sickness zone

The Kumari Mother Taleju

The Calling

She sat on a weathered bench and gazed at the quiet courtyard, watching shadows and light move across the ground, creating abstract patterns. It seemed just was just a few moments ago when her family laughed and played games, dreaming of a better future.

Now she was alone. She shivered as a cold breeze blew though her soul. She stirred from thoughts and wiped tears. She could not recall when the last time her eyes were dry.

She wandered into the darkened house and went a quiet room. Her eyes fell upon the small bed, dresser and a wilted flower in a ceramic pot atop bathed in sunlight streaming in from the window. The once, happy bright orange and purple walls now appeared old and neglected. Knelt, she reached for a painted with animals and flowers wood chest. She smiled. Her daughter decorated it a year ago because she complied it was too bland. Bishma loved colors. Undoing the brass latch she raised the lid. She bit her lip, seeing the carefully child's clothing. She swallowed. Mustering courage she rummaged until locating a leather bound book and a small bag.

She went to a desk by the windows, sat and opened the blank pages. She removed an ink bottle and pen and stared at the empty page.

A blue and red bird fluttered onto the window sill and watched her. She reflected on her family and the sudden loneness laying on her heart.

She sighed heavily and made her first entry.

Spring 1262 AP (After Purge) Month 9, day 12. Sofia, Italia Commonwealth.

I, Noora Al Monte, take pen to paper to begin this diary as promised to you, Ali my husband, upon your death two days ago. You insisted it would help me understand the many questions I have about our lives and eventually discover the reason for my persistent emptiness.

But, I confess I am skeptical. I barely have strength to place word to paper due to the depression hanging over me. My gloomy world consists of just sitting alone and watching the sun journey across our olive groves casting long, purple shadows. Perhaps I'm searching for meaning to all this or the will to continue.

I don't know if I have the determination. . . .This is my first sunset alone in more than 12 years. Not having you and Bishma to share our favorite time watching the sunset leave me empty and afraid.

Oh, Ali! Why this? We both hardly got over the loss of our Bishma when illness took you. Was it because your heart was broken, and you could not bear being separated from our daughter?

I pause, hesitate in words. I watch the sky paint rich gold and grays and the birds cease their daytime melodies. The humid air is still as our world holds its breath before taking another breath heralding the evening. Oh! This sorrow wraps me like a heavy blanket.

Then, I recall your smile and laughter and it warms my heart. Slowly, painfully, I put to my thoughts to paper. Perhaps it will be easier later, but for now it takes all my courage to cover these blank pages with my thoughts.

We received word that the 1262 Confirmation was officially announced by the Western Kumari residence. If selected, I pledge to keep a journal of my activities you so and Bishma will share these. I suppose I better have find courage to write about interest things instead wallowing in my gloom, otherwise this will be a very bore read!

I confess I feel awkward sharing my thoughts—even if it's just paper!

Day 13. Dear Ali. The air tonight is sweet. The night blooming jasmine you planted under the pear tree awakens with the stars.I can't sleep in this bed we shared and wander the house in the half light. I see you and Bishma in the shadows, and at times I reach for you but my hands my grasp empty air. These memories are vivid and hurt when I realize what they are.

How quickly our lives have turned into memories. One moment you and Bishma are solid beings interacting with me but the next instant they are but quiet, indifferent shadows void of life except for what I recall.

You said once this is all life is a collection of memories and thoughts. Therefore, do we only life in the past and our experiences comprise our reality, or is there more?

Day 14. Today was a blur as I moved though my life centered on our home and lost purpose. Without you there is no propose in my life.

Sometimes I feel I'm just sleepwalking through this dream called Life, numb to my surroundings and unaware of the resonance echoing from my past. I go about my task in mute resignation of what I am, guided by what is expected of me. Are we therefore just spirits imprisoned by our own expectations?

I can't help but sense undercurrents in my life. There, just below conscious thoughts moving independently of my surface world, like a river with many currents, but the surface looking calm and inviting.

I joined the village and performed the community Dedicational ceremony for the first time since your death. It felt awkward leaving our house and many wished me well. I spoke to our Alimajh about impressions or images just beyond thoughts, hovering like birds but every time I look, they are gone. They are strange faces, people with strange clothing. They are disturbing yet familiar. They started this morning when I meditated on Taleju's mandala.

He said they could be from into past life memories triggered by my traumatic event. I am frightened, I am afraid where they may take me.

Day 15. A restless haunts my spirit. It followed wherever I've gone. I've walked to the river four kilometers from here, hoping I left behind this feeling but it was in vain. Is because I'm alone? No, I concluded it's because I sense something in my future.

I spent this afternoon medicating on the Kumari's Mandala, seeking answers in the designs, but it left me empty.

You remember I complained it lacked something which bothered me, like it is incomplete and left me outside. When it magnified those impressions, I got frightened and quit after about twenty minutes.

Day 16. Today I placed your stone marker under the pear tree beside Bishma. You would love this, Ali. The mason did a wonderful job carving the Flower of Life and your Spirit Note on the blue and white marble. Now, anyone will know that my precious Ali and Bishma watch from the shade.

Kneeling, I gazed at our small yard and the stone fence we struggled to build during that hot dry summer to keep wandering animals out. My eyes lingered on our olive orchards and grape orchard harmoniously creating green patches in straw colored fields and purple shadows. Sadly, these were wilted because of years of drought. To the white horizon the undulating hills of purple and cream watercolors become lost in afternoon haze. I recalled your desire wanting to see where the hills end. Today I noticed how sad and weary our once vibrant world has become. Oh, and our stone house! How empty and depressing it is without you! Even Bishma's gold and purple bedroom brought to me tears. The blue sky and cloud painted on our living room ceiling no longer beckoned me to dream of happy life. I am wrapped in heartaches and your memories filled me with emptiness. I wandered aimlessly or sat beneath a sun drenched window, staring at the passing hours. I'm like an uncompleted puzzle searching for missing pieces. Sometimes I looked up and I caught my breath in expectation when I thought I heard you or Bishma calling me, only realize I am alone. I am deceived by my memories.

Day 18. This morning I found a dead robin beneath the fig tree. After burying it, I noticed branches rubbed off the walls' green and white stucco. It made our house look old and tired---like me. With the Spring Equinox a week away, I will try to repair it for our festival.

In the early morning I was disturbed by a vision and sat beneath solar lamp at the kitchen table. My heart raced, breathing fast because I could not calm down. My mind struggled to grasp a dream about you and Bishma. How shall I begin?

I walked on a beach. It was hot and sweat soaked my clothes and the glaring white sky burned my skin. I felt emptiness greater than The Great Desert permeated everything. These ocean waves were not blue but sickly brown and with each ebb and flow deposited garbage and black fluid around my bare feet. Pungent decay filled every breath of sticky, humid and salty air. To my left I noticed twisted steel rise like bones of a decaying, colossal beast. They stretched to the horizon. A profound sense of loss gripped me, a pain so immense it stretched back through time, drowning my personal loss in a sea of many losses. From the shadows I felt ghostly angry and grief faces watched me.

I ran up a dune, my feet slid back with each step as sand grabbed my feet. I struggled, desperate to reach the top and when I reached the summit I screamed.

I was high above the ground, looking at buildings so massive they blocked out the sun and sky. Black roads crisscross into confusing pattern. Steel objects moved upon these roads and they stretched in every direction like the vastness of the sea. Everywhere was people, crowding in shadows, in buildings and roads. The gritty air smelt of choking fires. The constant noise was horrible, confusing and frightened me. My head spun dizzily, my heart pounded with such force I thought it would burst from my breasts!

I can't take my eyes away from this place. Dread and apprehension paralyzed me. But why did it seemed familiar?

Then I tumbled into blackness. I screamed.

I woke back in my bed, covered in sweat. Vainly I reached for your comfort. What did this mean? Is this strange place from the Purge?

I dared not return to sleep for fear of returning to that horrible place.

My gloom was only dispelled by a nightingale's song. Dawn is coming.

Day 20. Ali. Today is the Spring Equinox and beginning of the Conformation. I can't believe you took your last breath in my arms a week ago. Under much fanfare we villagers gathered at the central market to receive the Kumari's representative. I confess I almost did not attend, for so depressed but was compelled to do so. I wore that outfit I bought when we visited New Iberia during our honeymoon. You remember? You were transfixed all day when I stepped out of the souk in this red and yellow and punjab outfit and boots and that black sash with silver specks. You stumbled on the cobblestone because you were so distraction by me, remember? I can still the sash wrap it three times around my waist and leave plenty of room for it to dangle. I found that yellow and blue kufi Bishma gave me and secured it to my long hair with mom's silver pin. Oh I wished you are here to see me!

In the afternoon we gathered beneath the Kumari flags. I've never seen one before. They had a gold background with red emblem of the crescent solar eclipse and an eight pointed star. I was surprised to see our Kumari representative was our old friend Joseppi. You remember him. He was our childhood neighbor who moved to New Iberia shortly after we married. Oh, how he's lost weight and his boyish face sprouted a beard! He even had the blue tika between his brows showing completion the Confirmation pilgrimage as a Mokti. He looks so regal in his red and gold robes.

When he completed his pilgrimage he earned this title, meaning Enlightened One. Beneath the banners he spoke about having followed Taleju's religion as Kumargi and it is our duty to have courage to go beyond just a devotee and prove ourselves by performing the Puja or 'Those who seek Taleju's Divinity.'

This call is to dedication and commitment.

Then he read the village roster, which was very outdated. It was sad listening to those families who were no longer and when you, Ali and Bishma were called out I felt a wave of sadness. I looked so forward to this moment but, without you and Bishma sharing this honor it seemed hollow and, honestly, trivial. Of the twelve on the list I was the only attendee.

At first I completely put the pilgrimage out of my mind, preferring to remain here on my beloved Sofia with memories and safe surroundings. But Joseppi sensed my apprehension and later when we talked he understood my reluctance. He told about his challenges and rewards, his doubt and convictions and the difficult journey. His pilgrimage took over a year and it changed him forever; likewise only about twenty percent survive. He said it would change me too in ways I never imaged and the person who began the trip would not be the same who finished.

Afterwards I pondered my present situation and the ghosts I've carried in my heart for long. You remembered my older sister, Aisha, died on the pilgrimage when I was nine. It so affected my parents they turned away from Taleju and insisted I could not perform the pilgrimage because I was different. Was it their fear or the fact I was not like the others? Since then I've wondered about my sister's fate and lived with my parent's guilt my whole life.

Despite my trepidation you know I've wanted this opportunity since childhood. You promised we would perform the Puja as a family. It was my greatest wish we all could make the pilgrimage together.

However. . .

Ali, I feel there is some greater need waiting on the journey, some unfinished business I must settle going far beyond the everyday task of the Puja.

After careful thinking and my role as a Kumargi I accepted Joseppi's invitation. But we will retrace The Awakenings path together! I will carry small, perfume bottles of your ashes. I have sewn small pockets in some waist belts and therefore we each will see the Nepal Commonwealth and Kumarisattva!

Day 21. Having made the decision to participate I feel great weight is lifted. As if fate agreed, for the first time in many years I witnessed brilliant colors and heard wonderful melodies at sunrise. I should have happy, but am not. My greatest fear rises from my heart, prompting dread.

What if they discover I am a Seer? I know it doesn't matter to you, but in our world it does. Normals fear Seers more than Djinn and we both know tales about Seer stealing children and eating them. Ridiculous! But many believe this. Remember the village in the Sardinia Region who found out they had Seers in their midst? They killed the family, including their new born and burned their house even though were renowned healers! It is my reality I hide by living as someone else, a self imposed lie. But no matter how much I desire to be a Normal it will not alter who I am. Taleju cautioned it is bad to live as others expect rather than being true to one self.

Sigh.

Ali, I long for peace in my heart. To live as whom I am, in the full sun, not hiding. Maybe this pilgrimage will, perhaps, gave me peace at last.

Enough rambling. I just had to get this off my chest.

I will include important passage from `Awakenings' in my journal not only to compare my pilgrimage with Taleju's but how our world changed since the twelve centuries since her adventures.

I will start by reciting the meaning of Taleju's eight sided star.

The Eight essentials of Life
Spirituality without religion.
Awareness without faith.
Knowing without believing.
Permeate without form.
Liberation without Penance.
Oneness as Many.
Impermanence is Permanence
Dharma as One

Day 22.   Today, Joseppi and six Kumargi s acting as his assistants led our small group for the coast.   There was excitement as we realized with was our first step as pilgrims. Including me, there were fifteen pilgrims from other villages. In keeping with the pious tradition we left before sunrise with no fanfare or goodbyes.   I managed to paint the wall and willed the house to our villages if I do not return after five years.   I felt sad leaving memories and all that I have ever known.   Oh, how our home looked so lonely when I passed it! Soon, Sofia disappeared behind the orchards.   Even though I looked to the road ahead, my heart returned to our home. Shall I ever see Sofia again?

Day 23. I am exhausted from our work today. Joseppi led us in guided mediation of the Mandala after reading and discussing the introduction of the Awakenings. I record this passage why Taleju went on her journey which we Kumargi pilgrimage are following. On The Awakenings first page is this introduction.

The Awakenings is the journal of our Kumari Mother, Taleju during her second journey to the Western Ocean.   When she left Kathmandu she was 35 (135AP) she and her followers left Nepal on her second epic quest. It was on this trip she recorded what she saw and her spiritual teachings.   By the time she reached

Italy, she had more than five hundred followers. During the journey she contracted sickness and was plagued by bad health. Finally when she was 43 (143AP) exhaustion claimed her. She died peacefully on a meadow surrounded by her devotees. Since then her words and compassion has been inspiration for those seeking spiritual guidance in this post Purge era. Within these pages is the tool for enlightenment. May you walk in the Light Taleju gave the Children of the Purge.

I was born Shakya Tian Nawari in a village outside Kathmandu one hundred years after the Purge and was chosen at age six as the next Kumari goddess. I took up residency at the Kumari Ghar, or House until age 12 and represented the goddess for devotees and those seeking my blessings. I did not like Kathmandu because everywhere was starving, disease and dirty. I was told the hills of Kathmandu were once green and the great peaks were covered year round with snow before the Purge. Now valley was brown like a desert and the peaks, once Nepal's pride, were piles of barren rocks. The river once was rich with life and water; now only its brown shadow trickled through our city. Sometimes I got ill when the Black Monsoons brought gray, acrid cloud for days at a time.

The Purge happened a century ago. When the Purge came we did not understand its meaning or how it affected us. Kathmandu was remote from the Nation States. However, its effect reached us. Landslides, floods and fires rained upon us; destroying buildings, roads and forests. A great fire brought darkness from which the sun did not shine during the Time of Cloud and Darkness, lasting ten years. Our green hills turned brown and most life died: the insects, birds, animals and us. The water was poisoned; great heaps of dust carried on the wind, bringing sickness to outlying areas. Then the lack of food followed. The Kathmandu valley was crowded with millions of souls and most perished. So many died survivors were unable to perform traditional sky bury or cremate them. Survivors were forced to move into the country to avoid the horrible disease and petulance.

Those who remained in Kathmandu hovered between life and death. Water and food were lean. I wanted to go home but I was kept in the Ghar for my safety and to give our people inspiration. I hovered many times on the verge of death, stricken down by malnourishment and sickness. Yet, the faithful came daily and sought my guidance and blessings in this insane world. I lived in isolation with my father and sister, the only surviving of my family. I experienced firsthand grief and hopelessness. I was afraid, but did not show it because my devotees, caretakers and family expected me to be strong, even if I was not.

Per the Kumari creed, when I reached puberty my role ended. We escaped the disease and misery by leaving Kathmandu and returned to my home in Bhaktapur. But even here all we knew was desolation and famine. My sister died when I was 17, my father a year later. Yet, the Kumari people, desperate for guidance continued to visit me. I was still considered the Kumari's representative even though I was a teenager. The faithful believed the living Goddess adapted to these changing times and found others Kumari. They brought food and offerings which was the only way I survived.

All these desperate people, their confusion, anger and questioned why we were victims of the Purge. They turned to me for answers. Their questions became mine and I resolved to travel beyond our mountains. Thus armed with news from the travelers, an old map, compass and my determination I set out west when I was 19.

I returned to Nepal on my 32th birthday; wiser, seeing the larger picture of what happened. I understood our spiritual connectedness and what went wrong. Kathmandu was recovering because the Black Monsoons stopped reaching here. Survivors came to consult with me. I stayed two years then my group of fifty followers left to share `The Awakenings' with other children of the Purge.

Here is the record of my journey. May future generations see what I encountered on this extraordinary trek into our past, present and future. ----Taleju-

Ali and Bishma I'll keep you in my thoughts and heart. Good night.

Day 24. Since leaving home I not felt well; nausea and fatigue plagued me for kilometers on these dusty roads beneath the hot, humid sun. We carried our individual packs while Joseppi's attendants handled our pack animals and set up camp. The afternoon heat was exceptionally bad; we huddled beneath sledge hats, covered our hands, eyes and faces and walked in shade to avoid exposure. We all wished for the relief of spring rains. I cannot recall a time when the threat of exposure was this bad. This weather was more like midsummer. This heat sapped my energy, making it difficult to concentrate or eat. Sometimes I needed help getting up in the predawn light because I was stiff and painful.

I was shocked how our world had deteriorating since our declining birth rate and this prolonged drought. When I travelled this route as a child it was busy with traffic and settlements. I even recalled picking oranges from trees next to the road, slept on the open, or at times danced in the sun when I got bored. Now we only met a few destitute people and stray dogs looking for food. We passed deserted villages and dying orchards being crowded out by oaks forests as nature slowly erase our presence. In a few years not a trace of us will remain. Even though we lost over fifty percent Sofia's inhabitants, Joseppi said we were but a handful of villages still in existence.

I thought about stories about life before the Purge and how the afternoon sun was not so brutal. People did not fear it but traveled in short sleeve shirts and pants and even partake a popular ritual called `sun bathing' to darkening their skin! Considering our present situation I find this hard to believe. The flagstone road were worn and broken in places, making walking difficult. Once I sprained my ankle and painfully hobbled until we rested. In places scrub grass covered much of the trail and afflicted us with spiky, dried burrs leaving painful welts under pant and socks. We stopped several times to and remove these. In the evening my legs suffered burning pain. Luckily Joseppi brought herbal suave which helped.

Since leaving Sofia Joseppi appointed each us as Alimajh, the duty of leading the Dedicational. He explained it would help us appreciate our pilgrimage. When it came to my turn I was so nervous and self conscious I stammered and could not complete the passages! He saw my embarrassment and intervened, sparing further anxiety. I hate interacting with the pilgrims in this role! I hope I do not have to do this again.

Day 27. I was so sad by what greeted us when reaching the coast. Remember that spring ten years ago when we visited my cousin who lived in a sea side village? Those white quaint houses, the manicured nut and fruit orchards, and their colorful boats had vanished. The sea level had risen and submerged abandoned dwellings. The salt water has bleached their once colorful walls and covered them with gray barnacles. The salt leached into the soil and killed trees along the shore. Boats rotted along the shore. This was very depressing.

Families either left or made another settlement on higher ground. The villagers look sickly. I was told my cousin left for New Iberia. Joseppi came to our villages by the land route further west and was not aware of the change. He was shocked. He could not hide his dismay when first seeing the coast. The last time he visited this area was when he was eight.

We walked another ten kilometers and reached Rossu-Santese and slept in a deserted villa overlooking the empty settlement.   Like most villages we passed, it was submerged. That night I could not sleep because I was filled with memories of our honeymoon, the colorful boat rides, the laughter, the singing and brightly dressed villagers who treated us as royalty. It was a magic time and for a moment I was back there. This new world superimposed over memories filled me with loss and despair. Oh, how my heart ached with sadness and loss. So many changes, so many years passed and look what our world has become. I will be glad to leave this place and just remember our good times, Ali.

Day 30.   For three days we followed the coast, passing more submerged villages. At some places our trail vanished beneath the sea. We were forced to take alternate paths which slowed progress. We hoped to get to New Alicante yesterday but had to settle for camping in the trees and watched the sunset over the ocean.

Day 31. Today my first leg of my trip from Sofia to the coast concluded when this morning our exhausted party reached New Alicante.

New Alicante was crowded with pilgrims waiting to continue to Neostella. I met devotees from New Iberia, Catalonia Region and the coast of the Great Sahara desert. This is a modest, coastal village of neat orchards and red brick buildings huddled around docks crowded with sailing ships.

Here we encountered music, dance and busy souk which reinvigorated our interest. New Alicante was crowded with merchants, travelers and pilgrims from across the Mediterranean region: in far off Iberia, North Italian Commonwealth, Anatolia, the Levant and the Sahara desert.   The visitors told of similar changes to their environments; the ocean levels were rising and babies not being born.

I spent the remaining day resting my aching feet beneath the shade of a huge fig tree and studied the map Joseppi gave me. At first I was overwhelmed by the depth of our pilgrimage and seemed far more taxing than I thought.   I imagined myself standing before a towering mountain, gazing up vainly to see the summit hidden in the clouds. Ahead the path was strewn with house size boulders and I heard you encouraging me by saying it is not as big as it looks, Noora.

Yet, my heart still faltered.

In retracing Taleju's journey we will visit lands seemingly from our worst nightmares. Names like: Holy Seer's Cauldron, Land of Volcanoes and Thunder, Realm of Glass, Fields of Black

Pools, Ghost March and Gray Skies painted vivid images of blight and desolation. We will start from the Italia Commonwealth and make our way across the sea to Syria, Arabia, the Persian Emirates, Hindustan Corridor and finally home of our Kumari Mother, Nepal Commonwealth. Joseppi explained it was like taking a physical journey through Taleju's Mandala.

In the comfort of our home I found the courage to take this journey. But now, away from Sofia, I am plagued by doubt since I face my dream directly. But now I am here and the responsibilities weigh upon me and question my ability to make the pilgrimage.

Sigh. . .

The night settled upon this village long ago. The singers with their drums, flutes, zithers serenaded us at sunset have retired. The village is quiet. The moon is halfway across the sky. I am alone with my thoughts.

Good night, beloved husband. Tomorrow we sail for Italia.

###

I woke four hours after my last entry. The village was still wrapped in sleepy darkness. The moon peeked through the trees on distant hills, casting its pale light and featureless shadows. I sat outside with solar light beneath a tree so not disturb the other pilgrims.

I had a most profound and frightening dream---or was it a vision? I returned to my room and fell asleep after reading about The Purge. The room dissolved in a dark chamber and I was sitting at a table illuminated by a fireplace. I shuffled large cards and placed them in front of me. The cards were color like rainbows superimposed over a circular design in the middle. Within this intricate circle, cursive script spiraled out forming Taleju's Twenty One Spiritual Precepts. As I turned it over I heard a flute echoes a haunting melody, making my heart ache. A faint, blurry image came into focus and I fell towards an ocean sparkling in midday sunlight.

I was a pair of eyes far above a black road snaking along a waterfront. Upon this moved hundreds of metal carriages. On one side were tall structures, their vastness so great they reminded me of canyons which blocked out the sun. This place was very noisy from millions of mechanical, angry shouts and a sea of people moving with chaotic, frightful pace. On the far horizon hundreds of those immense structures obscured the hazy distance. Metal ships larger than our village moved upon the ocean without sail or oars.

Then the scene shifted and I watched a woman riding in one of these metal carriages. She sat in the back, the windows were dark and in the front seat a man moved a circular wheel. The woman was in strange clothes—like those painted on the Caves of Marceilla from the Purge time—long pants, shirt and a tight fitting jacket. She held a small card to her ear and talked into it. She was young, blonde, and very upset. As she spoke she shifted the card to her other ear and nervously glanced at the man at the front.

I understand her strange language, and the voice coming from the card.

She angrily spoke into the card she called David. He replied in a mechanical voice.

Marty and Sheikh Neyhan were killed by a bomb at the palace during their meeting. The radicals claimed the responsibility and threatened civil war unless the loan was immediate terminated.

Until then she was assured the loan was approved because she thought Senator Hayden's covert operators were supportive of their long range goal. Now it seemed his radical team had other ideas. She instructed Marty to speak with Senator Hayden. Meanwhile she will contact her business associate, Curtis and she would fly to Dubai once things were settled with the Senator. She stopped talking and stared out the window at those big buildings covering her in long shadows. She felt her efforts slipping away and losing her job and commission. She quickly pressed on the box and in a shaky voice reported to a Mr. Blofeld the situation.

She was instructed to set up a meeting with Hayden.

Then she shook her head and whispered about two frustrated years wasted on ungrateful Rag heads, oil, money and their backward nation.

The dream vanished, leaving me sick with dread. Somewhere it sparked deep fear. I do not know what this means. But, what disturbed me most about this vision was the table card I selected. On the back was written: *The goal of incarnation is to neutralize past events that negatively affect other spirits.*

Ali, I wish you were here to share this and comfort my heart. I am truly frightened by this dream. It had an underlying terror greater than anything I faced.

Sigh.

The rooster announces the peaceful day. The morning air is heavy with pungent salt, sweet roses and baked bread. Golden light and deep purple shadows cast abstract patterns on brightly painted shutters. I sense peace here, yet I am possessed by gloom.

Time I prepare myself for boarding the ship to Italia. When arrive I will ask the Kumari Daughter about my dream.

Month 10, day 1, Italia Commonwealth. Joseppi and his Kumargi s were at the docks where they said good bye and draped us with vermillion colored silk scarves. It was a sad but joyous occasion. This truly marked the beginning of the long journey to Nepal. Bishma, you would love it here! You always wanted to take a trip on the ocean. I think of you now as I looked out across the waves sparkling like rows of diamonds glittering under the midday sun. Cool, salty breeze blew through my hair and brought relief from the heat as we sailed further from the coast. There were about fifty of us from New Alicante. Our things were stored below deck in places called `holds' and given blankets, pillows and rugs to either sleep below or here on the open deck. I found a nice spot near pilothouse. The captain's berth was underneath the quarter deck astern and in morning he climbed narrow steps to a pilothouse. Several times a day he took measurements of the sun by holding a brass disc and turning dials. His helper scribbled data in a book.

I and others lounged beneath an awning while crew in white baggy pants and long sleeve tunic, their faces and hands darkened by the sun, navigated the maze of ropes and tended billowy purple sails. At first the ship's pitch and bob made me queasy, but after herbal tea I felt fine. Meals were served below deck and consisted of flat bread, olives, cheese, pears and tea. It's bland. I missed the spices, but can't complain.

I spent time listening to others, engaged in idle chat or at quiet time read Taleju's Awakenings. Since that dream I ponder the Purge, hoping to understand this horrible event which changed our world. Even now when I close my eyes I envision what Taleju's wrote: great, black fires consuming everything, the years of smoke blocking out the sky, the disease, the water wars, the utter desolation and darkness that was everyday life until Taleju brought The Awakenings. I am proud to be on this pilgrimage.

I have strived to recite important passages and even tested it on other pilgrims when discussing certain entries by recalling text flawlessly. The pilgrims are impressed as you would be proud of me, Bishma. You used to smile when Ali and I had difficulty reciting passages that you remembered so easily. I suppose my determination to have deeper understandings is because of this pilgrimage. I promise I will commit to memorize the entire The Awakenings and, who knows, maybe I will best your recital! That will be a real accomplishment, right?

Day 2. Second day out. Wow. With moon light waltzing on the water, stars twinkling and green lanterns' glows these were sights from a wonderful dream! I was glad to be above deck enjoying this—even with the occasional, salty spray. The cool air was not uncomfortable huddled in my blanket. When the sun set passengers brought out musical instruments and serenaded us with flute, drum, chimes, singing bowls, mandolins and zithers. The crew paused in their buy schedule and enjoyed our singings and occasionally requested songs. A man, his wife and their teenage son are particularly talented; they are storyteller and musicians of some fame in their home, Anatolia.

We should be at our destination tomorrow.

Day 3. Neostella, Sardina. This afternoon we came to Neostella. This is the where the Conformation pilgrims begins. Devote followers from all the world converge on this spot to begin their arduous journal to Nepal.

As a child our family visited here on business because many our caravans started and ended here. I remembered being enthralled by the city's activities and the great, imposing Kumari residents upon the hill. My dad took me there just once when I was about five, but I marveled by the temples and gardens. And now I am returning!

Neostella is one of the first cities after the Purge. Chosen for its gentle sloping hills and protected inlet it was originally built fifty feet above the beach in anticipation of the rising oceans. Additionally, the people developed ways to grow fruit trees in hill caves, thereby saving tree species from extinction during the Time of Cloud and Darkness. Now, the hills are covered with healthy orchards thanks to a network of underground irrigation systems and date palms sheltering the groves. Neostella is the travel and trade hub throughout the Mediterranean world because it escaped the poisons of the Atlantic coast. Trade stretches from the Fog and Misty Lands to the Greater Sahara Desert. As we approached, I saw colorful stucco buildings nestled among massive trees. From a nearby hill the West Kumari Daughter's House overlooked the city. Purple and white prayer flags slowly waved in the breeze and shimmering wind chimes beckoned us. Yet, like all cities near the water the ocean claimed old Neostella and left dangerous obstacles. A red and white pilot boat guided us through the maze. Below the passing ocean life now took residence in submerged tree stumps, streets, walls and roofs. Bright red flags marked treacherous areas.

The crowded and busy wharfs were very busy with workers moved like well oiled machines. Lean, low lying ships took passengers or tubby merchant ships delivered colorful cargo from exotic locations. The din of activities, both human and animals, mingled with cultures from all over the world. Sacks of spices, dried fruit, wood casks filled with wine and beer, clay jars of honey, date juice, olive oil, sealed crates of building material, wood beams, flats of tile, marble; flat iron bars, copper, bronze; canvasses, red and yellow weave baskets, even chickens, pigs and goats added to the rich market.

The humid, salt air mixed a cornucopia of scents: body sweat, perfumes, incense, musty wood, pungent baskets, animal odors, and cooking onions. With sledged hat pulled low to shield against the glare I watched the activities with childlike wonder. Never have I seen such a gathering of people! From the far north The Fog and Mist men in brown pants, tunic, wide belts, pale skin men with blue eyes and blonde hair remind me of ghosts. From the coast of the Sahara Desert tall, lanky blacked skinned travelers with wide noses and coal black eyes move with grace in bright colored robes and turbans. From the distant lands of Han Federation short, slight built yellow skinned people with wide flat faces, narrow eyes and coiled ebony hair dressed in intricately patterns bespoke of this exotic land. White thobe men with gray and brown checkered head clothes secured by circular rope brought spices from the Levant; and finally, us pilgrims in our odd mix of dress. I must say we appeared rather bland compared to these exotic travelers!

After a busy day we were cloistered in a nearby inn and given a huge meal. Six of us shared a large, spacious room overlooking the sea. Tomorrow we will visit the Kumari palace.

Oh, how I wish Bishma and Ali could see this!

Day 4. We were up before first light as we given pilgrims clothing: long sleeve brown tunic, blue pants, black waist sash, leather boots short open vests and kufi hat. After completing the morning Dedicational we performed Purification by retracing Taleju's mandala which the palace grounds represent.

The ritual was led by a Senior Satori, named Altus, who made the pilgrimage three times. He completed his first when he was 15. He looked to about 40 and widowed when his wife and son died five years ago. Despite his enthusiasm and patience there is sadness about him.

This place is unbelievable! This was the first time I's seen the Kumari's House. I was overwhelmed by all the grand detail and grandeur of this most sacred site. The living, eating quarters, quest halls, servants and the central House were laid out according to the Kumari Mandala. The brick courtyards mimicked the bright, colorful Mandala and each building was arranged according to it. The buildings covered with hundreds of glass wind chimes on the eves are a vision from another, peaceful world. The Central Hall's circular gold dome dominates the place, and sat on a square foundation decorated with sacred symbols. The dome represents the heavens and the square foundation earth. Each window was richly carved casement and covered by elaborate screens. From the surrounding buildings hundreds of fluttering, red, yellow and purple payer flags attached by horizontal rope converged at the dome. The finial were three, upturned crescent moons and an eight pointed star. Altus explained the star is Taleju and the crescents are the two Kumari Daughters and Kumarisattva.

Each threshold, casement, door, arch, pillars, roof finial and sacred objects were covered with imagery, patterns and sacred numbers. There was not a place I looked that did not remind me of sacred passages or mimicked the Mandala. The House is designed with meditation and reminds pilgrims the Kumari, the living goddess's representative, resides here.

As per keeping tradition the buildings are three storied: Earth, Air and Heaven.

Our first assignment was to prepare your spirit by tracing the Kumari mandala. This represents our life's journey towards enlightenment.

Before sunrise we gathered in damp, salty fog at the North gate and recited passages with Altus. Then we sprinkled lapis on a granite stone carved with symbols representing `Universes' mandala entrance. We continued in a clockwise direction moving to each outer gate using our prayer wheel. These were small and attached to a stick and spun around by hand, generating delicate melodies.

When we came to the `Air' East gate the sun dispelled the mist shrouding us and washed the grounds in gold light and long shadows. We offered vermillion in a stone bowl near the entrance. At the South `Fire' gate we paused while Altus read about the Purge and sprinkling saffron on a bright, bronze disk.

The West gate, `Enlightenment' was shaded by ancient trees. At the entrance was a silver guilt Taleju statue seated on a lotus. We stood before containers, reciting passages and then took handfuls of jasmine blooms and sparkled on the statue. Then we entered the West gate.   According to legend this was the gate Taleju entered Kathmandu on her return.

Within the mandala are three energy parameters: air, fire and water connected by a web of nine `energy' centers that converge at the Kumari palace. As we moved through each center, we ritualistically opened them, creating a vortex which we connected to the others like an expanding circuit. Nine marble pillars divided into three connecting pinnacles of three primordial energies: red, yellow and purple. We attached these to our heart and when the circuit completed these energies offered unhindered access to the spirit, enlightenment and knowledge. The pilgrims thought they were imagery but I saw these energy bonds and heard them as hum, ocean waves and thunder. When we finished it was afternoon and we paused in a park for lunch after Altus led our Dedicational.

Having started in the `Air' circle and after connected the energy web we moved into the `Fire' boundary. This was a path covered by hundreds of bits of mirrors. We activated solar lamps which threw out soft light, reflecting the trail like a cluster of stars. They turned yellow and rose like fire columns as we moved through them, reciting and spinning our prayer cylinders. This lasted until later afternoon.

Finally we entered the inner square, the 'water' border. From our vantage point here buildings formed a wide courtyard and at the far end was a reflective pool. It acted as a perfect mirror of the Kumari's House and I saw the energies converge at the dome, twisting and ascending like glittering light columns into the sky.

We were giving time to wait for the evening Dedicational which would the Kumari Daughter would lead. Excitement and expectations lightened my heart. I read and admired the sounds of tingling bells, horns, wind chimes echo though the evening sweet breeze. I felt a peace from the restlessness I had lived with for these many years.

Towards evening we were given oranges. Bells rang and low drown horns announced the Kumari Daughter. Wearing red and yellow robes and covered with silver jewelry she sat on a yellow minbar, and spoke quietly and peacefully. She seemed to speak to each individual about the Puja, pilgrimage, our challenges, and our goal. She said that no one who started it would be the same afterwards. The Puja meant to different things to each person, its reward went far beyond earning the Mokti tika. She added through reading The Awakenings we would trace Taleju's path, feel her hardships, sharing her disappointments, loss and insights. It would be a very difficult trek and many would not live to see its end, but all of us in Taleju's eyes were special for having the courage.

Ali, Bishma, I go with great joy glow in my heart as I stand on the eve on my new adventure.

Day 5. Today stated with anticipation but ended in disappointment and anger. I have never thought this day would come or that I would find myself rejected by the one person I place all my trust in.

After the morning Dedicational and breakfast Altus and his Kumargi assistants guided us through purification rites. We circumvented the Kumari House three times and performed puja at the ninth `directional energies'. Here we opened the gates so their energies would surround the main House. This created a vortex for the Kumari Daughter to receive Taleju's spirit so we could communicate with the outer form of the living goddess. Shortly before the Kumari's visit we were given special incense from Nepal and, reciting the Pilgrim Pledge, sprinkled this on a bronze altar shaped in the sacred lightning bolt, the Vajra. The yellow flame turned into a beautiful, pale blue.

The Kumari Daughter's receiving chamber is on the third floor, the second floor her living space and the ground floor for general meetings and compound duties. Amidst chants and bells, and carrying incense burners we were led us to the third floor antechamber to wait for our summons. On a huge table Kumargi s huddled over wonderful art, reciting text and creating a colorful Mandala from rice and sand, It was nearly complete and each of us given tasks. With chants echoing through the room I carefully applied sand in the designated area, feeling grateful contributing to this wonderful art. The Satori leading our group observed our work and commenting all Taleju's Kumargi added to this great Mandala in which we live.

Afterwards we sat on red and gold cushions on the dark painted floor, reciting, mediating and performing mudras. Attendants served spice tea and bread, or hung colorful prayer banners at the windows in our honor. A gentle breeze fluttered the banners and serenaded us with tinkling of bells. The room's sandalwood smoke soothed my nervousness and aided my mediations. Although I tried focusing on recitals, I was anxious hearing Puja summoned and expecting my name to follow.

I was filled with great expectations. The West Kumari Daughter is the highest representative, chosen by our Kumarisattva and this would be her second pilgrimage. Since childhood I've heard about this compassionate woman from devotees who travelled thousands of kilometers to sit at her feet. My name was called and after given a bell I joined the other waiting devotees. Taking a breath to calm my nervousness I lowered my head in reverence as we were guided into the chamber, chanting the prayer of the Pilgrimage and gently shaking my bell.

The Daughter sat on a minbar in front of a massive Mandala tapestry partly obscured by sandalwood incense blue haze. Thangka, banners and religious objects surrounded her. Sunlight fell full upon her from an opening in the ceiling. Satori and Kumargi s chanted to the accompaniment by delicate thumb chimes, drums and low, echoing horns.

When Altus called each name from a scroll the summoned pilgrims set the bell on a table then, palms pressed together, approached.

The Kumari wore red and yellow long dress, heaps of silver necklaces, bracelets and rings. Her forehead was painted with the all Seeing Eye and accented by red jewel. Three sacred symbols decorated her chin and cheeks, showing her authority of the three Kumari Houses. Her dark eyes were outlined in kohl, their bottom line extending to her temple. Her ebony hair was pulled back behind a gold crown with its front pieces representing the solar eclipse and Taleju's eight pointed star.

We recited the Eight Flames of Life while the devotee kowtowed and touched the Kumari's feet. Afterwards the devotee rested on their haunches while the Kumari dipped her finger in red dye and pressed it against their forehead. This tika was her sign granting permission to precipitate in the pilgrimage. The devotee stood, with hands pressed together, head lowered and backed out. They paused long enough for a Kumargi to drape a purple, silk scarf before leaving.

I watched, nervous, anxious.   When they called me I monetarily stepped in sunlight. Kneeling, I touched her henna dyed feet, took a blossom from a nearby silver bowl and sprinkled on her feet, then kowtowed. I raised my head. I was so nervous I forgot to keep my eyes averted and invariantly looked into her eyes.   The world seemed to darken.   Her gold flecked eyes watched me not with compassion, but shock and coldness.   I waited and the more she stared at me the more uncomfortable I became. I waited for the tika but it never came.

Instead tense silence lingered.

She sat back waving me away, saying my kind are not welcomed here. Too stunned I sat there, unable to believe what happened. Finally a helper assisted me away. As I was led away Altus watched me, her eyes betraying astonishment behind his indifferent expression.

The reset of the day I sat in a secluded grove, wrapped in my shock, confusion and wept. Meanwhile the pilgrims celebration seemed to mock my fate.

I was heartbroken and confused. What should I do?

Day 6. It took another day to complete the ceremony. There are about five hundred puja on this pilgrimage. I spent today in a daze, torn between my feelings. Should I return home and to humiliation and personal defeat, or continue and be subjected to the Kumari's wrath and possible harassment. If the Kumari knew I am a Seer, then others would surely discover.

Since yesterday some devotees spoke the Kumari sensed trouble and refused me because I may bring hardships upon them. I vacillate between being strong and continue; or weak and retreat. I wanted this whole life. My older sister failed and now it is for me. Why am I so confused?

A Satori visited me, offering a return trip to Sofia. I was angry and shoved him away. Later a Kumargi came back and demanded I return the pilgrim clothes. This angered me more and in a fit of rage I tossed silver at him, explaining I paid for the stupid clothing and they were mine! Resentful, frustrated I retreated into the garden and watched the evening ceremony for the pilgrimage being held in the main yard. The sand Mandala we helped create was brought out and the after much fanfare and ritual the Kumari destroyed it. I could not hear what she said because my mind kept returning to that horrible memory. When the Kumari announced to the accompanied horns and cymbals all attendees were official pilgrims it fueled my anger even more.

This night I saw myself in the mirror. I looked so lost and sad; a stranger washed up on some distant land and unsure what lay ahead because my trust in the Kumargi was shattered.

Day 7. The Kumari's incident and her assistants isolated me more from the pilgrims. Reflecting on the encounter yesterday I think the Satori actually feared me or my presence may affect them. I kept going though stories about what Normals did to Seer. Even though I am in a religious group, my life means nothing if they decided their peace is more important.

They kept their distance for now and I focused on the preparation for the voyage tomorrow. After much heart searching I determined to make the Puja. I could not find anything in Taleju's writing excluding anyone from the pilgrimage. Why should I abandon my childhood dream and the pledge I made to you, Ali and Bishma? In reality I do not need permission, only a devoted and determined heart.

With this decision I steeled my will and vowed I will do what must be done to accomplish my Puja.

I forgot my gloominess and kept busy with loading sacks, crates and clay jars onto the ships crowding the docks. No one objected of me working. Most pilgrims lounged, preferring to remain idle and chat excitedly about the journey. I was glad for the distraction and being away from them.

In the afternoon I performed a private puja at the grounds. Towards evening I meet a family of musicians: Marcus, the husband; Lucinda his wife and their teenage boy, Duce. I found out they were famous in Anatolia. They were discussing the importance of music in meditations with a group of Kumargi. After Dedicational they noticed I was sitting alone and serenaded me with a melody from the Pre Purge days. The beats and cord arrangements seemed odd but it left me more cheerful.

Just before retiring Altus visited me and inquired about my decision. When I told him I wanted to continue the pilgrimage I assumed he would berate me. But to my surprise he placed a tika on my forehead and draped a purple scarf around my neck. He said all pilgrims seeking Taleju's wisdom are welcomed.

Day 8. A most trying and anxious day but I won! It began with a damp, salty mist hanging over the city. In the pre dawn we gathered by the designated ships' gangways and waited quietly while Kumari officials, on the main deck, shouted our names. I watched the pilgrims walked the gangway, paused while the man in charge checked the list then wave them aboard. Time passed. I anxiously awaited. When the last name called I was left standing alone. The official searched the list then signaled the gangway to be hoisted. I leaped on the gangway and tried to board, but he stopped me. He demanded my name and when I showed it was crossed off the list. He reminded me the Kumari did not give me permission. I shouted I will take the journey only for Taleju and did not give a damn about what the Daughter thought. We both got angry, shouting and he attempted to block my way. He tried restraining me and I defiantly stared into his eyes, my anger swelled and felt energetic rumble around me. He hesitated; his expression changed from anger to uncertainly then released his grip. At this time Altus appeared beside him and, taking the list added my name, explaining there was a misunderstanding.

I thanked Altus. The deckhand backed away and I stepped onto the deck. I was so upset I collapsed on a nearby crate, bowed my head and allowed my tears to pass.

The afternoon salt air was oppressive, like my heart, as we sailed to the hazy, milky horizon. As the crew tended sail and rigging, I sat away from the main group. I was nauseated and exhausted by the stress. I felt hostile stares and kept my eyes downcast, studying the book's Mandala and tried to image where

I was at. Taleju said the Mandala reflected our life and I imagined mine was stuck in the chaotic maze.

I heard Altus and the Kumari Daughter arguing on the aft deck. They were hidden from the others but from my advantage I saw everything. She slapped him before storming away, leaving him alone.

In the evening Altus visited me. We stared at the ocean. I noticed rose light radiate from his heart chakra. Feeling awkward by the incident I witnessed I kept my gaze downcast as we talked.

He inquired my skill with maps, star reading, compasses and geology and if I had experience riding camels, since these will be our main transportation. When he recited the languages we would encounter, I answered I know most them. He was impressed. I explained my family and husband were in the business of guided caravans across New Iberia and Sardinia region.

He said their group was short one scout and if I would help. I replied I was here to serve our pilgrims. He cautioned that I will encounter much unpleasant political fallout from today and I should take heart because I will prevail. Then he added I was a rare spirit, humbled of heart and Taleju's true devotee. My courage was commendable and he had no regrets about helping me.

I thanked him. Altus is a good spirit.

Day 10. As per tradition the Kumari held Majlis in the morning on the aft deck. This gave pilgrims the opportunity to meet her and ask religious questions, complaints and hear her decision. This served to keep open communication and involvement with the pilgrims and gauge problems before they occur. Pilgrims expected this and it was one of the most important duties she performs. It built trust and cooperation. I stayed away, observing the proceedings from the deck.

Afterwards she held readings and guided meditation on the main deck. In the afternoon I and other were called for a meeting with her. The scouting party was being assembled. At first she did not believe I was skilled but after a few tests reading sea charts, land maps and pinpointing our location using sextants and astrolabe, she was forced to acknowledge this. I did better than most others who had very minimal experience. Yet, although I was most qualified, we were under the leadership if a Satori named Patan who seemed more interested in impressing the Kumari than finding his way through a forest.

Throughout the meeting I felt her hostile stares and presence. It was an anxious and nervous event. I was glad when it ended. I removed myself to the forward deck near the prow and watched the ship cutting through the waves until dark and my mind cleared.

Day 11. The Italia coast came in sight this morning. It was obscured by gray fog and got worse until we were unable to advance. We anchored off the coast to wait for it lift. I spent time reading and attended a class Altus held about using the Mandala in meditation. Until starting on the pilgrimage, I did not realize how important the mandala was. I find it greatly enhance my meditation and understanding of Taleju's passages.

Day 13. Today we camped in hills overlooking the village near ruins called Tarquiniaon. A river once emptied here but now it just dry canyon and boulders. The village looks quaint in painted bright color with gardens and olive orchards. Yet this land had a tortured look beneath its apparent beauty. Many hills had patches of white rock and glittering glass mingle with scrub grass. This underlying despair and tortured land marked the outer boundary of the Purge firestorms. Altus said it gets worse further south and east we go.

We waited two days for the fog clear so our small fleet could safely navigated the submerged ruins. We have about three weeks of supplies for our journey to Atri, a coastal city which we transferring to pack mules. Lucinda, the wife of the musician I met earlier, was ill and the rest weak or sick traveled into the hills on mules. The rest of we walked in the sweltering heat. We made camp as instructed by our group leader and cautioned to keep our skin covered or travel in the shade to avoid the direct sun.

Pilgrims were divided into twenty teams, each with responsible for preparing camp, packing, secure provisions and cooking chores. Since I was on the Scout team we were given camels and spent our first day checking the road, selecting a camp and locate water. We shared laughs when some of our team had never ridden a camel made humorous attempts. Naturally I was assigned to assist these until they got the hang of it. Towards evening Patan briefed the Kumari on our findings and the next day's route. Per her instruction, only Patan could receive orders or report to the Kumari.

Our first meal in Italia was bulgur, onions and an assortment of vegetables. It was bland because our cooks had not discovered the secrets of spices, but satisfying. Lucinda, her husband Marcus and son Duce were part of our camp team. After dinner they entertained us with stories and song until the moon rose and our guides called us to sleep. I was exhausted by today's activities. I am happy to be on land again.

Day 14. Patan's leadership is a mixture of getting lost and uncertainty. Before his appointment he was a Satori in charge of the Dedicational. Therefore his working knowledge is limited to religious ceremony. The task of scout is left to pilgrims with varying degree of competence and experience. I am the most experience, but due my past trouble with the Kumari, he considers me a ghost. He does not acknowledge me or listen; rather he pays more attention to others who already had shown a flair for mistakes and misunderstanding. One example Patan believed a scout who was so incompetent with an astrolabe, he and our location in Anatolia heading for the Black sea! Another scout had never seen a compass and thought we still tracked by magnetic north. Never mind that changed hundreds of years ago!

I do what I can to teach others about maps, geological, land, instruments and remain outward calm when he does not include me in discussions. It's bad I must endure this humiliation because of I am an outsider, but it tries my patient when my experience means nothing. I fear they will blunder and naturally will blame me.

I quickly concluded I am here just to be out of the Kumari's sight and I suspect he reports my activities. Already I've frustrated him and know she gets an ear full. Instead of argue, I let Patan to make errors. Maybe he will choke on his arrogance. We travelled about eight kilometers ahead of the main group, using our metal boxes with dials to measure the Rad Sickness prevalent in these lands. If the dials indicated red, we have to find another way through. Yellow, we can be in only of a limited time. The green area means we are safe. We consulted our maps and explored where water could be found. Bird Handlers joined us and we sent messengers to the main group via carrier pigeons. By evening we selected a camp site, nearby water and shelter. When we returned to the main group, Patan shows the map and our next camp and what to expect.

The further inland we travelled, the more the terrain became hazy, muggy. Near the coast birds were noticeably absent now they serenade from the branches. About twenty kilometers from Tarquiniaon there were are no more farms or orchards. Everything had an unspoiled look. Yet I glimpsed vast ruins beneath the tall grass and dense undergrowth. I got the impression we were in land devastated by the Thunder, Flashes and fire storms Taleju spoke about. The road we followed was wide and worn; in spots bits of black surface were exposed from centuries of travelers. This was a Pre-Purge road we followed. Like many roads from that era mechanical beasts carried passengers throughout the world.

Towards evening we reached the hills of Lake Braccaino near our first destination: The Ascension. We camped in a grove and watched the sun set across brown and red splashes, obscuring the horizon.

Day 15. *I have travelled our world, seeing the horrors we inflicted, felt the scars we left on our home, and heard our Spirits pain and suffrage. I leave my gift, The Awakenings, so humanity will heal and walk the path we are meant to. I am blessed to have travelled this path. Remember we are all Spirits of the Universe--all we have to do is lift our eyes and see. ----Taleju's last words-*

In the morning we reached Lake Braccaino. By this time the sun burned off the haze and we spent time admiring the lake's glittering, blue mantel at the foot of jade colored hills. It made for calm, peaceful memories. Here, according to tradition, our beloved Kumari Mother and her travel companions rested for three weeks as Taleju's health failed. Then on Month 10, day 14, Alter Purge year 137, weary from travel and sick, laid her head down beneath an orange tree and died peacefully. It was said the birds gathered in the branches serenaded her and then went quiet, mourning her passing.

Her travelling companions, Sanjari, Pravati and Radha cremated and scattered her ashes in a nearby field. Then Sanjari, Taleju's first devotee and childhood friend, returned to Nepal where she became the First Kumarisattva. Parvati stayed in Neostella and taught The Awakenings. Later she was appointed the First Kumari Daughter. Radha travelled north beyond the Land of Mist and Fog, her fate unknown.

We visited the holy site located halfway up a hill dominated by a lone, rocky outcropping dubbed the `Crown of Tears.' Here, among orange grove a white domed building, the all Seeing Eye faced east and capped by a gold solar eclipse and eight pointed star. The orchards, rocky fence and stony fields covered with colorful clay pots were arranged as the Mandala, with the shrine in the center. Three Kumargi s in blue robes, gold sash and red kufi were caretakers.

We performed puja at nine stone monoliths representing the energy gateways which activated the Mandala. Three Kumargi caretakers acted as guides, leading us in chants and filled the air with blessing by ringing thumb cymbals. We paused at each circle and light incense or sprinkled orange peels, circumventing them before moving into the each inner circle until we arrived in the Ascension shrine courtyard. We lounged beneath orange trees heavy with fruit provided by the Kumargi s.

Because there were so many of us it would take two days to perform the ceremony. The Kumari divided our group into two and one was dismissed or returned to the camp. The reminder was divided into twenty and waited. I spent time reading and meditating. Our group was called, but The Kumari Daughter ordered me to wait until everyone had finished. I sat, feeling outcast and angry. Yet, I did react because she knew she was trying to provoke me. This was a very important Taleju temple and I would not allow my feelings to poison my experience.

It was near evening when I was summoned. I climbed eight steps representing the Flames of life and paused by the narrow, arched door. I took ashes from a silver bowl and spread it on my forehead before entering.

It was dark except for faint illumination pouring thought a ceiling opening, illuminating the floor and the complex mosaic of Creation. I studied the six interlocking circles and triangles. Since childhood I wondered about their individual meanings. When I inquired the Kumargi looked pleased and gave me a detailed explaining. The central circle and three swirls reflected karma, reincarnation, compassion; the six circles including the central and the border represent Taleju's Eight Flames of Life, and the triangles remind us of the three Kumari principles: unity, enlightenment, awareness

The Kumargi lit several solar lamps, filling the chamber with pale light. I directed my attention to the small chamber. In the center was a tree stump covered in sheets of gold. The stucco walls were painted with horizontal bands of blue, gold and red. The guide waited in the shadow while I approached the stump, head bowed, palms pressed and reciting the Prayer of Ascension. At the appropriate moment he rang a bronze bell next to the wall. Its delicate note echoed through the incense scanted, still air.

Taleju, you have abandoned all illusions
You possess the Eyes of Infinity.
You have abandoned Ego and the Mind
You possess the Voice of Clarity.
You has shattered the Glass Wheel
You dwell within the Moment without bonds.
Mother Kumari fill my heart with The 8 Flames of Life so I will
make them visible.
Blessed Mother Talejusattva.

When finished, the Kumargi took my hand and grasped it, smiling. I returned to the darkening courtyard where Altus was waiting for me. He lit a lamp and together we returned to the camp, not speaking a word. It was after the evening Conformation when I joined the pilgrims and Marcus' family and listened to their harmonious voices and instruments. Looking around in the black shadows cast by the solar lamps I glanced back at the shrine. It seemed forgotten; a relic from an age long since vanished. This place felt sad and lonely. I wondered if Taleju felt this too when she died.

Day 16. We rested today while pilgrims continued puja at the shrine. I spent time in the shade under orange trees and when dozed off. I had another vision.

Like the other it started with me seated before a table with cards lay out. This time the Tree of Life was superimposed on rainbow symbols. I selected a card which read: *Ego is but a play of Mind.* From somewhere the faint drone of singing bowls, filled me with a green light. I turned the card over.

Splashes of blues and whites leapt to my mind and faded until I was a viewpoint soaring in clouds high above the hazy, brown earth. I was terrified then realized I was only invisible eyes observing this world. I noted the unbroken blue heavens and the yellow sun. Then a shiny metal bird caught my attention. It was huge, with many windows and wings which did not flap like a bird. On its body was written ` W Blofeld and Associates.' This bird reminded me again of those drawings in the Caves of Marceilla.

My vision shifted and I was in this mechanical bird. Inside there was a narrow hall with many windows. I was aware of a background noise like rushing wind. Men in black and gray clothing sat around a table. That woman I saw earlier wore a black jacket, pants and white scarf around her long neck. She was next to an elderly man with a large nose and fiery, deadly eyes. I sensed she and the others feared him. As another tall, thin man entered the room they turned and looked at him, their spirits dark and cold. No one said a word and he sat and faced the hostile group.

The woman looked at the elder man then opened a folder. Her tone masked anger directed at the man who just seated who she called Senator Hayden. She indicated the elderly man as Mr. Blofeld and his stare never left the Senator who kept his eyes averted. She reminded him of their agreed goal then outlined what has happened since the bombing.

Covert teams supported by the USG were to drive the United Arab Emirates to bankruptcy by disrupting oil and imports, thereby defaulting on their loans. As agreed Sheikh Neyhan's nation would become a client State and hand all assets over. Blofeld and Associates would give loans to prevent bankruptcy and stimulate the economy.

The eldest son, Sheikh Maktoum, assumed leadership but it was still unclear where he stood about the loan

Meanwhile the radicals continued random bombings, threatening businesses and destroyed an oil refinery as a display of their seriousness.

She reminded Senator Hayden this was not acceptable to his business associates or his government. Mr. Blofeld represented a considerable business venture that wanted assurance from the Senator his group would be reeled in and the loan would go through.

Meanwhile Mr. Blofeld instructed the Senator to find why his group turned against them after two years of cooperation.

The blonde leaned back and folded her arms, scowling. She warned if he could not control his group, then Curtis `the Jackal' would make the Senators cooperated. The Senator tried to appear indifferent but his eyes betrayed terror.

He promised the USG would pressure the Sheikh to accept the loan. He assured the client State was guaranteed no matter what it took.

The vision vanished, leaving me weak and disoriented. That same dread I felt from the last vision shrouded my heart. I am afraid of something . . . but what? Shaken, I went to the shrine and sat in the shadows, pondering the dream's implications far into the late hours.

Day 17. Today we rode into rough terrain looking nightmarish as though giant beasts took bites out of the earth. It was utterly quiet, like the silence of death. Grass and trees grew in abstract contortions from scrubby, rocky and sometimes glittering ground. The pilgrims were warned to cover our faces to avoid inhaling travel dist, not drink the water from streams or eat the red berries along the roadside. I sensed great disturbance to this place and with each step it intensified.

I and two other scouts monitored for Rad Sickness. The dials moved to the yellow but sometimes they crept into the red. We found a safe place in a narrow valley for camping. A messenger pigeon carrying Patan's findings was released and we settled down to wait their arrival. It was near evening when the group joined us. Everyone looked exhausted and haggard. We walked 40 kilometers today—a hard push necessitated by the threat of Rad Sickness. Many fell asleep where they collapsed. Our evening Dedicational was postponed to allow rest. Tomorrow promised to be as demanding. We should be within sight of the Holy See.

Day 18. Taleju's entry when she passed through here.

It was once the seat of power for those who worshipped the Son of the Heavens. For two thousand years it held sway over the collective consciousness of the Old and New Worlds; wrapped in pomp and archaic ceremony and surrounded by aloof self deceiving importance and mystery. Here from its marble halls it took wealth from the innocent masses, slaughtered millions in its name, persecuted those of questionable devotion or tortured those who they deemed a threat. These were done in the Son's name; but it was excuse for ego's delusional importance and deep fear.

Now I walk through this land where once people lived in artificial canyons stretching beyond the horizon. All that remains in scattered ruins, sand, rock and an eternal grayness. Bits or concrete boulevards, forests of twisted metal reach into the gloomy sky, and walls punctuated by gaping holes looking like death's empty stare. It is utterly quiet and shrouded by clouds. A stench lingers in the humid gloom. I am aware of millions of spirits silenced forever. I am told before the Purge artificial lights lit hundreds of kilometers could be seen from space. Today only darkness occupies this place where not even the dead dare to trod. Sickness lingers here. I hurry to leave this desert plains of massive craters, home of the Holy See-

This morning two injured travelers returned to Tarquinia. We left the valley and gradually climbed into rocky hills. By late morning our instruments indicated the Sickness is nearing critical levels, yet we pushed on until finally coming out upon a most incredible and frightful scene. At the crest of the hill the valley sweeps away before us like a great bowl, consisting of hundreds of craters until it vanished in the milky horizon. From some outcroppings the surface glittered like green glass. Vegetation gradually declined the further south until barren gray and glittering, green glass remained. The air was humid, unusually dusty and the hazy sky tinted brown. This is the Sea of Craters Taleju spoke of; the handiwork of great upheaval by fire and storm that annihilated millions of people and poisoned our world. I struggle to comprehend the power which unleashed this curse. Why? What compelled them to bring massive destruction on a global scale? Were people of the Pre Purge insane, driven by forces they could not comprehend? Or they are no different than us? Do we still harbor this darkness?

Despite having covered my mouth and nose I coughed gritty air. I studied the map, attempting to grasp the magnitude of the horrors before us. We were still many kilometers from the Holy See but we could not get closer. Our map showed the Sea of Craters covered eighty kilometers.

In the evening we gathered at the ridge and lit candles in memory for all the people whose world was taken away in the blink of an eye. It was a solemn affair and many of us shed tears. The great quiet since entering this place emphasized the apocalypse. I thought I saw the victim faces and heard their wails across the eons in the gathering, sullen darkness. The violence still lingers here; permanently imprinted for all time. It left me restless, depressed and I had trouble writing. Ali, Bishma, it was best you never saw this, for the burden will haunt me the rest of my life.

Day 21. I am exhausted. We covered a hundred and twenty kilometers in three days to escape the Rad sickness zone. Here, the land healed, although traces of its violent past are still visible. Gentle rolling hill and sparse forests watched silently as we walked a path overgrown in places. The humidity lost its grittiness and the sun no longer shone from its smudged, steely perch. Because of the heat we're had to ration our water, which made the walk was made more difficult. Normally curious children who spent times darting in and out of our group could not keep up and, like the elderly, took turns riding mules. We could not afford to slack; we determined we had to walk this distance.

We came to sparse villas with meager olive and orange orchards small and frail compared to Neostella. People met us with bread and dried fruit. The Kumari blessed them and invited them to share meditations and noon meal.

Duce joined our scouting party after one member fell ill. He was eager to learn and quickly grasped the map and instruments. Although he does not display his weapon, Duce and his dad are swordsmen. I welcomed his assistance.

Some people developed fevers and blisters on their hands. We suspected they picked tainted berries. Today they were too weak and we left them at a villa to recover. We will wait a week in Atri for them. If they do not come, we will sail without them.

Today I borrowed a mirror and what a shock! Ali, I lost five kilo since starting this trip! My stomach is flat, arms lean and legs sculptured. Yet, I am more gaunt and dark from the sun. It seemed like my eyes grew larger!

In my daily dealings with the pilgrims the Kumari Daughter avoided me. To her, I am invisible. . .

At the evening Confirmation it seemed ironic when she discussed Taleju's 21 Tenants. In one passage our Kumari Mother said: *As Unified Consciousness we work as One for the many Enlightenment. Beware, whereas ego slips into its selfish world it is duped by its own illusionary importance.*

Day 23. A sad day. Our first casualty was an eight year old boy who spooked his mule and was trampled. The family cried for hours. The poor dad; he held the boy in his arms and rocked back and forth, his expression of utterly disbelief. In a fit of grief, the mom cut her arms and forehead and smeared herself with her blood—a tribal custom from the Levant, I'm told. The sight of blood upset many people. We built a pyre and after cremating him we scattered his ashes in a nearby grove. The dad piled stones up to mark the spot. We travelled in sullen resignation the rest of the day. Music, our evening ritual, was absent in respect for our loss.

Day 25. I wrote **Taleju's 21 Tenants** to remind me what I should hold in my heart and not be blinded by our petty self importance. Therefore, I will never forget what egocentric did to our beloved earth.

We have no possessions. Everything is on loan to us.
The planet is a living organism in which we can affect good or bad. Therefore, we must live in balance with our environment.
Consider all immediate and future consequences for your actions.
Act only in the best interest of other spirits. Be selfless.
Ego is but a play of Mind.
Ego destroys. Unity builds.
All manifestations are from the One Consciousness and interdependent.
There is no poverty, only selfishness.
All creatures share the bounty.
Spirit seeks to balance; mind and ego seek to unbalance.
All actions today have consequences tomorrow. Individual accountability is the key to enlightenment.
There is no death—only continuation in many forms.
All universes are interconnected and comprise the Omniverse.
What you do today echoes throughout Infinity and sets up conditions for future incarnations.
The goal of our incarnations is to neutralize past events that negatively affected other spirits.

All spirits work together towards Enlightenment. It is not a solely an individual journey, although individually we each walk the path.
Karma can only be neutralized by those who own it.
As Unified Consciousness we work as One in Enlightenment. As ego we slip into selfish disregard of the Universality.
We create earthly laws to manifest the Higher Consciousness. We do not to exclude, prejudge, control or promote fear. These latter are of mind and emotion which benefit the few at the expense of the many.
Every manifestation is a reflection of spirit and therefore, commands our respect.
We are melodies of light suspended in Infinity. Our forms are transient and always change to different songs.

We camped at a village halfway between the Sea of Craters and Atri. It was modest place on a hillside with olive and pomegranate groves. The orchard shaded aromatic herbs, millet and cucumbers. The locals made an excellent white cheese mixed with herbs and spread over bread. It was hearty and complimented our bland soup.

We met a Healer who treated our ill pilgrims. He prepared herbal plasters for those suffering from Rad sickness and travel. The villagers were hospitable and we were grateful for their effort. That evening I had a most disturbing encounter. While I sit beneath a tree a boy of about ten observed me from the distance. I sensed his inquiring gaze. Finally, I motioned him over. He reluctant approached me and cautiously he asked why I was with these pilgrims. Perplexed, I answered. Then I saw the faintest glint of green in his dark eyes! He replied I was not one of them. Suddenly, embarrassed he quickly fled, leaving me stunned.

Feeling self conscious I returned to the main group and for the rest of the evening avoided everyone.

Day 28. After two days on the road, we reached a plain of grass and mounds the Daughter claimed this was once a city. This evening we gathered and read out loud Taleju's account of the Purge apocalypse.

For nearly a month fire and thunder rained from the sky, transforming land to black ash and oceans into steamy fog. The pride of humanity's cities were gone in a blink of an eye; carried aloft in artificial suns which vaporized all in their path into rising columns of boiling, churning clouds. These mixed with other great fires consuming the land and oceans, creating dark clouds so thick they blocked out the sun. Black rain fell, depositing their poisons.

Those who miraculously escaped the carnage, death quickly followed, decimating land and animals by touching all with Rad Sickness. The world was shrouded by the Time of Cloud and Darkness for years; sunlight failed to penetrate and feed the planet, turning the once green realms into gray wastelands. When it lifted, the sun shone upon a different world; gone were the glittering cities, the clean lakes and the abundant oceans. Now only vistas marred by craters and void of life stretched to the horizon. The dream of Madness that walked for Millennia had completely transformed our world.

With the passing of so many centuries the Purge seemed like an abstract tale which we cannot fully grasp. It was like an old picture kept in our distant, collective consciousness—gradually fading, replaced by our current understandings.

Perhaps our future generations will wonder if this really happened or the product of soothsayers and story tellers. I believe the underlying purpose to the pilgrimage is really about preserving the Purge memory and reinforce that it *really* happened.

Day 29. High winds and rain this afternoon, drenching us and turning our hilly paths into mud. Although I was pelted, I was glad for the relief from the heat and shed my hat and gloves to experience this blessing. The rain heals this land and awakened smells of fresh greenery and earthy scents. We paused while waiting for the storm to pass. Later it settled into constant drizzle and we continued walking until late into the evening.

Day 31. Locals warned us these storms will increase and we must quicken our pace to reach Atri. After two days of frantic travel we failed in our objective. The gathering storm began as stiff winds and exploded into a gale by the time we reached the coast.

Then the stinging rain appeared and we scramble for the trees. We gathered our camels into small groups and secured our baggage as best we can. Wrapping in blankets we huddled closely for the storm to pass. Overhead branches swayed to angry howls. Occasionally thunder brought lightening As darkness descends it intensifies and many travelers were fearful, especially when branches snapped and carried away on the violent winds and stinging rain. I reflected on the Purge and realized this is but a glimpse of what it must have been like.

Having wedged between two camels I used a blanket for shelter. When storm ripped my cover away, the rain soaked completely in a matter of seconds, Duce threw his blanket over us.

Month 11, Day 1.   A party from Atri arrived around noon and assisted us with baggage. The frightful storm ended in the early morning, bringing sunshine and calm.   The air was crisp and salty; brown scrub grass transformed into green. Water dripped from branches and splashed the ground like glittering orbs. The earth was reborn. Some of our baggage was lost. I, Duce and our group spent most of the morning searching. We located about half our soaked items. By the time we reached Atri it was dark. I was wet, cold and chilled. A kind family took us in and we huddled around the fireplace for warmth.   We were fed and offered wine.   After this I felt well enough and sleep in the vegetable hut. I was so exhausted I barely could write.

Day 7. The storm delayed our preparation and we were forced to remain in Atri for a week. Two days later the main group joined us, carrying those left back in other villages. They reported a single casualty: a man died when the tree sheltering him broke and crushed him. Altus crossed him off the ledger and made a notation.   I mentally notes we had three hundred and seventy five.   I wonder how many pilgrims will complete the journey.

The original land or sea path Taleju took was buried by the ocean long ago, as was any coast cities she encountered then. The next documented location was   Duraykish near the Levant coast.   It is about two weeks travel by sea. Including passengers and provisions, camels, our little fleet consists of fifteen ships.

Our time was occupied by replenishing provisions, pack animals such as camels and mules, waiting for more ships, and taking on passengers.   It was a huge undertaking and I was impressed by how the pilgrims worked together to make this happen.

Since my group responsibilities include assisting with navigation we met the captain of the fleet to review the course. The information I got was grim. We will follow the coast near the Land of Volcanoes and Thunder.   A huge obstacle called the Anatolia   Great   Reef   has   many   shoals   and   treacherous undercurrents which can trap ships without warning. Additionally, frequent storms change direction which can blow us off course and into these shoals. The Captain remarked the currents and winds are influence by a chain of Purge era volcanoes.   Most these peaks are quiet, but some have been known to wake.   The sailing season ended early this year with the storm. This means our trip is risky since the weather pattern is shifting from south to north.

Later the Kumari Daughter reviewed our route with my group and heard the Captain's suggestion. She acted as if I was not in the room, directing her questions to my group. Her manner and tone towards me angered me. After much discussion she wanted to risk reaching the Levant, rather than wait for six month when the next season started.

There are three decks on our ship. The captain and his crew occupied the quarter deck. The Kumari, her Satori and navigators took the state rooms. However, much to my anger, I was not included but joined the pilgrims in the lower deck which we shared with the provisions, cook quarter.

The Kumari flag was hoisted, signaling prepare to depart. In the early afternoon our fleet entered on calm waters and sailed for the Aegean Sea. I am stationed on the lead vessel with the Captain and the Kumari. Each ship had large numbers on their red and gold sails and communicated via lights or pinions. The lead ship has red and white striped sails. Our Captain strolled throughout the ship, checking on passengers and observed his crew.

It was pleasant and warm sitting topside in the shade and I watched the sparkling, blue expanse. The air was alive with the calls of gray and white seagulls; the solar sails fluttered and moved to the salty wind. Soon land faded into hazy horizon and soon we were alone; colorful dots bobbing up and down.

We reach a beach covered in stinky slime and oily film. A world shrouded in thick fog that burns skin and chokes our breath. The stench of rotting vegetation, death, acrid metallic, sulfur, and pungent salt dominate this fog. It sting the eye and chases away hope. It is depressing and oppressive; a gray and brown cloak lying over this ocean once teeming with life but since the Purge is now vacant. At cliffs water churns and boils, giving off a dull, greenish glow. Hot steam rises up and chaises us away. I cough and wipe my eyes before turning back inland.

This is the same watery grave wherever the coast meets the coast..---Taleju's description of what was once Greece.

I set the book down and looked east into the gathering darkness. Now the Kumari Daughter and her Satori were visiting us. Her hollow, musical laughter was carried on the warm breeze. She stopped near me and, leaning on the railing, gazed at the ocean for a long time. She noticed my book and asked what I was reading. I replied. Her expression was bemused and remarked not everyone reading the Awakenings is capable of understanding.

I met her gaze as she strolled by, but her shallow words burned in my hearts. My cheeks reddened.

Later I grabbed my journal and let my hurt spew onto the page. *And not everyone who professes to wear the mantel of devotion is true to themselves.*

Day 14. For nearly a week we've been sailing. The weather was bright, sunny; the ocean calm with a steady southeast wind taking us towards the Levant. However, at times when I closed my eyes I sensed disturbance, like oil upon water that is invisible until seen at the right angle. It came from north where haze laid low and hid the Purge volcanoes we initially saw when entering the Aegean Sea. Since then I felt uneasy, but I was reluctant to speak to the Captain because I did not have evidence to support my concerns.

Since then I settled into routines which have consumed my days. Besides preparing meals, clean my berth each morning, rolling up hammocks and mop the deck, I was expected to be on deck at sunrise to take measurements of the stars and the electromagnetic lay lines. Sometimes the lay line instrument failed so I repeated readings. We noted the magnetic south, recorded these in the navigation log and plotted the course on the charts. This was also repeated after sunset. On days where clouds obscured the stars, we relied on just the lay lines, the astrolabe and compass readings.

Today I sat beneath the deck awning with Duce and his parents. I have not seen them since Lucinda's illness. Duce and Marcus tended her. She caught stomach flu and this day she braved the weather and came topside. She looked pale and miserable, but laughed and smiled as her husband shared engaging stories about their village life. The tale of a stubborn rooster in the tea house had me laughing so hard tears covered my cheeks as though I was in a shower.

Duce is an artist and added these sketches of you, Bishma and me to my journal. I admired the way simple lines create life and memories. He captured your nuances; Bishma's slight pout, of her hair falling over you left eye; Ali, he even caught your hooked nose and sparkling eyes and trimmed beard I loved so much! His sketches made me cry.

This evening they waited until I finished my chores before they serenading us with music from times before the Purge. They were sad, mournful and possessed different rhythms than I have heard. Their voices, the thump of the drum, the fitter of flute and the mandolin's harmonies left me with heartfelt loss as I envisioned millions of faces so long ago listening across the millennium. One song was about writing love letters of regret was particularly haunting. I believed Marcus called it Nights of White Satin.

It is now 2 am. I am exhausted. Sunrise at 5 am. I will keep you both close to my heart as I lay the journal across my breasts and protect it with folded arms.

Day 16. Taleju's description of the Clouds of Fire which we now call Land of Volcanoes and Thunder

It is barren, a wall of gray and black rocks stretching to the horizon. This desolation shone in diffuse, weak light peering through smattering of shapeless, dark clouds. The empty fields with twisted mounds and deep gorges bury the once lush greenery that inhabited this land. Far to the north jagged peaks hold up the sky with billowy, belching columns of fire and smoke. The mountain range is mostly obscured by sulfurous and fiery clouds. Low, angry rumbles echo across the distance as though the mountains are angry. My small boat stays clear of the shore where fingers of still smolder lava reach into the sea, sending up steam and noisy, angry hiss. The air is hot and grittiness clings to my clothes; occasionally glowing ash trickles down from the oppressive sky. Everything stinks of rotten meat, decay and death.

There is no life here near the Clouds of Fire. Earth is enraged. This land speaks of our foolishness brought upon this once utopian realm.

In the morning it was clear and a light haze hung to the north. Yet, I sensed dread, my stomach a tight ball of knots. I was constantly drawn to the volcanoes and after searching their smoky horizon my inner vision saw stormy, energetic patterns pulled together and distorted the lay lines, twisting them like ever tighten spring. After taking chart reading I told the Captain that a storm was growing. He inspected the sea, currents, wind direction and sky then shook his head and says I have an overactive imagination. The Aegean Sea was calm. We had but four days before reaching the Syrian coast.

His indifferent only increased my uneasiness.

For my whole life I have been careful not to tell anyone I saw energy, otherwise they would suspect I was not a `Normal'. Now I am torn between explaining why I knew and thereby reveal of myself, or hope I am mistaken.

Throughout this anxious day my inner senses watched the horizon build towards violence. It was horrible, its energetic activities danced to sinister low rumbles and distant thunder. These red primordial energies spun like a monsoon, reached skyward and dissolved into fine wisps, only to return with growing intensity. In the afternoon another energetic noise joined in: hundreds of gongs. Then, the horrible beasts wake.

Shortly, in the evening a hot breeze brought thick, black and boiling clouds of stinking sulfur. It came so fast we had little time to respond. The captain looked at me with amazement then explained to the Kumari's Satori that the Anatolia Great Reef, a continuous wall stretching for thousands of kilometers from Anatolia into the Mediterranean, prevented us from seeking shelter on shore. He said our only option was heading out to sea and ride out the storm. The Captain bellowed crew to their stations and ordered everyone below.

Below deck in the gray darkness we clung for our lives. The storm intensified, tossing or slammed our ship and sometimes knocking us from our refuge. Fear griped everyone. Eventually water poured between the deck hatches and down the steps leading to our deck. We scrambled out of the way as cold, salty water soaked us. I fight panic by recording in my journal to forget our plight. I wondered if I had spoken earlier if we may have avoided this. I felt guilty and helpless.

With great difficulty the Kumari Daughter clung to whatever she found and moved among our group, doing her best to assured we will be alright. Yet her eyes betrayed fear.

The storm grew, and grew and grew.

I feared any moment our fragile ship would splinter. It pitched and rolled under the angry gale's howl. Waves smashed against the hull, sending horrible, shuddering booms as the tortured wood strained. One moment we pitched skyward, pause and then plunged into the sea. We were tossed and knocked against the bulkheads like dolls in a giant's temper tantrum.

Most of the solar lamps are out. I hurry to finish this entry. The storm intensifies and I am afraid for my life.

Bishma and Ali, pray for me.

No matter what happens, I love you.

The Levant

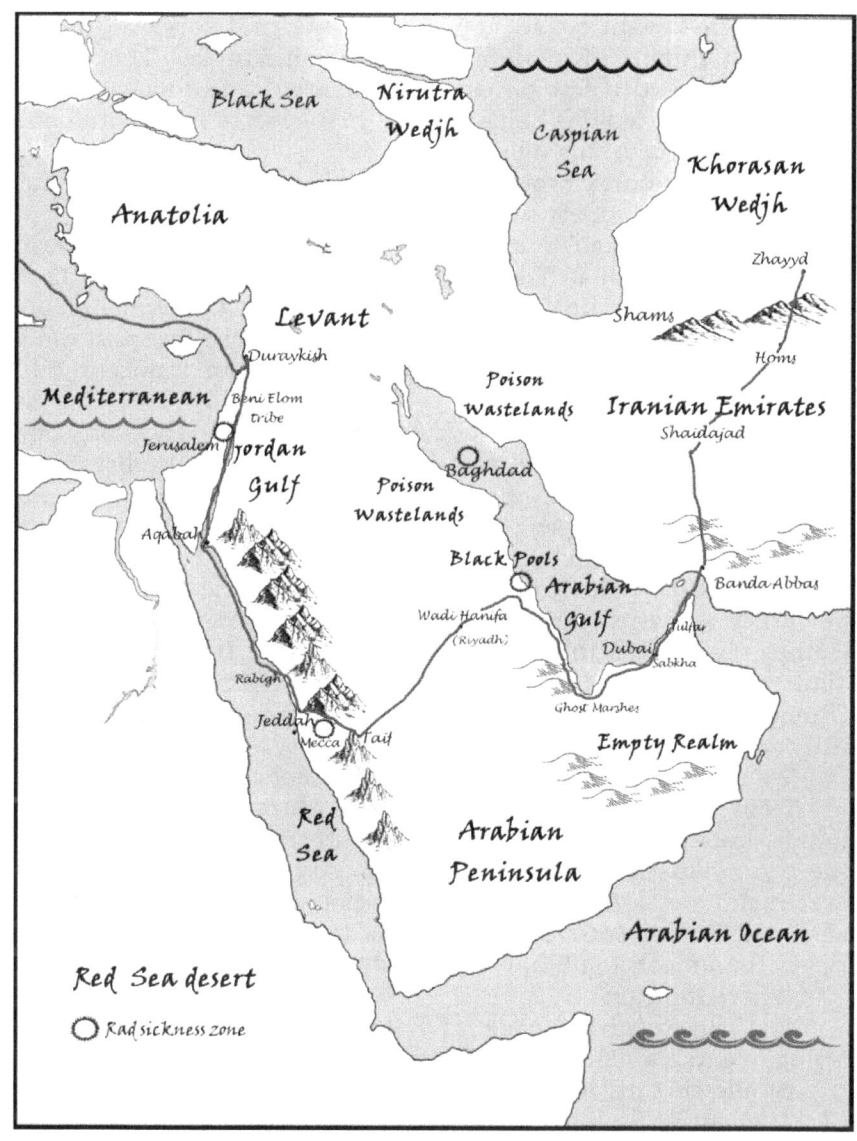

Day 21. The Levant coast.   My precious journal survived, having tucked it tightly in my clothing before the ship broke. The journal was soaked, and a few pages were smeared, and today the sun dried them out, leaving salt stains. I managed to find a quill and ink in an old chest this morning.

Since the storm brought us here, these days were frightful, filled with much anxiety and violent threats.

The sun is high overhead. I sit on a crate; one of many scattered along this hot, sweltering shoreline where distant, concrete walls rise up like grave markers from the sandy slopes and blue, sparkling waves. I cannot believe these five past days. It seemed like centuries ago, a different life, an innocent time when last wrote to you.

We are surrounded by our ruined dreams. They are now reduced to broken boxes, crates, sails, splintered timbers and, regrettably, those poor pilgrims who will not live to see their dreams fulfilled. Those of us whom karma spared cling to life beneath makeshift shelters assembled from crates, wreckage, and shredded sails.   The Kumari Daughter's broken leg was attended to by her servants and our physician. Some, with only ragged clothes clinging to their bruised and bleeding bodies, wandered aimlessly along the shore, searching for survivors and belongings. Others watched the sea; hoping what remains of our small fleet will come for us.

We are derelicts, lost on the Levant beach.

I am spent; my muscles ach, head throbs, throat dry. My hands, battered bruised and covered with sores, struggle to hold the pen. Nausea troubles me; I am forced to stop as dry heaves overwhelm me.   At times I subconsciously reach for my waist sash and touch your porcelain urns to reassure me that I am richer than most; I still have my most precious items. . .

Where to begin?

Pen hovers above page as I look towards Duce and Pavlo trying to catch a fish in waist deep in the surf and in the rocks.

Swallowing my terror, I start with . . .

The storm.

It intensified throughout the night; tossing our little ship like a cork. Items not secured to the bulkheads quickly became projectiles as the decks heaved and swayed. Crew members scrambled below carried faint, yellow lanterns frantically lashed down cargo, blankets and chests then the deck hatches. I felt trapped in this wooden prison. All around the ship creaked and groaned; waves pummeled our seemingly tiny hull with violent shudders. Cold sea water was forced through the hatches and we scrambled to plug the gaps with blankets or clothing.

We huddled together, mothers clutched their children, some wept, others whispered in frightened tones, a few coughed, others sang religious tunes to dispel our fear. But it offered little comfort. In the dim cabins terror etched our faces as we tried to calm our anxieties.

Outside crew desperately shouted and scrambled to tame the storm. I managed to secure myself against a bulkhead with my hammock. On the deck above the Kumari Daughter spoke earnestly with her staff. I heard scraping as objects were moved. A short time later Altus appeared, carrying a lantern and soaked from the water having poured thought the steps. The lantern made his face look drawn out like some creature from the Nether Realms. He reassured us the Kumari Daughter was praying for our safety and that the Mother protected us. Then he paused by me and stared into my eyes. He squeezed my hand, smiled and left.

After tucking my journal in my clothing I tried to sleep, but anxiety and expectation frayed my nerves as I envisioned our ship breaking any moment.

I think another day passed as we struggled with the elements and the captain tried vainly to cover the distance separating us from the Syrian coast.

Then, I think it was the afternoon on the third day I was aroused by a loud bang followed by sounds of splintering wood. The ship hit something and lurched violently and we tumbled among shouts and screams. Crew shouted as the storm howled.

We had only a single lamp working and watched in horror as water gushed onto us from the stairs, showering us with boxes and anything that had broken free. Above, pilgrims screamed as they scrambled for the stairs leading to the main hatch.

At that instant the ship rolled steeply and I feared we would flip. Panic ensured. Everyone raced up for the stairs, trampling each other and joined the Kumari's group trying to escape the hold.

The ship was struck violently and shuttered as timbers splintered. The upper deck hatch tore off, sending water pouring down, knocking pilgrims backwards where they tumbled onto the slippery deck.

I was struck by a falling passenger and thrown against the bulkhead. Stunned, I lay as passengers clawed and fought each other to escape. Walls of cold, salty water gushed from the ceiling and raced across the floor, pulling and tearing at whatever was in their path. People screamed as they were pulled into the watery fray. The ship pitched and rolled. The surging waters tossed us onto the opposite bulkheads, instantly killing many.

I struggled against the rising water and reached the hatch opening. The pilgrim ahead of me blocking the hatch was swept away and I pulled myself through the opening onto the deck. The deck was chaos. Another ship's hull had crushed the quarter deck and the constant waves pounded the two ships, quickly reducing them to splinters.

A large wave knocked me over. I slid towards to the opposite side and grasped a rope. Desperately I held on as the water pulled our ship down into the dark, chaotic water. Then the rope snapped and I was dragged into the churning sea.

I was briefly disoriented by pounding by timbers, crates, clothing and bodies. My lungs ached and my muscles frantically struggled against the violent thrashing as I used my all strength to reach air. My head poked through the surface where the angry ocean tossed me. The wind howled angrily, pelting my face so hard I had trouble catching my breath. As I crested the waves, I saw our and another ship in a death embrace. Then I dropped into a trough being bombarded by debris and frantic people. Someone grabbed me and pulled me down. I panicked and kicked at them, but their deadly grip was only torn away by a crashing wave. By the time I crested the wave I saw our ship briefly before it broken hull vanished below.

The shouts and screams were muffled by the storm. Everything was a blurred impression. I cannot recall when I found that crate and lashed myself with rope. Clinging half in and out of the water, waves crashed over me. I bobbed and swayed as the storm relentlessly lashed me. I drifted in and out of consciousness. My little raft left behind the cries of death until I was along with the storm's rage. I was thistly, hungry and terrorized by fear. Night came, increasing my anxieties. I prayed to Taleju, you Ali and Bishma or tried calming my nerves by mentally focusing on her mandala. I thanked the sun when it returned to a calming sea in the gray morning, In my delirium I thought I died and floated in the Neither worlds, it became hard to distinguish wake from dream state.

Despite my fate, that vision returned during those times when I slipped between sleep and wake.

Here I was in the same small room, at the same table studying the cards, wondering which to pick up, and knowing I am not ready for what it will reveal. I hesitated, I sensed dread. Then I heard wonderful melody. Looking up I saw Taleju sitting across from me, smiling. She told me not be afraid.

Unsure, I reached for a card: it read *Consider all immediate and future consequences.* Then I heard thunder and saw the Yantra of Entanglement rising from the card. I turned it over.

There was faded, sepia, tall building on a beach lined with palm trees. Shadowy, metallic coaches moved on black ribbons. People in robes walked beneath the palm trees and others in skimpy clothing lounged on a beach. I was shocked by this lack of solar protection. It was hot; the sun pierced sandy air of a world normally desert, but strangely transformed into something it was not.

My viewpoint shifted. I was inside that building. It was magnificent with red and brown, polished marble and gold trim. Blue and green mosaics and opulent carpets covered the floor. On a wall inlaid gold cursive writing dominated the room. Strange, glass and metal decorations hung from ached, dome ceiling, emitting sparkling light. The richness to this place was unimaginable.

From tall windows sunlight streamed in, catching an array of people in white robes and dark suits. Some sat at tables and, sipped from delicate cups, others lounge in overstuffed chairs, reading papers. Rich smells: exotic teas, pastries, all manner of prepared meals bespeak of a foreign, wealthy world I cannot comprehend. Gone were the simple clothes and minimal food or plain dishes; everything spoke of excess: from the manner in which these people conducted themselves to their oversized building and furnishings.

Now I was a viewpoint in a room overlooking the beach. In the distant haze massive glass and steel towers covered the horizon. An oval, dark table was in the middle of the wood paneled room; that blond woman, Mr. Blofeld and Senator spoke with a regal, commanding man in a white thobe and black cloak trimmed with gold. Beside him was another man, Curtis, in a black suit similar to Blofeld. This Curtis frightens me. His tanned, sharp features and thin lips reminded me of a jackal. His cold, calculating eyes were hidden by round, tinted glasses and never missed a thing. His close cropped hair showed scars, which I got the impression due to fights. His stout body bespeaks of incredible cruelty and menace.

On the table lay pictures and papers which they occasionally referred to. Their voices were low, flat, and emotionless. Although it was cool, the Senator's nervously sweat betrayed his nervousness.

I wanted to flee this place. Dread, fear, resentment gripped my heart. Yet, I was trapped; I watched this play, knowing the ending but helpless to stop it. Is this a past life or vision?

As they talked, Curtis held a slender object and constantly presses its top. It made clicking noises. Occasionally he used it to write on paper. The Senator was annoyed by his actions; the others didn't notice. Tense, underlying hostilities permeated the group. The woman spoke, the others listened. Blofeld never addressed to the group but the woman acted as his spokesperson, speaking as though having rehearsed a script. The group averted their eyes from Blofeld, except Curtis. His glasses hold steady on Blofeld like a trained, war dog.

The woman held up documents and remarked according to the Senator's report his radicals came under the control of a new leader from Mecca, a Saudi hothead named Qahtani, who wanted to free the Middle East from USG financial slavery. He was very popular with the group and abandoned their original task. Now they became fanatics spreading his agenda. He already ignited civil disturbances and several civil wars. Sheikh Maktoum agreed with him and threatened to cancel the loan.

Now civil war threatened the UAE. Since their last meeting several Emirates joined his cause. Bombings and violence escalated and several attempts made on the Sheikh's life. The oil fields were taken over by the radicals, and they threatened to use nukes to destroy the refineries if their deadline was not met. They demanded all westerner business and banks leave within a week.

Those in her government worried for the Middle East stability.

She reminded the Senator failed his duty which now called for drastic measures. The USG was not going to lose another `Allied' and stood by to send in the military `to protect their interests, offer the Sheikh protection and secure resources for the benefit of his people.'

Blofeld wanted to avoid trouble and pledged his government was a mutual friend but needed assurance from the sheikh that he supported what his father pledged.

Blofeld glanced at the woman who produced a contract. The Sheikh read through the contract with his advisor. He finally shook his head and returned the contract. He said the Kingdom offered loans without the stipulation he handed his nation to westerner bankers. For the sake of his people, he decided to go with them instead.

The woman's face twisted into anger, she felt her life crashing. She flung the folder at the Sheikh, saying she and the USG wasted two years settling this up. She reminded him her government looked upon this as a betrayal of friends and anyone interfering was considered hostiles.

Arguments exploded and tempers flared between the Sheikh and the woman. As accusations flew Blofeld touched the woman's shoulder. She instantly became quiet, fuming. Finally the woman threw up her hands in disgust.

She suggested someone should teach the Kingdom a lesson about interfering by bombing Mecca.

Curtis paused flicking his pen.

The sound of crashing waves grew louder and washed away my images. I woke. I was pitched forward and the crate rolled over me, pulling me below. Waves pummeled from every direction and got into my nose and mouth. I fought the heavy crate pinning me to the sandy bottom. I twisted my swollen wrists free of the ropes and pushed the crate away. When my head broke through the sea I coughed and choked. I used what little energy I had to stagger onto the beach and collapsed onto my knees, gasping. Waves splashed around me, bringing sand and that crate near my feet. Spent, darkness overcame me.

I do not know how long I lay near the surf. I think I reached the beach on the prior afternoon; now it was now mid morning. I rubbed sand away from my swollen eyelids and checked myself. My hair was matted, clothes torn and bloody and fresh cuts throbbed. My skin was red and stung from sun exposure and I was coated in sand and salt.

I heard voices above the waves and staggered towards them. I found many pilgrims wandered aimlessly, stunned, speechless or shouting for love ones.

I was very weak and it was difficult sitting. I and about ten other people occupied a makeshift tent constructed of crates, timber and cloth. We huddled in the shade. Some whispered quietly or stared out at the glittering ocean. A man remarked the many pilgrims sacrificed themselves to save the Kumari Daughter.

Later Pavlo found me and offered water. As I pressed the cup against my swollen lips and drank slowly I sensed great pain swallowing. He explained that his family and others were searching for survivors and trying to salvage what they could from the wreckage scattered along the shore. He said we were thirty kilometers from Duraykish—our intended destination.

Judging by the debris, I estimated that more than half the fleet perished. The whereabouts of the remaining ships are unknown.

I was sadden by our misfortune but grateful to be alive. I wondered if you or Ali would have been as lucky as I.

The sun moved closer to the horizon. My swollen hands struggled to write. Someone shouted from the ridge above the beach. Camel riders approach and they carry weapons. . .

Day 22. They had taken everything. I and a few wounded were left to fend for ourselves. This afternoon we huddled beneath rocks to avoid the sun and only moved at night. Yesterday bandits came here, claiming they controlled of the coast and as payment stole everything. They forced those well enough to load camels or pressed them into their services as porters, later to be sold as slaves.

Those resisted were killed by weapons firing projectiles called 'guns.' These long sticks made terrible thunder and spew fire and smoke; they left deep wounds. We were terrified. This was my first glimpse into the power of the ancients and horrors described by Taleju.

The Kumari Daughter and her group spent hours pleading with their leader, a youth in orange and brown robes and blue turban. His hate filled face never softened. I never saw a person consumed by such feelings before. To show his contempt he killed one of the Advisors then demanded she call upon Taleju to resurrect him. When she tried to explain he slapped her face. He was surrounded by crimson, stormy energies. Is this the hatred that consumed humanity before the Purge? His actions left me nauseated. I was shocked. I could not imagine this kind of behavior.

They gathered us in a line and their leader inspected us. Those who he deemed fit was quickly escorted to join another group. When the leader came to me he paused and I noticed the red energies surrounding him vanished as though sucked away. His eyes briefly lost that hatred, replaced by fear. Without a word he pulled me from the line and shoved me away. During this, my urn bottles came loose and fell onto the group. To my horror when I reached for them the leader scooped them up, admired the blue and white designs and tucked them in his robe.I protested and he violent slapped me across the cheek. My head rang and I was momentarily dizzy. As my vision cleared I saw rides pointing their weapons at me. I struggled with my rage and helplessness.

The riders placed ropes around the group's neck and beaten to hoist their burdens on their backs. Forming a long column, they waited under the leader watchful eyes. Riders slung their weapons across their knees and in menacing displays brought their weapons to their shoulder and fired.

Pilgrims panicked, wailed or collapsed onto their knees, begging for their lives. The riders killed a few outright and warned their captives to pick up their load. A few laughed or threw comments, sometimes whipping hostages with their camel sticks and those collapsing from their burden were trampled to death. I watched silently, my throat tightened as I fight back tears. The column disappeared beyond the concrete ruins just before sunset.

Nausea gripped me and I suffered a bout of dry heaves. I nearly passed out. The air where our pilgrims died was thick with dark energetic patches.

Stunned, feeling helpless I sat in the shadows, listening to pilgrim's wails and sobs. I thought of my plight, realizing we would perish if we stayed here. But this was not my concern at this moment. They took my precious urns and I would get them back!

I thought of the leader and his reaction. A plan formed. I would use his fear to my advantage.

Later I consulted a map and instruments I found earlier. I calculated our location. I had no idea if the news of our mishap reached Duraykish or even a search party was sent. The bandits headed south east; the map showed a settlement along a string of hills about fifty kilometers away. Since this was the only settlement, I concluded this was their destination.

It was evening. I gathered the pilgrims and I could not think of anything to say to settle my and their anxiety so I read from The Awakenings. I was surprised by how receptive they were listening to my voice cracked and paused when fits of cough disrupted me. When finished, I outlined my plan. We would follow the bandits and get our loved ones back. A few agreed to follow; most were afraid and too weak to travel. Throughout the early night I assisted those building shelters. It left me very exhausted. I have not eaten for two days and it was a struggle to even walk.

When the moon is at its zenith I and a dozen survivors will head into the desert. We have only water to carry, salvaged from the wreck.

Ali, Bishma, I go now.

Day 24. Ali, Bishma---with Taleju's blessing I am alive.

I am glad this day is ended. Never had I felt so helpless and feared for my life. I had pushed myself into places I thought impossible, I gambled with lives, not really knowing what I was doing. I am nauseated but emotionally stronger by this ordeal.

This day we covered thirty kilometers. The previous night's pace was grueling; I forced myself on, trying to cover as much distance night would allow. We continued into the morning until sweat soaked my clothing. The black rocks were deep, offering minimal shade on this rolling terrain. We huddled together; everyone was spent. I slept restlessly, ever fearful of discovery. I had hoped those who fell behind would catch up, but by evening they had not. We resumed our journey.

Because of our pace, our water was used up last evening. We had no choice but to continue. We left one person in the rocks with instructions to return to the beach if we failed, or inform our party if showed up. We covered our faces because we did not have goggles. The glair left me with throbbing, nauseating headaches. My weakness slowed me at times, but my determination compelled us to cross the sand and gravel field which to seem to stretch forever.

By the time we covered twenty kilometers before reaching their village we were near mad with thirst. Five of us arrived near dawn and waited in the rocks, gazing out at the shallow valley surrounded by rolling hills of shale and sand. Ahead were mud buildings, a few palm trees and smoke from cooking fires. Pilgrims shared an open pen with our baggage camels. Sounds of clanking pots, shouts and camel growls echoed in the still, sandy air.

While the others rested I read Taleju for inspiration and steeled my nerves. Duce wanted to bring his sword, but I said this would provoke them. Disappointed, reluctantly he complied. With the sun behind our backs I, Duce and several others walked towards the camp. I hoped this would be as threatening than if we rode into their midst.

They spotted us and camel riders sped towards us, shouting and waving weapons. The Kumari Daughter raised a hand to shield her eyes and looked towards us. I fight the urge to flee and carefully measured my step. I continued my purposeful walk, leading the others with soft words of encouragement.

The riders slowed and eyed us. I spread my hands, showing them we were not armed. I sensed uncertainty and their fear.

They stopped a few yards away and glanced at each other. The leader's camel continued a few paces ahead. He raised his weapon at us and for a moment I braced for the shot but did not hesitate. When I was a few meters away I removed my face covering and sat. There was apprehension behind his stern mask. He dismounted and we sat facing each other. He stared into my eyes then looked away quickly; I noticed the flashes of red and brown energies betraying his fear. I knew smatterings of his dialect and he seemed to understand as I struggled for words. But his reaction was outright confusion, as if a woman never talked directly to him. He tried to appear calm, but I could tell by his demeanor he was frightened.

When I spoke my anxiety and fear vanished. It was as if another being chose my words, articulating words, meanings. I remained strangely calm. I seemed to be here on this plain but also gazing back into the past and forward into the future. It was frightful, for I never experienced this before. He listened; gradually his face softened. During our conversation I kept my eyes downcast out of respect. He asked why I was with these people and if I worshipped the Kumari Daughter. When I explained I followed only Taleju and shared their pilgrimage, he stated the Kumari and her people were hypocrites.

When he gestured eastward and pointed at me, insisting I was someone else I did not understand. Exhaustion sapped my energy and I feared I could not continue this much longer. I then asked about my perfume bottles he took, asking them for their return. He looked doubtful and through hand gestures and carefully chosen I indicated them were very important. I tossed him a few silver coins at his feet. He watched me then handed them.

He gauged his emotions and sensed my opportunity. I asked if he would release our party so we can continue our journey. At first he refused and quickly rose. He stood over me, searching the eastern horizon as though expecting other would appear. Tense minutes followed. I expected to meet my end.

Finally the leader quickly turned his back. He walked to his camel, paused and raised a hand. A young rider stared at me, but it was due to . . . .admiration? Then they rode off. A few minutes later the pilgrims were released. Overcome with relief I buried my face in my hands, weeping with joy and exhaustion. My group knelt around me, placing comforting hands on my trembling shoulders. Their love filled my heart, replacing that cold emptiness I left since beginning this journey. I realized then that, though my motive had been selfish motivated, I my life was not mine but theirs.

I was too weak to rise so my group assisted me. We waited. A group of camels laden with our stolen possessions and the pilgrims came to us. The Kumari Daughter was at the head of the escorts. She glanced at me in passing. Behind walked Altus who embraced me, as did many others. The bandit who admired me earlier brought a camel and assisted me in the saddle. I climbed on as I had done many times when a child. The bandit and his escorts were astonished by my handling.

The bandits provided escorts, food and water for our return trip to the beach. We left shortly after, pausing throughout the day to rest and eat. When offered dates and water, I fought the urge to devour them quickly, fearful it would aggravate my cramps. Pilgrims walked beside me, staring up admirably and tried to engage conversation. I was too tired to reply but offered weak smiles.

That night we camped along tall hills where the ocean could be seen in the distance. My head aches and eyes hurt from traveling without goggles. This evening someone found a box of food and distributed them among us. Duce composed a song about their adventure had how I saved them. I was glad it was night; my cheeks flushed with embarrassment.

Later, the Kumari Daughter came by and spoke softly so as to not be overheard. I thought she was going to thank me but instead accused me of usurping her authority. I resented her implications and sensed for the first time she shared the same fear as the Bandit leader.

I waited until afterwards then wiped constrained tears. On that night I truly felt betrayed by the person who I held in unquestioning loyalty for my whole life.

Day 25. We have a new traveler. Yusuf, the rider who offered the camel, remained with us after his escorts left. For some reason he had taken a liking for me—which I must confess, is embarrassing. He immediately set into tasks: built fires, fetched things and made sure I was—all under the guise of helping the camp. I haven't the heart to send him away; I'm uncomfortable with the idea of servants but his smile and enthusiasm was infectious. Besides, all are welcome in Taleju's camp, even though many pilgrims distrusted him and found my attitude towards him confusing.

Yusuf is a Beni Elom, the tribe who lives here. He is about twenty, was raised by a bandit relative after his family died when he a child. He wears a Nepal Commonwealth coin around his neck that was given to by his father. He met many travelers with tales of the outside world and he drawn to venture beyond his realm. Then when he met me he saw his opportunity. He added that a traveler from the East is rare, although he did not elaborate its meaning.

Like us he performed prayer rituals three times each day facing east, but he recites these in what he called `the old language'. He was fascinated by Pavlo's family music and when not doing chores Duce teaches him the mandolin. Despite their cultural differences, he and Duce are quickly bonding.

Since returning, talk of the events spread through our camp and pilgrims followed me with many questions. I am weary of their behavior. After recounting a dozen times I refused further discussion. I am too tired to spend energy on this nonsense! Someone had taken to writing my words and shared these with others. I had noticed within camp there is a kind of unspoken gratitude and reverence wherever I go. I do not like this because it draws unwanted attention.

And, if they _really knew_ the reason for my visit they would not hold me in such esteem.

This evening the Kumari Daughter and I had another unpleasant encounter. It involved Yusuf. She asked if he intended to join the pilgrims then he needed her permission. I explained I instructed Yusuf to see the Kumari Daughter but he explained he assumed I was the group leader.

The Kumari Daughter was livid and threatened to toss me out of the group. This angered me and I said only Taleju could do so. I have never seen her face twist with such hatred! She replied in a cold, threatening tone that _she was the only_ Taleju Sanctioned Representative and I was only there by her grace. She added the Conformation did not include people like me and I made a mockery of everything sacred. Before I could reply she stormed away.

I stood as though bolted to the ground. Sweat soaked me, my heart raced, I clenched and unclenched my fists as my feelings washed over me. I screamed with pent up rage. I was glad it was dark so others could not see or hear me.

Or so I thought.

Later as I sat before my shelter, Yusuf joined me and asked if the night creature had harmed me. Confused, I looked at him and shook my head. He said it had red eyes and was at the place where I was last seen.

A cold chill filled me. I shivered, knowing the implication. I resolved to be more careful showing my feelings.

Day 26. A rescue party arrived this morning with badly needed supplies. The meager food stuff given by the bandits had run out yesterday morning. We spent most of the day tending the sick, transferring items and getting ready for the three day journey back to our original destination. Reports showed that about two hundred and fifty travelers perished, meaning only about one hundred and twenty survived. It was the Confirmations' worse casualties in more than two hundred years.

The rescue party was gravely concerned we met the Beni Elom bandits and were astonished by our good fortune. Some Satori proudly claimed it was the brave actions by the Kumari Daughter which prevented bloodshed. I and my original rescuers were stunned and angry by this blatant lie. Altus met my reaction and shook his head. He understood. It served no purpose challenging her

We left shortly after sunset. My heart was cold and empty while the Kumari Daughter led us like a triumphant mother.

Month 12, day 1. Duraykish. I write from a wood porch atop a hill overlooking a sweeping valley of rocky, white stone intermixed with low lying shrubs and olive orchards. About two kilometers distant was the glittering sea. The original city was beneath the ocean. This new Duraykish lay on a valley transformed into a bay. Tilled pomegranate, grape, and lemon groves hug the hillside and provided trade for travelers heading north and east. The souks were active and wealth flows into the communal coffers.

We were informed the Holy Lands are now safe enough to visit for short periods. We will be the first Confirmation pilgrims to see this area since the Purge.

The news of our encounter with the Beni Elom quickly spread the village. They are afraid that they may retaliate, leaving them anxious and fearful about our lingering presence. The Beni Elom is descendants of the original people who ruled the Holy Lands before the Purge and caused much turmoil throughout the desert nations. Inhabitants said they were arrogant, very protective of their territory and sneaky; although I have seen none of this in Yusuf. Even so, whenever he went to town he brought unwanted glances and resentment. I think some feared he is a spy on a scouting mission. Thus, I kept him restricted to our villa outside town.

It took until yesterday to salvage what we could from the storm. The material was distributed among the pilgrims, except me. I got nothing. However, last evening pilgrims visited with several chests in gratitude. Afterwards I performed a thank you ceremony for those who gave their lives so we may share their belongings. I stored clothing and everyday items, dishes, cups, pots in large, dark wood chests with beaten, brass accents. I placed them in the main room as in remembrance. The wood gave off a pleasant, sweet smells, despite salt stains.

The villa housed six pilgrims including Yusuf. What we called home these past five days was adapted to the environment so it caught the morning and evening light and afternoon breeze. Half the structure was stone, whereas the remainder was walls of lattice wood of intricate designs. This permitted cross ventilation through each room and kept the house comfortable. The entire villa's floor was built on stilts where we stored supplies, rugs, and other furnishings.

Thick, wool carpets covered the wood floors. Seating shelves were built into the stone walls and covered with blue and yellow cushions and bolsters. Each room was painted different, bright colors about half way up with the rest of the walls and ceiling finished with white gypsum. The morning and afternoon light shining through the lattice sparkled like waves on the ocean.

The kitchen area was outside in the back, sheltered by trees. It had beehive clay oven and carefully crafted cooking pits that distributed the heat onto metal plates. The stove was so efficient that solar discs along the base kept the surface hot for six hours.

We slept outside on the flat roof, wrapped in thin blankets and using cushions for head rests. Metal bird cages hung from branches near the stairs leading onto the roof. A particularly beautiful blue and white song bird offered delightful melodies at the beginning and end of the day.

Duraykish architecture and clothing styles were a blend of my world in the west, and this new, mysterious world of the desert. They were gracious and friendly and conduct business with expectations of socializing, tea drinking and haggling over prices. This was a custom from the Purge days and was a time honored sport. Not to engage in these activities brought distrust and dishonor for the buyer and seller. Their markets were busy and filled with gossip brought in by travelers.

Some town inhabitants wanted to visit with me this afternoon but when I greeted them they got frightened and left. I did not mind because I am still uncomfortable with strangers and shun attention.

The storm delayed us two weeks, meaning we are almost a month behind schedule. This is concerning since we've yet to cross the eastern deserts which are heading into their hottest season. This will force us to shorten our travel days, pause more often and worry about provision. Altus warned the Arabia portion of our journey can be grueling and frightful.

There was ugly talk about me as well. Some pilgrims claimed we were doing fine until I joined them; mishap after mishap has since followed us. I thought people gave nature more credit than to hold fast to superstition! I sense this may cause conflicts, possible divide our group--something we cannot afford. I entertained the idea that the Daughter may be behind these but I will not waste time on speculation.

Since coming here we were busy getting supplies, arranging the route and plan for alternate paths. I look forward to first pilgrims will visit the Holy Lands.

It is dark. I close for now.

Good night Ali and Bishma.

Day 2. I spotted a woman on the edge of a grove watching me for hours. Although she was nonthreatening, the fact that she did not move during this time bothered me. When I approached she vanished but not before I glimpsed her face and clothing. Her face was hidden by goggles and blue scarf. I judged she was in her early thirties, thin features. Her outer robe was loose and long sleeve; beneath this I glimpsed a long dress with patterns on front and secured by a waist sash. A silver dagger was tucked in it. Her impression was of a race I had not seen and wonders if she was from the deep desert.

I sensed she avoided me not out of fear, but we should not meet. What was strange about this encounter was the area where she stood vibrates with residual electrical energy sounding like humming of bees. It left me chilled and I hastened away.

Towards evening Pavlo and his family serenaded our hosts. After the music Altus took me aside. He was troubled by the Kumari Daughter taking credit for saving our group. I said it did not matter to me because I did not seek recognition or fame. He seemed fascinated by my answer and for a long time watched me. I forced a smile to hide my discomfort. Then as he left he remarked Taleju would be proud of me.

Day 3. Yusuf was all smiles. His progress with the mandolin earned him a place in Pavlo's family music session this evening. His fingers lightly touched the strings and the notes complemented the group. He was a natural and anticipated what chords to use. Even the few villagers complimented him. I think they were realizing that this young man was not what they initially feared.

I had a dream last night in us. Ali, and Bishma stood with me atop a mountain. Below were dark clouds; the sky was gray, there was no sound. Bishma took my hand and said `Hear the souls of a million pilgrims? They wait for Taleju to speak away the clouds.' I looked at you, Ali and asked when Taleju will arrive. You replied `She is already here.'

Day 7. Today we set out south along the `narrow ridge' to the Holy Lands. Those too weak or ill will return home. We desperately needed to make up for lost time and hoped to get through Arabia before the summer heat prevented us.

Our caravan numbered one hundred ten camels and ninety assistants—all recruited from Duraykish and surrounding villages. The Kumari Daughter traveled inside a red and gold palanquin carried by a large camel. Her entourage rode similar equipped beasts; the weak and some children hitched rides on pack camels—sitting high on the canvass crates, poles and sacks. Most everyone else walked, covering the kilometers on blistered, calloused feet wrapped in sandals. Most carried what little possessions and comforts in rucksacks; many used long walking poles to support themselves. Our pilgrimage group carried enough supplies for two weeks. By then we should reach the town of Green Sand on the shore of what was known as the Urdun Gulf and they will outfit us for the trip to Aqaba. Duraykish claimed it is rich with trade and fish. It is on the shore of what was known as the Dead Sea.

To reach our goal we will have to travel through Beni Elom land and are instructed not to deviate from the trail or approach villages outside our designated area. The Beni Elom is made up of warring tribes and anyone passing through their land must pay tribute. The Kumari Daughter carried a letter promising gold and other valuables for any tribe offering protection. I suspected Beni Elom really do not care and would prefer rob and sell us as slaves.

Yusuf travelled with me, teaching me the finer points of camel ownership.

I resumed my role as scout but in addition our advance party represented our group when we met strangers. We checked maps, compasses, took radiation readings, tracked our path via the stars and in the evening sent someone back with our report. I was ordered not to leave my group since I am in charge. Luckily Yusuf, Duce and his family were with me to ease my apprehension and anxiety. I at times resented not being with the main group, but I can do without the Daughter's antagonistic behavior. Over this past month I saw through her righteousness pomp. She was a frightened, selfish woman who really wanted to be someone else—perhaps the Kumarisattva.

This evening after a meal of rice, dates, cucumbers and olives I sat beneath a tree and watched the sunset. This was the first opportunity to enjoy the close of the day alone. My thoughts lingered on my home; the village, and Bishma enjoying the rope swing while Ali and I sat on the porch watching the light play through the leaves. That moment seemed like a different life; full of innocence, dreams and an unknown future of promise.

For a moment, just as the sun vanished behind the hills, I saw in my Third Eye gold and blue lines crisscrossing the hills. They hummed and pulsated like deep, drums. I sensed these were the earth's energy lines. When I tried focusing on them they vanished. I wasn't sure if I imagined these, yet their sounds lingered and permeated my being. I felt strangely peaceful.

Day 9: These two days travelling were hot. There was no need to wear protective eye covering because shade from so many trees kept away the threat of solar burns—although we still keep our heads covered in our sledge hats. This morning we passed the last of the tilled groves marking the boundaries of the Duraykish. Now wild trees and rocky slopes make our terrain. The trail was smooth, marked occasionally by upright stones in several languages. Yusuf said this was now Beni-Elom land. Although the area looked peaceful, I sensed we were being tracked.

Today our group came to a grove of trees. There was a stone well. Yusuf warned us not to use it. It was then I notice a carving of a skull and Beni-Elom writing. He said the water was good, but visitors must get permission and pay a fee. He pointed to a clump of trees and said we were being observed. As we rested and got our bearings I sent a messenger to the group.

As we broke for the noon meal riders appeared, carrying weapons. I was frightened and had visions of being tied up and carried off to a slave market. Yusuf calmly stepped between us, motioning to me to remain calm and show no fear. They paused several yards away, observing us. Their faces were hidden by blue face scarves. At this time my back was to them. When I finished handing out bread, I faced them. They were startled and talked softly among themselves. Yusuf and I walked over to them and Yusuf acted as my interpreter. I met their stares, pressed my palms together and bowed my greeting. I explain we were the Conformation scouting party and asked permission to cross their lands to the south to visit the Holy Land. They replied there was not much in the Holy Land but we could pass through their territory for a payment. When I inquired their price, they hesitated and rode away, talking among themselves. Yusuf watched briefly then shrugged. He said they were afraid to talk to me.

Day 10. This has been a horrible day. In the morning as we prepared to break camp a rider hurried up and warned us Beni Elom were holding the Kumari's group hostage and threatened to take our caravan. Yusuf and I immediately rode back and in my haste I nearly fell off my camel. As we approached, shouts and pleas echoed through the hills, followed by frightful boom.

The scene was chaos. Handlers, porters and pilgrims sat or ran around, screaming. A large group of Beni Elom riders surrounded the Kumari's immediate group while others stood over several figures near the well—covered in blood. The Daughter was screaming at an elderly man who I assumed was their leader. His white beard was dyed with red henna and his bushy brows were screwed up into deadly glare. He pointed a walking stick at her and swatted the documents she tried to show. Taking a breath of courage to still my anxious heart, I dismounted from my camel and Yusuf joined me. Immediately the Daughter accused me of not paying these savages for safe passage and blamed me for the death of three people who went to the well, thinking it was safe. I ignored her and faced the leader. He spit at the Daughter, cursing her and when his eyes fell on me became strangely quiet. He signaled and a dozen men surrounded me with bared swords; one gently jabbed me in the ribs. I felt warm blood but I dare not show pain or surprise. Meanwhile the Daughter kept yelling and was only quieted by Altus's firm hand on her shoulder.

I pressed my hands together and bowed to the leader. Taken aback, he hesitated and repeated this gesture of respect Yusuf taught me during our time in Duraykish. Through Yusuf I explained I sent word yesterday to avoid the well until the tribes were paid. He replied they had not and this woman—he indicated the Daughter—insisted her group had made prior arrangements, calling him a liar in front of this men. When he came to collect the fee he caught three people at the well and killed them.

He calmed as I spoke and all the while he watched my expression. If asked if I was in charge. I told him the Kumari Daughter was responsible and I was just with the scouts. He said everyone lied but that I and Yusuf were the only truth Sayers.

Yusuf quoted a fee for passage, well and the embarrassment we caused them. I protested. Yusuf warned me this was how his people saw it and to protest or show contempt meant disrespect and possible retribution. It was about facing face and tribal honor. With heart pounding in my mouth I swallowed my anger, turned to the leader and forced an apology. Ten silver coins were agreed and I placed them on the ground for his inspection. He knelt and carefully took each coin, weighing it in his thick palm. Satisfied he nodded and waved. His men pulled back, promising us safe passage to the next post.

Tension rose through the camp. I felt many eyes on me, sensing I was blamed for this incident. We buried the dead and gathering our things. After performing last rites, the Kumari Daughter quickly vanished in her palanquin. I asked Yusuf why Kumargi were so despised by the Beni Elom. Rather embarrassed he remarked that previous caravans promised much, only to lie and make trouble in his land. They felt their religious status placed them above the customs of others. I remarked that we were not religious, but spiritual and honored all things. He was surprised.

As we prepared to leave Altus took me aside and reminded me of my role and should have remained with my group. The

Daughter saw my return as challenge to her authority. Angry, I said if I had not returned things would not have gone well. He nodded, saying the Daughter assumed we had secured safe passage but instead I deliberately brought disaster. I held back a curse. I asked if my messenger arrived. He nodded. Then I asked why the Kumari Daughter hated me so much. Altus replied she was greatly troubled by something for years, and it seemed to be directed at those of not the Kumari religion.

I reminded him bluntly I am the most devoted follower and stormed off.

Day 12. Yesterday I heard rumors I was a Djinn in disguise and brought trouble. They conveniently forgot it was I who avoided a bloodbath and restored group honor. Some believed this, others did not—especially our Duraykish helpers who spent time with me at the city and heard accounts of my encounter with the robbers. I suspected the Kumari Daughter or her Satori was behind this. What's interesting was after this incident six Beni Elom joined my group; they were Yusuf's friends and spend a lot of time helping with chores and seemed to be genuinely interested in me. We were grateful for the help. They did not bother asking the Kumari permission, but assumed I approved. In the mood I was in, I did not care about she thought. Yusuf explained a woman as direct and brave as me was not seen in their culture. I'm an odd celebrity.

Afterwards I kept a ledger of messenger I sent. I vowed this would not happen again.

We camped overlooking Tiberius Elom Lake surrounded by lush trees. To the west the hills were rocky and barren. A river meandered to the south. There were recent dwellings among Purge era ruins. We were still in Beni Elom territory and dared not venture beyond our path to explore.

Since joining our group, Yusuf's friends not only have helped with chores, but in the evening they train with sword and spear. They come from warrior background and it is customary all men are skilled with weapons. At first I was uneasy but Yusuf assured we had nothing to worry. Their pledge was their binding honor. In these troubled time I reluctantly accept them. I have placed Duce in charge of security matters. The Beni Elom respected him and gives unquestioned dedication. Now I have guards stationed outside my tent and during travel. I am sad that my life has come to this. Perhaps they see something I don't. I have been a trusting spirit and only see the best in people.

The terrain we travelled though was vastly different than what Taleju described as hot, blistering, shrouded by perpetual, sandy gloom. This land threw off the Purge scars and life slowly returned.

This afternoon more pilgrims left the main party and joined us. Tensions between factions, the Daughter and her Satori were brewing unrest. Although I was only commanding a scouting party, they appreciated our team cooperation and looking out for each other. I suppose the stories and my recent actions contributed to their decision.

Day 14. Before the Purge this lake was contested ground by many cultures and religions. Great wars were fought here and controlling its shores brought wealth and prestige. The land felt old and tired; millions of souls walked its shores, leaving ruins in their passing. Evidence of its importance was carved into the broken land along the west; great upheaval and violence brought craters and green glass fields---most of which are now covered by sand and scrub trees.

I dreamt I wandered through a Purge city with wide roads, mechanical transport, noise and teaming masses. I stood on the city's shore and gazed out at a lake smaller than it was now, hearing stories about religious miracles and hoped for a better future. However, it only brought death, misery and beg the question: why do we seek to better ourselves spiritually yet insist destroying our world?

I thought our group would negotiate passage through Beni Elom territory to the Holy City but the Kumari Daughter insisted on doing this herself. It took most of the day to reach an agreement. The Beni Elom was not interested if it was an important stopping point on Taleju's journey, all they wanted was payment. They sensed our desperation and played it well. They got a stiff price for the visit and our passage to the wide, lush river to the south.

This lake was more than a hundred meters above its Pre Purge depth, erasing all traces of cities called Bethsaida. Korazin, Hippus, Magdala. Along the east side of the lake small villages offered boats upon smooth water where bountiful fish added to their diet. Along the west side among overgrown humps and mounds we visited ruins of a city called Tiberius; the city in my dreams. Here, Beni Elom huts made of stone dotted hillside of meager orchards and gardens. We were instructed to camp away from their main village.

According to Yusuf the Holy Lands were occupied only four months during the year due to the risk of Rad sickness. Our group came during the last month. We were the first Confirmation pilgrims to visit the west side of the lake.

The Kumari Daughter, wearing her finest red and gold robes, dress, sash and head cover stood on a mound, surveying the pilgrims eagerly surrounding her. Her face beamed with self importance. It was near sunset. Long, orange light marked by deep, purple shadows sculpts her into a hard, marble like statue. Her soft voice carried on the dusty, hot breeze. Like the Beni Elom I and a few others stood apart from the main group; I sensed they did not want us to share their moment. A few give me cold look. Beni Elom watched from the distant—some hostile, others with contemptuous tolerance. Our guide, an elder from the main tribe, ensured we were not harassed. It was obvious us strangers were not welcomed.

Most pilgrims had their red and gold copies of Taleju's The Awakenings open to the pages recounting her travels here.

This is the border of the Holy Land. Travel is difficult and I am only able to get close to the lake briefly before being forced away because of RAD sickness and breathing stifling, hot, sulfur laden air. The lake boils and steam columns cover this area. When the Purge hit, it tore apart the west bank and scorched the east. The earth broke apart and water long since trapped beneath ground gushed up to bury cites not yet covered in ash or mud. Angry north east volcanoes belch deadly smoke and ash. Nothing survived this place and I wonder what the future holds for this tortured earth. Visibility is limited to a kilometer which seems like I am trapped in thick, hot clouds. I must walk all night to avoid further delay in this place . . .

The Kumari Daughter read then spoke about the Purge healing humanity by casting aside the old ways and replacing them with Taleju's universal healing. She added that all who seek peace were welcome and she brings humanity's eternal awareness through the Mother's message.

I sensed her words were but deceit from a dark, troubled soul.

Later at my evening meal the Beni Elom elder came to me. He asked why I was not with the main pilgrims. I replied I belonged here with my small group. He added the Daughter's ramblings were from a crazy woman. The peace I sought lay to the east. His comments left me curious.

Day 15. Today we travelled twenty five kilometers, following the shore of Tiberius Lake and finally camped where the Urdun River began its journey to the Jordan Gulf. The trek was hilly and at times treacherous. Since we feared encounters with the Beni Elom, we monitored our progress and our scouts kept in contact with them using mirrors. A man from Duraykish was from the Great Sahara desert and his tribe developed a system of codes, which we quickly adopted. With training my group became proficient with it.

Even with the old man leading us, other tribes stood by to harass and occasionally throw stones at the Kumari's caravan. A pilgrim was struck in the arm. My group did not suffer this. I conclude it was the tribal leader escorted us.

We had hoped to reach the first Conformation pilgrims to travel the west bank of the Urdun river but Beni Elom tribe refused passage. Therefore tomorrow we will cross to the east and follow it to the Jordan Gulf, a trip by my calculations is about two hundred kilometers.

I sat beneath a big tree near the river bank and wrote by camp fire. Pavlo and a few others played music and told stories. Marsh flies and other biting bugs lay thick in the air. Their annoying buzz and bites were a constant annoyance. I do not like this place; it filled me with dread. I confessed the closer we got to the Holy Lands the more apprehensive I became. The long history of violence permeates the rocks and earth as though it was a living being. I feared it shall continue. The Beni Elom behavior support this consciousness and it is sad to see humanity still cling to ways that dominated this Purge world. My legs ached, stomach filled with anxiety and my head hurt from travel in this heat. My only comfort is you, Bishma and beloved husband Ali tucked inside my waist sash. You have joined me from what seems like centuries ago on this momentous journey. I will be glad when all this is behind us and see the snow capped mountains of Kathmandu.

Day 16. It has taken all day for our large group to cross the rapids to the west side. My party originally selected a point based on suggestion by one of our Beni Elom members. It was swift, with large boulders but it passable. When the Kumari Daughter saw this, she insisted it was too dangerous and went further downriver to a place she thought was safer. Despite our guide's warning she attempted the rapids, losing three people and eight supply camels went missing. She returned, very angry and with minor scrapes and cuts. We later found the drowned entangled in the brush along the river and the camels grazing nearby. Everyone was spent by the ordeal. I stationed our Beni Elom guests along the parameter to keep away hecklers. Yusuf said this land belonged to the Desert dwellers and we were safe. From here on the Beni Elom controlled only the west bank.

We did a tally of the damage: we lost all of provisions. All we had was what we carried, about two days of provisions. Green Sand was still nearly a week away.

The Kumari Daughter continued blaming me for our fate. Her group felt it was her right to hold me responsible for any mishap. I told her she can believe what she wanted but I will not be accountable for her bad decisions. I reminded her she cannot pressure me to leave. She claimed it was her group's decision. Although I saw through this lie it was futile to argue. I returned to my scouts, sullen.

When Duce inquired, I forced a smile and replied the Kumari Daughter and I had an ongoing misunderstanding. He then added that no matter what happen those around me will remain loyal and believe in my sincerity, not the Kumari's lies. I felt embarrassed but it encouraged me.

Day 17. Today was a solemn occasion. We buried the victims beneath a shrub tree: two children and an elderly woman who perished when part of the river bank collapsed. A stone marker was placed over the site; a crude Kumari's symbol, names and date of their deaths. The Kumari Daughter commented mistrust and bad information that led to their demise. I knew who she implied and felt hostile eyes upon me.

Later we found our camels. Their cargo was gone and I suspected the Beni Elom. Yusuf and a friend searched for those responsible.

Before resume our march Satori Patan returned with instructions he resumed command of the scouts. I was demoted to his Second. Without ceremony or explanation he took the maps, my instruments and reviewed our calculations before resuming our journey. I was visibly upset and this insult and it did not go unnoticed by my group. Yusuf whispered that he will only obey me. I reminded him we are a team and worked for the benefit for our pilgrims. We will do what was expected.

The travel was rough. The Urdun River was wider here, its banks steep and packed clay and sand. There was no trail through the dense, thorny brush covering the banks. Occasional trees, some dead, others thriving, also impeded our path. Sometimes we glimpsed white and blue Dhows plying the river with nets, carrying timber, clay pots and sacks. The mariners wore light robes, head scarves and dark goggles. Their movements across the deck and ropes were unencumbered and they paused to observe our large group walking or riding camels. When they saw the Beni Elom, they jiggled daggers tucked in waist sash in mock threat.

Towards evening we came to a trail and turned onto it. Instead of making camp we pressed into the hills because the Kumari Daughter wanted to make up for lost time. Many people were tired, weak, and fall behind until our party stretches for several kilometers. Our exhaustion forced her to camp in a sand field, scrub grass and small trees. Not the best choice for camp. As I laid in the shade, trying to ignore the itchy welts from invading bug bites, stragglers stumbled by. Everyone looked haggard. Yusuf returned empty handed. They located the supplies but the tribesmen told him this was payment for the men who joined us.

Day 18. I wake to a wonderful serenade performed by Duce, Pavlo, Lucinda and Yusuf. A group of travelers gathered around me and as Pavlo's booming voice recounted some of my adventures fresh bread, tea and dried fruit were placed at my feet. I was touched and eat graciously, listening as strings, horn and drum touch my heart and dispelling my resentment laying over me like a black cloud. When the song ended, the group ceremoniously knelt and placed palm reverently over their heart and whispered blessings. I was overjoyed and kept tears from upsetting my stoic present I felt I had to maintain.

Packing my belongings I mounted the camel and joined our scouts. Riding camels gave the advantage of seeing above the dense brush and tree thickets that otherwise would have created a nightmarish maze. The river twisted into backwashes, mudflats and marshes. Our path skirted the area where the flat lands met the bare hills rising like craggy barriers beyond. The stifling air was thick with swarming bugs. Everyone swatted and cursed them. Red welts covered my hands and face.

Our group came to a trail surrounded by date orchards. We signaled the main group and as evening descended we prepared camp. The pilgrims joined us. Night descended quickly. There was no moon and the stars painted brilliant splashes of iridescent white across the black cosmos. Far away frogs groaned and the river babbled. Despite exhaustion and the bugs, I forgot my tension and allowed the night to settle my heart.

Day 21. It has taken us a week to reach our destination, Green Sand. Satori Patan proved inexperienced and all the reasons I forgot why I did not like him returned. Although he relied on my leadership and our group suggestions, he took all the credit. Since he joined us, the Kumari has commented him on his skills and the 'tension' from the scouts was gone. Because of my group's mood and our contempt for her, he kept to his place which allowed us to tend our duties. He took the credit, while this token leader kept her off our back.

This evening I lay the flat roof of a white painted house in the middle of a date field overlooking the wide expanse of the Urdun Gulf. Green Sand, a modest village of scattered dwellings, orchards and a busy harbor populated with lateen sails. It lays beneath brightly tinted green hills plunging into the Gulf in the gathering darkness. Earlier voices, braying camels, carts and activities carried on the lime scented breeze, hinting activities and wealth sailing from Green Sand to Aqaba where the gulf meets the Red Sea. It is quiet now. Yet, despite this peaceful setting Purge violence is evident here and I sensed great, spiritual pain. We are twenty five kilometers from the ancient, Holy City Elom.

The Beni Elom settlements visible on the west bank disappeared several days ago as the cliffs were transformed into bare sandstone, volcanic flows and basalt cliffs. As we neared Green Sand, the Desert Dwellers heard about our plight and offered supplies, food and water. It was due to their hospitality that we had food enough to reach Green Sand. Our group was so gracious and thankful. When they encountered our Beni Elom companions, dismay and initial hostility gave way to grudging acceptance.

Day 22. Today was my first opportunity to observe the Desert Dwellers up close. They live in extended families; the elder stayed close to the home, tended small gardens, and fetched water, cleaning, while the men and women and working age children went to the orchards and groves. Everyone contributed to the families and their community. They are trusting, happy, sing and at times broke into spontaneous dance to make hard tasks more enjoyable. The men and boys wear brown or white robes, sandals, kufi and each male is armed with a dagger. The women and girls go around in brown, red and green dresses where ornate pattern which showed status. Some had silver jewelry and bracelets.

In the afternoon they shared a meal and rested for three hours. Refreshed, they resumed work and at sunset performed ceremonies which I'm told honor their deity whom they believed inhabits all things and bestowed blessings.

My group was constantly checked on throughout the day by family members who watched over our well being. These people reminded me of my own village and caused pain of loss when my mind returned to our home and the world I left.

Day 23. Yesterday The Kumari Daughter and her Satori met the Beni Elom representative across the river. Green Sand did not welcome him and his boat docked beyond the piers while sentries escorted the Kumari and armed boats prevented the Beni Elom from leaving their boat. The meeting lasted most of the day.

The Kumari Daughter reported that we were given permission to visit the Holy City Elom.

In the morning we left Green Sand and spent most of the day carried by ferry to the west side of the Gulf into Beni Elom country. The Desert Dwellers applied fresh white paint and decorated their boats carrying us with our banners and their flags.

I stood near the bow of the crowded ferry, peering into the haze and glare at horribly mauled hills mixed with green glass, sand and brown rock. The radiation sickness monitor dial touched the yellow portion, warning me our visit was limited by a few days.

We landed on a hastily constructed deck of a settlement with olive groves. Here Beni Elom met us and afterward the Kumari Daughter showed the letter written by the elder at Tiberius and the man he visited yesterday. Taking payment we waited in the shadows while we waited for the rest of our group. Our guide, a young man carrying a big sword and walking stick, explained that the world's oldest city, Jericho, was nearby underwater. He added his tribe was proud of their connection to this ancient memory. It was late evening when the last of the group arrived. We camped along the shore; huddled around our solar fires, cooking meals, some sang, others were in heightened anticipation of being the first outsiders to see this forbidden world. I, however, experienced increased anxiety and dread. I tried to sooth my mind by reading Taleju's Awakenings.

Great sadness fills me.

Herein lies what Pre Purge called the Holy Land. It was the meeting place of three, desert religions; a place of tears and blood spanning thousands of years. Here, holy leaders ruled by cunning, treachery, the sword—all in the name of self importance. Here is where the mind and emotions dominated spirit—great tendrils of hate, contempt and illusionary good radiating like spokes of a wheel. This wheel turned: grinding down spiritual freedom, encasing the mind in darkness and refusing to live in the present; always seeking the horrors of the past to justify their present behaviors; they were Self possessed by the belief they were victims of everyone but themselves.

Then the Purge removed their self important stone temples, moments and histories—burying them in ash and smoke as it cleansed the darkness that covered this land. The wails and prayers of millions echoed across the heavens for they believed this was their promised sanctuary---yet their deity was forever silenced; reduced to painful memories. The sands covered the past and this Great Vanity in which so many poor souls suffered. So many spirits placed their trust in these hollow words. . .

I travel over the mountains from the east; following the poisoned river called Urdun between this steep valley. Looking west into that sandy haze and glittering, green splashes of glass upon raw sand. The tragedy, sadness and desperation permeate the ground upon which I stand. Grief stricken, I cannot approach this place and turn away, hurrying from this sandy shroud and glittering glass as tears blur my sight . . .

Ali and Bishma, I am glad you cannot see this place we walk through. As far as I saw were deep mounds and jagged rims. Nothing grows here. We're warned even the water is poison and therefore our Beni Elom guides ensured we only visit safe wells. Being away from the Gulf breeze made the heat stifling; gritty sand painted the sky brown and got into the mouth, eyes and nose; coating the skin like a scratchy blanket. You would think me mad for coming here. I too wonder.

Day 23. Because we need to travel quick and unhindered if we are to complete our trip on time, we carried what we could comfortably on our backs. Our guide walked fast and many had trouble keeping up with him.

The Rad Meter neared the red, making me anxious. Travel seemed slow while we wind our way through canyons and climbed towards our goal. My feet and legs ached; many suffered blisters and cuts. Some fall by the side, sitting in groups under rocks offering minimal shade. Our time was minimal, task paramount. Our hopes seeing this place which for so many centuries were closed to outsiders brought hope of discovery and pride as first visitors seeing this Purge important city. What did I hope to see when we reached this place? I don't know. Maybe it was expectations or Insight to something greater.

I cannot imagine what this place looked before the Purge; nor do I understand why the Beni Elom were so proud of this Purge city. They seem possessed by some pretend importance. When I asked Yusuf, he shrugged and answered this was the Promised Land long before humanity occupied it. I wonder who promised it, and to whom?

I walked with the main group. I felt hostile eyes and some travelers fell back rather than share the trail with me. Yusuf and his friends, Pavlo's family and others stayed close to me, watching our surrounding and pilgrims like guard dogs.

We came to a rise and stood on a ridge of a massive crater; the rocky land swept away for kilometers, hinting to the magnitude of unimaginable power that created this place. In the haze and nearly obscured at the far end, was a small lake, surrounded by date trees and domed buildings. It was nearing dark and we were still kilometers from our destination. Disappointed, we will resume in the morning.

Day 24. Today I seemed to carry the full the weight of the Purge; dark, stifling, sickening, without hope; a world lost, seeking redemption but finding only nightmares. The spiritual sickness here was intense, although judging by the smiles and feeling of accomplishment expressed by our group they did not share my impressions.

The day began before sunrise and looking towards the city I saw gray, red and brown shadows swirled up from the ground like whirling dervishes. Sounds, resembling discordant machines; low, oscillating thunder and high pitch screeches layered upon layers pierced my head like arrows. They were concentrated this crater and were unlike any I heard or felt. Even now our earth was sick. What I suspected was true: the Purge could not erase this poisoned consciousness.

Yusuf came by with bread and tea. His eyes widened and for a moment looked away, startled. He then admitted my eyes glittered purple and it frightened him. I immediately lowered my head and forced those energetic impressions away. They faded, as did that light in my eyes. As I ate, Yusuf whispered proudly he knew I was `one of them.' He knelt and drew a symbol on the ground at my feet, tapped it with his finger and then left. I studied it: in the center was a spiral and either side crescent suns.

His comments made me very self conscious. We assembled at the ridge and as the Daughter's voice recited Taleju we studied the destructions, trying to grasp why this place supported and promoted such universal hatred.

Spirit seeks to capture that state of inner awareness buried deep behind the illusionary world it sees. Yet, many succumb to confusion and disillusionment and walk though life asleep. Importance is placed on mental or emotional trivialities which intensify throughout many incarnations, locking spirit is struggle and saturating the earth with these energies. Even when people are long gone, these disturbing energies linger, poisoning the

hearts of those who venture near. The old darkness prevails,
planted by former inhabitants.

Solemnity we followed our guide on the narrow trail and by
late morning reach the settlement. I felt as though I walked into
a maelstrom of conflicting currents. These gradually crashed my
resolve and I staggered under their weight. Nausea and
throbbing headache possessed me. It was all I can do to keep
moving. I saw and felt the former inhabitants reaching across the
centuries to speak to me, at times their intensity deafening By
the time we reached the settlement, I just want to scream and
run—but I determined to understand what this place was trying
to show me. I hide my feelings and stayed with the group.

The streets were modest with dome shaped buildings and
pomegranate trees. Beni Elom stroll by, their darken faces severe
and arrogant. A few cursed us and like the bandits in the desert,
our presence was not welcomed. In the center was a two story,
gold domed structure covered with blue and white tile. A modest
courtyard and a well were in a walled entrance. We waited in
groups as our Beni Elom guides led us into the building. Steps
lead to gold gilt doors surrounded by symbols. Inside was a large,
crowded room. Illumination was provided by colored glass in the
dome. Twelve support pillars covered with symbols were spaced
evenly around the room's outer edge. Gold and brown tile
decorated the floor. In the corner a large wall niche was a
rectangular stone that was part of a massive wall. Embedded
within this is a rusty metal piece. Beni Elom knelt before this,
their heads bowed, lips moving silently reciting from scrolls they
picked from a shelf below. Frankincense lingered heavy in the
blue, smoky air.

I studied the ancient stone which appeared to have melted
like wax. The Daughter asks our guide what was the significance
of the stone. He explained it was all that remain of the ancient
city millions worshipped. He added this was a Divine Sign that
the promised Judgment had prevailed. To the Beni Elom, the
Purge was known as The Blessing because it punished the wicked
and returned their Promised Land.

We lit red candles and set them in gold holders arranged on a
table spanning half the room's length. This gouged and worn
table was covered with worn carvings retelling the Purge: a huge
city; sky flashes; fire; death; Beni Elom on their knees praying
and looking skyward; entering the waste land, building this town
and finally the temple we were in.

Afterwards we returned to our camp just as the sun dipped
below the brown, hazy horizon. With each step I took away the

town my nausea subsided and the voices in my heads eased. I spend this evening recuperating and watched celebrative dances and listened to Pavlo's ballad about our visit. Never in my life was I so glad to be away from this sick, depressing, and evil place.

That is if evil really exists instead of just in our minds.

Good night my beloved Ali and Bishma.

Day 27. Well, here I am again on the wood and weathered deck of a lateen sailing ship as the brisk wind pushes us along the bare coast of the Urdun Gulf. It was hot and pleasant when the salty wind caressed my face. This was a blessed change from sweaty miserable we endured for so long. It is near the New Year and I feared our delay may exact a terrible price when we enter Arabia. By my calculation we are more than a month behind schedule.

In Taleju's time this was a huge, barren valley occupied by the Urdun river. Now, it was burial places for Purge cities, long forgotten in the depths of the beautiful sea.

When we returned from our trip to the Holy Lands many of us were sick by Rad sickness and took more than a day to recover. The Desert Dwellers spent time serving herbal teas they claimed quickening the illness from our bodies and strengthened us.

Our next stop is Aqaba, a settlement predates the Purge and forgotten until the Urdun Gulf formed. Now, it is the meeting point for trade routes from Italia to the Persian Emirates which brings great wealth for its citizens.

We sailed by brown, black and sandy hills, their sides jagged and twisted. They raised either side of our watery expanse like dirt encrusted rags. The green hues from fruit orchards occasionally break the bleakness along the shore. Sometimes small vessels greeted us from local villages. A few attached themselves to our small fleet and brought fresh fruit, bread and trinkets. Their visits made for lively times; bargaining was fierce, fun and carnival like. These people really like to engage us as it was both a custom and sport for them. Their enthusiasm affected even the most stoic to join me. I can't help but smile with gratitude. The profits are shared by their community.

Yusuf practiced the mandolin and composes song. He said his father was a musician but died early during childhood. He had three brothers, all who died. He was raised by his mother. They grew and traded herbs and then he was about 10 she died. One time while travelling to a nearby town, his group encountered Seers. He was surprised how accommodating they were and, despite Beni Elom distrust, they returned only kindness. What he remembered most was their eyes: gold flecks in the sunlight! I never realized that this was not 'normal' and thought they could be seen in everyone's eyes if conditions were right.

I am finding out my difference continued to attract strangers. People talked and I can no longer deny or pretend otherwise. Being confined on this small ship gave passengers and crew the opportunity to meet me. Throughout the day travelers shared their concerns about the trip and asked for my advice and encouragement. I was reluctant to offer council; I am but one of them and no wiser. Why they think otherwise baffles me.

Many were confused by the Daughter's attitude towards me and wanted to see who I am. Initially some were skeptical and fearful, but later realized I was nothing like the stories portrayed me.

It was ironic my parents discouraged any talk about seeing lights, color or hearing strange music. They warned me to keep quiet because people would think I was 'One of them.'

Yet here, unable to hide myself, I find people's reaction quite the opposite. I do not deny my identity but also do not announce it. This mystique draws the curious.

I asked Yusuf about Seers. He said they lived in near the Caspian Sea and can see things ordinary people cannot. They spoke a musical language and their writings supposedly contained hidden messages. It was believed they came from the west after the Purge. People despised them because they can supposedly read minds, levitate, and can kill with a word. He confessed he joined our group because of me.

But when he mentioned Seers believed Taleju was one of them it struck me hard. This is pure nonsense! Yet, it suggested a reason for the Daughter's attitude towards me and her underlying apprehension. For if Taleju <u>was</u> a Seer it would drastically threaten everything we believe.

I dreamt last night that I stood in front of a red wood door. Beyond I sensed rugged mountains. From somewhere the tinkle of glass bells resonated. I was afraid and hesitated to open the door. Then I woke. The dreams uncertainty lingered until first light.

Ali, Bishma. I leave you with a ballad lyrics Duce sang this evening.

She walks with us, our Mother Guide.
Threats do not touch her heart.
Even the Daughter fears her Light.
Taleju, we raise our voices in praise
As we walk into the future past together.

Arabia

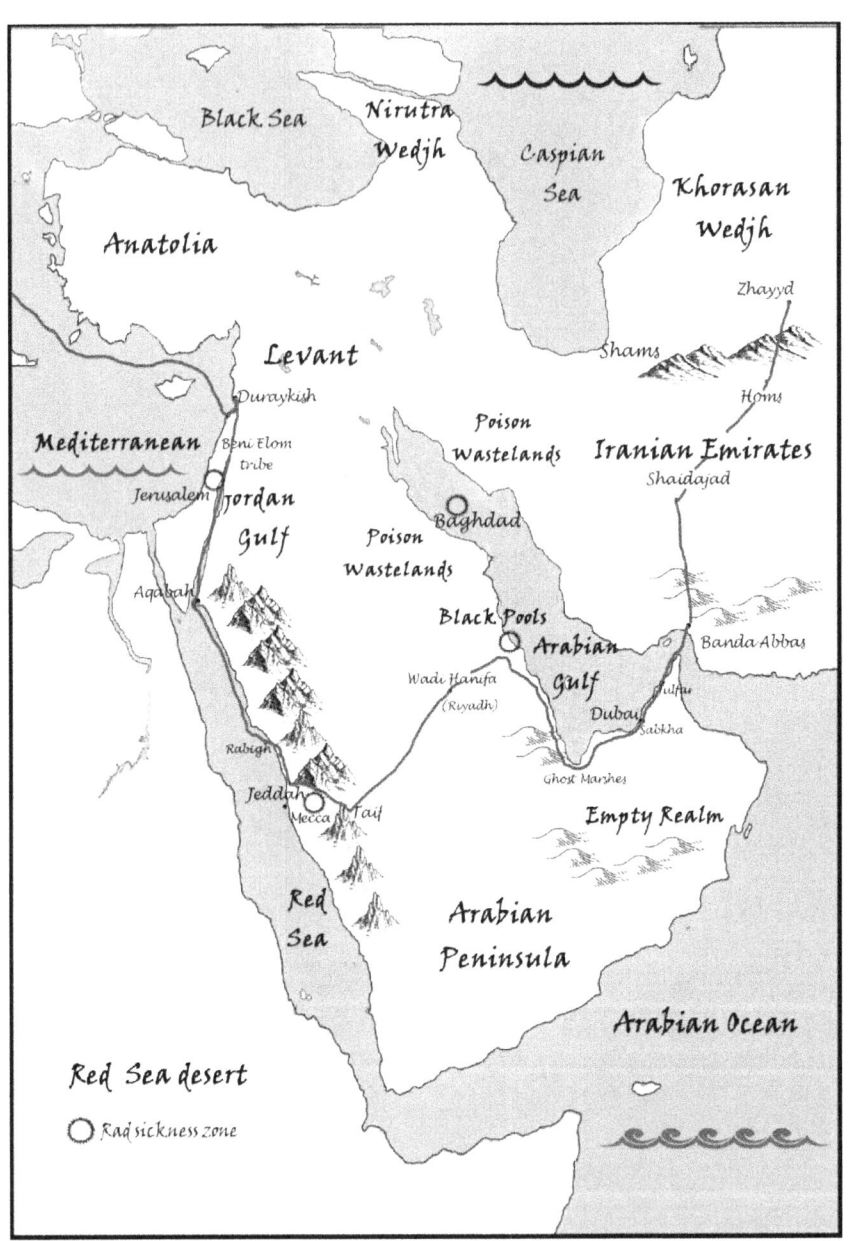

Black Sea

Nirutra
Wedjh

Caspian
Sea

Khorasan
Wedjh

Anatolia

Zhayyd

Levant

Shams

Homs

Duraykish

Iranian Emirates

Mediterranean

Beni Elom
tribe

Poison
Wastelands

Shaidajad

Jerusalem

Jordan
Gulf

Baghdad

Poison
Wastelands

Aqabah

Black Pools

Arabian
Gulf

Banda Abbas

Wadi Hanifa
(Riyadh)

Julfa

Dubai

Saikha

Rabigh

Ghost Marshes

Jeddah
Mecca Taif

Empty Realm

Red
Sea

Arabian
Peninsula

Arabian Ocean

Red Sea desert

⭕ Rad sickness zone

After spending two weeks our boat followed the Arabian coast and reached the remains of a Purge age city half buried in the rising sea. Steel and concrete rose through water; their sides encrusted with white salt and are scattered about like a great puzzle missing much of its pieces. On a cultivated hill nearby a village of white and green houses glittered in the hot sun. Simple brown robed people in sledge hats, their faces and hands covered to avoid the heat, tend to their chores.

We are met by friendly, curious strangers and invite us into their modest homes. Seated on dirt floor they offer tea and bread and rest. They want to know what it beyond their arid world and others survived. I reply yes, and have returned to the old ways.

People have inhabited this area for thousands of years. Prior to the Purge it was a resort city stretching many kilometers where visitors came to escape the heat. It also served as a military site protecting ships. The people call this place Aqaba. From here we will strike along the coast, following the Jordan River into the Levant and perhaps see the Holy Lands.

-Taleju-

Day 30. Aqaba, meeting where the Red Sea meets the Jordan Gulf. Shortly before dawn we arrived. This last day of this year found me thousands of kilometers from home. Aqaba's squat, flat roof buildings are painted white with accents bands of blue, red and green with lattice windows and balconies from which residents casually observed the passing world. The city is at the base of a jagged peak. Date and fruit tree orchards fan out along the slopes and reach the water front where many crowded ships wait to off load or load material. On this day the Gulf was clear and sparkled in the hazy, gold light. Its souks were busy and everywhere the scents of cooking, spices, incense, perfume, sweat and dust waft in the dusty air. The new city was built above the old Aqaba which was more than a hundred meters beneath the sea. The old city was on the edge of the gulf before the rise of the Urden Gulf which covered an intense desert called the Dead Sea. Legends of the horrific journey through the desert and the Beni Elom hostilities still occupied many local tales.

A most wondrous call echoed from the many minarets three times a day; their haunting melody carried like a mother's soothing voice. Many people paused in their activities and go to green tiled, domed buildings to perform rituals to a Pre Purge deity. These worshippers believed the Purge was the opportunity to throw off the old ways for simpler times. They don't consider themselves special but embraced the world as universal. They saw everything as being part of their deity and therefore by showing reverence for all life this reflects upon their sky deity. This, I believed, was related to the Mecca religion that was wiped out during the Purge. During the noon call I was invited by locals to observe their ritual. They recited in an unknown language; they sometimes raised their hands skyward or prostrated themselves on the floor covered with beautiful rugs while an elderly man led the prayer. He faced the gathering atop a minbar, a kind of decorated platform. It was decorated with geometric pattern representing a palm and camel which the citizens consider their 'Twin Blessings.' It was explained that all places of worship are oriented towards an ancient city called Dubai, where the Purge began and, in their eyes, the new Beginning.

Afterwards sandalwood incense was lit and fresh oranges handed out to those who weren't in a hurry to resume their tasks. The thick, orange peels released their damp, refreshing scent as I peeled it away and bit into the succulent meat. Sweetness gushed into my taste buds, fruity tang whiffed into my nostrils. It has been weeks since I had such refreshing taste!

The elderly man was interested in me and asked many questions about my home and reason for the journey. He was intrigued by Taleju and added that she was mentioned in their holy text. He added the Seers knew of her and wondered if I was related to them. Blushing, I shook my head. He escorted me to the door and said our group was always welcomed in Aqaba.

Today our activities were focused on celebration and I was glad for the change. Aqaba craftsmen spent hours making hundreds of red and gold paper lanterns, banners and transporting these to a site in the desert at the base of the predominant peak.

The place was selected by the Daughter as our gathering place to perform the Lights of Awakenings, marking the New Year. After a meal of cucumbers, olive and bread which represent what Taleju ate on this day, our group gathered outside of town. Those who could wore their finest robes and jewelry. I managed to wear a blue and brown outfit I got at Duraykish. However, most pilgrims had only faded, dirty travel clothes. The Daughter led us from our camp as the sun dimmed in the western sky. By the time we reached the plain, the full moon illuminated our way.

The night was warm and dusty. Aqaba lights sparkled and flickered. Singing and music fluttered on the breeze. It was a perfect setting.

Hours before, citizens arranged our banners in a large circle. In the center pilgrims assembled before crates and each worshipper was handed a red, paper lantern. Beneath solar lamps we applied our name in ink then set the lantern on the ground. Sitting crossed legged we listened to the Daughter recite Taleju. Above, the canopy of stars and silhouetted hills looked upon us. Her words seemed to echo across the eons, stirring my heart.

Upon this longest day of the year marks the passage of the Purge. For it was on this day humanity passed into a painful nightmare. Spirit woke and through teary eyes saw the destruction wrought by the greedy few. So to never forget that path, lanterns of Light were left in the Darkness to illuminate our new path where we will devote ourselves to understanding the Universal One, seeing Infinity unfettered by illusion or self importance.

Cleansed of the shadows which subjugated all to fear and slavery, the Purge brought clarity and a new reality.

Let each year remind us of sacrifices we gave to Understand.

Her words echoed briefly in the darkness. When she raised her arms, we went and placed our lanterns in the sand, creating a huge circle. Then her and her Satori paused at each lantern, reciting prayers and afterwards lit them. The line of lights grew like an opening flower. When they came to mine, however, she refused to light it and returned it without a word, waving me off. I was shocked, disappointment and anger filled me. I controlled my feelings so not appear affected by her behavior. Duce, Yusuf and others came to my side, still reciting the prayer. They accompanied me to the circle and waited while I lit and set my lantern among them. The Daughter looked back but her expression was hidden in shadow. As a group we stood defiantly away from the main group. Others saw what happened and came to my side. We raised our voices loudly towards the heavens, momentarily drowning her group. Satori Patan came and attempted to remove my lantern but was quickly prevented. Angrily he tried pushing though escorts but, with folded arms my friends stood defiantly. He ordered them to stand down. Yusuf shook his head and placed his hand on his dagger.

Duce reminded him that Taleju does not discriminate and the Kumari Daughter disrespected her and all pilgrims. Patan raised his hand towards his face to slap him, but hesitated. Eventually he cursed and left. We waited anxiously, realizing what this signified.

When they finished, The Daughter visited each person and gently touched them on the forehead as she recited a prayer. However, when she came to our group, she glared at us briefly and stormed away.

Thus, began this New Year.

1263 AP: Month 1, day 1. I will never forget this day.

Aqaba is alight with festivities: music, gatherings, feast, dances. Shops are closed. The only normal activity is the ritual call. Here, the leaders recite text and call to honor the past and embrace the future. Colorful banners fly from windows; citizens go about in elaborate robes, pausing to greet friends and strangers. I am surrounded by spices and rich food. By midday I am so full from being invited to dine at strangers' homes I can hardly move. Our small group celebrates with song and dance. I feel free among my friends and sway, stomp, wave my arms, and lock our arms as we shuffle in circles. The drums and flutes thumped and screech; the rhythm takes hold and guides my step and movement. I am an expression of the music! I saw many colored patterns flickered around the instruments and realized they are the musical notes! It was wonderful. By the time evening came I was so exhausted all I could do was sit in the courtyard and watch.

When the Daughter, Patan and Altus joined us I sensed she was not here to socialize. Her presence was clearly tinged with purple, red and brown swirling energies around her heart. When we gathered Patan read from a document while the Daughter and Altus listened. The Kumari Daughter announced I was banished from the Conformation and my name stricken from the record. She had hoped I quit, but my attitude and behavior created resentment in the main group. For their benefit I must leave. The others were encouraged to continue.

Stunned, I stared aghast. I never dreamed that I would be thrown out by the religion I worshipped since childhood! Cast out by jealousy, fear for `not fitting in.' Such shallow, callous disregard for devotees. My world crashed around me. My life did not matter to her. What made her think she had the authority to ruin lives over petty trivial?

My legs nearly gave out and I struggled to keep my composure. Patan held out the document for me. Shocked I ripped it and flung it at him. Patan avoided my eyes, his face cold. He and the Daughter turned and left. Stemming tears I dropped to the sand and bowed my head. Duce squatted next to me and placed a strong arm round my neck. Despite my effort not to show emotions I buried my head on his shoulder and wept. So distraught was I that I did not hear the heated argument a few meters between Altus and the Daughter. As the shock dimmed, I looked up at Altus and about twenty pilgrims watching me with sad faces before leaving.

Day 2. This morning as I was preparing for tea I was shocked to see Altus, Satr and a few Council members join us, wearing the clothing of devotees. Altus explained ever since my initial meeting the Council disagreed with how she treated me. Her charges were wrong, especially after my bravery and earning the pilgrims admiration. To many I was as a valuable member, but she seemed afraid and a threat of her authority. She constantly worried about my influence, even though I thought I had none, and sewed discontent, fueling apprehension and superstition.

She wanted to get rid of me but threats of losing some Satori tempered her until last night. Some of his administration could no longer stand by and support her behavior towards a pilgrim. It spoke ill of the Kumargi.

I was moved to tears, for I never believed I had these admirers. They scarified their standings and status for me and hoped I would have the courage to reciprocate in kind.

Until now I did not believe I had influence that affected those around me. But now I realize these people chose me over the Kumari. I am deeply touched by their action and swear to be very careful and not disappoint them. From here now I realize my word and act will have consequences for our group. I will carry Taleju's teaching in my heart—no matter how painful it may be. Her truth is all that matters. I owe it to Taleju and my group who believe in me.

Later after Altus and our new four Council members visited our pilgrims, offering words of encouragement, we made plans while the main group booked passage down the Red Sea. I would lead our group, following the same route several days behind.

Our group spent the day gathering things, appointing tasks and checking maps. With the help of Yusuf and friends they took navigational instruments and maps. My path seems to be clearer and strangely familiar as though I had walked this before.

This night I watched the main group carry solar lights as they boarded their ships for tomorrow's voyage. Loss tinged my heart.

Day 3. How sweet! Shortly before dawn I heard camel growls and when I inspected them I was reunited with the she camel Yusuf gave me when we first met! She and a few had broken their ropes and returned to us. With them I don't feel as lost. At least I have a connection with our past and I don't to worry about training her.

There is much to be done for our trip. I spent the morning meeting with merchants and suppliers. W paid for pack camels and provisions, planning to get more assistants and provision for the inland routes when we reach Rabigh. I fear the heat will be terrible and our travel extremely challenging. This will be my first test being leader.

In the afternoon I had a most unusual encounter. On the outskirts of town we met a group of desert travelers going to the main souk. They were completely covered up in dusty robes, faces wrapped in headscarves and wore dark, thick goggles and had the appearance of being in the desert for months. They rode tattooed camels. Their decorated and colorful wool blankets possessed geometer patterns I had never seen. Their camel tassel bells generated melodies as they lumbered over the sand. These riders were laden with thick carpets, bags of incense, cooking gear, tents, and jewelry and books.

Each rider carried a big sword, although their presence suggested non violence. I sensed energetic, golden lights and heard gentle music radiating from them. This impression overwhelmed me and it took a few moments for my mind to clear. When their leader passed me standing by the trail he stared at me. Yusuf said these are Seers.

Curious I followed them. They paused by a well and spoke in a musical language I had not heard before. The leader watched us then motioned for us to join them for dates and bread. We sat on carpets beneath shady trees. The leader spoke in a heavy accented and introduced himself as Shams. He pointed to a woman in the shadow. I recognized her as the one who observed me at Duraykish. She said something which I guessed was a greeting in that musical dialect. I must have presented a surprised look, for Shams laughed.

Then leather bound books and scrolls were set before us and Shams invited us to choose a gift. We thumbed through pages with cursive, ornate script; some with pictures, other text and poetry. Shams explained they were gathered from across the world and each year they visited Aqaba to trade them.

They were in many languages and our group voted on a book with many pictures. During browsing, Yusuf opened a very old book with rainbow colored pages. He quickly set it aside.

I was about to make our choice but instead took the rainbow book. I scanned its pages. My eyes immediately were absorbed by the delicate, hand written script that seemed to leap from the pages. It shifted, each time looking different as though sentences were overlaid in a host of colors. Jumbled images like pictures from a great puzzle flowed and danced. The sensation was so intense I quickly shut it and looked away to clear my mind, for the book filled me with layers and layers of music and faded images.

Shams slowly removed his goggles and observed me with dark eyes sparkled with gold and purple. I gasped. He took the book and pressed it into my hands and sang something which caused gold light to radiate from his heart area. The group pressed palms in front and bowed their heads. Stunned, I watched them return to their camels and vanish behind the trees.

Yusuf called it the` Rainbow Book' and they spent time looking at, their faces reflected disappointment and curiosity. They wondered why I selected this book instead one they could read. I looked towards the Seers, confused by our encounter. However my heart glowed as if I found lost friends.

Day 4. I was up before sunrise making final preparations. Our group is organized and everyone works together. By noon we broke camp, packed our tents and belongings, loaded them on camels and entered Aqaba. It was towards sunset when three ships we hired left the pier. I watched the stars until late in the night, mulling over the tasks ahead and my responsibilities. I am still unsure about my role and my group's trust in me leaves me apprehensive and nervous.

I had another disturbing dream. I was at a red door. Someone shoved a mirror in my face. I stared but only a blurry image. I knocked it away and tried opening the door. The mirror reappeared, blocking my entrance. Each time I attempt to move it, it returned. My fear grew with each attempt. I woke, startled. This dream is a nightmare.

Day 6. We left on at noon of the 4th. It was hot and humid, all of us huddled under the shade provided by the deck awning. We were several kilometers offshore; following the undulating, bare peaks as they vanished in the white haze. From what I can tell, no one lives along the arid coast; it is empty; even the birds that accompanied us from Aqaba have vanished, leaving the sky strangely vacant. Nothing but the sound of waves against the hulls and our voices broke this eerie solitude.

We are nearing the heart of the Pre Purge world. This place was unimportant for thousands of years until empires came to drain Black Blood, to power their machines, fed the multitudes, fight wars, and created products poisoning the earth. This place felt empty and discarded. Yet it is here where the most difficult part of our journey begins. The map showed settlements and water is sparse; we must conserve our energy and travel only at night. Being a month behind schedule adds to our dilemma. This is the season for the deadly heat, sand storms and floods. The sailors tell me these storms can strip flesh from bone.

In the afternoon the next day our group asked if I would be our Aligarh, or someone leading the Dedicational rituals. I deferred to Altus's group but they insisted I fill this role. They are interested in my interpretation and sometimes it counters what the Daughter taught, leading to confusion and debate. I am weary of debate; Taleju's words impart universal wisdom if people just shut their minds and listen! (SIGH). Splitting hairs over a phrase is a colossal waste of time.

I started to hold majlis on the main deck because I was asked to decide personal matters. At first I declined, but they persisted and explained this is what a leader is expected to do. Both parties seemed content with my decision. Yusuf was convinced I had greater wisdom than an ordinary person for this task. I was quick to scold him because it goes against Taleju's teaching. This is dangerous thinking.

Day 8. On a ship off the Arabia coast. Frightfully hot when the breeze dies towards the evening, humidify soaked our clothing, leaving us sticky and miserable. The shade provided by deck awning seemed futile against the sun's steely, blistering heat. We dosed between lethargic awareness and restless sleep.

This evening was my first attempt to study the Rainbow Book.

I immediately realized this was an old book. Its pages were heavily stains and discolored. Stitches bound it and sections of the leather cover warn off, revealing worm holed wood. The cover art faded long ago.

Names and dates of previous owner were carefully listed on the inside cover in old Nepalese script. It started with Radha, one of the original Companions, and kept ten centuries by a dozen families. The last entry was someone named Jasmine bint Laxminath.

I was confused by its orientation until discovering its orientated is backwards, reading from right to left and not written in Taleju's native Nepalese but a Pre Purge language all but forgotten. At the beginning of the book cursive script is overlaid with rainbow patches but progressively replace the writing until only continuous color bands remain.

Swirling colors and music spun through my mind as I inspected it. It left me nauseated and I had to stop.

Day 9. The faint writing was unlike any I've seen. I assumed text orientation was right to left but quickly discovered it is not. Instead text orientation changes every other sentence. Thus, it was read by continuously scanning, from right to left and then changing direction. It was done in fluid hand; kaleidoscopes of colors formed what I suspect were whole sentences rather than single words and possessed a three dimension quality. I was left with the impression I was reading two languages simultaneously. I struggled to grasp them then realized my mind had to be clear for these 'impressions' to flow. To see this extra layer of information required my inner awareness. Here, I do not read but rather 'feel' and 'see' energies.

In my first few attempt I could only decipher bits of information. Some pages were jumbles of incoherent colors. A few even emitted bits of melodies like incomplete song. Yet, like composing a song, the book gradually revealed its secrets.

On the inside cover was the Flower of Life divided into twelve, colored sections. Below read: *Dream and Echoes. In my own hand I, Shakya, former Kumari of Kathmandu, Nepal, write this knowledge to share with my Children.*

Then a faded, gold cursive done by a different hand: *I Radha Bint Sanjahr, First Devotee, attest the truth of Taleju's, our Kumari Mother's authorship this year 142 AP.*

The contents were supposedly written by Taleju, although our Kumari Mother supposedly died at 137 AP. There are diagrams and illustrations begging for understanding. If this was our Kumari Mother's words I will be curious to see if it is different teachings than what survives today. I am unsure about its authenticity, knowing fakes exist. I will proceed but with a cautious mind.

My mind swam with possibilities.

Day 10. Rabigh, Arabian Peninsula. In The Awakenings Taleju wrote: *Time stands still since my traveling companions and I reached the coast more than three weeks ago after horrible months travelling inland. Desolation, sand, rocks and ancient lava beds make up depressing scenery along the sea's edge. Solemn waves lap the shore; mounds of concrete and twisted, rusting steel bones reach up from heaped mounds. Some huge buildings still retain their shape; vast mausoleums to the Pre Purge world. Ancient roads peer like black ribbons though encroaching sand. These we follow when permitted.*

The heat, humidity and sticky salt air cling to our clothes; bathing us in sweat and promoting layers of scratchy, caked sand. I am in utter misery riding my camel. Looking out at this waste land I wonder how anyone could live in this environment. I will be glad when we leave this place.

After following purge roads we finally reached a submerged city called Ribagh; evidence of it is seen from buildings along the hills and in the sea. We've encountered ferocious sand storms forcing our delay. They appear suddenly, turning day to night; we cannot see a meter distance and the sand tears at our clothing. We are prevented from continuing on the road due to violent storms and black smoke covering the horizon. I saw similar clouds near the Black Pools.

Everywhere are bones. We found a warehouse with canned food which supplements our diet. We plan to build a boat to continue on the sea to Aqaba, our next destination.

This evening we landed at Rabigh, and expected it inhabited but found this small village deserted. I am dismayed, since we have barely supplies to resume. I am reluctant to set out with limited water but have no choice. A camel rider, drawn to our activities, said the local inhabitant returned to the hills after the Daughter's party landed and will not return until the fall trade season. Because this is the time of the Great Heat, no one would risk venture from the hills and getting caught in the sand storms. We are on our own. He volunteered to be our guide. His twelve camels piled with goods are headed for Ta'if, another five days from Jeddah. We welcomed his company and purchase supplies for our trip.

This is a lonely place. No activities. Nothing inhabits here but our grumbling camels and our crunching feet on sand. Our map shows us about sixty kilometers from Jeddah. There are no Purge cities or roads remaining since the rising oceans covered them.

Day 11. Illuminated by a quarter moon, our caravan followed our guide on a coastal gravel and sand trail for a short time before detouring into the mountains where we found part of a Purge road. Although sand and rock long since covered it, it was wide in places and affords good travel. We walked through jagged, black rock canyons, brown cliffs and large expanse of pebble fields. The map showed that this was a major inland route to Jeddah. By our estimation, we are five days behind the main group and their tracks are easy to follow. We paused at a fresh grave and gave ceremony of honor. It reminded everyone about the hazards and price we each may pay. Traveling by moonlight afforded relief from the deadly heat; the silvery world seemed like a dreamland. Our path snaked and twisted through the wastelands, the sounds of passing echoed softly against the canyon walls. Sometimes Duce or Carlo would break out into song, making the drudgery lighter.

Shortly before sunrise we made camp. Altus and I met to discuss the Rainbow Book. He inspected it and was intrigued. It was unlike any he'd seen. When I mentioned the dates he was puzzled because when the Kumari Mother died Radha traveled to the land of Fog and Mist. After that her fate was unknown. This book presented disturbing possibilities not in accord with the traditional history. He cautioned me not to place much faith in this until it could be proven genuine.

In translating the book I found I could sense these words and they are strangely familiar to me. Now I am learning to read this again. I cannot explain this, only its impression is strong and lends to confidence.

Day 12. After a long, night travel this dawn I have translated a few pages. It was an introduction by Shakya so profound I doubted my accuracy.

Dream and Echoes: Our Kumari Mother's discussion on the Nature of Incarnation and humanity's future.

I, Taleju Shakya Tian Nawari, was born in a village outside Katmandu one hundred years after the Purge and was chosen at age six as the next Kumari goddess. I took up residency at the Durga Hall until age twelve and presided over our spiritual affairs. My reign was difficult. Our city inhabitants endured horror and unimaginable hardships and diseases carried by black clouds from the Subcontinent. Survivors moved into the country to avoid the horrible disease and petulance. I lived in isolation with my father and sister, the only surviving members of my family. I hovered many times on the verge of death, stricken down by malnourishment and sickness. Yet, for the faithful I performed my Kumari duties.

Per the Durga creed, I was replaced at puberty and returned to my village, Bhaktapur When I was seventeen my sister died, and my father a year later. Though I was no longer associated with the Durga house, people continued visiting and addressed my as the Kumari. I realized my time in Katmandu was but the beginning of my journey to understand the Purge. I met travelers who spoke of the Purge world beyond the mountains. At nineteen I left Nepal and headed west, eventually reaching the west Mediterranean Sea coast eight years later. I returned to Nepal on my twenty seventh birthday and spoke of the things I seen. People came from great distances to hear my words and what the Purge meant for survivors. Three years later I and a group of eighty followers left Nepal on a mission to spread hope in our dying world.

Wherever I went people listened. By the time I reached the land called Italia a cult had grown up around her. My followers were divided over interpreting my teachings. Some incorrectly insisted I was Spirit's Representative to guide humanity away from our past. Others viewed my words as spiritual dissertations into the realms and energies making up our world, thereby leading to Spiritual liberation. These two thoughts came to split our group into two factions: one wanted to adopt a spiritual hierarchy based on that of Kumari 'Living Goddess' with her teachings presided over by her representatives. The other insisted my teachings was an individual path and only through understanding Spirit and its many Realms could we grow beyond our destructive Consciousness.

In Italia our disagreement resulted in a split. My closest Companions and former Kumari Sanjari and Pravati insisted The Awakenings will be established in the Durga House. Sanjari would be the first Kumari Sister. She and Pravati returned to Nepal with most of the group. I was heartbroken and never got over my shortcomings. Radha and a few accompanied my northward where we hoped to reach the Land of Fog. But due to my failing health we stopped at a settlement at the Bay of Biscay where we met survivors struggling to rebuild their world from the ash and desolation. It was gloomy and very hot. The ocean was a sterile, poisoned expanse. Very little vegetation grows; the once green hills are barren rock and gray haze hangs over the area. Sometimes the salt air fills with the stench of decay or pungent acrid from large fires hundreds of kilometers away. We live in concrete ruins with piles of buried garbage mixed with the smelly soil. What unopened food cans we couldn't find in dumps, we supplement with wilted vegetables eked from the contaminated ground. People are covered in sores and tumors; the product of a disease that swept through here last year.

We are few; ten devotees of all ages and some have been with me since the beginning. All are devoted and apply my teachings. We work together to rebuild our world. We occupy a few huts of concrete and rubble. We have cleared away the sand, made repairs, built porches and did what we could to make this our dwellings tolerable.

My home is atop a hill. It is small, but clean. The door looks out at the ocean; two windows let in light. Heavy cloth cover the windows and door. Heavily chipped, faded green and white paint decorate the walls. In one corner is a wood frame, straw mattress and old blankets. My wood flute hangs on a nail over the bed. A repaired wood desk and shelves built into the wall is at the other end. Bolters rest on the raised divan running the length of the room. Tea pot, cups, plates and utensils wait in a niche by the door. *The Nepalese rug I carried since childhood covers the floor storage hole. Light is offered by candles but we don't use them unless necessary since few are available and costly. Banners and gifts from our travels hang from verticals poles in front of our hut, fluttering in the forever hot breeze.*

I am age 47, 163 centimeters tall, weighs 54 kilos; is slight frame with large, inquiring black and gold fleck eyes. Sometimes they change to rose, green, blue, purple and gold, depending on my mood. My naturally wavy and black hair is now streaked white. I have six tattoos on my face and four on my torso. The torso tattoos are honorary tribal. Those on my face, show my mastery of six levels of spiritual Realms.

I sit cross-legged on divan pillows, wearing my familiar and faded red and gold, long sleeve dress and brown waist sash. With color pallet, water and brush I write my memoires on parchment as I sit at my desk huddled over the dim light streaming in from the window. What follows is my testament.

I take brush and write not in the language of now, but for our children's children who will comprehend contents unforeseen by us. We are `Seers' the next evolution of spirit and can read color and hear Infinity's sound. Additionally we speak without words, hear without ears, see without eyes and walk both in this realm and many.

This is our Dream and Echoes, our foundation for our future.

Here I am with my devotee and childhood companion who share the end of my journey. Radha Bint Sanjahr; First Companion and Seer of Five Realms

This 23nd day, Month 3, year 147 After Purge
Biscay Bay, near the Western Ocean

Day 13. Taleju wrote.: *All manifestation is energy in form. Consciousness is energy aware of Itself. Energy is consciousness in motion. Energy has two distinct characteristic. They are sound and color. You could say reality on all levels is nothing more than these twins in various guises.*

Despite my exhaustion, I cannot sleep, for my spirit is restless after translating this passage. Tired and drowsy I secured myself to the camel saddle. We plodded onward while I, Duce and our new visitor led through the relentless desert. Since my effort, my awareness is shifting and my Third Eye opening. This new understanding, this perception goes far beyond mind.

I am aware of complex melodies shift in and out like whispers on the breeze. They come from the rocks, cliffs, and sandy plains. I asked Duce if he heard them and he replied no. Are they in my head? Am I imagining this because I'm exhausted? I wish they would leave me in peace so I could sleep. The space between my brow throbs, I sense purple energies expand, carrying my awareness into the invisible.

The book's contents connect on very deep levels and are nothing like I've read. This is so vastly different on many levels than The Awakenings. I suspect Taleju wrote for two audiences: those wanting guidance, such as the Kumari path, and those seeking deeper understanding.

Day 14. *This is Arabia. The hub of the world was born in this wasteland, that for millennium few dared to live here. Ironically from these sands the abundance of the Pre Purge Black Blood connected the world like delicate spokes. Nations fought over this Blood to created their vain cities of glass and steel, overpopulated the earth, devoured dwindling resources and took all within their grasp. These became the veins, muscles and soul of this beast. And here too, in this vast desert was born their apocalyptic blueprint. For they falsely believed their action did not demand payment. Now, the rocks are silent as they were before we came. Time erased their cathedrals of slavery until only memories occupied our campfires.*

Herein lays sand, lava fields, gravel plains, brown, craggy hills, black mountains stacked upon each other under unending heat baking the hardest stone into shards. Black ribbons stretched into the horizon, connecting mechanical carriages with crowded cities whose lights banished the night. Massive towers rose towards the heavens, their glittering glass could be seen far away. Ships not powered by wind brought riches from across the world, fattening the wealthy and impoverished the poor as they built their glittering moments from the sand.

Now I watch the blue ocean beneath the hazy sun. Vast concrete and steel clutter the sea, resembling a massive beast's bones. Herein was the Mother of Eve, or Jeddah, that greeted these ships for hundreds of years. As with all Pre purge cities along the coast, the sea claimed them in effort to erase the scars of our foolishness. ---Taleju near Jeddah-

Even at night the heat and humidity cling to my clothes, soaking skin and pressing the forever misery against my flesh. My joints are raw from fine sand rubbing against my flesh and cloth, aggravating my persistent headaches. We have enough provisions and water for two days. Our map showed a well in the mountains near ruins called `Ta'if. To get there we have to pass near Djinn's Breath. Altus says it is kilometers of glass and during the day reflects blinding light, making travel impossible until night. Travelers caught in here lose their way and die from thirst or burned by the reflection.

Night travel was more difficult now because the waning moon. The great, starry, opal band arching across the heavens was our guide as we followed the sea. Terrain was blocks of varying shades of black shapes. In some places the gravel fields resembled dirty snow. Heat radiated from the ground, causing continual sweat and discomfort.

Jeddah was out there somewhere in the vast, watery expanse. Our group peered from a cliff at the black waters but could only make out instinct shapes. The map said Jeddah was more than fifteen kilometers away. This land felt tired. Altus recorded our location in the logbook and updated our map.

Our guide led us to the trail from the coast into the mountains. Here the terrain changed dramatically. At dawn we reached a narrow canyon where we hid from horrible, greenish glow getting more intense with each minute. I spent time translating the book before the glare forced me to stop.

Day 15. *Our physical manifestation is but a part of our greater self and within each Realm we walk, we are part of the energy grid which sustains all. Listen and you will feel and hear the melodies and your own melody as you interact with the world. Look and you will see the energetic colors and patterns become and permeate your body. Know your patterns and that you are interact: these are Infinity's cornerstones. See these on all levels in each Realm we exist in: Physical, Emotional, Psychic, Mental, Causative and Moment. Each comprises these sounds and colors unique to their Realm. Herein is the genesis of All that we encompass. By understanding these, we know where we are and how to move freely in Infinity's House.*

Sleep continued to evade me. I was hot and miserable resting in the shadow, waiting for night to come. Even at night the heat increases with each kilometer and I envisioned we were walking into a furnace. It was deathly quiet and no breeze disturbed this hell. In my anticipation to be rid of this place, time seemed to crawl.

This night I saw distinct, colorful patterns superimposed on the land and heard distant sounds reminding me of distant drums. I was shocked when I looked skyward and glimpsed this same patterns in the heavens! These hexagon filaments glittered like filaments of fine glass.

These impressions came and went, teasing me as I shifted my awareness. Taleju's book mentioned these impressions are the Flower of Life's fruit. All manifestations consist of this energy mesh, hanging like delicate flowers on background of Nothingness. Yesterday I was confused when I first read this, but now I understood what she meant.

Shortly before dawn we came upon a fresh grave and a grieving woman. She was shocked to see us. She said her son died four days ago and rather than continue she chose to stay with him and die. She was delusional, weak hungry and her face covered with blisters. We took her in, tended her blisters and shared out meager supplies. After much coaxing she agreed to join us. My manner and attention I showed surprised her. I offered her my camel and secured her to the saddle. I and Yusuf walked with her. Her name is Sarah.

Day 17. Taleju wrote: *Mecca. Here the world looked to the huge rectangle block dedicated to their deity. People journeyed from afar to prostrate themselves and lift voices heavenward to connect with their inner selves. Here, masses sought spirituality while this land exported Black Blood to the greedy Nation states, feeding selfish empires and corporations. There was nothing left of that rectangle wiped away by fire storms and upheaval. The ground was barren of even the smallest plant. Rather, it was replaced by a vast, glass bowl reflecting brilliant domes of light like sun's reflection on water. Its touch blind and burns all even across great distance. We are twenty kilometers away and our Rad meters reading are off the scale.*

We call this area the Djinn's Breath and dare not enter.

We passed into the heart of Djinn's Breath. Black, craggy peaks surrounded us and the earth's bones lay bare, stripped of soil and life. The sickness meter read red, indicating we cannot venture closer to Mecca. The world beyond these mountains is torn and smooth; covered in glitter glass creating millions of individual sparks reflected from the stars. I sensed energy red and brown swirls upon this land; a great, gaping wound from long ago. During travel our guide hurried us to canyons for protection before sunrise where we rested in the sweltering heat. I am thankful he is here because we had not sense of direction or where the shadows would lay. The day was filled with blinding light and burning heat. It is an awful place filled with sadness.

On the 19th we consumed the last of our supplies. Our guide shared his food with those needing it the most. It was another night at least to Ta'if. Many of us are weak, sick and some can hardly walk. We burdened the camels with riders.

My evening speech was filled with hope and our enduring dedication to Taleju. We knew the journey would be difficult and will demand fortitude and group support. Taleju's children who must keep her light lit.

While speaking, I saw colorful lights around the group; some red, green, gold and purple. Those weak and the sick radiated dim lights mostly of brown hue.

Shortly before sunrise we passed two more graves.

Day 21. After travelling all night we reached Ta'if this morning. Many were weak and fell ill from the exhaustive trip's exposure. Ta'if was surprised by our appearance. Unfortunately, what extra supplies they set aside were taken by the main party. Consequently, we are now delayed while they try to accommodate our needs.

When Taleju came through here this area was covered in a sea of bones and vast ruins. Through the centuries they were changed into barren mounds which dominate the far end of the valley.

About three centuries ago people returned and settled in a small enclave overlooking the valley. They terraced hills, planted pomegranates, dates, grapes and roses and worked hard to start anew. Trade with new coastal towns flourished until now Ta'if is a major stop along the trade routes to Aqaba. Like Aqaba, they are peaceful and generous. We were housed in a complex of mud houses on the town's outskirts. Our guide who was the caretaker, was genuinely interested in hosting us and worked together to ready us for Riyadh.

Despite being diligent covering myself, I suffered sores and blisters. They were painful and I carefully applied healing suave and avoid irritating them.

Again Yusuf met trouble wherever he went. Ta'if people hold ancient hatred towards the Beni-Elom. Therefore Duce and Altus escort him. I hope these people realize that Yusuf is a gentle soul void of the Beni-Elom traits.

The man who guided us asked if I was from the Deep Desert, implying that I am a Seer. Unlike most people I met, he was not afraid but later I found out it held them in high regard. When I said I was from Sophia, he was intrigued. He hoped to visit the Italia commonwealth in the future. He wondered why we were not with the main group and I explained the Kumari Daughter and I had disagreements. I am leading my group and making the pilgrimage without her approval. He said he admired our courage.

Since taken the roles of leader and the Alimajh I realize our group bonded closer. During our Dedicational pilgrims asked for my interpretations of Taleju's teachings. I am still reluctant, refusing to accept my words are special; however my core group sough answers to questions the Kumari Daughter discouraged. They are spiritually hungry and looked to me for their meal.

After the evening dedicational, I showed Altus a drawing of Taleju based on my vision. He was startled, and must have thought I was crazy because he was quiet for a long time before remarked she looked like a Seer, not human. He then inquired about the translations and when I answered he could not hide his dismay.

He cautioned against sharing its content. Our group may not accept it and brand me a heretic. Unity is our upmost importance now.

Day 23. Yesterday I managed to spend precious free moments wandering Ta'if's terraced orchards and farms. Date groves near the wadi spread out across the valley. Camel caravans crowded the trails to make their last deliveries in this horrible heat and seek refuge in their homes. The souks were busy and trade in spices, textiles, rugs was brisk. Our group is recovering. I gathered supplies, coordinating packing and assembled our caravan. We purchased extra pack and riding camels for the three week trip inland to wadi Hanifa. I was cautioned that warring factions jealously guard their wells. These constantly shift so travelers do not know which tribe controls the water. Since the Great Heat is here, they will be more vicious protecting their resources.

According our map the nearest well was twelve days away at a village called Wadi Madina. However, with the main group ahead, I wondered if their presence will compromise our appearance. This was Altus's fifth trip and he knew this area well. He said the tribes can be violent and warned if we stay on the path we should be alright.

This evening during the Conformation I spoke about our upcoming trip and I observed how my words changed our audience energy patterns. I knew words can have profound effects but until now did not clearly see why. Words too are charged energetic patterns of light and sound. Energies embrace other energies and mingle like artists mixing new ones, creating new colors and meanings.

I decided our evening dedicational should end from passages from my translations but wrapped in The Awakenings language. That way I won't overwhelm or distract them too much.

We are Infinity's orchestra. Together each of us provides our own melody, adding to Life's symphony and our Cosmic Dance.

Afterwards Yusuf commented my eyes flashed purple and green during my talk. Shocked, I asked how the group responded. He replied it did not bother them.

Day 25. Several Ta'if families joined our pilgrims because they heard about me and were curious. I welcomed them and hope they will make the entire journey after the newness wore off.

In evening our pilgrims and camels set for wadi Hanifa. Ta'if inhabitants came out to say good bye. Our guide gave us special dates and thanked us for accepting him. He did not know until meeting us pilgrims could be compassionate and accepting of other beliefs. His tone hinted that his previous encounters with Kumari pilgrims were bad experiences.

Although the upcoming trek is difficult, we are eager to get on with journey. It's about eight hundred kilometers to our next goal.

Day 27. Hejaz desert. Desolation stretched ahead as we walked. The stark, black hills accented by gravel plains and rolling rock hills. The ground radiated heat, leaving us sweaty. The breeze brought sand that at times choked us.

On the second night we encountered a violent sand storm. It caught us on an open plain and played havoc with us. We dropped the camels and huddled behind them for protection. It lasted until after midnight. It left pilgrims with wind burns and scattered our belongings on the plain. It took an hour to retrieve these before continuing.

Day 29. I'm not sure if my effort to translate the book or the severe desolation contributed to last night's lucid dream. Or, was it a dream? Can spirits reach across time and connect with the living? Her book to hints this.

It occurred while we crossed a lava plain under the stars. I rode ahead of the group and Yusuf, Duce and Sarah walked a hundred meters ahead. Our way was illuminated by the heavens. Earlier I forced my head to clear colorful patterns underlying everything because it distracted me from my surroundings.

I wiped sand from my eyes and closed them but for a moment. It was daylight. I was in a small room. The room was decorated with horizontal green and white paint. In places the white and green paint were peeling, stained or cracked. Blanket covered two windows and heard the ocean outside. The air smelt stale, a mixture of incense and salt. From somewhere the sound of tinkling of glass chimes blew in a hot breeze.

In one corner Taleju sat cross-legged on a cushion, huddled over the very book I now read. Her brush quickly raced across the pages, adding color; occasionally pausing to add pigment from a bowl at her feet. She wore simple, green robes and a gold kufi hat on her black and gray streaked hair. Around her slender neck glittered a silver and amethyst necklace. Nearby a worn walking stick leaned against the rock wall. She looked up and our eyes met I detected gold flecks. Even though her tattooed face was gaunt, she smiled; her hands trembled when she set the book down. She motioned and I sat before her. She studied me for a long time and said the past and future finally meet. She stated understanding our spiritual matrix is paramount now and I, Noora, am to prepare humanity for our next evolutionary step. I asked why. She replied in time I will understand.

Then I woke, riding as before. Only seconds passed, yet this seems like days. Her warmth and her sandalwood incense lingered with me. My head throbbed; multilayered images filled my head and my Third Eye ached. I sensed to have just returned from a great journey. It was joyous and frightening at the same time. I recalled her necklace symbol and realized I have seen it before—but where? It is not in her new book or any of the Kumari material. I am stunned and am loss for words. Did I journey across time where present meets the past, or did this desolation played tricks?

Day 31. This night after following gravelly plains and entering a narrow gully, I sensed we were being watched. When I focused, I detected soft energy fields of half a dozen people in the cliffs. They trailed us through the night, being careful to stay out of sight.

At first light we camped in a cluster of sandstone punctuated by many holes sculpted by the wind. As I looked out at our flat trail winding into the shimmering horizon I sensed the trackers headed north on camels.

Sarah came by and offered bread and dates. She sat quietly with me, attentive to my needs. I slept on the carpet in the crook between rocks and woke once. Once I woke, Sarah's head was bowed, a spear resting in her lap. She looked frail.

At the evening Dedicational I decided to speak about spirit's journey into these realms and how everything was composed of light and sound. The group asked about how to differentiate these things. I replied that all manifestation is individual, yet connected by the root sound and light matrix from which they spring. All the while Sarah sat next to me, recording my words in a small book. Afterwards I inquired and she said my words should be read by others. Her answer left me embarrassed.

Later when I showed Altus the sketch of the necklace he said the only time he saw this was at the Kumari Sister's resident in Nepal. According to him it was highest authority and denoted a Kumari Sister. This symbol was never shown publically. I explained it was the symbol on Taleju's necklace.

Month 2, day 1. Near Wadi Medina, Arabia. After a night's travel and being watched by those strangers, we sought refuge from the heat in rocks along the shore of a dried lake. It a brown carpet cracked into many patterns. At breakfast travelers huddled around Sarah and eagerly read what she wrote. They fondly looked in my direction as I quietly sipped tea and sat on the carpet, trying to clear my thoughts for sleep. An elderly man faced me, pressed his palms together and bows reverently. I instantly recognize it as the greeting reserved for a Kumari official. Stunned, I stared at him but did not smile. Embarrassed he quickly turned away. I do not like this tribute. It implies more than what I am.

Day 4. The thermometer is 57 C when we started our trip shortly after sunset. This heat settled into our bodies, minds and spirit; making us groggy and numb. To combat this we were forced to use our water rationing greater than anticipated. In this heat we would dehydrate quickly if we did not drink. The children suffered most. With the heat, constantly breathing sand, and the demands on our bodies it was a constant struggle. No one in their right mind would travel in this heat.

We paused briefly but this aggravated our weariness. I insisted we continued with minimal breaks because the nights were shorter during this time of the year. We had to cover the thirty five kilometers a day. Time and limited supplies were against us. I had never experienced this damning heat. I felt we are travelled through the Nether Worlds of Hades. We must press on.

Day 7. Yesterday was terrifying. In the early morning we used up our water and still had many hours to our destination. The seriousness of our plight forced the pilgrims seek refuge in a cluster of boulders while I, Duce, Sarah, and Yusuf trek across the gravel fields to wadi Medina. During the six hours we travelled, the sandy haze and heat was torturous; even our goggles barely dimmed the sun's glare.

Our hopes were quickly dashed when finding the village deserted and the well's foundations collapsed into a dry hole. Judging by the condition Wadi Medina was empty for years. Additionally we found discarded belongings from the Kumari's group. Disappointed and despairing, I sat on the ground and studied the map, carefully tracing our route. The nearest water was a small oasis in the mountains two days away. Our map was very old and things in the past did not exist, as I discovered on our trip to Ta'if. Even this oasis was still here we would never make it and if was gone, we'd die. My heart sank.

As I pondered our fate, Sarah brought our single water container. I sipped only enough to wet my parched throat. Then, defeated I glanced at the brown gourd, searching for solutions. Then I recalled what I read the evening before about energetic foundations of the physical realm. My mind shifted and I watched the gourd morph into blue and green mixed with brown and gold patterns. It took me a few minutes to realize I was seeing its physical energetic matrix and a melodies of sounds accompanied them..

I asked Yusuf about the terrain and where he thought water might be. He studied the hills then pointed towards a group of hills. Quickly, I led us to higher ground. At a cliff overlooking the valley I squinted against the glare, my eyes sweeping the plains. I focused on shifting my awareness with great effort, for I was so exhausted. My vision was like a telescope focusing until the image was clear. Then, gradually multicolored grids appeared superimposed over the ground and near a cluster of black stones; a faint melody narrowed my search until I located the same blue and gold pattern in the gourd. I could only hold the image for an instant until a crushing headache overcame me. I hastily indicated the location on the map, handed it to Yusuf and sent him quickly back to the group. Meanwhile the rest of us pushed on.

I led Sarah and Duce into the burning noon. Our destiny lay beyond a sand field near black rocks. I still had my doubt and prayed I was right. Several hours later we found the cluster of rocks but to my horror my inner vision faltered. Plagued by headaches and nausea I was able to faintly distinguish only their melodies.

The heat sapped my strength. I was covered with sweat, dizzy and I tumbled off the camel. I frantically searched the area and, falling to my knees, and scooped sand away from a huge, shady rock. Sarah joined me. Duce brought a shovel. Hot sand burned my hands; I and Sarah scooped; Duce used the shovel. Gradually a hole formed driven by madness. We continued digging. After about a meter we came upon moist sand. Sarah screamed joyously and Duce laughed. Soon water pool gushed into the hole. Further efforts awarded us with enough water to fill our containers. Although it was brackish, it was the sweetest thing I've ever tasted.

By evening my party reached us. The well was expanded and those who had not drunk in a day were served first. Far into the night we dug, filled containers and rejoiced. Many asked how I found water, I muttered Taleju guided my hand.

Yet, I was not comfortable sharing the group's joy. I could not share their smiles and song while I kept thinking about the Kumari Daughter's plight. Their faces flashed through my mind and, even though the Daughter banished me, I could not abandon the pilgrims to their fate. I was determined to help. I discussed my plan with Altus who indicated on the map the direction they went. After filling jars I, Sarah and Yusuf and a dozen camels led a rescue party. Altus and Safr were in charge. I expected to be gone three days.

It is now two days since I slept. This morning I write this entry after we hurriedly rested. The day promises to be hot and ahead the flat plains and tortured mountains stretch to the diffuse, hazy horizon. We have no choice but to travel whenever we can.

Day 9. So much has happened since my last entry. To keep our selves going and reduce the risk of falling of our saddles we secured ourselves. We rode day and night, resting briefly and took shifts guiding our party. We followed the ancient trail which at times were made of black ribbon from the Purge era; sometimes the sand buried them beneath massive dunes; other places it was black shards. It wound like an abandoned snake carcass, stretching forever to the horizon.

By day the heat tortured us; by night the vast heavens made us feel lost and alone. Along the way we passed Pre Purge foundations and signs of the pilgrims: fresh graves and discarded containers. Their desperation grew as we neared. The silence was broken only by the hot breeze's whisper and blistering sand swirling around us. The distance shimmered on transparent waves, distorting objects, hiding others. Near the crotch of two hills we reached the oasis indicated by our map. Like Madina these were ruined brown houses, wilted date palms and new graves. Nearby lay the main camp. The pilgrims looked very weak and despondent. Pilgrim and the Kumari Daughter's tent rested in the shade of tall rocks.

We were greeted by outstretched arms, emotional pleas and tears. While Sarah and Yusuf tended to the group, I rode to the Daughter's tent. Several men appeared, haggard and sun burnt, their fancy robes dirty and sand coated. They watched me with hostile eyes as I struggled to dismount. In my weakened state I fell off the camel and went to my pack camels and groped for the water jugs. When the guards realized what I was doing they assisted me and as they carried water jug to the Kumari's tent I followed. In the corner lay the Daughter on cushions, surrounded by her Satori. She propped herself on an elbow and watched me with hostiles yes, cursing me. A guard set a jug at her feet and explained I brought water and could take them to the source. Patan knelt and pressed a cup to her parched lips.

She commented weakly she hoped I did not leave Aqaba. I reminded her that despite her efforts, I would live to see Nepal as Taleju wished and, that if was because of me she will survive. Angrily she waved me away and whispered to her attendant. She was more concerned with my fate than her pilgrims!

Outside a Satori escorted me out and as we watched the pilgrims gathered around Sarah and Yusuf. Despite our differences, his eyes shone gratitude. H he unfolded a map as asked the well's location. When I pointed on the map our eyes met and he remarked I showed true compassion. He added my action proved the Daughter's claim against me was false. They had sent out a party two days prior looking for water and had not heard back. He feared they perished or got lost.

As we spoke pilgrims came up and fell to my feet, kissing them and pawing at my dress. Feeling awkward, I placed my hands on their matted hair and forced a smile. They looked wretched and my heart went out to them. Sarah and Yusuf could not hide their dismay at their behavior. I smiled and nodded it was alright. I appointed Sarah would remain here and guide them to the well. Quickly we gathered containers then I and Yusuf left.

It was a grueling time, completing the trip in two days. Exhausted, we returned just as sunrise. Altus reported armed men watched us from the hills and came to inspect our camp. They were hostile and never spoke. They carried swords and shields. Altus recognized them as a local tribe who brought trouble during a previous encounter.

Yusuf set up defense parameters and separated the camels into several groups, placing them and our supplies in the protection of rocks. Under tense anticipation our group settles in and, no longer able to resist, I slept. Duce and Yusuf took times guarding my tent.

Towards evening I climbed a hill seeking solitude and sat quietly, looking down at our camp. I was glad to be alone. The constant demands and worry frayed my nerves. Carlo's music drifted on the hot breeze. As I watched the gathering darkness my vision shifted and I soared above the ground like a bird. I saw half a dozen shimmering etheric bodies in the rocks a few kilometers away. I instantly recognized these men who I detected earlier.

Day 12. Like the previous days, these have been filled with trial and tribulations as I took it upon myself for our pilgrims' welfare.

For two days we widened the well and sent water to the Kumari's group led by Sarah. In the late evening the Kumari's pilgrims began trickled in.

Despite the heat and my utter exhaustion I sensed it was time to face the trackers. Since we arrived they had not left their camp and continued observing us from the nearby rocks.

I left instructions with Altus and decided to see them alone because too many would alarm them. Duce protested, but I held my ground. I explained these men had been following us since Ta'if. They knew the main group's desperate situation but choose to remain with us. I could use this to our advantage. I concluded them were not threatening.

I know they were scouts for the local tribe controlling this area. As I rode, I swallowed apprehension and steeled my courage. I rode to the rock outcropping near the base of nearby hill. They were surprised to see me and back away, expecting a trap. I dismounted and in a show of defiance I sat on a rock under the sun. I adjusted my goggles and coverings, observing them. The heat was furiously, sucking my energy and seemingly cooking my bones.

I heard music radiate from them and a first mistook this for instruments, until I realized this was their energies. Instead like before these were not indistinct images but colorful geometric patterns, bursts of light, gently flowing streamers that formed globes surrounding their physical form. Seeing their etheric bodies left me confused. My third Eye throbbed as though being stabbed by a hot poker.

After about a hour an elder man, a hand on his big sword, cautiously approached, his cold stare intent on me. He paused, whistled and shortly riders appeared from the rocks, riding to me and surrounded me. No one spoke, just stared. I felt their hostile eyes and violent intent. Eventually he signaled and they rode away.

I moved into the shadow and cooled off. I drank water and ate dates before forcing myself onto my camel. I returned to the camp and Duce assisted me from my camel. I waved him off and determined to appear tough, I walked unescorted to my tent and collapsed. After checking me, Sarah gave me herbs to aid recovery from the heat exhaustion.

Later, as my strength returned my group asked if I would lead the evening ceremony. By the time we assembled orange and purple shadows faded and the last color was drained from the dusty, brown horizon.

I reminded them Consciousness is not static but evolves and we should accept these. The old ways, even our assumption of the Kumari Mother's role and our place as a Kumargi change. Spirit awareness is not static but dynamic. Change and courage march in lockstep. We should be ready to accept this truth and have the courage to do so

Day 13. Today the Kumari joined us. They travelled all night and entered our camp at sunrise. They looked horrible. Five people died in route. Her assistants divided the group into sections and each took at turns at the well. These waiting we attended, dressing wounds, offering food and water, and assisted with shelters. The Kumari kept her pilgrims isolated from us and soon two distant camps appeared. Most pilgrims were glad for our assistance; the Kumari seemed to be the only person bothered by us. I did not interfere with her, wishing to show unity in our time of need. Many people were too weak move. Exposure and lack of water took some close to death. We attended them as best we could, but a few did not survive and when time permitted in the evening we held a ceremony honoring them.

Some of the main group were curious about our evening Dedicational and attended. However, the Kumari kept her distance, looking sullen and forgotten in the gathering darkness. Afterwards while we sang and danced, the Kumari held a separate Dedicational. The tension between our groups is great, like a storm lurking just below the surface, but I am grateful we are back together.

Day 14. It was in the late afternoon when camel riders came. Led by the elderly man wearing a dusty, gold trim black robe the heavily armed riders entered our camp, scattering pilgrims, kicked up sand and waving swords. They put quite a show on for us! Surrounding by his riders they dismounted and the old man strode to the well, knelt and scooped water with his callous hands. Holding them up he watched me defiantly, allowing the water to slip through his fingers. Then he spit and glared us, daring us to act.

The Kumari Daughter and assistants stood in front of her tent, watching. The man led his group to her and paused by a Kumari standard. He grabbed it and defiantly tossed to the sand. He watched her indifferently and when someone started introducing the Daughter he was cut short by a flick of his hand as though dismissing a slave. He muttered, under his breath.

Then he saw me nearby in the shadows. His intense stare froze my heart, yet I dared not show fear. Here was a face hardened by the sun and life spent chasing food and shelter and defending his tribe. One man with him I recognized from our previous encounter. Their menace was directed at me.

Tense minutes passed. Then Altus stepped forward and introduced us in their language. The man watched him briefly then spoke impatiently with a clipped manner. Altus translated. This was their property and no one could drink without his permission. Our behavior dishonored and violated tribal customs which demanded retribution.

He demanded how did I find water, for this area was dry from centuries. Then he accused me working with the Djinns and therefore it must be cursed. He waited for me to speak. When the Kumari Daughter tried to answer he quickly silenced her by raising an impatient palm. He warned her that he had not given her permission to speak. The Kumari face reddened.

I was so taken back by his accusations I struggled for a reply. I sensed our fate depended on my answer. I slowly removed my goggle so he saw my eyes and replied Taleju guided me here with the hope all would share it. He stared incredibly, hardly believing who I was. He momentarily hesitated then asked why she spoke though a Seer working with Djinns and not the Kumari. I replied that she understood his tribe needed water and so brought a gift through me, not Djinns. He was quiet, baffled. Then he accused the Kumari Daughter of harboring a Seer, which are enemies of his people and that I should be punished.

She explained I was not from her group and our group was heretics. He could do whatever with he wished. With her words I felt as if a heavy rock struck me in the head, leaving me momentarily stunned.

Then an armed group led by Duce advanced towards me, hands on swords. I ordered Duce to stand down. Tensions mounted. I asked Sarah to fill a cup and bring it to me. They watched quietly as Sarah went to well and returned. Dropping my knees I held the cup for him, head bowed and remarked that by his kindness I brought this water for him to see if it's worthy of him. I beg for his forgiveness because we were desperate and failed to consult him first. By helping us it demonstrated he was a wise and honorable man. He looked around then took the cup and drank slowly. He dropped the cup by my side.

He studied us. The leader said sparing our lives was his gift for finding water. He stressed all were welcomed to share his tribe's water, expect me.

After they left, our groups, stunned and anxious fell quiet and did not mix. Shaken and nauseated I retreated to my thoughts. I felt humiliated, angry, but glad I prevented an incident. Later the Kumari Daughter came to me and said because of my effort everyone owed me their lives. She would invite everyone back to her group--except me. She would call for a vote this evening.

Sick of her behavior and filled with anger I replied I will reach Nepal alone if be even without her blessings. I was first of many Seer who would make this pilgrims so the Kumari should prepare. Her face twisted and she slapped me. I wept.

The Daughter spoke to our groups, imploring them to return to her guardianship. She reminded them the pilgrimage was always guided by a Kumari Daughter and is the only recognized path to Satori.

She claimed I was an upstart, a false promise, a mutant that the Kumari warned against. Although my words appeared sweet, they hid discontent and Taleju's disapproval. Those who followed me were doomed to failure because I did not understand protocol, procedures and religious rituals demanded at historical sites. By missing these, the pilgrimage would not be recognized.

The Daughter promised those returning they would be forgiven; otherwise they would be banished and names removed. They were given until evening to decide.

Apprehension and dread darkened my heart. My group was reminded of the price for defiance. Would they cave in? I sat in the shade, head lowered, not wanting anyone to see my tears. Humiliated for my belief weighed upon my shoulders, I felt unworthy. I am a Seer, it's not of my choice but this is who I am. I was angry that what I thought a peaceful, enlightened pilgrimage would turn into a racial contest. The Kumari religion was fine for everyone expect for those who they chose. This hypocrisy sickened me.

Some quietly joined me and shared their concerns with Altus and Safr. Was this what the Kumari Mother intended, a test of faith. We waited. Time stretched. The heat made us miserable. My headaches worsened, I suffered violent attacks of nausea. I sat speaking to no one. Towards evening a girl took my hand. Raising my head our eyes met. I wiped tears and stilled my heart. I looked beyond my tent at the crowd gathered. She took my hand and we joined them and in a shaky tone I explained our puja was not about accomplishing goals, or visiting mandated places but understanding Taleju's teachings and finding our spirituality community. Through our puja is how we honor Taleju.

The Daughter came to us. Our pilgrims turned away, not speaking. None joined her group and after an hour she left, vanishing behind the hills.

Day 15. The hot nights lingered. We travelled in two groups although a few from the Kumari pilgrims joined us. Rumors of my magic powers circulate, which I tried unsuccessfully to stop. We were being tracked. So not to compromise our safety I took water in private.

After the split with the Daughter and despite my protest my personal guards were 'officially' created. They argued it was time I had escorts wherever I went. Until they explained I was not aware how much our pilgrims looked at me for leadership, which also could attract potential threats. They were convinced the Daughter meant to end my life. My death would be a great blow to our pilgrimage. I only agreed to this because I believed this is in the best interest of our pilgrims. They call themselves Red Sash because of the unmistakable sash they wore. There are eight members.

This evening came their first test. A man from the hostile tribe hid in the rocks and tried to attack me while I joined our evening Dedicational. Duce was with me and after a scuffle the man was disarmed. Duce would have killed him if I did not stop him. I realized these attempts would not end because Altus warned their honor was at stake by having me travelling through their land.

Therefore, I used their superstition against him. While Duce held him down I called for Altus to translate. I grabbed him by the chin and stared into his frightened eyes. I summoned all my pent anger and rage. When my eyes flashed red he screamed and begged for mercy. I reminded him I was a Seer and could summon Djinn. They would curse this land and take all the water; nothing would grow for a million years. Additionally, I will instruct them to steal their children. After a few minutes Duce released him. He vanished, screaming. Despite Duce and Yusuf praises this left me sick. This dishonest, cheap deception went against everything I believe in.

Day 18. Today we turned off the old road and followed a narrow trail into the craggy hills, taking us north of Riyadh to Wadi Hanifa. We did not find water where the map indicated and our weakness slowed progress. We were about day behind the Daughter. The land was barren, hot and empty. Wind 'Djinn' created by heat rising off the sand produced columns danced over plains, carrying brown sand into the sky. Desperation drove us on. Once, a person from the Daughter's group came by, asking for water because an accident broke half of their water jugs. Reluctantly I spared a few, only to later regret it when our own supply ran out this evening.

Day 19. More Daughter pilgrims joined us, but they were ill or weak. We could not make concessions because time was against us. We were driven by anxiety and desperation. Our pace was grueling and we had no mercy for those who could not keep up. It was heart breaking, but if we did not travel the distance, then we will perish.

We were all exhausted from our travel, lack of sleep and this hot and sandy environment. On this journey from Wadi Medina we endured two sandstorms, hardship, and sickness and getting lost in a canyon. These responsibilities left me no rest. During this trip I am plagued by doubt and at times cursed my role. I never wanted this responsibility but the more I run from this, the more it seeks me out.

I do not confide to anyone because I must appear committed to our task. Even to entertain this attitude is dangerous. Once I doubt myself, the Daughter wins.

I won't give her the satisfaction. . . .

No water or food or meal since this last night. We are a day from Wadi Hanifa. Clouds gathered on the western horizon, obscuring the moon and a breeze picked up.

Day 20: *We came to Wadi Hanifa valley in two days after reaching Riyadh. We came to a place where the wadi's deep canyons shielded an empty village from the main destruction. A storm came up and flooded the canyon. We made camp in buildings on higher ground and shielded us as best we could against black, slimy sand carried by violent winds. When the storm ended three days later everything was coated by black, oily film.*
   -Somewhere in Wadi Hanifa-

Because of our plight we rested very little, wanting to push to our destination. We started at mid day as the heat was cooling and travelled all night. In the early morning we experienced our first rain since leaving the Italia Commonwealth. We paused and lifted our faces in rejoiced. Raising my face the warm torrent quickly soaked me. It felt good. Later the ground woke with the smells of acrid damp, wood, sand and life. After months facing rainless days we were reborn in purpose and spirit. Brown water swelled the river banks we followed.

Late morning we reached Wadi Hanifa. Many pilgrims were weak and delirious. Yet, we were proud. Crossing the desert meant a test of devotion and endurance.

Wadi Hanifa has greatly changed since Taleju's time. It is a blessed place here in the high desert after enduring our horrible journey. For centuries the wadi cut deep channels through the sandy rock and three canyons creating Wadi Hanifa. Within its shaded banks farms produce dates, oranges, pomegranates, figs and olives groves. Tilled fields of herbs and wheat grow on tilled slopes. Wadi Hanifa's population is about five hundred citizens, surrounded by massive walls and round battlement towers atop the highest point where they see anyone approaches. Here, merchants gather from all corners of the world; bringing goods and returning home with incredibly complex, clay and reed baskets this city is famous for.

Officials met us at a predominant rock formation just outside the city gates. They were confused by our appearance because the main party arrived yesterday and did not mention us. I explained we were too weak to keep up with the Daughter's group. Later they got a message claiming the Kumari did not acknowledge us because we were impostures. Her answer left our host in an awkward situation. We could not join her since we were not part of the pilgrimage, so after much talking, we were taken to the walled enclosure for visiting merchants. The camp was crowded but in our sorry state we were grateful.

Per tradition, the cities along the pilgrimage outfit the pilgrimage for the next part of their journey. But because of our situation we are on our own. Some travelers saw our plight and offered food and water until we could get this sorted. We spend the remaining day recuperating and rested. A persistent headache frayed my nerves. My restless angry became difficult to control and isolated myself with instruction I would not see anyone. Altus and Duce went to town to arrange supplies. I tried to sort my emotions out.

Day 21. Altus and Duce returned. A city's merchant official accompanied them and said he understood our situation and agreed to payment of two kilos of jewelry. We now had enough provisions for about a month and an introduction letter to the eastern village of Al ain where we could get supplies there. I was very thankful for his generosity. Additionally, as per custom the city extended hospitality for 3 days. As a show of good faith he offered an invitation to visit Wadi Hanifa.

After the morning Majlis, Sarah convinced me to accompany her to the market. Yusuf took change of my security and our small group ventured into the hot summer afternoon.

We came to one of the main gates. This opened onto a wide boulevard intersecting three others at the city's center. Here we found the marketplace busy with travelers and traders from across Arabia and offered baskets, pottery, spices, fruit, vegetables, rugs and cooking utensils. Camels heaped with goods competed for shade in the narrow market while merchants conducted their business. I was surrounded by shouting, exclamation, curses and idle chatter. The sandy air was alive with cooked food, sweat and incense.

I could not stand the commotion and noise. After so long with silence, this irritated my nerves so my escorts headed to a marble and tiled, green domed structures just beyond the souk. From steps we watched Sarah visit an incense stall. Curious students glanced at us as they hurried up the steps, carrying scrolls. From somewhere a string instrument played. I caught a hint of sandalwood. Peace settled over me.

An official I met yesterday joined us on the steps. He was dressed in white thobe and gold head scarf and carried several scrolls. He is a teacher and scholar at the city's Madrasa, a renowned learning center. These centers gathered knowledge from all over the world and their goal is to keep alive information about the Purge. These libraries are the main attraction to Arabia. Like our Pustakalaya centers, they are single compound housing temples, library and learning centers.

Wadi Hanifa has many date trees and small gardens. Except for the stone boulevards dirt streets and white and green buildings with intricate windows make up the bulk of the city. Many dwellings are connected by covered bridges arching above the street. Inhabitances use these and rarely venture outside.

Like most people I've meet in Arabia they are friendly, gracious, but disagree with our religious ideas. Like those in Aqaba they believe the desert spirits reside everywhere and their wellbeing is dependent upon their moods, which they spent consider time to offer thanks and prayers. They dislike Kumari ideology because it was based on a dead woman. They saw this as clinging to the past rather than living in the present. They insist that by living in the present and trying to understand life, the faults of our past could be avoided. I confess in some ways I agreed with them.

When we returned evening time one merchant gave me a splendid carpet to replace old my prayer rug that was torn and faded. He explained it was a gift from his home Homs, a city in the Persian Emirates. In appreciation I give him a silver mirror from Sofia. He was appreciated and remarked his wife would love it.

Much to my disapproval my group sung me praises and stories about Taleju guiding me to the well. During our travel I heard stories where some claim I appeared in dreams, spoke over long distance or appeared as Taleju. Despite my attempt to discourage they will not stop. I suppose people still needed to believe in greater myths than themselves. I worry a time will come when a decision may bring great harm and realize I am not the infallible person they believe. It will be a harsh session, especially for them and me.

During travel these stories reached the main group, causing bitterness between us. At times tensions were high. The Kumari accused me of heresy and the product of insane minds; those in my defense argued I am compassionate and represent what the Awakenings really teach. It sickens me we have been reduced to squabbling like crows.

I close this entry with a comment at our evening meeting. *The Purge turned our world into ash. But from this ash we make mirrors from which we see ourselves as Spirit.*

Day 23. *We each carry our spiritual records with us; through all lives and incarnations. It is an open book. You want to know if a person is ill, look at their physical energy field; if they are angry, see their emotional field; do they believe in an afterlife, it too is written on their Psychic body; are they self serving and vain, their Mental body tells; what karmic patterns do they abode by? Look to the Causative body for the answer.*

Nothing is hidden by Infinity; spirit only has to see and understand. -Dream and Echoes-

Since camping I am filled with underlying dread, a vague shapeless threat leaving me no peace, much like a persistent fly. Until today I attributed this to my exhaustion and the weight of responsibilities, however, I discovered otherwise.

It began after we handed our supply list to the officials then I, Altus and Yusuf checked our maps, lists and reviewed tomorrow's journey. It was evening. As they left my tent I stood over the table, sipping tea and prepared for our Dedicational.

I was so preoccupied I barely heard someone enter. Thinking it might be Altus, I called to him and faced the entrance. But instead I found a stranger brandishing a dagger. We were both startled. He lunged at me and immediately felt pain in my left shoulder. His momentum sent me, table, maps and instruments to the floor. Raising the dagger he lunged over the table. Screaming I deflected his attack with my tea cup and rolled away. Leaping up I ran for the entrance but he grabbed my sleeve. Terrified I raked my fingernails over his face. Our commotion alerted Altus, Yusuf and Duce who were outside talking. As they rushed in the attacker pushed me towards them and ran out. Duce and Yusuf chased him but he vanished in the gathering darkness.

My arm bled and a sickening numbness of shock morphed into intense pain. My arm hung limp and when I moved fingers the pain shot into my head. I collapsed onto the ground and Altus lifted me.

Shaken, frightened and angry I composed myself. Sarah came in and she and Altus assisted me to my bed and cleansed the wound. Sarah insisted I should cancel our dedicational but I insisted our group is expecting me and I will not disappoint them. Weak, dizzy and nauseated Sarah helped me change and changed the dressing again before she and Altus assisted me out into the night air. I hid my wound with a scarf and managed to struggle through the ceremony. When the Dedicational ended I noticed blood oozing through the dressings and down my arm.

Afterwards I returned to my tent and I sat on the bed and, wrapping my arms about my knees Sarah used needle and thread to sew up the wound. The cut hurt, I bit my lip and tried not react but despite my effort I let out a few cries. I stared beyond the tent and shivered, not from cold but fright. The shock sickened me. The wound was minor pain compared to the insult I felt in my heart.

Sarah finished and whispered something and pressed a cup to my lips. I sipped the warm, bitter liquid. I don't remember when I fell asleep but was surprised to wake among the pillows and Sarah seated in the corner, spear in hand. She looked at me, her face gaunt from exhaustion and offered an encouraging smile. Sunlight shone in through a small opening in the door flap.

Yusuf drew back the flap and came with tea; his face showed the strain of being on guard all night. Outside an excited group gathered and Duce entered, hauling in a young man covered with blood and dust. His hair was matted, his clothing torn, and he had been beaten; welts and blood encrusted his arms and swollen face. He limped. He looked more scared than anyone I've ever met. Duce brandished his sword. Altus stood at the entrance, holding back the group who shouted and waved fists.

Duce pressed his sword against the man's neck, forcing him onto his knees. His dark eyes darted around, frightened. His face twitched, his cracked lips quivered. He watched me and knew I could end his life with a command. They waited for my response while I sat across him, sipping my tea and weighing his fate. I did not speak, for so shocked was I that anyone would want to harm me. Yet, I would not react to the violence emotions surging through me.

Then, recalling what I read a few days ago, I shifted my awareness to his Etheric Bodies. Multicolored spheres jumped out and surrounded him: wonderful patterns, geometrics, streamers, flashes and blurred pictures; each a different layer, moving to the front then sinking back, like a wave ebb and flow. Images formed in my head; I could distinguish the melodies of each sphere. I read his past, his mood, and the event leading to the fated attack.

He was not an evil person; his heart was good if given a different path. He was poor; no family; desperate. He spent his time making bricks. Someone offered him the chance to earn respect and wealth by killing me. I could not see who that was.

I was shaking inside with rage and the awkwardness of determine his fate. I forced myself to finish my tea then quietly set the cup down. Then, I spoke to him, revealing what I read. Fear turned to astonishment, and disbelief, then terror. He glanced at Duce's sword. I asked his name. It was Sami. I inquired to why he wanted to harm me. He glanced quickly outside at the crowd and then confessed the promised of money.

Yusuf joined us and Duce relayed what he said. Yusuf cursed and draw his weapon, raising it. I held up my hand, Yusuf lowered his sword.

Pleading in a shaky voice he explained if we handed him to the city, they would behead him for dishonoring the town. I replied his fate was up to him.

After consideration options I decided to go against what the crowd wanted. I had Duce and Yusuf sheathed their weapons and said Taleju welcomed him if he forgave himself. No harm would come to him as long as he remains here but he must swear not to harm us. I reminded him that I could tell he was deceiving us. He looked around in disbelief then dropped his forehead to the sand and in a quaking voice promised me. Duce and Yusuf did not hide their amazement.

I did this only because by observing his Etheric bodies I understood his heart and the role he may in play in my life.

When he crawled to me and grasped my hand, Duce pounced, ready to pull him away. I shook my head. Sami clasped my hands and looked up with tear filled eyes. He swore that the life I saved was now mine to command. He was indebted.

I instructed Yusuf to watch over him. Some in our group did not understand my clemency but later its new spread beyond our group. Duce questioned me and I said that it is what Taleju would do.

It was night. I sat in front of my tent, watching the play of the river current in the moonlight and listened to music and soft voices. Sarah and Altus were by my side. I ate dates and savored their sweet taste.

Yet, my thoughts wandered to what lay ahead.

Tomorrow we resume our travel and in four days we will leave the main Dubai road and travel northeast, following Taleju's original route along the coast to Dubai. This near forgotten route will lack inns, settlement until reaching Al-ain. We will enter the Poison Wastelands and, even though this old map shows wells, I have my doubt. This will be our most severe test of faith so far.

There is a vague dread stirring in my heart. I know my dark fears will return after been absent these weeks.

Day 24. We left Wadi Hanifa after sunset like passing shadows. I suppose they were glad to see us go. The Daughter's group started midday and with the moon's aid we followed their tracks. A rumor circulate that the Daughter was disappointed when hearing my fate. Rumor says she was behind this; I do not believe it. Sami said the man was a local and he never mentioned who was behind the plot. For now Yusuf kept him away and watches his every move. Sami assisted with camp duties and although quiet and reflective, is grateful for his new life. I confess I don't trust him and despite what I noticed in his energy field, am reluctant and keep my distance. I know in time our barriers will diminish.

The stab will leave a scar. Sarah had medical background and checked it constantly. She said my shoulder will be stiff and achy; full range of motion is doubtful since several tendons and muscles were permanently damaged.

Day 27. Taleju recorded this about Riyadh
The Rad meters points to the red, warning us to stay away. We reached the Nejd valley at noon and pause from hills looking at

ruins stretching to the horizon. Here lay Riyadh, Heart of the Purge. This desolation is empty of life, the sky is black, forbidding and chokes away our breath. Great fires light the heavens at night; by day rain brings sticky, black drops clogging the skin, ruins clothes and sticks to hair. This rain is foul and coats everything until all is black. Decay and stink is everywhere; the road we travel is littered with rusting hulks; windowless buildings stare at our passing; reminding me of skulls. Here and there gray bones mark the spot where human and animals fell. We move as fast as possible through this death valley.

The weather is changing and the extreme heat is getting notably cooler. Therefore, we decided to return traveling by day.

For three days we have followed a wide path used by merchants and travelers where markers indicate distance to Wadi Hanifa. Sand mounds, steel and concrete surround us, stretching to the brown, hazy horizon. In some places twisted metal and elevated concrete bridges rose up from the sand like some nightmarish sculpture. I glimpsed bits of black ribbon where Purge vehicles once choked the roads. Nearby steel monoliths reached a hundred meters into the sky; their massive heights blocking out the sun. These were remnants of artificial canyons Taleju observed in her travel and which I saw in my dreams.

At night we camped beneath towering ruins and sand hills reminding me of ocean waves. There was no evidence of habitation and I suspect this desert cannot support life because of poisonous residue. Though the centuries all color was bleached out as though life was sucked out by the desert. Our world has been reduced to indistinct shapes, tan hues and black shadows, creating a contrast playing tricks with the eyes. We were constantly harassed by sand carried on the breeze; grit invaded everything: our clothes, water and food. It left a foul smell that made many sick and aggravated throats and chaffed skin. Even my goggles failed to keep sand out, forcing me to be cautious when clearing my eyes.

This harsh emptiness and lack of life reminds me of a huge cemetery.

We are still in these ruins with no end in sight.

This was my first glimpse of the magnitude of a Purge city. Millions of people once inhabited this valley. I cannot image the chaos and noise Riyadh created or the massive logistics required to house, feed and transporting this sea of humanity. I cannot grasp this magnitude; its size defies explanation or sanity. Should I admire the Purge for having the technology to build this, or curse them for their foolishness?

Day 28. We came to the Dubai road juncture, leading south to the Arabian Gulf coast. Our pilgrimage turned off and headed north east to Hades Cauldrons and the Black Pools. This trail was small and unmarked.

Today it was stormy and sand obscured travel. We found sheltered in old buildings and wait for the storm to pass.

Ali, you would be proud of my determination to unlock Taleju's book. I managed between my duties to translate nearly half. It is very difficult and only possible as I delve deeper into its contents. To unlock the hidden language in the rainbows was only accomplished by applying what I gleamed from previous knowledge to the new. Thereby characters, colors and even the sounds determine how sentences are formed. It is tedious work and leaves my head throbbing for hours. Many Taleju's ideas are still beyond me and create more questions than answers. I carefully record my translations word for word so future generations will have her undistorted message. This is radically different than the Awakenings and written in deeper levels on matters of how Consciousness works. This book is meant to be applied, rather than ritualized and meditated.

The book is stored inside that sandalwood box you gave me on our fifth anniversary.

I seem to be living two lives: by the day I read the book and have my duty to the pilgrims. At night I am Shakya's student. With each session I get glimpses of awareness far beyond those established by Taleju's religion which we have followed by hundreds of years. It is so simple and so profound.

Sarah has taken upon herself to read my words at the Conformation gathering when I am tired or preoccupied with duties. When hearing them I am amazed for I have little recollection.

A thought linger from my recent translation: *Spirit walks between two Worlds. That which it sees and that which is hidden. One binds, the other liberate.*

Day 31. I do not see them but sense we are being observed. They were careful to hide themselves and despite my effort to `detect' they are invisible. At times I felt pressure against my head, as though someone tried to invade my thoughts.

My arm continues to heal, however throbbing pain interferes with my range of motion and strength.

Midday we finally left Riyadh and trudged across undulating sand plains, following the tracks laid down by the Daughter's pilgrims. They are a day ahead. Later we descended into a shallow canyon and encountered stone markers left by them. These contained letters for us, inquires about pilgrims' health and spiritual advice. They are welcomed distraction from our travel. Everyone is emotionally drained by the desolation and silence of Riyadh.

We followed the undulating path until we reached a canyon which opened into a ridge of buff hills and rust colored rock. At dusk dark clouds obscured the eastern horizon. Altus said this is our destination: 260 kilometers to the Black Pools.

Month 3, Day 2. The sky turned gray with threatening clouds and worsened as we continued east. Now distant thunder echoed and greasy, pungent smells carried on the breeze. In the distance rain cloaked the desert like veils. The Daughter's group continued leaving notes, revealing the pressure she under. Her camp was divided between those who sympathized with me, and those who championed for drastic action to prevent us from continuing. Many from both groups still clung to the belief the attempt on my life was her doing.

The terrain gets more tortured, showing scars of great upheaval even many kilometers from Riyadh. In some places we came upon concrete foundations nearly buried by time. We have not seen a single creature or plant since leaving Wadi Hanifa. This is a gloomy, sterile realm. On the map shows beyond Riyadh is called Poisonous Wastelands, an appropriate name.

We encountered rain, but our joy was shortly lived. At first we tried catching it but quickly discovered it was slimy, gray particles. It stunk like rotten eggs and so foul it left dark blotches on skin and our clothes. We were forced to seek shelter when the rains came. Even between bouts of rains, the hot, humid air was filled with sticky, gray particles. I fear exposing my journal so I postponed entries until safe. The same is true with Taleju's book.

Day 4. Sometimes between riding, the camel's sway, and the monotonous dulling my sensing I detected distant background sounds coming from far beyond: low rumbling thunder, tinkling glass, a mournful breeze, even the angry hiss of snakes. When I looked around and concentrated on hearing my surroundings, they were absent. These sounds happened only when my vision shifted and my physical reality lost its form and changed to shimmering gossamer. It is so vivid I fear stepping through it! I had to close my eyes to clear this vision. Shakya's book mentioned this, but experiencing this frightens me; this is because my mind cannot grasp these unseen things stretching far beyond my visible world. At times I envision myself swimming against a storm pushing me towards the shoals.

Late afternoon the rain clouds moved south, bringing sun's heat and low lying ground fog. It choked and stung my breathing. Even covering my face did nothing to ease the discomfort. In the east, dark patches covered the horizon. I realized they were not clouds, but smoke; I am filled with unexplainable dread. There waited the Black Pools.

Day 6. Near sunset we came to a stone obelisk standing like a lone sentry in a vast gravel field. It appeared very old and long ago its sides were covered with letters and brightly painted, now cracked and nearly erased by sand. Other travelers added their messages or initials, creating a curious history of who passed through here.

We curiously studied it, unable to read the ancient, cursive script. Altus said he passed this many timed and no one could translate it. Near the bottom the same karma symbols in Taleju's book caught my attention. Knelling for a closer look, I discovered writing was similar, however the `letters' were different and incomprehensible. I concentrated on the bands that once covered the sentences. I was able from the color traces to sense what they meant. The puzzle opened for me. As I read my finger moved across the text and altered directions.

> Herein our Demise was given birth
> Long ago when we bled our earth.
> Madmen promises enslaved us
> charmed us with their spell.
> But their dream soared and collapsed
> The Purge Beast was released
> Now we are orphans' children
> Condemned by our parents
> Upon this Wheel of Sorrow

I explained Seers probably made this. Sarah recorded it in her book. A few pilgrims left tokens, performed puja and lit incense.

This was the first Seer monument I had seen. I am surprised by my ability to translate it.

This evening our camp was usually quiet as the sober message hung over us.

Day 7. This wounded land will take many centuries to heal. Great discord hangs in this place. The scars left by the Purge went deep into the world's foundation. My inner senses underlying disharmonious, bubbling up like restless spirits. This land is angry and since setting foot in Arabia I am aware of residue violence is greater than anyplace I visited. At times these feelings constant grate my nerves.

As we got closer to the coast the disharmonies and storms intensified. At places the ground was hot and seeped foul mist. We were forced to seek alternate paths. Breathing stifling, stuffy air thick with grimy sand irritated my lungs and my cough worsened. We were yet several days from our destination and I wondered how my group will hold up. We seemed to be entering the Hell believed by the ancient religions. We covered our mouth and noses with cloth and frequently paused to wipe accumulated coating off goggles. We did our best to protect the camel's nose and mouths but forced to save our precious water prevented us. The poor camels suffered. Blankets hastily thrown over our belongings failed to prevent them from being soaked by persistent gray rain. A tarry, rotten stench grew stronger with each kilometer.

Altus said that when he visited ten years ago it was not like this. He doubted we will get close enough to see the Black Pools. That night I asked if our group wanted to continue and they said yes.

Day 8. This night I had a very vivid dream of Taleju. We were in a small, dark room with small window looking at snow peaks in the distance. From somewhere soft voices droned, heavy sandalwood incense cast blue mist over the room. There were many rugs. Taleju was a girl, about ten, wearing red dress, gold crown and her eyes outlined in black, her ebony hair pulled back tight behind her head. Her forehead was painted red and gold in the shape of a down facing crescent moon. She hummed to herself and wrote in a book. She grimaced and rubbed her left arm.

Our eyes met: hers flashed gold. She stopped humming. Taking a mirror from a nearby desk she held it up so I can see my reflection. I look tired, pale and sickly and as I watched my image she commented in a young, sweet voice Consciousness and all Its Realms are not static but Consciousness constantly shifts Awareness, life comes and goes like closing chapters in a book. Old replaces now. The same is for ideas, thoughts and beliefs. Despite my effort to stem the current, this river cannot be stilled. As she spoke I watched my reflection in the mirror. My eyes irises glow purple then pink; wonderful melodies radiated from me. The dream frightened me, I woke.

Day 9. *Herein is the center of the greed which enslaved humanity: this Heart that pumped the earth's Blood; this sacred Hall of illusion with its cathedrals steel pipe, tanks and towers; this congregation of power and madness. Its tentacles stretched across the earth, touching everyone and enslaving humanity in its transparent dreams. The desert dwellers who lived in these arid lands became willing slaves for their dominating masters far away. Although the desert dwellers had riches, their hearts were troubled, spirit confused. Nations cast lustful eyes to this place with intent to consume more, steal if necessary or send great armies if threatened. Black Blood arteries covered the world; powered their great cities of steel and concrete, consumed resources, overpopulated and fueled hatred and fear. Wealth was taken until only a few possessed it; yet they still sought to bring suffrage and blight upon the world, bending life to their foolish will.*

Then, the Purge reminded them. When the black Blood stopped, the rage came: sweeping across the world in its all consuming firestorm; opening new wounds, closing others.

This is an awful place; black smoke chokes the air fueled by great fires covering a sea of Black Pools. Thunder and lightning shake the ground and the rain brings the Black dust. It covers everything; the sand, hills, my cloths, skin and hair. I struggle to breathe against the stinking haze. Only fire and smoke inhabit this place. I can see but a few hundred meters.

Humanity has transformed this place into a nightmare that will for eons remind us of our folly.---Taleju near Dhahran, Arabia-

We are near the heart and soul of the Beast, the nightmare of insanity. For us pilgrims, the Kumargi, we wanted our life to get the chance to visit this place and see, as Taleju did, where it all began.

Yet the horrors far exceed our worst nightmare.

Today our travel was relentlessly filled with choking and black smoke obscuring daylight. Last night I saw distant, amber glows. Many were sick but determined to get as close as we could. Along the way, we picked up half a dozen pilgrims from the Daughter's party. They suffered breathing problems and weakness. We placed them in abandoned, rock shelters built to accommodate the pilgrims and promised to return in two days.

Everything lacked color. The ground was black, the hills were black and heavy smoky clouds were black.

On a gravel and boulder plain we fought an easterly, roaring hot wind carried on columns of oily smoke. We entered a canyon and the slippery rocks slowed our pace. Later a thunderstorm broke, drenching us. Altus pressed us onto higher ground. We scrambled up the gravel and rock, struggling against cascading water and tar. As we reached the summit black waves cascaded through the canyon, sweeping away packed sand, boulders and nearby cliffs. It exposed the ancient road before ripping it to pieces.

Our map indicated we entered Hades Cauldron, about twenty kilometers from the Black Pools. A band of hills separated us. While we made camp in the rocks I led a group to the summit. Looking into thick, smoke columns it temporarily shifted, showing black, fiery cauldrons dotting rocky slopes and boiling sea. The Kumari's camp was above a canyon about five kilometers away. We only remained a few minutes within this blistering and suffocating before returning to camp. Our camel prints left brown prints upon the black ground

Taleju said huge cities covered this land; now they were gone. I cannot imagine why humanity chose to poison our world in such magnitude.

We were too exhausted to hold a Dedicational.

Day 10. Hades Cauldron, Arabia. We can go no farther and turned south. The pollution and our sickness was too much and I fear this place will claim lives if we persist. The Black Pool, even after all these centuries, is still an obstacle we had to respect. I send riders back to get those we left just as another hideous storm drenched us. From the hills I observed canyons melt into brown, black mass and filled with angry sledge, completely burying the trail. The storm intensified, the blistering winds made it impossible to continue. We set up a hasty camp in a cluster of large rocks and waited out the storm. Camels were nervous and complained. We had to restrain them and covered ourselves as best we could. I worried the storm would carry our belongings or wash them into the canyon.

Towards evening when the storm subsided a messenger from the Daughter's party came with grave news. Her camp was washed away into a canyon. She is feared dead.

Leaving Altus in charge, I and Satr led a rescue party, fighting treacherous terrain, floods, rains and complete blackness. Our solar lanterns were ill equipment to illuminate much beyond a meter so I guided us with my inner vision studying the planet's energy field. Soaked, exhausted and hungry we reached them camp before dawn. When we arrived a few people stare at me in horror and quickly move aside. Later Duce remarked that my eyes glowed as though possessed.

Their camp was in shambles, laying in deep mud and large boulders. Dead camels mingled with scattered supplies and broken crates. People were in rags, covered in tar, mud or blood. A group came to us and indicated the area where a group gathered shouted, crying frantically and clawing at the mud. We hurriedly up the canyon. The floor was soft, hindering progress as our camels sunk and struggled against the mud clinging them like glue. Twisted bodies poked through the maze of rocks, boulder and sand, being illuminated by our weak, blue lanterns. I cleared my head and that point between my brows expanded. Geometric patterns superimposed over the ground and mingled with faint rose, green and blue energies in the rocks near a group of huge boulders. It was here I concentrated my efforts and directed our group. Desperately clearing the mud and rocks we found unconscious survivors. In a space where two massive boulders collapsed we located the Daughter buried up to her head, blood and mud covered her head. Carefully digging her out we carried the unconscious woman back to camp and set up a shelter.

We conducted an assessment of the camp: twenty five pilgrims and five Satori perished; about half the camp was destroyed.

As the survivors pick through their belongings and we attended the wounded they turned to me for guidance. I make sure the Daughter was cared for by Sarah then assigned duties. This time they did not hesitate or protest. Many were weak and wounded. I inquired as to why they sent for me and a pilgrim confessed I could see invisible objects. Although a few regarded me with contempt, most were grateful.

Satr was in charge of the preparing the camp for return to our camp. The rain and the choking air increased, making it impossible for them to stay. We worked all night searching for survivors. By dawn I, exhausted, led them and what supplies we could salvage to our camp. A few stayed to assist Sarah and the Daughter. We sent another party in mid day and by evening all pilgrims were together and crowded in shelters. While I assessed our situation the victims recuperated as the storms continued. Some pilgrims were thankful, others suspicious. After all our efforts, most pilgrims feared me and kept their distance. Even in this mishap old divides linger like chronic sickness.

Day 11. Patan, the only surviving Satori, held a dedicational for the dead. Pilgrims performed rites and puja. I and Altus spoke, but the Daughter's pilgrims left no doubt they were not pleased. We performed sky buries per custom; however I suspect it would be many years before the sky would take their bodies.

The flood left only Altus' map. Our group had two navigating instruments and three Sickness meters. After inventory remaining supplies Altus calculated we have enough water for eight days.

Al-ain is on the edge of the Empty Realm, which Altus warned is one of the most inhospitable places on earth. But it is ten days travel. Our next destination, Sabkha is another month.

Difficult travel ahead.

Day 12. Travelling through Hades Cauldron and dirty storms weakened us but we must press on. Lingering could spell our doom. We made special palanquins for the Daughter and her attendant; Altus recovered the ledger and updated the list. Patan is now in charge of the Kumari's affairs and wellbeing. Although I did not want the responsibilities, I and Altus filled the role of leaders because the majority pilgrims expected this. This meant my headaches and problems increased tenfold.

Once we loaded the wounded and supplies we journeyed towards the Empty Realm, following the pilgrim trail. Additionally, our camel train was reduced by two third, meaning we used camels for carrying supplies and many, already weak, were forced to walk. Our numbers were reduced to one hundred and eighteen.

It is ironic that I, a recluse who wanted only to travel by myself and devote my time to The Awakenings am thrust into this role. I suppose I should be grateful to be alive but at times I am resentful. Tending the pilgrims and our camp leaves little time for me. Perhaps this is what the dream meant.

The rains stopped yesterday. Near evening we camped at concrete foundations. Everyone was covered in grimy filth; our faces scratched and dirty. Our ripped clothes clung like sticky blankets. But, we are back together again as a single group and this is important. Ali and Bishma I hold your smiles as I finish writing.

Day 13. That dream! It disrupted my sleep and now I fear to close my eyes because I may enter it. I lay here in the first glimmer of the day, huddled over the lamp and compelled not to forget this and write furious before it vanishes.

It began as a viewpoint rushing across desert emptiness until reaching an artificial canyon of steel and glass buildings on the edge of the ocean. Black ribbons crisscross and upon these countless metal carriages sped at a maddening pace. People crowded the sidewalks and all open spaces between buildings. Metal birds populated the brown, hazy sky. One building stood out; dwarfing all other structures. This glass, slender tower stretched to the night heavens. Twinkling lights like billion glowing eyes look down upon these busy activities.

This city was a cauldron of deafening sounds, choking air and frantic movement. My heart pounded, I tried calling our but only strange silence permeated here. I seemed to be trap between realities.

My vision changed and I was in a large room with many tables. That same blond woman sat alone and watched the marina and boats through large, glass windows. Multicolored, night lights from the surrounding buildings reflected long, shimmering bands upon the water. Outside the night air was hot, humid and oppressive. But in here gentle music played, the cool, mechanical air was scented with sweet incense. People came and went, some whispered or attendants brought meals heaped with quantities that started me. The excess was intriguing and appalling. The woman took a glass goblet and sipped red wine. Her earlier tension was gone, her features softened. She unfolded a slip of paper and studied it. It had numbers: deposited Eighty million Dollars to . . . Her face beamed.

Then, something distracted her. She and the others in that room stared in horror at the far wall where a huge screen showed images of violent fires, roaring smoke and ruined courtyard with a rectangular object in the middle. Surrounding it laid thousands of bodies in bloody pools. In thick smoke veiling things people scurried in panic; their faces twisted, screaming, weeping. Some on their knees, imploring the heavens with clasped hands and tears. Chaos was everywhere

The woman's face drained color. Her heart raced, her fingers tightened around the glass until it shattered, drenching her in wine. Startled, she looked at her bloodied hand. She whispered. She fumbled for a slender, dark rectangle in her bag and quickly taps it but tries again when it slipped from her grasps. Her voice shook so bad she had trouble speaking into the object. Then, tossing it into her bag she quickly ran out into the night.

The image faded into painful, white light and I stood at that same door. As I tried the knob the mirror appeared, blocking my way. Dread and fear intensified each time I pushed it away. A billion voices wailed, their echo shook me to my being. I woke and screamed. My head throbbed. A few moments later Sami appeared and inquired. I mutely waved him away.

Here in this dream waits my greatest terror.

Day 16. In the afternoon the breeze shifted, the sky cleared briefly and had relief from the nauseating smells. We and everything we carried were covered in sand and tar. My matted hair and clothes were so stiff that it felt like armor. The stench of tar clung to my nostrils and our meager meal of the water, bread and fruit tasted sour.

We were miserable and exhausted from lack of sleep. I pushed our group on, even though I hobbled due to pain and weakness. Our only desire was to forget our ordeal and reach Al-ain. This land stretched ahead, gradually losing its tarry, black film. Ahead, gray and rust colored rocks stood to the hazy hills. White hot, blurry sun hung in the sky. The ground looked the same as that we passed earlier. No breeze; it was quiet; this land still. I watched the dust devils spinning and carry sand particles into the brown sky. Sometimes I wished I was one of the particles so I would escape my misery. I kept my mind busy by checking our party and anticipate our reaching our next destination.

Patan filled the duties of the Alimajh for the main group while Altus or I led our group in the Dedicational. This was the first time in more than a week we felt well enough and had time. The Daughter's Mandala was damaged and covered with tar and mud and unusable now. We lent ours, which sufficed.

Day 20. Al-ain, Empty Realm. After four days of hope, they are gone. We arrived at Al-ain in the early noon and found the town had been deserted for years. Sand covered most buildings and brown, wilted date palms. We inspected the well and it only contained dust. We found camel carcasses managed to find grains and dried fruit in saddle bags. I attempted to locate water via my inner vision, but I was too weak.

Ahead lay the Empty Realm, a vast expanse of sand and rock. According the map no wells until Sabkha, still weeks away but indicated an oasis about three days ahead on a trail connecting with the Dubai road. From there we had to cross searing desert for a week to reach it and towns and help. Our pilgrimage along this trail had now come to an end. We had no choice but to try reaching the Dubai road. I suggested we travel by night and the pilgrims were glad for the rest. At sunset we will resume.

Day 22. *Fires, black smoke, heat, sand and desolation is the world we travel through. If there is a hell, then this is it. Unbearable heat we are forced to travel at night. No water and sand storms blocking our path.. We are alone with our thoughts. I cannot comprehend how humanity lived here. Even the scorpions have taken flight from this place.---Taleju- in the Empty Realm-*

Our group is exhausted and nearing the end. Sickness prevailed from exposure to the Black rains, tainted food and little rest. Pilgrims collapsed by the trail, too weak to continue. We left them by the roadside and they can join us in Dubai. But without provisions, which we cannot part with, we know their fate. There is much waling and imploring. My heart burst with sadness and helplessness. They curse us, the Kumari, their lives. The cries were only silenced by distance.

The Black Pools left its poisonous mark. The Empty Realm barren hills marched on; punctuated occasionally by sand dunes and white, salty plains. Nothing grew. We struggled against the oppressive heat by wrapping our mouths with scarves.

Because we are so weak I insisted we pressed on, hoping to reach this oasis before exhaustion overcomes us. We rest little, continuing through the day and night. Time is running out. Yesterday the trail vanished and we had to rely on our bearings. Trudging through sand and soft gravel slowed our progress.

The Daughter is running a fever and delirious. Sarah said she ingested poisonous black water and mud. Her lungs were coated with Black Blood and it was a struggle for her to breathe. Once she cried and thrashed so violently she nearly fell off the camel. I reluctantly ordered her tied to the palanquin. Those who did not trust me surrounded her camel and did not allow anyone near unless Patan insisted. Even when we camped her assistants refused to join or speak with us, whispering about 'these heathens'. I do not understand this; everyone's welfare depends on cooperation; this petty stuff annoys me. I got the impression no matter my role, even if we reach Nepal, I will always be the heretic, the unbeliever, the unworthy.

Even hopeful I tried using inner sight to find water but my weakness prevented this. Oh how I wished for a shower and clean food!

Today, two camels died. We took their meat and packed theses in the salt sacks. The camels were overburdened so we carried what we had the strength for. However, as we weakened, so was our ability to carry. Many sacks were abandoned by the roadside.

This day I had great difficulty walking and after arguing with Altus who insisted I ride I reluctantly agreed. Even riding was uncomfortable. This afternoon my stomach burned in fiery pain; I suffered nausea and dry heaves. Later I developed dizziness and headaches. I am too weak to ride upright and secured myself to the saddle. I managed to put on a good show when my pilgrims demanded it.

I hope we will reach the oasis tomorrow. Duce and a group were sent ahead last night to get water. After half night travel we were too weak and spent to resume. No information about Duce and his group. We collapsed in a gravel field. We were quiet, waiting for death's merciful hand. Dawn broke over a hazy horizon, promising more heat and misery.

I am afraid this may be my last entry. Forgive me, Ali and Bishma.

I failed you. . .

Day 26. Eye in the Sand, Empty Region. I am told it has been four days since my near fatal collapse.

During this time I hovered in a state of darkness with memories of intense dialogue with Taleju like bits of an incomplete painting. The Black Sickness nearly killed us but thanks to our host who scrubbed, cleaned or replaced our dirty clothes and administered herbs we are recovering. The storms that caught us at the Black Pools were the worse in more than a century.

Altus tried to wake me in the morning but Sarah said I will die unless we get help. Sami convinced Altus to set our solar generators on a hill and use their mirrors as a distress beacon. Meanwhile at noon Duce and his group returned after meeting Seers who trailed us since Wadi Hanifa. They tended to us, gave food and water then led us to a Seer settlement deep into the Empty Realm.

These people are the Deep Desert dwellers, the feared Seers. Their village, called Eye in the Sand, exists in a huge hole in the ground, thus protecting it from the violent storms. Single story, white washed buildings huddle within the opening. Surrounding the village date trees offer shade and moisture for a variety of herbs and cucumbers. They have two wells; one in the opening along the cliff which is used by visitors, the other in town, reserved for inhabitants. Colorful flags dangle from the trees; each house has glass wind chimes which offer sweet melodies. Although the settlement is isolated they traded with the coast and inland towns.

They wear green red or white sash accenting deep blue robes covered with intricate patterns, turbans, thick goggles and carry large swords. Their faces are covered with blue woads; wear many finger rings, bracelets and each possess unique necklace embossed with design representing Taleju and her mandala. They speak a musical dialect rather pleasing to my ears.

In the town's center is the 'The Pavilion:' a blue and gold, domed building surrounded by lush courtyards. Each afternoon Seers gathered in the afternoon to study the Awakenings.

My group readily accepted them. However the Daughter group regards them with suspicion and hostilities have developed.

Despite this, the Seers were perfect hosts by carefully tended our needs. They did not interact with us beyond required and were cautious with their interaction. They made it clear that when I regained consciousness we must leave in four days because the land is very fragile and could not support greater numbers.

Several customs of note. They do not show their eyes to strangers and wear goggles in public, even inside dwellings. Another is their musical language is reserved for Seers and outsiders are forbidden to lean it. Attempt it is the most serious breach of respect and honor, which they hold in esteem even beyond what I am used to. I found out this has to do with the use of sound combinations. They seem preoccupied with sounds affecting their surroundings.

For his act, Sami earned our group's respect; and Duce invited him into his Red Sash escorts. He was very proud and always very attentive, meeting his obligation with enthusiasm and devotion.

Altus, Satr and Patan worked together and putting our affairs in order for the upcoming journey.

This morning I felt well enough to hold a Majlis. I was surprised when a Seer elder attended, quietly observing from the shadow. Afterwards many pilgrims visited me expressing gratitude, praise and offered gifts. Afterwards I requested they share these with our group and hosts.

This afternoon I had my first hot meal in days. It was spiced rice with vegetables. It lacked the sand, sulfur stink and tar bits. It was the best meal I've had or a long time.

At the evening Dedicational the Daughter's Mandala was used. I led our guided meditation, angering some pilgrims which left during the ceremony.

Day 28. I meant to visit the Kumari's Daughter yesterday but camp duties called me away when I tried seeing her. Today I finally did.

She was housed in a small courtyard outside the village. Her banners and flags were repaired and cleared, lending gold and red to the surroundings. Her assistant tents stood nearby. Since they had exclusive right to her and control who could visit her, they turned away our group. Since I specifically appointed Sarah to check on her, when Sarah told me what happened this aroused my anger. Sarah, Patan and Duce and Sami joined me when I confronted them. Despite Patan's order they still blocked us. I reminded them I was still in charge and it was my duty to help the Daughter. When they failed to obey and showered me with abusive words Duce took a menacing step. I shook my head and he stopped. Removing my goggles I stared at them with rage until they grudging moved away. I felt sick and shook with anxiety but did not show it. I entered the dark room where several devotees sat holding the Daughter's hand. Patan ordered them away and they watched from the shadows. Sarah inspected her.

She was ashen, breathing slowly. Her head was bandaged; she seemed to have aged considerably. As I stood over her my mind settled. Gradually her energetic images filled my awareness; making note of color and sound based on what I read in Shakya's book.

Her life energy was dim; blurry images locked into her emotional body drew my attention. I sensed great importance in these. I waited, and eventually they crystallized; impressions: sad, forlorn, low esteem and anger. This was tied to events I could not access because my ability was not great enough.

Afterwards I and Patan performed puja and ceremonies for her. Then I anointed her forehead with sandalwood, whispering Taleju's blessing. I did not realize how much our ritual affected me until I was overcome by profound grief. I shivered as waves the Daughter's emotions washed over me. I shook and was overcome with tears. Patan led me back to my tent where I wept until the feelings passed.

Day 30. My session with the Daughter left me spent and confused and I did not leave my tent all morning. Here was a skill I discovered but have no idea how to control it. I am consumed in a storm; a doorway opens and I am pulled inside. I realize I would have to be more careful. I carried residue the Daughter emotions and have no clue to take me out of this.

Near noon I was visited by the village elder who attend the Maljis. I was still very weak when he came. Sami assisted me up from the bed. He stretched out his hand and for an instant I thought we would grasp it. However, with palm down he scanned my heart energy. After several minutes of this I sensed rose and green energies radiate form his hands. They mingled with my gray heart energies and felt a sensation like snow melting. When he finished, my depression was gone, replaced by a warm glow.

His stoic face smiled approvingly and introduced himself as Zal. He explained it was their custom only closest friends or relatives addressed them by names because they believed names held power. Outsiders addressed them only as `Seer.' I felt he bestowed a great honor.

He explained we will be provided with a new map and provisions to continue our pilgrimage to Dubai. We will pick up the pilgrimage trail in about three days.

He took me to the blue building with the gold dome. Delicate hint of sandalwood permeated the dimly lit room illuminated by sunlight shinning through the dome opening onto ornate rugs. Interspersed were pillars decorated with Purge scenes and Taleju's journey. In an alcove facing southwest a marbled wall displayed the Taleju mandala.

The Guardian removed his goggles, saying was an honor seeing his eyes. They briefly glow green and rose before settling to black with gold flecks. I gasped. Sitting cross legged on the rug, we drank tea and talked about the Purge, Awakenings and Taleju. He answered my questions in a voice that seemed to echo through the ages.

Seers never believed in `Taleju' because this refer her as a `hidden goddess'. She was not a goddess, nor hidden. Seers knew her as Shakya, a tortured spirit seeking to make sense of her world. With the Kumari religion adopting her teachings she became an icon; a strange mix of fact and fiction and from this `Taleju' was born.

Shakya knew humanity's survival looked bleak. Survivors did not understand the Purge group Consciousness and there was real danger or repeating it.

Humanity had already gone as far as it could with this Consciousness. However, it now had to break the old cycle and embrace the next phase of our evolution. This means we had to abandon the old ways. Although Shakya spoke of Consciousness, Light and Sound, Spirit, Incarnation and the Balance her meanings were changed and adapted to the understanding of her time.

The Kumari text `The Awakenings' was limited to the Mental and Emotional realms. They were concept building, an introduction, whereas Dream and Echoes will prepare Spirit for our next evolutionary journey and assist us beyond the Purge Consciousness.

Shakya's companions suspected she was the link to this next step in human evolution. Later she wrote Dream and Echoes specifically for us.

Seers appeared from where Shakya settled. Although she was Nepali born, she, Radha and her kind marked the beginning of a new age. She understood the problems future generations would have integrating with `Normals' and the struggle each will have to evolve into the next step.

There were three copies of Dream and Echoes. The book I have is the only complete example and kept in a family for centuries because, being a relic from Shakya, no one knew how to read it. Until now its teachings were passed down by oral traditions. That day when I chose the book, many Seers knew I would eventually translate it. They suspected unlocking the words was tied directly to an inner capabilities far greater than Seer are capable of.

I inquired why I and he replied I will know in time.

Curious, I asked how they found me. He explained through a boy I met in Italia. A woman, a Fifth Initiate had been following me since I arrived at the Levant. Eventually we will meet. She will be my guide at a critical time in my life and complete a karmic cycle set up centuries ago.

It was getting late. Finishing our tea he took an object from the desk and showed me a square silver object. Undoing the clasp I gasped.

It had a painting of Shakya exactly how I see her.

He explained this is how Shakya really looked. Even as he spoke Shakya's large, black and gold flecked eyes burned into my mind.

Afterwards I felt I had finally come home to my people. Living as an outsider my whole life had ended.

That evening I discussed our meeting with Altus. He was genuinely interested and shocked. He sensed the Kumari religion hid secrets, especially regarding Taleju's origin. He suspected Shakya's identity but it did not change his love for her.

With our provisions replenished and most of us stronger, I was invited to speak to the village before leaving. I spent two hours sharing my knowledge and my adventures. They were grateful and turned out for our departure. I am sadden to leave them, but inspired to accept my destiny.

Month 4, Day 5. *Somewhere in the Empty Realm, Saudi Arabia. Weeks we travel through waste lands, punctuated by black roads partly buried in red sand dunes. It is hot, the sky cloudy with black clouds and the blistering winds brings scent of rotten sulfur. We've seen vehicles and skeletons. The maps indicate there are no water and luckily found a trailer in one of these places filled with rusty, but drinkable water. We let the camels drink and we found extra containers to store water. Since beginning our trip we have been luckily to supplement our meager supplies with canned goods---gifts from the Purge. I hope our good fortune holds out as we follow the Purge roads and each our destination---wherever that may be. I came through here eight years ago. It is eerie that the only thing changed is the ocean has risen. We passed a Purge vehicle yesterday and I remember it still has the same green paint I saw before. Time seems to stand still in this sandy and empty world as we continue towards the black clouds marking Dammam, heart of the Black Blood.---.Taleju-*

For two days we travelled by night then it became cool enough to brave daylight. We traveled through this barren land. Our only worldly view was the hundred meter high sand dunes, black crags, lava fields and salt plains. We kept to places our updated map showed, gradually moving southeast towards the Arabian Gulf. The black haze is far behind us now; a smug on the faded, brown horizon. The heat was punctuated by mid morning to mid afternoon cool breeze. I am hot and sometimes miserable, but clean clothes made it tolerable. Our map showed we had left the Empty Region at last.

We salvaged our Pilgrimage banners and now displayed them. As a parting gift, the Seers made a banner representing them: a rectangular banner with the gold flower of life superimposed on individual red, blue and yellow panels. This was carried next to my home flag, Sophia. We promised to present it to the Kumari Sister. I counted ten different Commonwealths encompassing New Iberia in the West to Chen east, The Great Sahara south and Sardinia Region in the north.

The Daughter was tended by her devotees. To protect her from the constant sand I placed her in the front of the column. After weeks of hostilities they were grateful for my attention.

I started the journey weak and walked only a few kilometers but as healing continued, my stamina grew to almost half a day. I rode ahead of the group, joined by Sami and Yusuf. Sarah stayed with the Daughter's palanquin while Altus supervised the supplies and Satr visited pilgrims and offered encouragement.

The conversation with Zal filled me with hope and renewed acceptance of my role. Although I harbor self doubt, I do not curse my plight but regard it as the role bringing the change Taleju wants. I walk tall rather than anxiously hide it. I am accepted me and the pilgrims place great importance on my tasks. Leading theses people I, a Seer, is discovering my destiny.

One another note, one man from the village joined us.

Sometimes while riding and conditions permitted, I translate passages from the book. Shakya discussed past incarnations, their meaning and how spiritual law of cause--and-- effect karma work. She gave insight into understanding karma as energetic patterns and differentiating between this and imagined karma or `projections.' I was impressed by her details. Until now karma was a `concept,' not energetic science. I now see the world and myself as living examples of this great Echo.

Towards late afternoon on the fourth day we climbed a ridge and saw the Arabian Gulf under a hazy sky. When Taleju came through here she mentioned concrete and steel monoliths of massive cities on a great peninsula. So many, in fact, at places they choked the shoreline. Now, only a few twisted metal skeletons dot the ocean many kilometers off shore. When the ocean's raised the kingdom of Qatar which occupied this huge peninsula, vanished. Now only a small island marked its location.

We found a stone marker showing coordinates. We reached the pilgrimage road leading to Dubai. We paused, offering thanks to Taleju and our Seer hosts.

That night I joined our group singing romantic or melodies about home. Many were saddened by their losses but their spirits lifted, thanks to Carlo, Yusuf and his family.

Day 9. From the hills we headed south, following the shoreline road and shimmering ocean for three days. Scouts reported the beach was covered by tar, in some places several meters thick. Scrub brush which dotted the hillside were notably absent near the beach. Several pilgrims braved the tar and attempted to catch fish, but only caught slimy creatures unfit to eat.

The hills gave way from packed rock to crumbling rock and outcroppings. The blinding, salt field was gradually replaced by the ocean and shallow, foul pools emitting horrible stench. Since nearing the coast the air turned hot, humid and stuffy. My clothes clung and I was drenched in sweat.

One our fourth day we reached `Ghost Marsh.' This was a continuous salt marsh with tufts of black grass, gray sand and green slime. It stretched beyond sight and forced us inland in search for a way around it. It was only when we came to rust colored sand dunes that we had enough elevation. From the summit the stinky marsh seemed to go on forever. While camped as darkness descended we were treated to an eerie light show. The marsh was alive with dull, pale blue light interspersed by dark patterns marked by the grass. Later, the warm breeze caused the dunes to hum like mourning spirits It left us on edge and we did not sleep. Many thought spirits were here to do us harm. By dawn it vanished.

During our rest the Kumari Daughter was taken from her palanquin and laid in the shade. She was very pale and thin. She only muttered and when opened her eyes stared into nothingness. I sensed her spirit will depart soon. The party asked me to watch over and comfort her. Since our last meeting I only felt an empty awareness of a tortured spirit. Altus held her hand; occasionally gave me sad looks when I visited.

I scanned her energy fields and discovered I could peer deeper. One event was locked within her Causative body; it was blurry and she held onto it. After talking softly to her, she relaxed and I saw a little girl asking her mother about becoming a Kumari. She was upset by her mom's answer spent the rest of her life struggling with this. Here was the root of what I saw earlier. I leaned close and whispered passages from The Awakenings. Even though she did not outwardly responded, her energy field shone gold and white, indicating my words healed her on a deeper level. The realization our spiritual bond spanned many lives weighed upon us both. I struggled to find closure and free us both from these obligations which shackled us.

Day 11. It took two day to cross the Ghost Marsh. By evening we camped on rolling, gravel plain. Far off were more red sand dunes. Streaks of red and orange laid to the west. People huddled around solar cookers, chatting or singing. Everyone was glad to be out of the marsh.

I don't understand why but dread fills me when I try to translate the book. I'm not sure if the rainbow layer has unlocked something inside me, or I am fatigued. Perhaps I am blocked and I have to evolve into the next comprehension level. Frustrated, I set it aside. I have been stuck on the same page for two days. The text is jumbled when viewing it though the rainbow it blocks me. . I suspect it relates to my dread. I will try later.

Before giving my evening talk, Carlo played the drums while Lucinda's flute carried a light melody. Their music calmed the air and eased our hearts. Later Lucinda remarked she created this particular melody as a summons to my Dedicational.

I end this entry with the passage I used in tonight's meeting.

Incarnated Spirit experiences only transient and immediate outcomes, unaware these set up consequences echoing through many lives that entangle individuals and nations. An example is the centuries fight over what some have called `Holy Ground.'

This is the trap of mind and emotions; snaring us through image and feelings. They are illusionary and once Spirit realizes this It moves outside Its self contained prison towards universal balance.

Day 26.   My emotions struggle to find courage to face myself and write this most difficult entry. Words sometimes cannot express my feeling or what happened, but I will try.

I have seen my dreaded past life and it price came with crushing consequences; this curse which I can never escape.

Ali and Bishma this was what happened since my last entry. We camped on the rolling plains above a rocky cleft after travelling south east towards the gulf to an oasis.   The evening was peaceful and pilgrims prepared a special meal of fruit, bread and dried meat celebrating nearing Dubai, an important goal in our pilgrimage. Altus produced several bottles of wine.

Thus I lay upon my rugs, confident of our accomplishments and the wine's warm glow in my body.

That dream started differently this time. From black depth swirled red, blue and yellow that coalesced into many images surrounding me. Some blurred and others sharp and as I watched them they moved. I realized I was watching my past incarnations. I moved though these with frightening speed and sensed I was drawn to a particular life. Jumbled sounds from a billion sounds and impression bombarded me.

These faded and I was back in the room where Taleju and I met before. She sat across, her eyes closed, hands resting quietly on her lap. A distant sound grew louder. Was it thunder? Suddenly frightened, panic overwhelmed me. I tried to flee, but I was paralyzed. Taleju asked I should see what brought me here. This intensified my dread. I watched Taleju, hoping she could take me away. Instead she opened her eyes.

They were pools of black, like death.

From them purple and gold light radiated, carrying melodies of flutes, drums. The sensation of crushing waves followed. I was pulled into warm light.

The light faded into chilling awareness. It was night at the same marina in my previous dream. I was observing the blond woman again. Her face reflected sick, anger and fear.   In the hot night hundreds of people strolled, others sat on benches and completely oblivious to her. Beyond the marina a million lights twinkling from buildings. One structure towered dwarfed the rest, seeming to support the heavens. She reached into a leather bag slung over her shoulder and removed a rectangular object. She stared in horror at the small screen of moving pictures of fire, explosions and dying cities. Everywhere was chaos.

Panicking, she looked around, searching for a place to run, but knew it was useless. So she waited, captivated between those images and this peaceful marina's slender boats gently bobbing on the water. She was here to meet the man she called earlier.

Someone approached.

It was Curtis: his wire rimmed glasses reflecting the nightlights and hid his eyes. Dark energies surrounded him and his menacing, stoic face held unspoken hostilities. Enraged, the woman rushed him. She screamed and cursed him. Weeping she pummeled her fists into his big chest. He looked down indifferently then grabbed her wrists. He cold, emotionless, blue eyes peered over his glasses. A cruel smile betrayed his feeling. He reminded her in a flat tone his group only did what she directed and even though the events did not turn out as planned, her plan succeeded. The USG would have two client States, Blofeld Associates would make loans to enslave the nations for generations and she will be wealthy beyond her dreams.

She would share the fruit of her labor and retire on a remote island, taking comfort knowing she reshaped the world.

A blinding flash.

She looked up and was instantly consumed by blinding, burning light.

As the light faded I found myself back at the red door. Desperately I tried opening it but was locked. Someone again shoved a mirror in my face and I shoved it away. But every time I tried the door the mirror returned. In a fit of desperate anger I knocked it away. This time grasping the handle, it turned and the door opened. I took a step and heard the mirror crunch under my foot. Taking the mirror I turned it over, and stared into a cracked reflection.

The blond woman' distorted image stared back . . .

I woke screaming. Consumed by blind terror I fled, driven by my hysteria. I burst from my tent and ran. Night swallowed me; my wails became cries and painful whimpers. I did not recall where or how far I ran across the dunes and gravel fields. All I thought about was that dream and its crushing meaning.

Memories, impressions of being alone; I cried, pleaded while hearing a billion screams explode in my head. Oh how I wanted to die! I begged for the desert to swallow me; I asked Taleju to kill me. I threw myself against the rocks until my face and arms bled; I ate sand until raked with painful spells of vomiting. I clawed at the ground, attempting to bury myself forever.

In my delirium they found me and carried me back to camp. Impressions of thrashing and screaming, refusing food and unaware of my surroundings. At times I sat arms wrapped around my knees, rocking back and forth and muttered, pleading with Taleju to end this madness.   In my numb state I stared without speaking. People spoke but their voices echoed from a million kilometers away.

I wanted to be taken away for this revelation. I remember finding a dagger and trying to pierce my throat. Sarah prevented me and I was restrained. I cursed Sarah and spit and tried hitting her whenever she got close.

When not drowning in my wretchedness I was trapped in nightmares. The moonlight shone on massive sand dunes which I ran though, trying to escape. Black ooze suddenly gushed from the ground and I struggled on a violent, tar ocean while the skies were filled with smoke and flames. I attempted reaching nearby rocks but no matter how I tried they were forever distant. I wake choking if I was drowning. The nightmares repeated unmercifully.

On time I remembered dreaming Taleju was in the room I stepped into, watching me with understanding eyes, sadness etched on her face. She listened to my plea, my supplications, and my confessions, but she reminded me is this is who I am.

How can I ever rationalize this insanity? I, Noora Al Monte, from Sophie Commonwealth, in a fit of self indulgence greed was responsible for the Purge. I, whom in this life considered gentle and compassionate but am really worse than all evil spirits who ever incarnated.

My past actions are here for all to see: in the ruins, countless deaths, Black Pools, Black Clouds and the poisoned earth. I will always be remembered in history as Beast's Mother to previous and future incarnated spirits.

Damn my name for all Eternity!

After what seemed centuries the night mares ceased. Later I dreamt I was exhausted and covered in tar crawling onto a beach. Ali and Bisha you were there. I implored you to take me to Taleju so I could beg for forgiveness. Bishma took my hand and looked into my eyes.

You replied Taleju is already here.

Your words sparked something inside and gradually life returned to my troubled spirit. I became aware of my surroundings: the camp, daily routine, riding, pilgrims silently walking, assisted on my camel, taken to my tent, being watched over. I now recognized those who I mistook as threatening strangers in my madness. I allowed Sarah to attend me. When Altus, Duce and the others visited I met their concerns with forced smiles. I could not speak, because my voice escaped me. Rather I seemed to move in a world void of color, emotions or time.

I had the strength to force myself to nibble food Sarah brought. Sarah said I was missing for more than a day after running away, wandering in the desert, my clothes ripped nearly off, my body covered with self inflicted wounds.

It took two more days struggling with my feelings to have courage to speak. When Sarah and Altus heard the reason for my madness, I feared they would leave and never come back. However, after a long silence both embraced me. All my pent up grief exploded and I wept for hours. I wept for the loss, the sorrow, and humanity's tragedy.

This evening Altus, Sarah and Yusuf assisted me outside to the waiting group. Pilgrims eagerly waited for me to speak after days waiting for my improvement from my `sickness.' The evening was warm, the stars glittered, the dunes created abstract patterns in the moonlight above the cluster of tents. Sarah's melody announcing my arrival echoed like a haunting voice. I felt like a stranger here, but also a weary traveler who returned.

I thought of my revelation, the world, the Purge and the Awakenings. I thought of this present moment, our pilgrimage far from home with these brave spirits. My weak voice carried on the breeze, speaking from beyond time and space. I said Taleju had shown me many things and promised she had not forgotten and she walks with our pilgrimage.

I am not sure if I have courage to work on the book for some time. It frightens me and feel I am not worthy for this task.

Ali, Bishma, I hold you closer to my heart. I miss you both terribly. I feel all alone in this world of my creation. . .

Day 31. We came to the oasis today. Near the trail and beneath palm trees we found the stone marker telling us we crossed into the Dubai region, birthplace of the Purge. After gathering water and our camels drank, we camped on a rocky ridge overlooking sand dunes sweeping away to the horizon. I glimpsed the faintest image; a black spire nearly lost in the hazy distance. Below, our camp was alive with song; we were within sight of one of the most important goals in our pilgrimage. Today I twisted my left shoulder; it limits my already restricted motion and I have to rely on others for assistance into the saddle.

Reaching this goal give me renew hope and my gloominess dims.

A pregnant woman and on the verge of death but recovered gave birth to a healthy boy. She calls him Shams. This is the first birth since we arrived in Arabia and the mother is proud by this distinction. Her husband died in the flood.

The Kumari Daughter was assisted from her tent and watched the waning day. She was silent and briefly opened her eyes. Her spirit weakens daily. She will die soon but fighting to hold on until we can reach the Island of Awakenings.

Yesterday Altus showed me our new banner. It combined elements from ours and the Kumari religion. In the center of the white background with vertical purple stripes on each end is a multicolored Flower of Life above an indigo crescent moon. This will be carried immediately behind the Daughter's banner.

The dream occupies my waking moment. I tried ignoring it but it compels me to reflect and ponder, no matter how much emotional anguish it causes. I am at a pivot time in my life, realizing who I am and the changes coming despite humanity and my resistance.

Rumors about my illness abound: I went mad after seeing Taleju, I fell into Devine fits, Djinns possessed me, saw visions, and spoke in tongues. Fearing disruption of our fragile alliance with each other I confessed publicly what happened: I went mad when facing my karma (although not revealed its contents). Others may be faced with these during the pilgrimage and must have courage to accept their past deeds.

Month 5, Day 3. Sabkha, Dubai coast. I sat cross-legged writing on the beach as the sun cast long shadows above the western dunes. The salty air mixed with camp preparing meals, incense and fish. My muscles ached, shoulder throbbed but I am filled with a sense of accomplishment.

These four days we journeyed through this empty desert, drawn by very tall steel beams many kilometers off shore. Towards the west showed hills scared great violence; indicative by shards of green glass glittering at a place the map named `Glass Graves.' Scrub brush grew everywhere. The ocean was no longer gray but sparkled rich blue and the white beach was free of tar. Yesterday we passed a camel caravan heading southeast along the Dubai Road. The travelers gifted us fresh bread and dates.

This morning we sent messengers ahead and by the time we reached the beach inhabitants come out to greet us. Joining them were excited children in brown robes, shouting and held out hands. We broke sacks of dried fruit and distributed it. Many were grateful and shared with their parents accompanying them.

Since we were several months late the inhabitants assumed the pilgrimage was postponed this year and had not prepared for us.

About a kilometer outside Sabkha we passed a stone monument intersecting the Dubai road and coastal trail. Many travelers left their faded names on its brown, smooth sides. Perched atop the monolith was an ancient transportation machine, rusty and filled with holes. A hot breeze fluttered colorful streamers attached to it.

Sabkha is on the spot where a Purge existed far inland. Dubai, some thirty kilometers east, is now buried by the ocean.

Along one side of a half moon bay lay Sabkha: a cluster of squat two story buildings, date trees, herb and vegetable gardens. Dwellings are decorated in blue and green horizontal stripes; decorated panels serve as windows. Blue cooking smoke hung over the city, treating my senses to a host of spices and tempting meals. Occasionally the hot breeze added sweat and salt to the mix. Inhabitants in green robes and head covers wandered the shore and narrow streets. I glimpsed thin dogs lurk in the shadows; watching passersby or lounge in the shade.

On the opposite bay mango groves tended by workers used boats to reach their crop.

Dhows anchored a hundred meters off shore rock gently on the tide. Small boats ferried goods to the shallow beach where workers unloaded cargo waiting on the sand while others filled the boats. Shouts carried on salty air. People crowded around the goods and inspected or conducted business. Camels waited with their handlers forming trains loaded with merchandise. Blue cooking smoke hung over the city. I glimpsed thin dogs lurk in the shadows; watching passersby or lounged in the shade.

Our camp was set up in a walled enclosure intended for weekend souks. A wonderful causeway covered with red and white roses connected us with the village. Singing and laughing our red and yellow tents and red carpets soon occupied the empty lot. Some ill pilgrims was visited by the town physician, Sarah assisted him. I set the Kumari Daughter group in an isolated grove of trees and then met the Sabkha officials. They promised to send our requirements to other villages tomorrow.

Today was a sad occasion for us. Our gracious guides who journeyed from Aqaba returned to home. We gave them incense, rugs and valuable camel saddles as gifs.

As I write, flutes, strings and drums accompanied songs and dance. Looking across the azure sea I reflected about my life I left. It seemed like a different life. I had changed so much. Ali, you would be impressed by my assertive manner. I never thought I would be anything but shy and recluse. Bishma, you would be delighted to hear the many wonderful stories I could tell of my adventures. Maybe someday I will write a book and when I'm old, sitting around campfires will weave this magical time for listeners---if anyone wants to hear.

Day 5. Yesterday I was busy with meetings and arranging our trip to Dubai. Today, I had the opportunity to visit a curiosity: mango groves.

Arabia is void of trees except in sheltered areas. There this was the first time I had seen coastal trees. What was intriguing is they grow from salt water. Yesterday I had my first mango at the souk and engaged a merchant in conversation for an hour. He said mangos appeared about a hundred years ago and stretched from the coast to the Hindustan Gulf. Because of them coastal settlements and trade developed along the Arabian Gulf. Bandar Abbas is the main importer for the Persian Emirates.

The souk merchant took me, Sarah, Altus and my Red Sash escorts on his felucca. The mangos grow from the water to many meters in height, spreading out and creating shady, cool canopies. Hundreds of roots form the massive trunks and glossy green leaves sheltered clusters of yellow and red mangos. I sighted brown, slender creatures the size of a cat cling to branches and watched us curiously with wide, gold eyes. From the canopy green birds fluttered and filled the pungent air with shrill songs. Colored jars hung for branches, marking areas for harvest. Each year they rotate harvest zones.

Seeing this brings joy to my heart. Nature is healing, adapting to the change. I pondered my own issues and I will find courage to do the same.

Tomorrow we will visit the Purge origin.

Day 6. Island of Awakenings. Dubai

Our boat reached the Dubai coast. Beneath a hazy sky Dubai is a maze of steel towers stretching towards the horizon. Some structures are intact but most are twisted and broken as though a giant's club went on a rampage. Sometime I noticed buildings with heat damage, looking like melted candles. The black ocean covers the ground floors and the streets are clogged with debris, steel, concrete and rusting vehicles. A great tower, missing its top, dominates the skyline, a mad monument for those insane dreamers.

Pieces of bridges and roads arch from the ocean like great, concrete serpents, creating crazy mazes going nowhere. The stench of this place dominates the salt laced, humid air. Far beyond the city the desert turned into the same green glass we have seen much in our travel.

We cautiously navigate, looking for a place to land before our boats sinks due to heavy storm damaged at Ras AL Khaimah, another Purge city along the coast.

Here is Dubai: artificial city built upon wasteland. Like a ravaging beast it consuming every resource for its artificial fountains and fake abundance. They ate in frenzied decadence and lived in caves reflecting their disregard for balance while each day their waste filled the surrounding desert. Within these glittering canyons of glass and steel were hallmark of abundance, greed and their grandest illusion. The wealthy coveted and took everything whereas the poor had nothing in this artificial plenty. Greed and poverty lived by side by side.

Here was born the Purge, the place where humanity's six thousand years nightmare ended. From here the Beast woke, spreading rage filled fire storms and the horror embracing our world.

After spending a day in Dubai, we eventually found a place to abandon our boats and continued our journey north along the coast.

Future generations will not curse this place but praise it.

With excitement we boarded colorful dhows in the gray of the morning and, with banners fluttering and pilgrims singing we made the four hour trip into the heart of Dubai. We would soon stand at the place where devotee faces during our Conformation: the Temple of Awakening.

Dubai is vastly different than when Taleju visited. Over twelve centuries passed since her visit and, as with all coastal cities, covered by the ocean which nature sometimes transformed into beauty.

Clusters of twisted and rusting beams cast morning shadows above the sparking, blue ocean. Our ships approached a massive tower dominating the ruins which I recognized from my dream. In places sand had accumulated in and around ruins to support acacia and date trees. Gulls and desert pigeons screeched and fluttered among them. Occasionally our voices echoed like faint whispers. Sometimes I sensed millions of people staring back from across time. It is unsettling for I felt they singled me as the cause for all this. Perhaps just is my imaged guilt?

Near the great tower our captains carefully guided us through mango trees huddled around a small island. It was ringed by palm trees and in the center a blue domed building covered with many symbols. Our dhows secured to stone docks and we spent the morning unloading our supplies. The island was laid out in as the Kumari's mandala.

The dock led to a stone arch painted in relief text and scenes from the Purge. It once had many wind chimes but after ten years most were gone. On the arch left side was a stone rendering of the Purge Mirror: a spiral in the center of flame shaped mirror. While on the right the Purge wheel: circular spiral with at ends two crescent moons facing outwards. This gate represented the entrance into the mandala. Stone obelisks, carved rock fences, trees and the building created the maze. Pilgrims appointed to repair and make the grounds ready for us quickly fell to their duties.

Attendees placed The Kumari Daughter in beneath trees near the temple and even though it was hot, she was covered in robes. Her dim gray and brown etheric energies replaced vibrant yellows and blues. She no longer wore the red and gold, long sleeve dress of the Daughter. Rather, her frail body was covered in simple white dress and a blue outer robe. Her ceremonial crown rested on a rug by her side. Her silver and lapis bangles, rings and necklace were too big and hung awkwardly, making her look like a little girl.

While Patan directed the repairs, it fell upon me to conduct the Alimajh, and even though I am a not Satori, because of my position in the group they thought it was best. I was reluctant, not believing myself worthy, but after discussing these with Altus and Satr they assisted my preparation.

The preparation for Ceremony of Awakenings took all day. Those not on the repair party made paper masks representing themselves and prepared the feast. I Altus and Satr poured over text and choreographed events. Yet things did not go as planned.

First, there were the clothes. They insisted I should wear the Daughter's red and gold ceremonial dress and jewelry and facial make up. I told them this was a mockery of the Kumari and I would not have any part of this. Instead, Sarah modified the brown clothing of a pilgrim and accented it with red, gold and blue embroidery. Instead of the silver crown I substituted my red kufi.

Patan was the only Satori appropriately dressed for the ceremony and joined us and we led the pilgrim puja as we traced the mandala. Starting at the island's corners we gradually made our way to the temple. Pausing at each prescribed spot I read text before pilgrims performed the ceremonies. We started in early afternoon and took until evening to complete.

I reviewed the text as pilgrims assembled outside the domed building. Preparing myself, I sat on the carpet in the center of the crowd. They waited eagerly for me to speak.

And waited.

From the beginning I sensed something was not right about this planned recital. For hundreds of years these rituals were done the same. Now it was time for change. My heart stirred and as I surveyed and read the crowd energy fields. Sounds, like rushing water filled me; from my heart I observed gold light spread and touch them. I seemed to float above and around them. Then my world shifted and I joined Taleju in that room beyond the red door. Her purple eyes hold mine then extended her hands. Clasping them an electric jolt went through me. Words formed and I spoke as her. I do not what I said, but I was aware of the audience reaction. Some leaped to their feet and pointed at me, shouting I am Taleju. Soon others followed. Some bowed to the ground and clasped their hands in front, whispering Taleju's name. Others cried and wept. After I finished the pilgrims rushed me. My Red sash surrounded me and I was quickly escorted away. Altus, Satr and Patan went among them and calmed them.

Earlier a large, ceramic bowl near the temple was cleared of sand and incense bark placed inside. Solar cookers were positioned and their energies focused on the bowl. Altus and Satr activated them. Moments later perfumed surrounded us and the pilgrims formed a line, holding their masks.

Duce and Sami surrounded me while I stood apart and recited the Awakenings.

Our spiritual journey never ends; our struggle to balance our past, present and future is like a melody we constantly rearrange to achieve that song that will echo our greatness throughout Infinity. By taking all that which this illusionary realm binds us and committing them to the flames of Awakenings, we transcend time and space and briefly touch the Moment, the Eternal second, in which all dwell.

Patan tossed the first mask into the flames representing the Kumari Sister. Then I followed, whispering the Blonde woman's name. Behind my escorts I waited while pilgrims said their name before adding mask to the flames. Solemnly we watched the roaring fire carry away our surrogate illusions. Having completed, candied fruit and flat bread spiced with cinnamon, allspice and dates were shared. I retreated to the shadows and watched our pilgrims, envious they had but to worry only about getting to Nepal, not the demons I faced each day.

Later I visited the Daughter still lying beneath the trees. Kneeling, I placed her silver scepter in her bony hands and pledged I will continue the Confirmation pilgrimage as the Kumari prescribed.

Ali, Bishma, it is late now. Many pilgrims had retired, leaving me with my thoughts. I feel this day marks a pivoting time for Taleju and us Seers.

Day 7. Last night we were treated to a most wonderful sight! The beach lit up as soft blue, sparkling illumination with each wave. The light was captivating and pilgrims scooped the water, intrigued by the glow. We discovered they were small, jelly pods creatures. The dance of light lasted until just before sunrise.

As custom we continued cleaning the grounds, painting and made repairs. This was our symbolic cleaning of ourselves and what the Purge represented. I spent free time devoted to the Awakenings, visiting pilgrims and briefly sat with the Kumari daughter in a small tent erected for her. Her attendants thought ill will of me, but they knew better than to protest.

A blue and gold song bird serenaded us from the tree. In the afternoon a pleasant, cool breeze came up. The Daughter looked peaceful.

Day 8. Today is a sad for everyone. This afternoon the Kumari daughter transcended.

Before sunrise we held our Confirmation and afterwards the day was devoted to performing pujas and meditated on the Purge and our surroundings. This is the day called 'Reflection of Spirit' where this day is devoted to pondering the pilgrimage and each individual connects with Taleju to gain insight.

I sensed mood changes among the pilgrims. They watched me with almost god like admiration and at times some called me Taleju. I was very quick to correct them and they looked as though the Purge Beast spoke to them! I will not let them fall into this trap. It's been happening since we left Aqaba and after yesterday it got worse! I am at wits end of how to stop this.

We concluded our ceremony by adding our scroll containing names of surviving pilgrims to those tucked in the temple's walls. There were hundreds of scrolls at a various states of preservation, hinting to the centuries we had visited this place. Sunlight shined from the ceiling and illuminated the niches. In the temple center stood a black rectangular rock with silver chased edge. Altus claimed it was part of the great tower of Dubai. Atop the stone were carved these words: Our eyes open, our hearts pure. We follow the Kumari Mother.

We crowded into the small chamber and performed puja while Altus added our pilgrimage year and number to a list covering the rock. We pilgrimage was one hundred twenty six.

As I lead the group out, an assistant said the Kumari daughter called for me. Our group found in front of her tent and beneath the tree. Altus, Yusuf, Duce and I thought her dead until she opened her eyes. They were clear and focused and for an instant I saw flash of rose light. I gasped my sleeve and I knelt by her.   She placed a trembling hand on my forehead.   When I leaned close she whispered with her dying breath we will never fit in.

Our eyes held.   They briefly flashed purple and then dimmed. Her arm slipped from my face.

Stunned, I lowered my head and grasped her lifeless hand. Grief and guilt overwhelmed me.   Weeping I placed her cold hand against my wet cheeks.   How could I've been so blind?

Altus joined me and placed a comforting hand on my shoulder.   I leaned forward and kissed her forehead.   Overcome by guilt and remorse I fled, weeping and tears blurred my vision.

Day 9.   Today I find it very difficult to write with the mixed emotions churning through my heart.   Riddled by guilt, loss and low self worth I pressed on with the duties at hand: the Antyesti, or the Ceremonial Cremation of a Kumari Daughter.

This ritual is very specific.   The Daughter is cremated by wood because this represents the earth from which she is born, and the flames and smoke send her elements to the heavens.   Her ashes are returned to nourish the hallowed ground of Kathmandu.

The dhows showed up shortly before sunrise to return us to Sabkha. However, when getting news about the Daughter one was sent to get wood for cremation.

While we waited Altus and his helpers took the body into the temple grounds and directed preparing the body.   Because there was no fresh water, ocean water was used to wash her.   Next her arms were placed atop her bosoms and wrapped in white cloth. Then prayer streamers wrapped around the body.   We used sandalwood and clove oil to sprinkle the wrappings. Gold and red cord, representing her connection to Taleju, bound her feet and midsection.   While this occurred pilgrims performed puja and recited text.

When the dhow returned Satr and Patan supervised the unloading of wood and constructed a pyre facing east in a clearing near the tree where she died and the temple.   A yellow skirt surrounded the pyre foundation and four modified solar collectors circled it.   Beyond, our pilgrimage flags flapped in the gentle breeze.

It was noon when we were ready.   Both male and female energies were presented: Satr and Patan in front, I and Sarah in back.   I originally did not want to participate, for I was so consumed by emotions but Altus reminded this would be the greatest honor I could bestow on her.   With Altus leading the processing we carried the body and placed it on the pyre.   The pilgrims gathered; most wept, a few wailed. Altus drew three lines in blue ink on her forehead: symbolically meaning Taleju's Companions.

In supplication we four circled the body three times while Patan recited a phrase which we repeated.

Everything is changeable, everything appears and disappears, thus is the transient nature of All Things. Go into that realm of wisdom and share your love with our Mother, Taleju. May you be reborn as a Sattva.

When finished Altus quoted Taleju.

The measure of an enlightened person is not by the wealth they have, but their compassion and sharing. Here you blaze greater than all the heavens and your spirit song dances in our hearts.

The solar collectors bathed the pyre in blinding, white light. Soon the wood exploded into flames, consuming the body and carrying flames and smoke into the sky. By the evening the body was reduced to ashes. Altus gathered them in jar. Many pilgrims wept into the night.

A stone mason carved a marker with the Kumari symbols, her name, dates lived and where she died. It was placed beneath the tree where she took her last breath.

Kumari Daughter, forgive me for not understanding. May you find Enlightenment in your dreams yet to come.

Day 11. We departed Dubai today. None of us really thought our experience on the Temple of Awakening would hold such sorrow and for some of us, confusion. For the Daughter and me this pilgrimage was a trip through our tormented spirits, each fearful of self discovery. I supposed we hoped for unity and personal accomplishment instead.

Since my Purge revelation I have difficulty distinguish between this world and those 'behind the curtain.' The mirage separating these seems great but in reality they blend like watercolors. I picture myself walking between two worlds: never here, never really there either.

After returning and without consulting me I found to my horror our Satori and pilgrims elected me as the new Kumari leader called the 'Daughter's Deputy'. This was a quantum leap from just being a reluctant leader to grand religious titles and honors which I *never* wanted. I saw the ramifications and I was very angry, creating bitter arguments with the Kumari officials.

By making a 'pretend' official carry Taleju's mantle is cheap and insults the religion I love. This shows a lay person with no experience living a Satori's life has more value than someone who dedicated their life to practice and living Taleju's mandates, thereby earning the titles. I reminded them Patan is now the senior Satori and should have the title instead.

My anger intensified when they tried to hand over the Kumari specter and jewelry. They assured me they exercised the law by holding the election. I warned this was a dangerous move which would end terribly. Altus argued none command the same respect as I. It is to me, not them, the pilgrims look for inspiration and wellbeing. He pursued this matter until I, in a fit of rage, rebuked him and tossed the specter and jewelry at his feet.

Surrounded by my Red Sash escorts, pilgrims were kept away and I rode the rest of the day in seclusion, lost in disappointment and fury.

When camped, I was trapped inside my tent by pilgrims gathered outside. Sarah went to talk with them but they did not leave. It was near midnight. I wanted to sleep but I was too upset to relax or clear my mind. I feared this time would come and here it is.

Finally, I joined them and with emotions quaking inside my heart ready to explode I controlled myself. I thanked them but I reminded them I did not deserve this because I was just a pilgrim Rather, I insisted the Daughter's Deputy was Patan. I ended by reciting Taleju.

The greatness of understanding Spirit lies within us and no single person holds its key, promise or is greater than us. We are all equal in Consciousness. Dance your own Life's song, not what others have written. We all take the same journey.

Day 13. A crisis hit us today. I thought the storm of role playing was settled. I tried to stay in the background, giving Altus and the Satori opportunity to handle matters religious. I refused to participate in the Conformation ceremonies because I wanted it make it clear the Satori were in charge of the Kumari's affairs. I sensed their disappointed and anger but they grudgingly accepted it. This lasted two days before the pilgrims refused to cooperate. They sat quietly, unmoved or shouted my name during the ceremony. When I stayed away many left. This was the first time our precious ceremony was not held because of this behavior.

For the sake of our pilgrimage I gave in. I temporarily accepted the title of Daughter's Deputy to keep the peace until a Central Region official would take over. I reminded they I was only a pilgrim and the burden they placed on me was only deceiving themselves and Taleju. However, I did not accept the religious vestiges. With that the camp settled into unity and calm. I performed the ceremonies, all the while anxious and wishing I was somewhere else.

Day 14. Taleju wrote.
Somewhere on the United Arab Emirates coast.
We are at the mercy of nature since these two vessels are wind powered. After running south at the Persian coast the winds shifted and it pushed us west across the Straits. For another day we followed north along the coast where massive brown and black peaks plunging into the sea, making landfall impossible. We searched for a place to land while a terrible storm brought black, boiling clouds and the stench of sulfur. It picked up and, fearing being caught, we found shelter at a Purge city called Ras Al Khaimah. Its decaying buildings rose from the sea and offered protection against the lashing winds and turbulent waves. Here we waited for the storm to pass. By morning it was calm enough to land and search for food. We located a cache of can goods and spent the day replenishing our stock and repaired damages.

Ras Al Khaimah is a massive city. Its ruins are partly covered by the rising seas and stretch beyond a flat beach to roughed peaks. A white stone mountain dominates the area. This place is littered with Purge vehicles, trash and covered with a thin layer of oil. The stench is horrible. Towards evening another storm approached so we secured our boats and sheltered in a large warehouse.

We travelled four days, following the coast south. We encountered more coastal settlements and mango groves. A network of small dhows connected trade and spread the news we are here. Our presence drew the curious, mostly these wanting to glimpse me. Judging by their behavior they believe the stories. A few bowed reverently. This angered me, but I knew they had no idea what happened and, like all, were victims of fantasies. Not wanting to seem ungrateful, I acknowledged them. Some claimed knowing my exploits and I cautioned not to believe everything.

This is dark times for me. Ali, you have no idea the hells I face within my heart and camp. I see myself as a monster, but to these pilgrims I am their savior. This extreme poles work on my nausea and anxiety; I can't sleep or concentrate, leaving me depressed and isolated. I question myself: am I running from Taleju's wish and responsibilities because I do not trust myself? Do I doubt my role because I am afraid or unworthy? Do I suffer illusions and am thus deceiving myself, or fear I will deceive others? I am so afraid to face myself I do not work on the book because it reminds me of who I am.

This evening I found Taleju's advice.

When our lives are filled with confusion and self doubt remember this is spirit urging us to embrace our fate. No one ever said walking the enlightenment path would be easy. It is filled with fear, doubt and darkness with each step. This journey to self discovery is only for the brave and courageous.

Day 15. We reached the last city on the Dubai coast: Julfar. It is where the ocean met the mountains steep, rocky crags impossible to cross by land. The city of Julfar occupy a narrow beach and cove with a prominent, sandstone brown formations and white granite peak punctuated by many holes and black layers. On surrounding bluffs abundance of date, olive and pomegranate orchards paint serene pictures in this brown wilderness. In the harbor bobs green, hulled ships with a large sun and cross swords emblaze upon main sails. Altus said this are Persian Emirates ships, our next stop.

We camped outside Julfar in an open courtyard on the edge of an olive grove. While Sami and Yusuf prepared my tent, I presided over disputes at our Majlis. When evening descended I sat in front as Altus read then I shared comments about the passages with eager pilgrims. Sarah took notes. The pilgrims were calm and peaceful and I felt guilty. I did not share their mood.

Day 16. Julfar, Dubai coast. Today I met the Persian Emirates representative. He was a balding, middle age man with a thick moustache. His wide girth, green and gold silk robes and turban hinted to the opulence he enjoys. A pair of hard faced, armored escorts in spike helmets escorted him wherever he goes. Although he spoke softly and with refined manners his tone betrayed his demanding demeanor. The villagers tolerate and feared him.

With him was a Central Kumari Satori, Gurung. His presence I do not trust or like. He wore his clothes like a strutting peacock and displayed contempt for Altus, Satr and me. The Central Kumari heard the stories about me and he reminded us that he was sent to execute the Kumari's wish. He gave us a letter establishing his authority over us. He expected Patan, the only remaining Satori, to assume leadership. His arrogance angered me and Altus rather bluntly, I was legally the Daughter's Deputy which only the Central Daughter could rescind this. Until then none of us would recognize his order.

He became enraged, threatening us with imprisonment and torture. My impatience grew and after seeing explosive, red and brown energies in his aura I had enough. This insult had to stop. I ripped off my goggles and stared intently at him. My eyes smolder red. I reminded his behavior dishonors us, the Kumari and Taleju. As the Daughter's Deputy I warned him we will not tolerate this display, especially from a Kumari representative. He knew nothing about the struggle we endured and had no right to show much pettiness.

Speechless and frightened by what he imagined I may do he backed off. Our encounter left me shaking inside and nauseated.

In the afternoon I was calmer when the Persian Emirates official saw us. He reported in five days ships will arrive and take us across the gulf.

After sharing a meal he presented us with a finely woven, silk carpet. Its flowers and geometric patterns seemed to leap off the surface. I assured him this great gift would be shared by our camp and placed the carpet front of my tent for guests. He was confused until understanding my gesture.

A group of forty who had waited for our arrival joined us for the pilgrimage. Altus included their names in the ledger. Since anyone joining the pilgrimage after leaving Italia, those completing the journey will earn the honorific title `Satori Champion' and not allowed to wear the tika but given a special hat.

Today a vendor came by with Hindustan Gulf oranges. I tasted this for the first time. Its fruit was sweet and succulent rather than pulpy and sour like those from home. I was so impressed I bought several cases for our group.

This evening's discussion began with a comment by Taleju.

Like each thread contributing to a carpet we weave our incarnations into a complex picture of who we are.

Day 19. During this time we prepared for our trip. Two days ago I had a most unusual experience. While visiting the spice souk near a Awakenings temple the prayer was announced by ceremonial two meter long horns. Its deep, drone echoed through the streets. In front of the arched doorway a middle age woman in the red and gold robes and red hat of the Kumari priest, or Pujari, stopped me and invited me to lead the Alimajh. I was tired but did not want to disgrace her so I accepted. She led me inside where people gathered in a modest chamber covered in rugs, ceramic accents on the wall and heavy with sandalwood. Next to the gold and red minbar the arched niche facing Dubai held the silver Purge Mirror: a flame shaped mirror embossed with the

Purge symbol. She introduced me and handed me a copy of the Awakenings. Not sure about our safety, Yusuf and Sami stood beside the minbar as I ascended the three steps. Tucking my skirt under my knees, I sat. I felt self conscious and nervous and led the mandala ceremony as I've done for many times.

Afterwards, I read from the book. A hundred faces waited quietly while struggled for words. I commented on the passage about karma and we all share this common bond. I reminded them our current life was the blue print for our future dreams. When I finished some came up and touched my hands. A few asked permission to join our pilgrimage.

This was the first time I addressed the public outside our group. I was invited back the next day and shocked to discover the crowd grew beyond the temple and filled the courtyard. I felt so humbled!

When I returned I met a family waiting most of the day for me. They are Seers. I invited them in and showed them where they could camp. They had come from a village in the Empty Region and covered four hundred kilometers in six days, hoping to catch us before we left. They are the first Seers to undertake the Confirmation journey.

Day 21. During our remaining time the Seers kept to themselves while they adjusted to living among `Normals' who regarded them with curiosity and apprehension. In gratitude they gave me an heirloom brass coffee pot. It was etched with family names, dates of birth and death going back several centuries. At one time a red carnelian capped the lid but had long ago vanished. It was dented and heavily used. I sensed this gift was very special which I reserved for special guests.

After attending their first evening Conformation the husband confessed he was impressed by my tact conveying Taleju's mystical side as a matter of fact. In their minds I spoke closer to Shakya's truth than the Kumari's popular teachings.

Yesterday the Sheik's personal vessels arrived: large, high decked dhows with spacious quarters able to accommodate nearly a third of our party at one time. Their green, white and red stripped, crescent moon and phoenix emblem sails created a vivid contrast to the blue, sparking ocean. Their crew wore long, green shirts and baggy pants and white vests. It took all day to load. The Persian official and Gurung joined us and in the afternoon haze our five ships sailed from Jufar to our next destination. Bander Abbas, Persian Emirates.

Part Two: The Returning

Noora's mandala

Persian Emirates

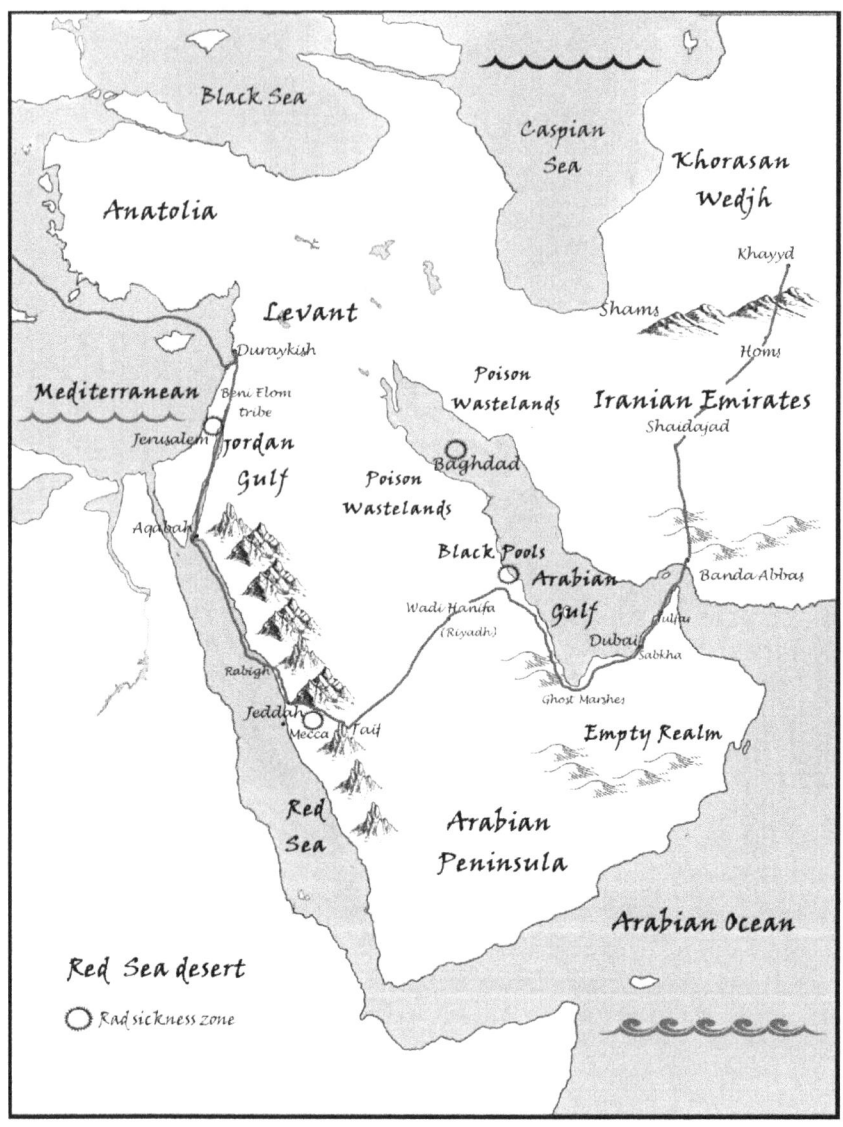

Month 5, Day 24. Arabian Gulf. For several days we followed the coast, travelling beneath empty, torturous mountains that plunged into the sea, their rugged isolation inspire awe and fright. Vast shadows contrasted with hazy, brown sky and the harsh sun. I thought about the storm and our good fortune to land on a beach. Here, there would not be such luck. Not only would there be no help, but these steep cliffs would crush us between the currents and rocks. This was the edge of the known world, for nothing existed along this coast but the Empty Region.

Towards evening we left the coast and turned northeast into the open waters. Gurung avoided me, but spent time with Patan. He was shocked when I held my daily majlis, checked on the pilgrims' wellbeing and consulted on religious matters. One particular comment upset Gurung when I reminded pilgrims no individual can claim enlightenment as their own exclusive right. He made his displeasure and after a heated argument I reminded him who I am and our pilgrims look to me, not him, for answers.

Later   I tried to translate the book, but being upset and inner pain was still too much.

Day 25. In ancient times this area was known as the Strait of Hormuz, a major route for Purge vessels taking Black Blood to feed humanity's thirst. When Taleju travelled here it was barren and the sky filled oily, black clouds. Now we saw merchant ships on the hazy ocean trading with along settlements from the Hindustan Gulf to the Persian Emirates boundaries. Our map showed to the north is the Poisoned Wastelands and a submerged Purge city called Baghdad, which Taleju failed to visit.

The winds calmed in the afternoon and we switched to solar power. We glided gently beneath the milky humid sky. Our ships rocked gently as waves splashed against our hull. I spent my free time on deck, staring at the water. Despite my anxiety born from my responsibilities and my personal dread, in the Arabian Gulf with the only sea to surrounds me, I felt more at ease with the salt air in my face.

In the evening our captain entertained us with stories about massive beasts powered without sails that could travel when and where they choose, and the crowded coastal cities---all now buried beneath the sea. For all his good nature and sense of humor it seems out of character when he confessed admiration for the Purge technology.

Day 26. Taleju's journal entry when arriving at Bander Abbas, Persian Emirates.

 Our travels bring us to the western coast of what was once Iran: now reduced to tribal fights for dwindling resources. Like all Pre Purge Middle East nations Iran suffered terribly both through regional ancient hatred and death by corporate nation states. Its once fertile land is now transformed into sterile desolation covered by black smoke, ruined cities and the stench left by millions of dead.

 Bandar Abbas was one of these places. Once occupying many kilometers of coast is now gone except for a few shelters dug into the hills surrounding the original harbor slowly being drowned by the rising sea. Death and decay linger as far as I see. Ruins, pollution and debris make travel impossible to the surrounding hills or harbor choked with twisted hulls of mighty ships. It is sad that this old grand city should meet such an end. Bandar Abbas had been settled continuously for five thousand years.

 We are hoping to travel along the coast to reach Baghdad and cross into Arabia and trek to Dammam, the city where the Black blood came from. However, to the north the sky is covered with black clouds and I fear it will be impossible to pass. We met a few travelers from the north and said choking fires, immense fires, destruction, decay from so many cities and Rad sickness poisoned these lands for thousands of kilometers.

 We are forced to abandon our original course and find boats to cross the Strait of Hormuz here instead. I calculate it will take a month before we can resume our trip.

 Ali, it had been a busy day filled with ceremony. Today I was the center of the Persian Emirate's attention. I felt self conscious, yet fascinated by this place unique for its ruler and accomplishments. Unlike elsewhere, they adopted Pre Purge style of government: a Sheik. His affairs are guided by ten officials elected from the representing tribes, with the Central Kumari Daughter as State Advisor. It is like a Commonwealth of sort, but instead our regional representatives acting in group, the Sheik makes the final decision that can be contested only by the Kumari Daughter. The Sheik, a regal, middle aged man, seems sincere and concerned for his subjects.

 Our first glimpse of Bandar Abbas was long, green strips of mangroves along the shoreline. We sailed into the port city at midday, being guided by a pilot boat through dense mazes of tall, mango trees. The sun shone on many colored, domed structures huddled close together along rocky hills covered with thick orchards and crowded harbor. At the waterfront a wide stone avenue lined with animal statues was crowded with merchants loading and unloading goods. A coastal road was busy with camel caravans bringing merchandise. Bandar Abbas is surrounded by a thirty meter wall from the hilly summit to the harbor beach and accessible by two gates. Persian Emirates flags flutter from many roofs and avenues. Bandar Abbas, like the phoenix, has risen from the ashes of its former self, reborn and from what I am told, the center of trade and education for the Arabian Peninsula and points east.

We were treated to a royal reception by the Sheik and the Council who, under banners and armed sentries paraded us through the streets to red, blue and yellow, terraced buildings upon a bluff. The dwellings were spacious inside, covered with rugs and white gypsum walls decorated with colorful, floral scenes or embossed with geometric patterns. Ornate bronze lamps hung from wall hooks.

When we entered servants stood behind wash basins, waiting as we washed our hands and faces then offered towels. Resting on bolsters or raised divans we were treated to spice tea mixed with milk; fresh melons, oranges and honey cookies. Servants brought silver incense burners that refreshed the salty, humid air with pleasant sandalwood.

I wished I had changed out my plain blue and white long shirt and baggy pants. Having lived with a week's accumulation of sand, sweat and dirt made me feel like a beggar. I dared not remove my kufi for fear showing salt incrusted and grimy hair. Out or respect I took off my goggles and as we exchanged pleasances my eyes changed colors to match my mood. Caught in the moment, I was too tired to control them. I don't think they minded at all.

The Sheik and Council listened to our stories and my role recounted by Sarah, Yusuf and Duce. To me, this sounded like they were talking about someone more competent and patient than me! This left me uncomfortable and when asked to elaborate I was awkwardly quiet. Although Gurung tried to divert responsibilities and credit to Patan it did not fool anyone because they read the dispatches Altus sent earlier. The Sheik was fascinated by my courage, determination, group's welfare and that I am a Seer. When the Sheik inquired Gurung about the Kumari's stance on Seers his awkward silence betrayed what he suspected.

Our meeting ended before the evening ceremony. The Sheik gifted everyone new clothes and the servants prepared our bathing chambers. It felt good to sit in hot, perfumed water, soaking off days of travel. By the time I cleaned, set my hair and changed into fresh clothes I felt reborn to ready to lead our dedicational. The pilgrims waited in the courtyard, as did the

Council and I led the guided meditation. Tonight's topic reflected conflicting emotions I carried since my revelation.

Spirit is independent of those transient attributes called personality we commonly identify with. Rather these are merely masks we shed with each incarnation. Although we are ultimately responsibility we should not condemn ourselves for the roles we've played. Instead have the courage to embrace ourselves as Spirit for the greater Consciousness community.

It is early morning. The moon rests quietly in the east. I had a dream where I sat in the middle of ruins, wailing and cursed myself for the death I brought. I asked why? I want to know so I could lift this burden. Then you, Bisha come to me. Wiping my tears you took my hand and led me to a bluff where below waited a sea of people. With a brush you painted my dress. Curious, I placed my hand over my heart and looked at my palm wet with rose colored paint. You said they were ready. I asked for what?

You replied for my new Heart chakra color.

Day 28. After the dream last night I felt the most peace in many weeks. The anxiety about my self esteem lifted and I attributed it to you, Bishma. I may not forgive my role but at least Taleju's book drew me to explore my feelings. I was surprised I could again read it where I left weeks ago. It took awhile but I translated this passage.

Since childhood we are taught the Kumari Sacred Triad represent: Incarnation, Karma and Enlightenment. Other ancient religions placed great emphasis on them and claimed this Triad was either people, deities or ghosts. Taleju says it is none of these but is the Primordial energies of Life.

Energy comprises the Sacred Triad: three primary colors and sounds from which all things rise: They are Red which brings change; Blue which create and yellow which sustains. Or to put it another way: Red is negative attribute; Blue is positive; yellow is neutral. From these all Creation is born and depending on the percentage of each primary color determines the lifespan of everything from subatomic particles to universes and Realms. They forever change: red becomes blue, blue becomes yellow; yellow turns into red. Onward and outward this Great Wheel turns; the Destroyer and also the Creator and Sustainer of life.

Day 29. When I am not busy with tasks I study people's energy matrix. I am aware of their age by observing the percentages of red, blue and yellow in their root energies as they blink and shimmer like fine mesh overlaid upon their physical bodies.

Younger life forms concentrate more blue, while the aged, redder. These are not the Etheric fields belonging to the Aura, Emotion, Psychic or Mental bodies. What Taleju described are the Primordial energies underlying Manifestation. I compare it to a song's basic chord arrangement from which its melody are born.

At times I sense their underlying tone: red harsh; Blue liquid; yellow soothing. Their inner play fades and return like waves crashing on the beach. Underneath is a sense of profound connection to all things past, present and future.

I found this evening dedicational challenging to stay focused and not be distracted by all the wonderful melodies and colors! Hah! At times I lost my train of thoughts and stumbled to speak. How embarrassing.

My inner vision was crowded by pilgrims' splendid symphony of color and sound. So entranced by this, I did not realize the ceremony ended until Altus shook me.

Day 30. Once a week the Sheik or his Council visit Persian's major cities and engage in a Majlis; whereas during the other days it is held by a local official. This was the same event I held, but on a much larger scale and conducted more formally. Within our government, this is a citizen's right and established as result of the Purge. I understand before then nation states did not allow this.

People gathered in the courtyard at the official's residence then escorted into a spacious meeting hall. There, visitors enjoyed tea and waited to see the presiding official who received their petition in writing. A scribe recorded the meeting and decision. At the conclusion the visitors left food and objects on a table. When the sessions concluded the offering was distributed to the community. The officials never accepted gifts because it was considered bribery, which brought dishonor.

Today the Sheik, dressed as a common man in simple green and brown robes void of jewelry, listened patiently and made decisions in his quiet, even tone. I, Altus and Sarah sat to one side, observing. I felt self conscious and so I kept my head bowed to hide my eyes. One time the Sheik asked for my opinion. I was shocked and although it was a great honor, I felt uncomfortable. This placed me in an awkward position. I could not refuse but did not want to participate in his affairs. I briefly studied the visitor in question, noting his energy field, seeing darkness over his heart. The citizen was mortified when he watched my eye color change. Nervously he shifted his stance, looking around quickly. At first I thought he would flee but remained as though a great force rooted him. Carefully choosing my words I agreed with the Sheik's observation: the petitioner was lying. The Sheik waved and the man was unceremoniously escorted from the room. He remarked he brought dishonor to his family and us. After that the Sheik warned visitors to be truthful or leave. A few hastily vacated.

Afterwards, the Sheik said honestly was permanent for good community relations. He had no tolerance for deceit and likened it to the Purge mindset.

Even though I agree with him I am upset my skill is used in this manner. This show of the Sheik's authority is unnecessary. If a visitor lied, that is his business.

That petitioner's expression burns in my memory and it only reinforces how Normal fears Seers. I see horrible consequence if this continues.

Day 31. In our preparation for the trip the Sheik presented a gift for the Kumari Sister: two lemon starts from his ancient tree planted by his ancestors may centuries when they migrated from Hindustan. With it was silver plaque claiming these were gifts from the Persian Emirates for the Commonwealth of Nepal.

This evening I shared a meal with the Seer family who joined us from the Empty Region. Our conversation centered on Taleju's teaching and Seer customs. I discovered they observed strict social interaction, customs, and behaviors to keep `self' from interfering with the `universal' communities. One never read another's energy field unless invited or made this intent known. A common greeting is `My Eye is closed'—meaning the person will neither influence nor view guest's energy fields.

Since the Sheik's session I've been looking for behavioral guidelines Normal would not interpreted as threatening. Having these skills pose great danger for us: not only fostering pilgrims fear but my own potential for abuse.

Because I am the first Seer pilgrim I am anxious to avoid issues and support behavior Taleju expects. Therefore I will adopt Seer customs.

Month 6, Day 1. Today the Sheik brought documents introducing a Satori named Deva, a soft spoken, slight frame and in her mid thirties. She wore red and yellow clothes. kufi and a purple waist sash indicating her status as the Supreme Satori in the Central Kumari region.

She was supposed to meet us in Julfar but she is deathly afraid sea travel, so Gurung took her place. Deva is the second most important official. Her role, besides duties as head Satori, is the Daughter's official representative during the pilgrimage.

Although I am the Daughter's Deputy I was not a Satori and technically not sanctioned by the Kumarisattva. With Deva joining us the pilgrimage was brought back under the Kumari leadership, although I fear her presence may open deep wounds and foster tensions if she is not cautious

She is friendly, cautious and fascinated by me. I am the first Seer she had interactions with and quickly discovered I was not what she expected. She stated she will not interfere with me and wishes to share responsibilities. Time will tell how she fits into our group.

We discussed the route and I showed a petition from three hundred pilgrims wanting to join us when we reach the Central Kumari residences, a city called Homs. Homs is a nearly two month's journey near the Hindustan border. There I would meet with the Central Daughter receive the second half of the massive thangka.

In public the Sheik praised the decision. In private he cautioned me to remain in the background because the Central Daughter fears my potential as a Seer.

Day 4. The day before yesterday, and with Deva beside me, we informed the pilgrims our arrangement. I stressed its important and reminded them we were still on a pilgrimage under two banners: the Kumari and ours. The Central Kumari gave us her blessing by having Deva with us. I then outlined our duties and responsibilities. To support this, Altus and Patan gave her the West Kumari's Jewelry and clothes, which she accepted. Later, indicating her status as the recognized Kumari representative she wore the Kumari' necklace and one bracelet on the left rather than the right which would signify a Kumari. She led groups in puja.

I confess I am relieved by this. I can now focus on my own pilgrimage.

With much fanfare our caravan left the coast and followed the road inland. Along the path we were greeted by cheering crowd, rose petals and festive bread. Surprisingly Deva rejected the palanquin supplied by the Sheik and instead rode a camel. Upon her request we created a special holder for the West and Central Kumari's banners which she proudly displayed. She led our procession. Next came the Sheik's representatives, escorts, me, our flag and multinational banners then the main group. Baggage trains brought up the rear.

We have a thousand kilometers travel to Shaidajad, meeting place for the north, south, east and west trade routes. Our route was hard packed rock with stone markers every thirty five kilometers indicating distance from Bandar Abbas and the Emirates we traveled through. Orchards and farms rested like emerald patchworks against the sandy and rocky terrain. We encountered a caravan from Hindustan who told about rain storms drenching the higher elevation. I feared we will not make the passes before the winter monsoons.

Locals invited us to share meals. Many were Taleju devotees and wanted to know about our travel. A few requested if I would speak at the evening dedicational whereas others were more comfortable with Deva. For the first time since our journey many locals attended our evening discussions because they have heard of my reputation. Some claimed to see lights around me when we met. During the evening ceremony when I talked, Deva sat with the other Satori and listened quietly.

Someone from the audience asked about relationship between sound and color I mentioned. I drew from memory from a translated passage from Dream and Echoes.

We, as Spirit, are both artist and musician. Taking the Sacred Triad we build our realities on each Realm we reside; adding a colored note here, taking away one there until a wondrous symphony merges with the Greater music. We each contribute to Infinity's melody, at the same time paint our unique picture.

Day 9. This land we traveled was green but the distant peaks roughed bare rock. When Taleju came through here, a great plague left desolation. Now the world was alive with fields of wheat, millet, nuts and even peaches. We met mounted soldiers in armor showing colors of their Emirates. They bowed their heads reverently and a few paused and receive Deva's blessing. Sometimes they gave us supplies.

Over these past days Deva observed our camp, Satori and pilgrims interaction with me as I went about camp duties, leading the evening dedicational. As she promised she kept away from my affairs and concentrated on her duties as the Kumari representative. Sometimes privately she read Sarah's recording of my meetings.

We added two hundred pilgrims at Bandar Abbas, doubling our size. Some pilgrims were drawn by curiosity about me but the majority wanted to show their dedication. However, having two leaders made things confusing until they understood our roles. Many newly enlisted pilgrims confided religious matters with Deva whereas I was looked upon as an 'advisor' and 'administrator.'

When she had time she and Patan held mandala classes for the new pilgrims. Later, from what she observed, she admitted the Daughter's fears were unfounded. Even some things I spoke about unusual topics, they were not blasphemy.

However, I have not showed her or mention the Rainbow book. When I had time, I started again translating it. I still harbor misgiving about my skill and emotion attachments to my karmic past overwhelm me. Despite my personal feelings I know my task is far more important than my personal reluctance.

Day14. At each village we created excitement and were met by minor sheiks and their councils. With visiting our ranks grew with pilgrims, families, camels, and provisions. Today we did not camp outside a village because the Persian Emirates had many way stations called caravanserai.

These caravanserais provided everything travelers need: shelter, food and provisions, and each Emirate tries to overdo each other in hospitality. These caravanserais are protected enclosures with arches stalls, stores and sleeping quarters. The stalls and rooms formed a rectangle that faces a wide courtyard. Here, we set up banners and conducted our meetings. The main gate and building for the attendants were at one side. Ten meter tall, round battlement towers stood at each corner. At sunset the gate was closed and locked and we could not leave. The Emirates flag flew above each tower which can be seen for many kilometers, acting as a destination marker. While traveling in the Emirates we had no fear of tribal war, extortion or robbery. The eldest member of the caretaker family was very helpful by reviewing our map and sharing information what to expect.

We left gifts of food, supplies or silver in gratitude.

Day 18. This morning when performing the Majlis I was surprised when Deva joined me. She sat behind and to one side between Duce, Sami and Sarah. I feared she would interfere. However, when a traveler asked her for advice she directed him to me.

Unlike the Kumari Daughter, Deva took genuine interest in our group. She was quick to help and refused to eat until all pilgrims were fed. She rarely stayed in her tent but visited travelers and made it point to spend time with new devotees. Sometimes she conversed, sometimes she was quiet. After evening dedicational, she wandered the camp alone or with Altus and Satr. Many newcomers attended her guided meditation. Unlike the Daughter, she did not conduct teachings during my evening dedicational. She and Altus knew one another from childhood and occasionally sat around the campfire exchanging stories. She did not talk much, preferring solitude and when she was not reading Awakenings she meditated. Altus said they both went to the same school in Nepal. I suspect they are more than friends and sense their bond. Deva's husband and son drowned at sea while travelling back to Persian, leading to her fear of the sea.

With regards to me, she is cautious. She witnessed my influence and at times showed curiosity, although she never asked me to elaborate. We shared only minimal words. I was glad she had an outlet for her piety and devotion, which seems genuine. She led the morning and afternoon Conformation while I conducted the evening ritual.

I confess even though I still did not trust her, I am glad for someone sharing camp responsibilities. Lately, demands have been so great I either did not have time or was so exhausted I could not devote myself to this journal or the book. I would love several undisrupted days to attend to the book.

Day 20. After more than twenty years I discovered my sister's fate. It happened when we came to a hill shrine overlooking a village of red, blue, orange, green, purple and white buildings. This shrine was built from colorful, clay pots; a tradition started when Purge survivors returned and gathered the bones of loved ones and took them to the hill. They had only clay pots for internment and after inscribing their names they buried them. This tradition continues and over the centuries the cemetery expanded. Now fruit trees and peaceful courtyard enclose the cemetery. Each anniversary the villagers returned to repair the site.

Because of its history, travelers visited to paid homage or added their loved ones to the hill. All of us lost loved ones and today we honored them. We spent the afternoon painting vases and wrote names. Then, the caretaker loaded them on a cart and led us to the hill where we buried them at a designated area. I discovered this was the place where previous pilgrimages honored their dead. In clearing sand I found this memorial: Aisha Al Zoghb, Italia Commonwealth. Died 1241AP

I sat utterly shaken with grief. I cried, thinking of my fifteen year old sister dying in this lonely place so far from home and the heartache and disappointments she must have endured. Now, many years later, my husband and daughter joined her. I performed puja and recited a dedicational.

I am but the whisper in the wind, the sun's warmth upon your cheek. My life is Transient, my dreams fleeing.

Nearby I found a dedicational for a twelve year old boy. It was for the West Kumari Daughter's son.

Day 23. Our journey brought us into the rains while traveling through rugged mountains and valleys. Gray clouds lay heavy upon us for three days, drenching the earth, feeding fields and orchards. Afterwards, heavily scented sweet and pungent mist lingered on the ground like a soothing blanket. In some places large pools a kilometer across sprouted. Several times we detoured because our road was completely submerged.

Deva and Altus were together most of the time. I think they were in love. How cute! Altus's wife and child died years ago from illness. At the beginning of our trip Altus seemed so lonely and lost. Now, a spark shone in his dark eyes whenever her name is mentioned. He and Deva cannot hide their joy.

When Altus sided with me back at Aqaba some pilgrims branded him a heretic and many did not hide their contempt. However, this did not bother Deva. However, I cannot say the same for her escorts. They avoided him and do not interact with him. To me this shows the religion attitude towards anyone questioning their teaching. I wonder if Deva feels this about me. I could very easily read her Emotional body energies; however, I refrain because I now follow Seer's ethics.

Deva was getting more involved with my group. Sometimes she visited in my tent or rode with me. Occasionally we talked about the teachings, the trip and Taleju. I confess I am still cautious and not forthcoming with much information. Additionally, she regularly attended the Majlis and evening discussions; quietly watching. I knew she was very observant and caught everything I said. At first I was resentful, expecting her to respond like the Daughter. So far she had been supportive.

Sarah continued to record my evening talks and accumulated a small book which, through volunteers, made copies. Called `Noora Sayings,' these are in great demand. Groups conducted their own classes and discussions. It make me so uncomfortable. I fear they will place importance in subjects I never intended or misunderstand what I said. This could lead to personality worship and dogma which I sense is the core problem with the Awakenings.

Each day I cautioned them they must understand my words not from their mind but hearts.

Day 28. We crossed a salt flat surrounded by black pinnacles and barren hills. The blinding glare left me with horrible headaches. Additionally our progress was marred by creating salt clouds in our passing. This got into our clothes and lungs. I developed a dry, painful cough and my skin was rubbed raw behind my elbows and knees. Everyone was miserable.

It was a bleak world and I wanted to press into the hills before we camped. However, our pilgrims heard about a Purge cave painting at a village and, being a destination visit on our travel, Deva consented.

The village was on the edge of a Purge city consisting of hundreds of mounds and bits of concrete walls covering many kilometers. The locals took us to a sheltered building where we washed the salt from our faces and hands. We were given fresh fruit and bread then we divided into several groups and the locals took us to places of interest.

Behind a mud house decorated in faded red and blue, and sharing space with goats we entered a field of black stones. After walking about a kilometer through this maze with our guide we came to a concrete and steel gully.

Here our guide showed us a building foundation and the narrow hole where he entered. I was hot and just wanted rest in the shade but I had to be supportive and followed. The air was dusty but cooled when we entered a narrow, darken passage. The farther we traveled, the darker it became. Our only illumination was bits of sunlight and the lamp our guide carried. We crawled, crouched and carefully crossed narrow, concrete beams spanning deep holes. Eventually we paused before a small opening.

This was an entrance into a cave about ten meters square of crumbling concrete and rusted steel. Our guide held high the solar lamp. In the dim, blue glow I saw walls covered with many layers of images; some distinguishable, others long since faded. The skyline of a Purge city; people in strange clothes; vehicles on roads; strange weapons; things in the sky resembling a kind of bird; fire and mushrooms. In one corner were hash marks and circles. These, our guide speculated were marks showing distance to the coast or directions to the next settlement. I recognized some images from my dreams. They were more than a thousand years old. When Taleju visited she mentioned Purge ruins covering this entire valley.

When exiting, I slipped crossing a beam and my kufi fell into the hole. When we were back in the village our guide offered his bright, saffron colored turban and showed me how to properly wear it. The material was so long it extended to the middle of my back so I draped the excess over my left shoulder.

When I checked myself in the mirror I was startled by my transform. This turban made me look gentler, young. I retired this day feeling proud of my new fashion statement!

Month 7, Day 3.   The weather had turned noticeably cooler and gray clouds covered the azure horizon.   In the Persian Emirates we entered 'winter' which, until a few years ago in Sofia before our regional drought, our winters brought rain and hot weather. This weather was not to my liking. I hate cold.

The further north we went, the roads became more crowded with travelers trying to get across the mountains before winter. We still had to cross the Hindustan Corridor but Altus said this time of year it flooded, closing the passes.   The possibility of waiting out the winter and further delays depress me. I just want this trip to end!   Homs is the last major city in the Persian Emirates and we will consider camping there until spring.

Today we reached the Shaidajad valley, the second largest city and hub for routes converging from all corners of the Emirates.   Taleju mentioned when she came here only Purge ruins and bones covered this wide valley.   Now it is filled with life.

In the center of a great plateau the city stood atop the only hill, protected by tall walls and battlements.   Outside the walls the roads wound upward through terraced fields and orchards. In keeping with Persian tradition, dwellings are painted bright colors to invite auspicious blessings.   Emirate and local tribal banners lined the roadside many kilometers before reaching the city.

Near the city's base we found caravanserais clustered in dense date groves and fruit orchards. We camped in two spacious inns.   Our arrival created much commotion; residents and travelers brought gifts.   I and Deva were invited to take residence at the Council's residence.   Even though it was a great honor, I decline, explaining I must remain with the camp when Deva left. In reality I preferred to be with our group, instead of chasing accolades.   I was very tired and trip's anxieties worn my hospitalities thin.

Deva and Altus took the offer and before evening they left with city escorts and much fanfare.   In the crowded courtyard my tent was setup; Sami and Yusuf assisted me with chores and shared sentry duties.   I did not touch my evening meal and passed on the Dedicational.   Huddled blankets against the cold Sarah spoke for me.   Later Sami lit a brazier and I wrote in my journal by its warm light.

Day 6. Since camping, the clouds looked threatening and the night cold breeze constantly reminded me of my misery.   This morning the rain came, followed by the sun.   It washed the dust and luckily the inn's courtyard was covered with flag stones so I did not contend with mud and muck. Despite my aversion to this kind of weather, I was greeted by a most wonderful surprise. Along the Shaidajad River a few kilometers from our camp a great abundance of wild roses grew along its banks, their orange and yellow flowers filling the air with intoxicating perfume. The sudden appearance of this socked us. Excited pilgrims went to the river and created garlands of roses, wearing them or laid them out to dry. Sarah gave a rose which I placed in the pages of my journal.

Altus returned with a gift of a heavy robe. After wrapping myself and, invigorated by the roses and a afternoon meal, Sarah and my Red Sash guards joined me for a trip to the city.

Like all people in the Emirates, Shaidajad inhabitants share the bounty for their toil and trade. I found them friendly and helpful and very curious about me. It seemed my stories travelled faster than I. Their markets reflected the vast connections flowing into their domain: Italia Commonwealth, Land of Fog, Levant, Bengal States and Chen Union. Home sick, I purchased spices from Sofia, including my favorite perfume I lost during the storm.

Had dinner with a Shaidajad Council member at his modest home. Met his family and while young children ran through the room his older daughters served tea and our meals. He and his wife were very interested in my stories. Although I am a Seer, they were not fearful. In fact, she mentioned a land to the north called Khorasan Wedjh is a Seer domain. It was off limits to outsiders and very little is known about it. This piqued my curiosity and my hope to contact them.

Day 8. Having spent more time in Shaidajad I discovered it is the home to other religions, including some Pre Purge I had never heard about. One temple I visited kept a flame in a silver bowl in the middle of a large, circular chamber. This flame was reputed to be over three thousand years old and watched over by men called Maji. They made sure the flame never died. The flame represented the Sun and their god.

Another religion believed a Sky god resided over and protected them. Images of crosses decorated this domed building. and non members were not allowed inside. Taleju spoke about this Pre Purge belief as nurturing the mind and emotion rather that spirit. The followers of both religions were peaceful and sincere. When explaining their beliefs it confused me.

This evening Deva and I led the evening Confirmation at Taleju's mandira (temple). It was a splendid building with three, gold and red, tiled domes and covered with colorful tile, flags and wind chimes and the grounds represented the Kumari mandala. Statues of important Kumarisattva lined the steps. At the top a Taleju statue greeted worshippers passing through its richly carved doors. As I entered into this gold guilt temple with its dark wooden floors, colorful thangka and bluish incense clouding the chamber I wondered what Taleju would have thought of this. As Deva and I waited on minbar draped in red and gold cloth deep, melodious notes created by horns, booming drums and finger chimes echo throughout the crowded chamber. A sea of people sat on the floor waiting. First, Deva was introduced as the Senior Satori spoke first; sharing her thoughts about the journey and what it meant to the Kumargi. Then, when she introduced me as the Daughter's Deputy I was shocked. I briefly explained my background than shared a quote from Dream and Echoes.

Intent is what we desire. Aspect is our manifestation. Becoming is our true self as spirit within this Aspect.

After further discussion I concluded many were confused by my words. Afterwards Deva wanted to know more so we spent time sharing thoughts over tea. I did not tell her about the book, only that I discovered this through meditation. She was very impressed and wanted to know more. However it was getting late and by the time we returned it was past midnight. Inspired by my words I worked on translating the book until dawn. As I concluded this entry the morning Dedicational is called.

Day 10. Ali, oh how I wish to be embraced in your protective arms! My head throbbed painfully, my hands bloodied and my fingers struggled to grasp the pen. I squinted by lamp light in my tent, huddled over this journal. My fears made it difficult to put these events into coherent thought. I need your comfort more than ever!

These past days we concentrated on getting provisions before resuming our pilgrimage onto Homs. Our atmosphere was relaxed and peaceful; many visited the city. Our ranks continued growing and too our reputation. We now have another fifty pilgrims. Unfortunately it also brought unwanted attention.

After a morning of shopping I had completed the noon dedicational at the same Taleju mandira I spoke earlier. Wanting to get last shopping before leaving I passed a clearing house where merchants brought their goods. The crowded courtyard was busy with shouts, growling camels and workers unloading goods for inspection. I was so interested in spices I got separated from my escorts in the jostling crowd and failed to see men closing in on me. Then I was pushed violently into a camel. Someone stuffs a foul smelling rag against my mouth and nose. I became nauseated; I vague remembered being tossed into a crate before blacking out.

When I woke I was in a dark room with faint light from a narrow window high on the wall. My throat was swollen and when I breathed my lungs burned. The rag's stench filled my senses. I quickly removed the rag and then vomited. I could not get my breath and passed out.

Later I experienced the most frightening and unusual sensation. I rose from where I lay and effortlessly walked through walls, up steps and out of the building. It was late afternoon and I stood on a narrow street, looking at a two story white building with four wind towers. Two orange trees stood outside a square gate painted blue. I had a strange sensation of detachment, like a viewer without form. Then I rose into the sky and looked down the city's main gate at Altus, Duce, Sami talking with sentries. Then I was hovering above our camp and pulled into the Seer tent, observing the family sharing a meal. The boy looked up when I touched his mind.

Then, I was back in that room and as this viewpoint observed myself lying among sacks and crates. My face was swollen, my hands bloodied; I breathed slowly and painfully. The vision shifted and I wake back inside myself. Scared, I pulled myself up. My head exploded and I gasped and coughed. I sensed hours had passed. In the dim illumination I saw two men sitting on crates, their features cloaked in black clothing. Their faces were covered by turbans and eyes hidden by goggles. One held my ashes bottles and the other had my the Awakenings book. My head cleared and fear replaced anger.

When they saw me wake they spoke with malice and threats. One man rose, ripped the Awakenings and flung pages at me. He shouted I was an apostate and he should cut out my tongue. The other tossed the ash bottles into the air, catching them, taunting me and threatened to smash them. I was warned to stop this pilgrimage and return home or harm would come to me. As he talked I glimpsed a tattoo on his right hand.

Their behavior enraged me. I felt violated! Consumed by rage I sensed a vortex open deep inside me. I drew energies into me until stormy energies filled my heart chakra. Around me, the ground rumbled and hissed like a million snakes. I sensed I was in the center of a crimson sea of swirling light. My vision narrowed until only these two men filled my senses. Then this energy lashed out from my eyes, drowning them in a cocoon of intense ruby light. Their faces twisted in pain and they screamed, fleeing from the room. I collapsed onto the floor as the energy faded. Horrible, throbbing pain filled my head. I retched and blacked out.

Later, hovering between wake and exhaustion, commotion outside the door roused me. I sat up, whimpering while headaches ripped though me. Moments later dark figures carrying solar lamps entered the hall, the door was thrown back. I screamed, expecting those men. Instead it was Duce, Sami and Altus, city sentries and the Seer boy. Duce threw his muscular arm around my waist and they escorted into the cool, night air. In the shadows I saw the same building in my vision. Sami met us, he was bloodied. Altus returned my urns. I cried, filled with joy and anger.

Deva led us back to camp in the chilly, night air. She did not speak a word. I sensed her pensive mood. Later Deva heard of my account she assured me the Kumari had nothing to with this. Since my disappearance many people searched the city. However it was the Seer boy who led them to me.

I have tasted this energetic ferocity and am frightens me. Taleju warned about this. This is a demon I must keep caged or great sorrow will befall everyone.

Ali, Bishma; I leave you with this passage from the Awakenings.

Those who do not understand their individual spiritual greatness fear those who do. This has been Spirits' struggle ever since we incarnated as humans. It has fostered a thousand ideologies, killed billions and lay waste to our homes. Our turmoil, our inner battle to See who we are is our Curse; locking us into the karma Wheel we trod round and round upon our wail and tears.

Day 14. We camped at the edge of the valley as the sun set over Shaidajad's glittering buildings far to the west after two days following the river through the Shaidajad Valley.   Since this morning the road took us through kilometer after kilometers of undulating ground and thick forest of dead trees making up an usual cemetery.

Hundreds of stones with the name of the deceased hung from these trees. This practice dated to shortly after the Purge when the valley was covered by dead trees. As inhabitance built the city, the deceased was taken far away so their ghost would not haunt them. Back then people were superstitious cutting down trees—even dead ones-- so families tied stones markers to branches, believing their ancestors spoke on the wind. This supposedly soothed the deceased's desire to haunt their home.

Now grave keepers lived in this `Orchard of spirits' and tended this place; replacing broken and worn stones, fallen trees, rewrote faded names, and gathered stones for future use. When a person died their family added their name on their clan trees.

When the wind blew the valley was alive with the song of sharp clacks as stones hitting each other. Some trees were painted red, yellow, blue and green, signifying a religious sect. Red is that of the Kumari devotees. Special markers designated families and clans.

Since the incident at the cave some pilgrims had taken to wear saffron turbans, thinking this held religious meanings rather just a replacement for what I lost. Some claimed it differentiated them from the Awakenings devotee, which I discouraged. I confessed though, it adds color and liveliness to our generally somber looks.

We did not identify my abductors or their fate. Someone went to great trouble getting them out. Even though I was quiet about my experience, rumors spread, claiming I could walk through walls, punish with my mind, move objects, became a bird and communicate over great distance. I suspect the boy is behind this. In private I asked him not to speak such nonsense but it did not dampen his enthusiasm. I conclude this old struggle between truth and fantasy is human nature to believe others have greater spiritual insight than us.

Day 18. Two days ago a storm rolled in from the northeast and bought lightning and rain. We sheltered at one of the roadside inns. We met a merchant who crossed Kabul pass before the heavy storms closed the road. He said winter came nearly this year and caught travelers by surprise.

The days and nights are noticeably cooler and we all wear heavier clothing. At times our trail was obscured by fog but mostly the sky was clear and crisp. The mountains we travel through are bare, consisting of rugged crags and peaks.

Taleju's book revealed more secrets. This was what I uncovered.

As spirit we dwell in Infinity. As spirit we walk within the Six Manifestations of the Six Realms. They are: Physical, Emotional, Psychic, Mental, Causative and Moment. We call this The Shadow Realm; for it is but an echo of the Genesis of all. From here The Secondary Echo births the Shadow Realm. This is Consciousness's Primordial Dream in which we live and ARE.

From this she explains what The Awakenings briefly covered and the real meaning of her mandala. It states they are 3 pillars of wisdom; 6 cycle of life and the 12 attributes. However, this is different than the physical or natural seasons and concepts we are taught.

Rather, these numbers 3, 6, 12 are combined and divided into infinite combinations which became the foundation for Consciousness to interact within Itself through manifestation.

Number 3 is the most important and creates the foundation from which realities are built upon. This is the number of Consciousness realities: Primordial, Secondary Echo and Shadow Realm.

Additionally, 3 is the basic energetic component for the foundation for all life: the tetrahedron, the three sided pyramid. This contains energetic properties and corresponding colors: positive (blue), negative (red) and neutral (yellow).

Number 6 represent the combined Universes within the Shadow Realm: Physical, Emotional, Psychic, Mental, Causative and Moment.

Also the Psychic's 6 sub realms: Twilight, Upside down Reverse, Hall of Endless Possibilities, The Golden Realm, Akashic Records and Dream.

12 is the Shadow Realm's combined total universes.

This combination 3, 6 and 12 can used to understand a host of combinations and meanings which I have barely touched. It is so deep that whenever I discover something, it leads to others. There is no end the secrets they hold.

Taleju states by understanding these building blocks spirit we can manipulate them and travel throughout Infinity. Additionally, the key to all this is shown on the Flower of Life; of which I adopted in our new flag and the center in the Kumari's mandala.

The book shows the realms' colors and patterns, our Etheric bodies and relationship within our universes. Now I see why Taleju's insisted understanding Spirit via direct perception rather than trying to grasp it using mind. It is far beyond what I can comprehend otherwise.

Day 20. Taleju in Persian. *The road we follow gradually drop us into long valleys broken by mountains. There is a noticeable difference between Persian and the ancient lands of Afghanistan. Where large cities were almost nonexistent in Afghanistan, almost every valley we come to has ruins stretching for kilometers. This country was very populated. Bones, rusting vehicles, trash and tall buildings rise like bony fingers to the still sky. The Purge signs are everywhere; nothing remains; desolate land where not even weeds grow, no bugs, no birds. It is silent and absent of life. I fear the Rad sickness, for our instruments occasional fail. Our desperation, like our road, stretches unbroken to the dusty horizon.*

When Taleju came here desolation brought great hardships. Low on supplies from the journey they spent weeks searching for water and food. Water they found in isolated spots or rusty storage tanks. Food was discovered in metal cans dug up in ruins; it was risky because her group suffered a high percentage of illness afterwards. They came here in high summer. To them, this was the most difficult part of their trip, not because of the isolation like in Afghanistan, but the sea of death and disease still present.

Now we walked in a transformed land and passed stone markers listing villages and their Emirates. Villagers came out to greet us with flatbread and fruit. Children walked along side, dancing and shouting. A few people followed my camel and recounted my stories and deeds to their friends. They asked if I am Taleju returned as some claimed. I hide my dismay and remind them I am but a pilgrim.

Day 22. Two days ago we deviated from Taleju's original route. She did not come through here but a road further north through the mountains. However, through the centuries weather erased the original road and now our long history of pilgrimage created another road.

We entered a flat, broad valley with a constant chilling breeze. Yesterday we followed a line of wind banners towards the distant hills. In this desolation they seemed out of place. Shortly before reaching foundations of a huge Purge city, these banners changed into wind generators, marking a settlement. I expected a traditional village. However an entire village was carved from solid rock by using naturally occurring ten meter holes deep and thirty meters wide below the rocky plain. Each subterranean opening served as dwelling, courtyards and orchards or gardens. We encountered many travelers from the Emirates. Their camps resembled tent cities; the tents were colorful and brilliant banners flutter in the breeze. There was singing and dance. Their activities reminded me of our weariness. Like them, we could not hide our joy at accomplishing another leg in our pilgrimage.

We have arrived two months behind schedule but in time for this village Festive of Deliverance. Some of our pilgrims think this is an auspicious time and they were eager to join.

Alerted to our arrival a village elder met us just outside their village where ruins dotted the hillside near a cluster of flat stones. Here we descended a hidden trail carved from the rock and came to large caravanserais connected by tunnels. Thankfully, the steady cold breeze we endured for days was absent.

We were taken to our rooms. They were modest spaces painted brilliant colors, windowless, covered with rich carpets, bolters, pillows, futon and a desk. Attendants took our camels and graciously carried our baggage. We were weary and hungry. I can't think of anything by a bath to wash this dust away. I looked forward sleep in shelter beyond the cold wind.

However, after the evening mediation I was too restless and sat with Sarah and Duce in the courtyard watching the stars. We talked about other worlds and wondered if other beings looked to the heavens, wondering if others looked back.

Day 23. After a meal of fruit, spiced bread and tea our host took me, Deva and Patan on a tour of this unique settlement.

Rafjan is a small village of about three hundred inhabitants and shows their ingenuity when adapting to an arid and hot land lacking trees and water. Four hundred ago they came to this valley and realized the brisk wind was too harsh for growing fruit and vegetables. Thus they used the natural sandstone openings and created their village. They added orchards and corrals for planting pomegranates, spices and manufacturing sheep wool rugs.

Dwellings are connected by colorful tunnels and navigating this complex system is aided by color coded passages: red lead to private dwellings and green to the orchards, both which are off limit; blue is for the public souks, and white lead to guest rooms and outsides. Visitors stay in elaborate caravanserais and public access is either through tunnels or guest courtyards connected by steps or paths. Visitor lodging, public souk and wells are separated from the village, which can only be visited by invitation. At each dwelling, brightly painted doors face the courtyard and are covered with colorful and intricate tiles. In the center are two requirements: a pool honoring water spirits whom they believe nourished life, and a sky god altar that brings the wind and sun. Each morning inhabitance light incense and recite prayer for their deities.

Far from Rafjan a complex system of underground channels gather rain and channels water into cisterns below the village. Wind mills pump the water, while wind catchers supply cooling during the summer and power lights and cooking.

After our evening dedication we and other visitors gathered in a large field protected by high wall and between the village and Purge ruins we joined the Rafjan festival. Under the illumination by many light orbs we enjoyed a shadow puppet show about Taleju's defeating the Purge beast. The battle was epic, with lots of flash and booms that sent some children running, screaming or laughing. Deva, familiar with other religion, said `Deliverance' was based on a very old story about struggle between good and evil.

Then, with an invitation by the local musicians, Duce's family joined them and accompanied children reciting this tale. Afterwards we feasted and danced far into the night. The food, sweets and wine loosened my spirit and for awhile I forgot myself. Back in my room, my head spun and body glowed. Despite being exhausted, this has been a good day.

Day 24. According to Altus Rafjan supplemented their income by catering to tourists. Whereas other places we visited had religion or Madrasa as their centerpiece Rafjan created a Purge museum. Entrance was by a red gate beyond pomegranate groves, spice gardens and where families manufactured rugs.

In the morning our host took us to a `Purge city' which he claimed had a Black Blood refinery. It was no larger than an average village, completely walled so outsiders could not see inside except by paying admission and enter via a gate. The museum was dwarfed by massive ruins spreading for kilometers across the hills.

We strolled on wide, stone streets painted black to resemble a Purge road. Ancient, rusty and painted hulks sat along the road or in front of buildings. These I recognize as mock ups of vehicles that moved on the black ribbons under their own power. A maze of rusted pipes stretched along the ground and into the air; some attached to huge, metal and clay tanks, others connected to metal objects and gears. The scale boggled my mind. The Purge scale was huge, but seeing this recreation gave me the impression it had taken over the whole world. The maze of pipes was wider than my camel and more than numerous than the sand!

In another area beyond the refinery and representing a typical Purge street buildings painted in bright colors hinted to their local tradition rather than the Purge sober colors. Some ruin foundations were buried in sand up to the first floor and additions built upon these, creating a false front several stories tall. Wood panels covered gaping holes and then painted to resemble windows. A few pretend signs hung above the doors or painted on the buildings in fantasy letters meaning nothing.

Inside a building intended to show a working space I found haphazard metal frames and furnishing arranged with no regard for function. In our time, since we sit on cushions or divas, the notion of a chair was foreign. At one area I saw a chair propped upside down with its legs holding a kind of platform. It reminded me of a child's play house thrown haphazardly.

Of more interest was the museum displaying bits of pipe, rusted gears, metal wheels attached to elbow shaped objects, few glass bottles, rusty cans and lumps of a substance that was neither metal, wood, nor clay. It is labeled 'unknown.' Behind the displays wall murals depicted a Purge era city, the refinery, vehicles on wide roads and everyday life. The whole thing made me chuckle as our modern world tried grasping a foreign and long vanished world. I was amused by our innocence.

The Purge world was more sinister than they envisioned. However, I doubt they would comprehend this if I explained.

As with life, the legend is far different than the actual event. The gulf separating truth from fantasy only widen with time, as shown here.

At the nearby souk Purge souvenirs sold alongside richly crafted, red and white carpets, wool overcoats and quality brass cookware. We bought all the coats and heavy blankets we could find.

After the evening Conformation locals asked me if I thought their Purge city was accurate. This placed me in an awkward situation because it assumed two things: those stories of my past association were true and if I answered truthfully it would insult our host.

Instead I replied it was a fair representation but they should never forget the horror and darkness of that era. There was nothing quaint about it.

Afterwards someone brought a gift: a drawing from the Purge era. It was a sketch of a city street done on parchment. The buildings, people or vehicles were remotely accurate but, like their mock up city, a fantasy representation for tourists. The gift was given in humble gratitude and I thanked him.

Day 26. Leaving Rafjan we picked up Taleju's trail yesterday and followed it into a desert where white crusty plains heavy with salt we had to cover our faces. White salt drifted up and covered every crack and fold, getting under the skin and leaving raw, painful rashes. Sometimes we passed bleached bones lying on the surface. This place Taleju dubbed 'Plain of skulls.' A massive city once sprawled here but it was buried during the years of Sickness and Darkness following the Purge.

A valuable, opalescent, blue stone called 'Taleju's Tears' is only found here. Legend said the Kumari Mother cried when she came upon this valley.

Pilgrims braved the salt flats searching for these precious stones in places where sand uncovered bare rock. None were found.

Day 27. We left the salt flats and came to a small village of white buildings hidden in shady groves seen for many kilometers before reaching it. The well was in the main yard surrounded by souks and inns.   It was busy with traders heading south to the Hindustan Gulf or north to Anatolia.   We decided to rest here tomorrow.

After nearly a week without food and water exhausted, famished, and near death we come off the mountains to a small grove. Sensing water we use our remaining strength to dig and by nightfall find it. The trees are heavy with figs; the ground thick with muskmelons. We spend a week recovering but alas, one of my devoted Satori, Bhramsnapu dies as does a dozen other travelers. We bury him on the hillside and mark his grave with the pack he carried from Nepal. A camel platform in which we stored provisions is broken up and used for kindling. . .

  ---Taleju on her travel through Persian-

Day 28. I was curious about this burial place after Altus spoke about it.   In a hillside I visited a modest temple supposedly marking the spot in Taleju's stop. It is square with white and gold walls and capped by a blue dome. Earlier, local pilgrims heard about me and gathered here and when I walked up the steps they rushed me. Yusuf and Sami gently held them back but several managed to touch my clothes in passing.

Like all temples I visited in Persian, sunlight illuminates a modest circular room' painted pillars and ornate floor rugs.   In a niche facing Dubai was a scrap of wood, its paint having long ago faded and a cracked ceramic object. Silver incense burners sent inviting blue smoke and soothing sandalwood. Along the walls were depictions of Taleju's travel and their tragedy.

The temple curator, alerted by the outside commotion, rose from his divan and accompanied us. He explained these relics came from Taleju's party. The wood item came from her cart and the remains of a candle holder belonged to Bhramsnapu. My attention was drawn to the wood.   There, impressed on the surface was the same faint symbol on Taleju's necklace and our flag. I indicated it but no one else saw it.

After leaving the temple I paused to drink from a well in the front courtyard and rested beneath shady trees. The sunlight warmth felt good as it dissipated my constant chill. A shy boy offered me freshly baked bread and pomegranates. I appreciated his effort although I was not hungry and took a few bits. My bones ached and, wanting to forget my misery, I rested and read Taleju's account.

Since my encounter at Shaidajad my mood became pensive. I resent my role, waiting nothing but to be an ordinary pilgrim so I can concentrate on the Awakenings and Dream and Echoes. At times it is so bad I just want to be left alone with my thoughts. Sarah understands this and makes it a point not to speak or hover around me when am in this state.

But because pilgrims have expectations of me, I cannot share my feelings. Taleju said it was very lonely being a leader.

It is more difficult for me because I always preferred being alone.

Sometimes I envision I am a caged animal who just wants to be released from this fate. I know this won't happen, but I still can still dream. Right?

Deva and her group showed up and, sensing my moodiness, she visited with the crowd. Later I forced my pensiveness away when encouraged by pilgrims waiting all day to see me. I spoke about Taleju's challenging on this part of her journey.

As I spoke, I stood in the light where tree branch shadows danced to a sudden breeze. Several people in front pointed at me and I suddenly felt self conscious. I fell quiet when several pilgrims exclaimed I had levitated. Excited voices joined in and soon the temple echoed with their chatter. I tried calming them but gave up when my escorts hurried me away before the pilgrims could rush me.

This evening Altus and Deva came by. Deva was confused by my sudden departure and we discussed the event. I assured her the shadows played tricks because I am incapable of such things. She is sympathetic.

Day 29. Despite nightly cold requiring extra blankets, travel through the high desert during the day was hot and blinding even with goggles. As far as I saw atop my camel nothing moved in this vast, yellow and brown expanse. We were still days from the capital, Homs. As we get closer, apprehension lying in my heart intensified.

Deva confided her love for Altus and looked upon me for inspiration. Often she shared her problems, her disillusionment with the Kumari religion and her uncertain future. She fears if she marries Altus, who was branded a traitor, the Central Kumari will banish her as a heretic. I told her that her heart is pure and should not to worry about this.

Yesterday she warned me about secret correspondence from the Central Kumari. She was upset by my presence and accused me of dissention, blasphemy, and the West Kumari Daughter's death. It was hoped Deva's appointment would `polarize' the pilgrims back into order.

Deva explained even though the Sheik and his Council are subordinate to her, they have held back interfering even when she requested they act. The Sheik fears Seers more than her authority and wants to see how this will play out before making a move. I am a Seer and thus far it has protected me.

Deva knows the pilgrim relationship with me will not change. I have too much influence and leadership qualities. She even heard that some think I am Taleju returned, although she will never tell the Daughter this. That, she added would result in my immediate execution.

I realize after reflecting on our conversation I am more concerned with getting our pilgrims to Nepal than for my safety or gaining status. Yes, I fear violence might destroy our group cohesiveness, but I cannot believe that after all we've been thought this is our fate.

We are more than three hundred strong; only about fifty distrust me and remain loyal to the Kumari Daughter. Taleju's haunting words about the mind and emotion clouding Aspect ring true. I am entering a struggle for truth within this religion, this is why the Kumari fears me.

Long ago when I questioned the West Kumari's behavior this set up echoes and shook the Kumargi religion to its core.

I realize with much apprehension this may not end peacefully. However, I sense time is running out as I rush into a confrontation with the Kumari Daughter at Homs.

Day 30. On the empty plains today we were joined by a hundred mounted soldiers tasked with escorting us to Homs. They wore full battle regalia: peaked helmets, hardened leather, chainmail and vests of the Emirates' colors. Their commander, a scar on his forehead and a bear of a man with a disarming smile assured us they were a show of the Emirate's support. Their presence caused concern but I explained the Sheik honored us with his troops. They took position as lead and rear guard.

When we camped the soldiers kept their distance, staying behind well organized tents and sentry. Despite this unexpected gloom, the pilgrims' mood was light because they basked in this notoriety, whereas I hid my pensiveness. Deva returned after meeting the commander and encouraged me to flee because she feared for my safety. I reminded her I am but a pilgrim journeying because of my devotion to Taleju. The circumstances which I became leader were not of my choosing, but I accepted my role and will see it though the end for the pilgrims' sake.

I am tired of this pettiness. All I want to do is complete this pilgrimage and be left alone.

Month 8, Day 3. *Mind and Emotions are the Twin Sisters of Slavery. We as spirit realize this. It takes great courage to see beyond their colorful, dazzling chains.---Taleju-*

Over these several days our travel and camp were peaceful. Singing and dancing chased away the cool evenings and fatigue. I even met a young soldier and we chatted. He heard about me and admitted I was not what he envisioned. Seers are horned beasts can take the guise as human and steal traveler souls and children. I should have laughed by this, but I did not. Even though Seer families are on our pilgrimage so many people still harbor superstition. I think this trace back to their tribal roots or subconscious trauma left by the Purge. Back then it was us against them. Humanity has not really changed despite our effort.

On this part of our journey we were shadowed. They kept to the hills but I sensed their eyes. They were not soldiers as I originally thought, but Seers. Several times I touched their minds filled with impressions. This was similar to my connection with the boy earlier, but on a larger scale.

My awareness has expanded; perhaps this is why I could detect their minds. Now I am cognitive of intense physical energies to this land. The sun and moon produce distinct energetic music, gradually changing as the day or night waxed and waned. The cold breeze fills me with vision of long ago which overlaid upon the present as though seeing the past and present with two set of eyes. More than once I've been terribly distracted by this new found ability and nearly fell off my camel!

Taleju's book talked about all creatures having energy vortexes. I can see these much easier as circle of colorful lights spinning within pilgrims' etheric bodies. A beautiful rose hue connected Deva and Altus's heart energies. When they were together their auras flashed and filled the air with delicate melodies. Sometimes I noticed shadow around others and conclude these are illnesses. My perception grows each day.

Day 7. Homs, Persian Emirates. I am very apprehensive. My spirit is heavy. I am restless because unshaped threats hover just beyond my inner vision.

Homs, located at the base of roughed mountains, overlooking rocky expanse vanishing to the horizon. Tilled fields and orchards spread out from the city and are tended by small clusters of huts. Four main roads converge here; trade is active but now that winter comes had fallen off. Mostly locals travel here; bringing late harvests, pottery, textiles and rugs. People gathered in front of their homes and watched curiously as we passed. Banners of the Emirates fluttered by the roadside or hung from city walls. Thousands of wind chimes filled the air with delicate music, giving this place a surreal feel.

When we came into this valley two days ago frost covered the ground. By mid morning it was gone, only to return at dusk. The mountains were absent of snow but someone remarked that was not the case before the Purge. My body ached, my shoulder throbbed constantly and I began limping in pain. I have never experienced this kind of cold and do not like it. It causes me to pull deep inside myself and all I want to do is curl up next to a fire and think of those pleasant spring days of home. I relive those moments when you, Ali, pushed Bishma's swing under the massive, orange tree. Her musical giggles warm this lonely heart and dispel my misery.

Being this Emirate's capital and the Central Kumari Daughter House, Homs boasts many gardens and estates. Both religious and political bodies command the city's center. The Emirates administration is a collection of blue and gold domed buildings surrounded by rectangular walls and wind towers. The Central temple is above the palace; its red and yellow, tiled roofs, wood structures, and open grounds contrast with the city's mud brick buildings. The Sheik and his staff left for Bandar Addis during the winter months, leaving this Emirate's Emir to tend to State affairs. I was told he opened his palace to guests while the Central Kumari sponsored many roadside inns and was generous to travelers.

We were greeted outside Homs by Emir Hajaiz, riding a speeded white camel and escorts from the Central Kumari residence. After navigating wide streets and waving to enthusiastic crowds we camped at a pomegranate orchard behind the Kumargi temple. Temple helpers assisted getting our camp ready. The pilgrim mood was joyful.

This evening I gazed upon many solar fires dotting our camp. Music and laughter carried on the cold air scented with herbs and meals. It has been a long trip getting here and I looked forward to our brief rest before setting out in three days. Maybe my concerns will have been for nothing.

As a side note the Seers observed from the hills above. I sensed a dozen, some armed.

Tomorrow I meet the Central Kumari Daughter.

Day 9. Today my group was instructed to wait in the meeting room anti chamber while our pilgrims entered the temple and paid homage to the Central Kumari Daughter. Wearing her formal attire she sat on her minbar and draped yellow scarves over the shoulder of each devotee waiting in a long line with bowed head. Chants, horns, finger cymbals and heavy drums accompanied the Ceremony of Compassion and special horns announced shrill notes when the devotee was blessed by a scarf.

Afterwards pilgrims sat on cushions around her and waited. When finished, and in a soft voice, she said: *We as Consciousness are forever. Our form is but flickering shadows upon the dunes.*

With the ceremony's conclusion our pilgrims quietly, and solemnly, left. The Daughter invited all but me to participate in a special ceremony. I hid my disappointment and anger with cool indifference.

They must have sensed my mood, for Altus, Duce, Sami and Yusuf refused, despite my encouragement. Altus reminded her they were pilgrims of Taleju and did not recognize exclusive dogma.

The Kumari Daughter's face turned angry but she never lost her grace. Without a word she stepped from the minbar. We kept our heads bowed and palms pressed until she vanished. Shortly afterwards servants offered us fruit and tea. Deva joined us, looking worried as she led us into a private garden behind the main temple.

The Daughter, surrounded by her staff, sat in chairs while I rested on ground pillows as was my custom. Our conversation centered on the events, the West Daughter's death and my impressions. We touched lightly on Taleju's mysterious book but she confessed after reading a report sent by the deceased Daughter explaining it, she believed it was fake and a mockery to Taleju's personage. She was careful to avoid discussing my interpretation of the Awakenings. Although she seemed indifferent, her heart chakra and Third Eye shimmer with the stormy red and deep purple--- color of anger and dominance. As a show of respect I kept my head lowered and when I looked at her, she avoids my gaze.

Then she switched to Nepalese dialect when conversing with Deva. The Daughter's tone was clipped, impatient, threatening. Deva replied reverently, timidly and at times stumbled in her response. The air around them was charged and I saw red and brown energies. I shuttered. I felt a cold breeze blow through my soul. This meeting left me sick and I was grateful when it ended.

In the afternoon I was escorted back to camp and spend the rest of the day going over the trip and translating Taleju's book, hoping to forget my gloominess.

This evening Deva returned, visibly shaken and requested I do not speak at our dedicational. I sensed her apprehension and knew this came from the Daughter.

Great anxiety stalks our camp.

Day 10. In the afternoon the Kumari Daughter visited and spoke about dedication, the Confirmation and the blessings it bestowed. She then said that since the beginning it had been the Kumari reasonability to ensure safety and leadership so those completing the trip would return home as Mokti. With a leader not recognized or sanctioned as per the Kumargi creed, meant our pilgrimage would not be recognized and all effort would have been in vain.

She added that although my group had shown dedication by leadership when necessary, my title of Daughter's Deputy is revoked and Deva is now the Kumargi representative. She gave the pilgrims a choice; pledge to the Kumargi or return home.

I felt as though I was kicked in the stomach. I feared showing my reaction so retreated to my tent.

All these months of leading the pilgrims; the sacrifices, the uncertainty, all my doubts and to cast aside like a worn cloth! This is heinous, but threaten the pilgrims in the same breath is unforgivable.

My motivation was never about me! It was for them, the devoted pilgrims wanting to walk in Taleju's steps. All of us on this journey dreamed our entire life to make this.

Not for the Kumargi.

But Taleju.

No longer able to shield my feelings I wailed. My anger and uncontrolled wrath spewed like a storm. I heard deep rumbles and red light swilled around me. One cup lying on the table suddenly shattered and things flew about on invisible hands, slamming into the tent or tossed onto the ground. Sarah came in, she saw what was happened and left, her eyes wide in terror.

I screamed and screamed and collapsed to my knees. I glimpsed my reflection in a broken mirror. My eyes smoldered red, my face twisted with hatred. The shock dispelled my rage as quickly as a wind blew out a candle. I sat in the middle of the broken items scattered on the floor, defeated and spent. I wiped tears and sobbed. My world crashed around me. If there was ever a time when I felt taking the sword up against those who questioned my devotion was now!

My hand trembles. I must stop or the pen will tear pages.

It is now past midnight. My energy is gone. I am weak and sat, defeated. Deva and I discussed our options. She fears for her standing in the Kumari hierarchy. Should she disobeys she will be banished. Yet if she assumes the leadership I am betrayed. She does not agree with the Daughter and despite her objection the Daughter launched into threats. She reminded me that the Kumargi has an ugly side, and I had seen it.

With tears we decide that it is more important to show her loyalty in the face of this threat. She is the Supreme Satori and with the exalted potion comes responsibilities and unquestioned loyalty.

I would not want those who risk their lives to have their efforts discounted. I reminded her we are a team and eventually I will return. I encouraged her to act in the best interest of the pilgrims and get them safely to Kathmandu.

I thanked her for her support. She was tearful and we hug. I do not know when I may see her, if ever.

Day 11. After tea this morning Kumargi soldiers gave me with a document signed by the Central Kumari Daughter, charging me and eight my closest friends of sedition. We were arrested on the spot. I entertained the idea of resisting them, but realized many would die, so I summoned them to my tent and instructed them to surrender. Duce and Sami were the most difficult to convince but after assessing our situation they stood down. We listened as the charges were read out loud and then a dozen soldiers were posted around my tent, with instructions no was to leave.

Standing outside my tent I watched with great sadness as Deva, mute and in shock led the pilgrims away under heavy escorts. Some came by and asked for guidance and I reminded they are on a pilgrimage and their success is more than loyalty. Smiling falsely I assured everyone I did not hold a grudge.

But really I do!

Only about a hundred pilgrims refused to join and sat in front of my tent, watching quietly the group. Altus, Patan and Satr were given the choice to renounce me and be free. Altus came by, looking sad and distraught. With much prodding I convince him his role is to be with his love. Satr and Patan remained with me.

With the last pilgrim gone the guards closed the gate and stationed outside. We were now prisoners. The orchard backed up against the massive, city wall and this camp site enclosed by smaller walls. Enough supplies were left for a week. In the late afternoon a message arrived saying the Daughter will decide our fate in a week. Meanwhile, we will be treated as guests.

I lead the evening ceremony then afterward Sarah, teary eyed, ran up to me. One of the guards said all the books with my saying were to be burned. I assured her several copies were hidden in my tent. This calmed her but fueled my own resentment and rage. It was not the destruction of my words that upset me, but the Kumari's insistence only their sources is true and all other opinions are false.

Day 12. It has been a sad, lonely day as I take pen and write in my journal. I feel responsible for my friends trapped here with me.

Sarah and Yusuf sat in the corner and copied my sayings. Duce and Sami trained with sticks under a tree, their clack clack clack breaking the silence. The Seer families wandered the orchard and picked pomegranates. Some women huddled over a beehive oven and made bread. Another worked on a reed basket. Pavlo and Lucinda practiced mandolin and flute. From atop the wall sentries watched the gathering, cold darkness.

Although I am trapped here, this gave me opportunity to develop my skills. This afternoon my awareness touched Deva. Although I settled into her mind and vaguely saw what she did, I sensed she was troubled and scared. Her group was climbing the trail leading towards the Hindustan Corridor many kilometers away. They were quiet and sullen. Soldiers escorted them.

I have not eaten since my imprisonment; my appetite discouraged by nausea and bouts of stomach pain. I forced down water but I choked and gagged. My strength was only sustained by my determination to right this injustice. I am frustrated by my lack of courage to stand up to the Kumari, to challenge her, their teachings and state my issues. Since leaving home I have backed down, desiring only to complete this journey with hopes not threatening my life. I took it upon myself to guide us to Nepal because no would do so and our pilgrims looked to me for leadership. This, I confess was misguided; I falsely believed it did not matter who filled the role, only that Taleju's essence was maintained.

I've seen the warnings all along, yet in my optimism and ignorance about human character, my own fear of self worth, and wanting to avoid conflict I let this happen. Now it has affected nearly four hundred friends—friends who trusted me.

Is this how Taleju felt when her Companions split up? Was she cursed by doubt, loathing and fear?

My hand shook; the pen fell out. I must stop and . . .

Day 26. *With these words I impart my understanding of all Things within these Infinite Realms we, as spirits, dance and sing. Many will not agree, some will question and few will comprehend. They are here for our Future as we try to understand our Past.*

I have travelled through the Purge world. It was one hundred forty seven years ago that our world forever changed. To many, nature is cruel; but I say Nature, or Consciousness, is perfect in Its desire to return to Balance; It will, by any means, seek to undo that which the Twin Sisters of Slavery: Mind and Ego, try to manipulate even as these disregard universal balance. Many times we were warned but we chose to ignore these because we were trapped in self delusion. Our actions, our thoughts, our intent is ruled by the same karmic law governing us and all Realms. We were foolish to believe otherwise.

Live in balance; realize everything we do, say and our intent echoes for many lives though Infinite times and realms. There is no escaping: what happens today has consequences tomorrow. Each of us is the convict and the Judge of our own doing.

The Purge reminds us.

Understand my words and these will guide us to Awakened Spirits. We are blessed to live these Dreams; let not our Echo disrupt this Balance.----Taleju-Dream and Echoes-

Thus, after ten days of furious writing, which Sarah claimed I was in a trance, Dream and Echoes' is translated.

My memory since then is sketchy. I am only aware of my intense, desperate effort to complete it.

Sarah recounted the events. It started shortly after our sentencing. She found me huddled over my desk late that night writing furiously by a solar lamp. I continued writing for ten days and night, pausing long enough to sleep and barely touched the food offered. When anyone spoke to me I muttered incoherently, kept silent or just stared at nothing. Those around me thought I had gone mad or possessed by a Djinn. After over a week of begging for help, the Kumari Daughter sent a healer who unsuccessfully tried to break my trance. Despite repeated requests, the Kumari did not respond.

Two days later she visited and was alarmed I was still incoherent and unaware of my surroundings. She worried if I died in this state I may be martyred. Therefore she decided carry out my punishment that night so if I died I would be officially a heretic. She placed heavy guards around us and left to prepare the punishments.

The punishment for heresy or sedition is brutal. My face will be branded; my eyes and tongue cut out then returned to Sofia in chains. If I perished reroute, I would be left for the wild dogs.

As for the others, they would be banished from the Kumargi and branded on the forehead as heretics and any member of the religion who helped them would risk death.

The sentence will be enforced by Kumargi soldiers. She appointed a particularly vicious leader named, Bramaputra, known for his fanatical devotion to the Central Kumari.

Shortly after the meeting with the Kumari several men in black turban, robes, faces hidden and wearing goggles appeared in our camp and explained who they were and plan. The leader, Batu Khan, said we were going north to his tribe in Khorasan Wejhd where we would be cared for. He emphasized the importance of speed because once discovered our escape, Bramaputra would be relentless in his pursuit. Bramaputra would kill us, even it if it was not sanctioned by the Kumari Daughter.

Sill in a trance, I was carefully wrapped in thick robes and with our belongings our group were provided with many camels for our escape. We mounted camels then our rescue party led us out the gate. Sarah claimed the guards just stood there, staring lifeless and let us pass. We left the city by a trail into the mountains and numbering about one hundred and fifteen, rode for two days.

I was not aware of these events until waking the afternoon in confusion. The fort was gone, replaced by cold breeze, black shrouded men, deep gullies and camels. Their camels I thought covered in tattoos until realizing their hide was shaved into intricate patterns. Duce and Sarah calmed me and as they explained what happened, I drank water and ate cold rice and dried fruit as I shivered from the cold air. The numbness of my trance faded away.

Here I sit in gathering darkness, desperately trying to write what happened before our light vanish. We cannot use lantern because this may attract pursuers. The precious Dream and Echoes manuscript is tucked in my camel saddle, wrapped in a yellow sash.

The group who saved us are Seers.

Day 27. Until now I did not realize how simple or superficial the Awakenings message is. It is deep, but more akin to abstract thoughts associated with the Mental and Emotional Planes rather than delving into the Spiritual mechanics of energy manipulation. Having dwelled in the Mental Realm with its electric blue energy grids and watched thoughts solidify, I find it more importance to understand _how_ the Shadow Realm works, rather than explaining it via quaint concepts. For us to evolve into the next stage, we need to investigate energetic operations unique to each Realm. We should be students of Light rather than students of thought. I am convinced Taleju's new book is intended for the next step in human evolution—of which I am a part.

My head and my Third Eye throb until these sensations dominate my world. At times I think of nothing else but this new realization. Bit of images, like torn pieces of pictures stare back when I peer inside. Are they from the Realms I visited, past incarnations or my own, jagged feelings? They block my ability to see beyond. I suppose they are barriers but are they meant to protect, or hinder my ability to travel further into Consciousness?

Our Seers escorts emitted beautiful, blue and green light with soft melodies. Our group was surrounded with rose, purple and bits of red; our melodies heavier. I had not noticed the difference between our species until now.

Quite by accident I discovered I can move things by concentration; or at least affect them. I accomplished this by staring at a cup and sensing my energy surrounding it, something inside shifted and the cup rose a few centimeters. I can only sustain this for a few moments before it left me in horrible pain. I recalled when my anger trashed my tent and am very careful not to have any emotions when doing this.

Our group moved fast; taking little time for rest and travelling further away from the main road. We headed deep into a desert of brown gravel fields and lava hills. I sensed our trackers: about fifty, heavily armed. They were slowly closing in. Our leader, Batu Khan, said once we crossed the salt flats it marked the boundaries and they will probably stop. They are afraid of Seers and the fear of meeting them may outweigh their objective.

Yet, since waking from my trance I am not inclined to run again. I find the Kumari behavior infuriates me and I have little patience to scurry about like a mouse. They have interfered in my Confirmation. Why could they just leave me alone? All I want is to be allowed to perform my pilgrimage. I am being suppressed by the religion of my heart and it is time we stand up as proud followers of Taleju.

Batu Kahn sensed my mood. He remarked Seers hold me in high esteem but we must be cautious in our dealings with the Normals. They already distrust us and to provoke them could lead to trouble. I don't care. Let their fears consume them. Taleju's word is more important than dogmatic institutions holding sway over those seeking Truth.

This evening I presided over our first meeting in weeks. It felt good sharing my knowledge and answering their questions. Batu Khan and his men joined us. I spoke about Spirit's struggle to manifest higher ideals in a world filled by fear and ego. I quoted Taleju.

It is necessary for us as Spirit to constantly be on guard against our illusions so the shadow does not replace the sun.

Month 9 Day 2. Today I have discovered my potential. Other Persian soldiers further north east joined our pursuers and we met on the open plains within view of the jagged pinnacle marking the border of the Persian Emirates. Had the second group not joined the chaise, we had enough distance to lose our pursuers near a place called the White Plains. However, they forced my hand.

Until we met they had no idea we were traveling with Seers. They assumed I was responsible for our escape. Much to their dismay, they found out otherwise.

My Far Sight had limited range, about a day's distance. In the morning and at the very edge of my ability, I discovered the identity of our trackers.

Using his Far Sight, Batu Khan discovered their plan and had watched their progress. The Persian group came the east and rode all night, planning to delay us until the second party arrived. Batu Khan wanted me to lead my group to the White Plains and they would remain behind to confront the soldiers. Much to his anger I refused. For the first time in months I put myself in harm's way when, riding high on my camel, led my red guard to confront the soldiers. Batu Khan sensed trouble and reluctantly joined us. Some of Batu Khan's group waited in a ravine to protect our rear.

We assembled on the open plain and observed riders towards us. Eighty determined men with spear and sword carried the Persian Emirates and Kumargi banners. When the neared, I removed my goggles and waited. Batu Khan sat high on his camel, watching; his mind clouded and although I tried penetrating it, he was careful to shield his thoughts. His cold eyes met mine to cease my effort.

The rider next to Batu Khan quickly shoved his tribal banner in the hard ground. The Persians slowed and I sense surprise, then fear. They paused, observing us. Anger filled me as my gaze rests on the Kumari's banner. When Batu Khan held up his hand and rode forward, my rage explodes in ways that confused and delighted me. I think of the hurt and humiliation I suffered; of the Kumari's contempt; her deliberate lies. To them Taleju is by a rug to be trampled on when it suits their purpose. Swelling, ruby tinged energy swelled from my heart and clouded my vision. My eyes burned and looking through a red energy gauze at the riders the closest men choked as invisible hands squeeze his temples. Low, violent rumbles filled my ears. Their camels bucked and spun around, either running off in panic or tossing soldiers onto the ground.

Batu Khan glanced back at me and immediately a heavy presence struck me full in the chest like an iron fist. I gasped and my anger and that ruby power vanish. I vomited.

The riders immediately gathered their fallen and fled. Batu Khan sternly faced me. He warned my act would bring dishonor and further isolate Seers from the Normals.

Defiantly I watched the riders vanish. There was no reluctance but a profound feeling of accomplishment. If the Kumari wants a war she has it. The time of Seers has come.

I vowed then and there, in this morning on that gravel plain looking west that I, Noora, would no longer run!

Let all know I make this promise.

Khorasan Wejdh

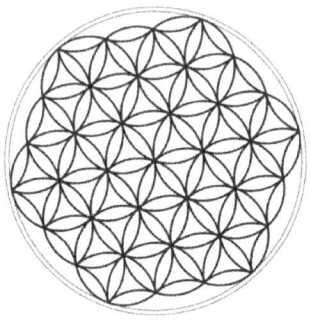

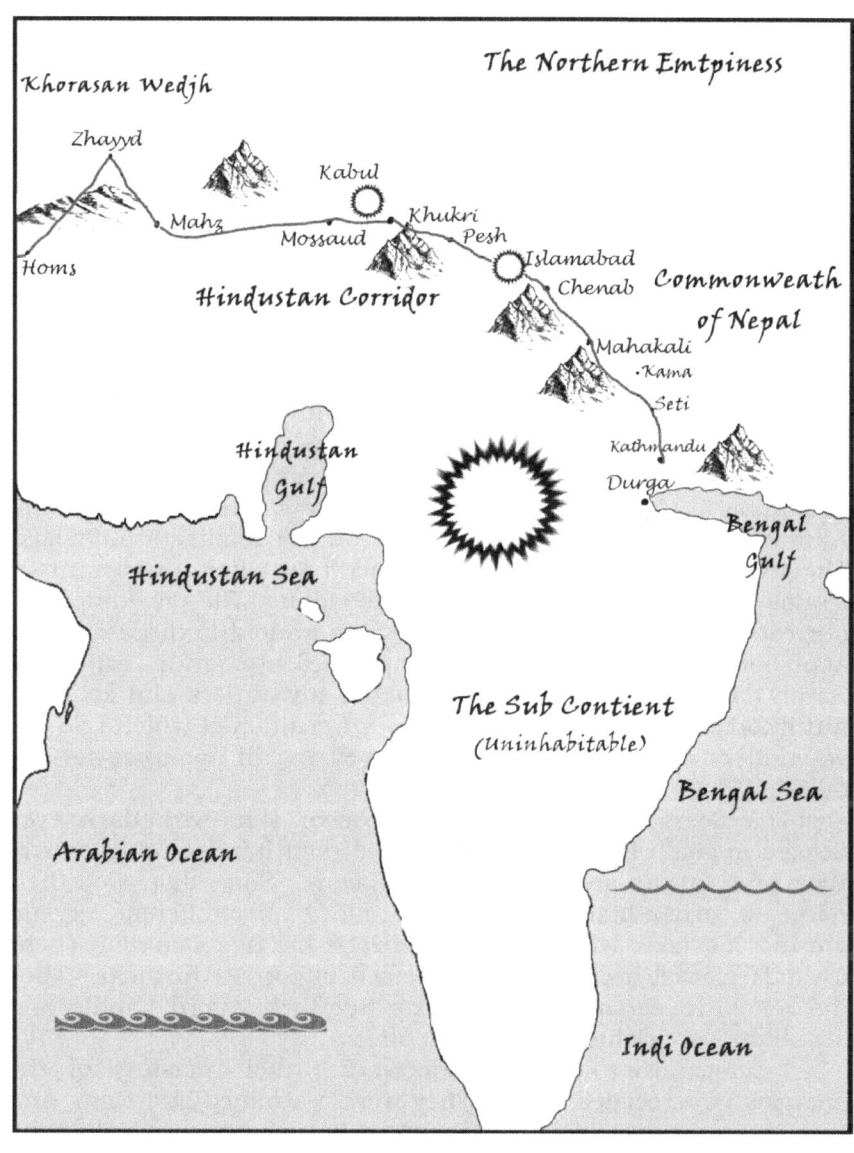

Month 9, Day 3. Khorasan Wedjh. How different our world is since dropping out of the mountains yesterday. We descended towards a continuous expanse of salt called `Vulture's Wing'. The stuffy air was heavy with fine salty particles that sting with each breath. While crossing, fine white powder rose from our passing and covered our bodies, causing pain and itching. Later thunder brought rainstorms, drenching us for five solid hours and transforming this powder into caked, sticky goo. The white flats we travelled through had been transformed into a shallow lake stretching to the horizon. The smell of salt, brine and even sulfur clung to my nostrils. Black and angry, brooding clouds watched over us and threatened to unleash their misery. Batu Khan remarked the Sub continent sent warmer weather this spring, promising more violent rainstorms.

Two meter tall rock and cone monoliths marked the beginning of Vulture's Wing. This was the boundary into Khorasan Wedjh, home of the Seers and off limits to outsiders. The groups had been chasing us turned back after our encounter. I know this is not the end to their meddling. The encounter left our escorts sullen. I sensed Batu Khan wanted to discuss it but kept his distance. I may have impressed our group, especially Sarah and Yusuf who whispered about my powers and courage, but it forced the Seers into an awkward position of which I do not yet understand. But, I did not regret or will apologize for my decision.

The Seers were swarthy and brown skin with dark eyes flecked in gold. Blue tattoos decorated their hands and faces and their blue turban accented by silver beads. Some displayed their name on turban badges. Each man wore different crystal around his neck which he hid beneath his black tunic. These crystals glowed iridescent and seemed important to them. They did not have personal adornments but their sword handle and scabbard were richly decorated in silver.

I realize they were very powerful; their mastery of the energies far exceeded mine. They were restrained and calm, and their customs discouraged foolishnesses energetic use. They did not read minds, and, as far as I can detect, do not project awareness beyond their bodies.

To them words were powerful; only Batu Khan shared his name. Rather, they called to each other by whistles associated with that person. They spoke fluid melodies, sometimes two octaves at once. Sarah, not knowing their dialect, thought they were happy because they always sung. Because I translated Dream and Echoes, I had a smattering understanding of their dialect.

They avoid contact and did not speak to us except Batu Khan, who carefully chose his words. Although I am a Seer, I am still an outsider. Being our group's leader, he only communicated with me. Whenever someone in our party greeted them they silently acknowledged without speaking. At first we attributed this to arrogance rather than their custom.

Towards evening we camped at a craggy hill in the center of this artificial lake. Everything was wet or damp. White and black birds with long legs and thin, curved beaks filled the cold, damp air with mournful cries. The Seers called them `Loons' and believe they bring good luck.

This evening I concentrated on seeing the Causative Realm, trying to understand more about my previous lives leading to my present situation.

The Causative Realm resides beyond the Mental; that place where all our incarnations wait our discovery in the Hall of Life. There, it is presided over by the Guardian A'nusha who assists all seeking answers. Here, we find our Seed Karma, or Original Intent: those acts which lay the root and our many echoes thorough these incarnations in the Shadow Realm. Unlike the Akashic Records that only show events from the Psychic Realm and below, the Causative encompasses all in its entirety.

I now realize my early visions selecting cards were attempts to reach this realm.

Batu Khan sensed a lot about my past I am not aware of. I am hopeful I can understand more about his people.

Day 4. We reached the lake's end at a place called `Blood Steam.' This was the most foreboding, hellish spot I've seen on my trip. Here, the water was a permanent mass of bright, red gooey, mud bubbles which boiled and churned up great pools of yellow steam that choked and burned. The stench was overpowering and we had be cautious about setting camp upwind in sheltered rocks covered with green slime. The pools' constant hiss reminded me of a angry beast and was quite unnerving.

Legend said a terrible battle happened here, transforming this once fertile land into a Netherworld. My inner vision saw the earth's energetic grids twisted and warped and the impression of many spirits who shed their bodies. Violent impressions still permeated here even after so many centuries.

Batu Khan met our Seer pilgrims for several hours before visiting me. He was interested in Taleju's book which I showed him. He said I have a very important mission to share her works and emphasized needed to resolve darkness entangling my

Awareness if humanity was to accept me. I felt slighted and a bit upset after our meeting.

Sarah and Yusuf continued making books of my sayings because pilgrims wanted this for our Dedicational.

Despite best intentions, the foul air prevented this evening meeting. We will be very glad to leave here.

Day 6. These two days we followed desolate ravines and narrow valleys through black, jagged hills, gradually heading north. A line of continuous gray peaks loom on the distant horizon. This is the boundary into the Hindustan Corridor. They look forbidding even at this distance!

Today I felt presence of many minds. Yesterday we passed colorful banners strung along a canyon marking the border of Batu Khan's village. This morning a large bird with blue wings and black and brown body followed us. At one time it rested on Batu Khan's shoulder. It wore a large crystal around its neck.

Yesterday Batu Kahn and I studied Dream and Echoes. He cannot read the text, noting it was a very archaic language but was intrigued by the diagrams and pictures. He said the Flower of Life is the Seers' universal symbol. When he saw Taleju's portrait, he explained she received six facial tattoos and became known as `She who is master of all.' A title no other Seer held. He added that some Seers are very spiritually advanced are initiated into color categories corresponding to their understanding. Presently only a handful Seers received four.

We shared a beverage called spiced coffee; a dark, brown liquid with cinnamon and chocolate. It tasted wonderful and was mildly stimulating.

As our camels prodded into this strange land, my thoughts lingered on last night's dream. In this Bishma held my hand as we stood atop a mountain, overlooking a forested valley. You said I will die but also will lead my people to Nepal. You added Taleju will be waiting there.

There is urgency to this vision. I am compelled that I must join the pilgrims soon.

Day 7. Yesterday we left the emptiness and joined a main road crowded with Seer merchants heading into north Khorasan Wedjh and towns along the Caspian Sea. It took us to a small village called Zhayyd, located in a modest valley covered with walnut, pistachio, lemon, olive trees, wheat and herbs.

Because it is late spring, travelers crowded the road. Beehive shaped dwellings sat inside walled enclosures nested in fruit orchards. These accommodated workers, farmers and laborers which were busy with planting and tending orchards. Irrigation came from underground channels, and cisterns built in the hillsides provided water from a lake many kilometers away.

Zhayyd is atop a predominant spine shaped like a shark's fin and overlooks two gates at each end of a road passing below. Within this space white domed homes decorated with blue symbols and geometric designs cling to the very steep rock face interspersed with thick fruit groves. Above each red, yellow, blue or green door glass mirrors caught sunlight and sparkled like hundreds of stars. Each door is a different color and painted with the names of families going back three generations. Batu Khan remarked this showed a family history and identified occupants. Undulating, tiled walls and narrow path or steps connected these dwellings. The valley is filled with a million different melodies created by banners with bells sewn on them, wind chimes and quavering kites flow from many dwellings.

Zhayyd proper is private and off limit to the public. At the main road a Long House' open at both sides serve as public souk and meeting place. Its golden, central dome is surrounded by blue six smaller domes. Ancient trees with massive, twisting limbs line the road as so many colorful banners.

Inside the Long House local and traveling merchants sat on rugs or stood behind tables heaped with fresh bread discs, spices, dried fruit and wares from across the Persian Emirates and beyond. Rug, pottery and curios occupied the other side. Sunlight streamed through ceiling colored glass, creating a Flower of Life on the ground. When we passed, I sensed gold energy radiates from these visitors and citizens.

So many impressions, individual and wonderful scents overwhelmed my awareness. Travelers gathered along the roadside and watch with quiet curiosity whereas, the citizens avoided looking directly at us. At first I was annoyed until Batu Khan explained it was their custom and a sign or respect.

Exhausted, aching and looking to ending our ride our group was led to a private guest area above the market overlooking the orchards and distant mountains. Tall walls surrounded the entrance and as we passed a gate we came into courtyard where our camels were unloaded. I nearly toppled off as my camel dropped to its stomach so I could dismount. Here we were assisted from our mounts, porters carried our supplies on their shoulders and Batu Khan led us up steps to domed entrances which would be our quarters. These dwellings carved in the rock lead into a complex city connected by narrow passageways, halls and steps. Wondrous murals depicting everyday life, geometric patterns and scenes from Taleju's teaching covered walls. Wall lamps produced frankincense scented yellow light. Ornate wood grates covered ceiling ventilations. Batu Khan explained Zhayyd had six levels and stretched more than two kilometers.

I and Sarah settled into our room, illuminated by a soft pleasing yellow glow by small lamps. Tired, I stretched upon pillows and rugs, numb and oblivious to my surroundings. I was covered in weeks of dirt, salt and mud. I lacked sleep, my muscles ached and my riding left sores. I just wanted to sleep and be alone with my thoughts. I needed to make sense of all that had happened.

I welcomed the rest. Goodnight, Ali and Bishma.

Day 11. So many things I have done since these four days. I am glad to have this opportunity to record my activities living among the Seers.

I will describe our room, which was really a sky cave. One end of our modest living quarters opened onto a balcony. From here I observed the passing world. On the opposite side our door was only a heavy drape. This led into a hallway with colorful ceiling murals and the communal kitchen. Another short corridor painted in blue and white tile went to the bathing chamber. Halls were painted different colors to indicate where they went, just like at Rafjan.

Rugs covered the stone floor; bolsters and blankets provided comport on a raised divan spanning three walls The white walls were covered about a third by branches, trees and bushes of various fruit and herbs. The arched ceiling was decorated with blue with yellow and white stars. Tables, chests and dressers skillfully crafted in dark wood accented with brass inlays stored our belongings. Sarah kept her book collection on a wall shelf. We hide Taleju's book and my translations in my travelling chest. Sarah attached our white and purple banner on the ceiling above my sleeping space. Fresh breeze blew into the room in the morning but by afternoon we closed windows when the rains arrived. Despite this, our room is cozy and warm after so many months living in tents and inns. There is more permanence here.

The Seers claimed they originated at the Black sea and Caspian Sea about three hundred years After Purge and moved south to avoid disease and famine. They believe their ancestors helped Taleju and brought her teachings from the west coast where she lived. They portably meant the ancient Bay of Biscay village her book mentioned. It vanished under the ocean long ago.

Zhayyd's population is about a thousand. This is one of the later Seer settlements, about three hundred years old. It was selected because its energetic alignment support crops in the middle of a lifeless desert.

Khorason Wejdh is the largest of six Seer Commonwealths, inhabiting areas around the Caspian Sea and north Anatolia. One city, Shams, is located at the Caspian Sea and on the fringe of the Northern Emptiness. A treacherous road connects Shams with the Red Deserts in Africa, Chin Sea and even Land of Mist! It is called the Sun Road, named after the valuable crystals traded along this road.

I never heard of this road while living in Sofia.

Seers monitor Normals through communicating over long distances by using telepathy or a series of complex sun mirrors. Both species keep to themselves except through trade for sun crystal which powers our solar gadget, and special incense only found in the Seer domains. The Seers have adopted these Sun Crystals far beyond the Normal's: they not only use them for heat and light, but measures earth's energies, ceremonies and giving off color and melodies when placed near certain metals.

Strict, cultural mandates rule their world and how a person behaves in public is the measure of character, trust, and personal worth. From sunrise to sunset everything they do revolves around codes of conduct and adherence to protocol and behavior. Social honor is paramount and any transgression is frowned upon. Any careless act or words bring disgrace and immediate condemnation. I've already incurred disapproval stares and painful headaches from Batu Khan for violating some creed. Although Seers are friendly, giving and possess calm demeanor, they expect us to abide by social etiquette and quick to correct transgressors (me).

Their day begin at sunrise. They gather at a place called the Knowledge Hall where they read Taleju's Awakenings, tell stories and pay homage. Everyone faces west and perform confirmation ceremonies like us, but with differences. This are repeated at noon and sunset. After the morning session they eat then tend to chores. Their last meal is after the evening ceremony and always includes olives and dates which they believe Taleju subsisted on during her last days. If they only knew she did so only because she was extremely ill and nothing else was available. She hated black olives but I do not have the heart to tell them.

There is no sense of `I' or 'Me'; in fact their vocabulary does not contain words denoting individualism but rather self connection to everything. They have some customs like those from home: communal sharing such as raising children, farming, herding and other tasks which benefit and enrich the entire community. Although businesses are run by the most skilled, these are treated as community trusts and all share the wealth. Individual hording or getting rich through the work of others is not allowed. Property is commonwealth, even dwellings; but families, living quarters and their domain are sacred and respected. I have difficulty relating to this lack of boundaries. What is amazing is no one takes advantage of others and lives at peace within their parameters. This is due to Seers outlook on life—which they spend considerable time studying Taleju's work and applying her knowledge.

Everyone spends daily time in the communal `Knowledge Hall' training and learning Taleju's inner secrets. Many are aware of past incarnations, the different realms and their energetic make up. To attest to understanding each person goes through tests and initiations and once deemed successful, receive blue tattoos on their faces and corresponding colored waist sash proclaiming their initiation level. Like us, babies receive marks but unlike us they do not show which tribe they belong. Rather they are given the mark of a Seer; an all seeing eye on the back of the neck. Later as they grow up, more tattoos are added their spiritual progress. A few have reached the fourth initiation, that of the Mental Plane. Only Taleju earned the title `She who is Master of All' which had six tattoos.

Besides newborns getting the mark, each baby is given a crystal or precious stone attuned to their energetic fields. Everyone wears these and keeps them inside their clothes. Only the individual owning the stone is allowed to touch it. These gems are believed to possess great power and Inner Sight.

When someone dies the family create a 'Life Rug' a memorial honoring their life. The families attaches this to the home door and displayed for a year before taking it to the family section inside a communal building. This sacred place is called `Hall of Memories.' Ancient trees surround the walled garden and building. It is isolated from outsiders. Herein are stored carpets hundreds of years old tucked in wall niches dedicated to each family. Families who no longer exist have their niche covered by decorated boards identifying the families.

In any emotional state they never resort to their energetic powers because they believed this would upset the balance of physical and spiritual worlds. They are very aware and their entire society revolves around protocols to temper one's temptation. Customs are so ingrained they dictate one's thoughts, greeting, personal and public interaction. At all times they are cognoscente of their acts and their far reaching effects. It is as though they can see the ripples of present behavior echoes though their future incarnations. In addition, they train their entire life to be a sword master because they are seen as mastery of self through etiquette, discipline, patience and skill. It is their goal is never drawing their sword, but just by reputation alone result in victory. They are feared by outsiders and avoid conflict. As with their society, they do not abuse their status but work towards universal common goal bringing Taleju's vision to life.

They view our Normal as a species giving way to mankind's future: Seers. They say since the Purge humankind's new physical and spirit models are evolving. Although they use their minds and show feelings, they always keep these separate because, as spirit, temptations for abuse are but a breath away.

The Purge was an example of extreme blending Mind and Emotions.

I have so much to learn from them

Day 13. Dear Ali and Bishma. We grew up believing Seers were savages who ate children, stole infants and commanded Djinn to do their evils. They were feared and anyone associated with them was shunned. I spent my life hiding my racial identity because my parents tried to keep it secret—even from me. They insisted I be a `Normal' and should fit in with others despite my difference. I compromised my truth for them.

Joseppi was right. This pilgrimage changed me in ways I never dreamed of. It forced me to confront myself and no longer hide from my destiny.

It was only through you acceptance, Ali, I began feeling safe enough to begin accepting who I am. You provided the key and I unlocked the door into my heart. Until this pilgrimage, my life was lonely in many ways—having lived a lie for so long it is difficult to live in the truth. Maybe it was my own fear, my doubt of who I am. This is the struggle I face each day of my life.

Now I am among _my_ people. Yet, I feel out of place; not really at home but yet not quite an outcast either. They exist in Taleju's realm; they have, within themselves at least, accomplished what I envision for our pilgrims.

Batu Khan said I am the only Seer born from Normals—but what about the Western Kumari Daughter and Taleju? To Seers I am unique and having translated Echoes and Dreams attest to skills they do not have. They attribute greatness to me which I do not have, and come for advice or questions about Taleju.

I am just a Kumargi pilgrim making a pilgrimage.

They are now fervently copying my sayings and Taleju's book. When asking specifics about Dream and Echoes my mind blanks and I cannot speak. Most of what she said is beyond word and can only be comprehended directly. Yet, my uncertainty and loss for words does not diminish my standing among them.

Some said I will speak when Taleju is ready.

Some even changed from wearing their colorful kufi to match my yellow turban. They think by mimic my mannerism or dress it will take them closer to Taleju—I discourage but, like my group, they ignore me.

Two days ago I met representatives from each family at a long house atop the village. Here, windows were arranged to catch the morning and afternoon light, offering a splendid view of the rich valley. Like our apartment, the great hall was covered with locally made rugs; crystals hung from ceiling and small niche lamps bathed the place in soft, yellow glow. This symphony of lights and crystals splattered artificial stars across the hall.

I was offered the place of honor opposite the doorway. They believed those seated furthest away are less likely to be harmed by wandering spirits. Everyone sat along the walls on raised dais scattered with big cushions. The only one facing the entrance was the guest of honor or the group speaker. The entrance wall was decorated with sacred writing, whereas the rest of the chamber painted in intricate geometric patterns.

After much tea, dates and socializing the meeting started when the mediator tapped a wood mallet against a brass bell. The bright, delicate sound sent off wonderful, rose patterns permeating everyone and soothed like washing one's face after a long journey. The presence from many minds reached into mine and a subtle shift happened whereas I connected to their thoughts all at once. Then, Batu Khan turned to me and said the group will honor me with their voices. Suddenly their minds left my head and they spoke in their musical dialect.

They were interested in my past, pilgrimage and my intent, which I explained is to complete the journey. Later I was informed they received a message from the Kumari warning me that if I left Khorasan Wejdh my life will be forfeited. By escaping and not returning home as instructed I violated their conditions. As though I had a choice! Get my eyes gouged out or flee.

Hearing this, I became very angry. My smoldering rage shocked everyone. My energy field flared up like a ruby exploding star! I shouted I will not be deterred by a corrupt religion and since Taleju scarified herself for our spiritual well being I will make sure her word is known.

Maybe I should have controlled myself because I said something I regretted later. I stated Seers are the new inheritors of the earth and Normals have to realize it. Either Taleju unites everyone, or separates all.

My outburst causes much awkwardness. Unable to deal with being uncomfortable and stared at I as though I am a leper I quickly left and for the rest of the day stayed in my room, sulking. So much for making a good impression!

That evening Batu Khan came by and, still upset and angry, we argued. I told him I am Taleju's representative and will bring her message to the world at any cost. No one will stop me. The Kumari has distorted her teachings long enough!

Batu Khan reminded me that we all Taleju's representative and I was deceiving myself for believing I was her only voice. When he compared my behavior to the Central Kumari, I was hurt deeply. Speechless, wrapped in my anger, I dismissed him with an angry wave as though he was an annoying fly.

This day passed. For the first time no villagers came by. Good! I was too upset to put on a kind face.

At night I ventured outside, sitting beneath the stars, struggling with my thoughts. I do not believe that all the sacrifices I made and the Netherworlds I crossed were in vain. I will not be deterred from my goal.

Day 15. *Fear is this color and its corresponding sound is a sickly yellow with splashes of gray created by sharp, discordant notes. It stems from the heart and gets tangled in the Emotion and Mental chakras. These in turn affect their corresponding Etheric Bodies. Fear is what motivated the Purge and fear is what enslaves us. Fear wears many faces: some ugly and frightful, some childhood like and beautiful. By shining a light on that darkened corner where it resides you will see not a creature, but emptiness.*

---Taleju's Dream and Echoes-

I had visions of Taleju after being been absent since completing the book. After the argument with Batu Khan, I was back at her village at the Bay of Biscay and I was shocked by her appearance. Since my visions, she has gradually slipped into illness and now her once beautiful, assured voice was but whispers. Her life energy was weak; that wonderful gold light dimmed. Rawdha tended to her and confessed her hopelessness to me.

Although I think I am a spirit only, they have always interacted with me as though I was a solid visitor. At first I wondered if the book brought me here, or I imagined it, but now I suspect I am from the future and visiting the past. But they spoke as though I am that which will come. At times it is disorientating.

Taleju watched me with stern, but understanding eyes. We conversed but I recalled only bits of our conversation. My Spirituality can only wake through me; it is time I step further into who I am to fully awaken. To do this I must break my chains and walk proudly in the sun as the One who is the Master of All. She encouraged me to continue bridging Normals and Seers into a single spiritual community but, she cautioned I must walk lightly as though dancing a delicate tune. Like glass, it could shatter.

Last evening we had a visitor. The woman I saw in Duraykish followed me here. She was a Seer from the Ninurta Wejdh; a Commonwealth north of the Levant and isolated by mountains. She heard about me encounter with the Aqaba tribe. During her trek she posed as a camel guide to keep her identity secret. While I was in prison she joined the crowd at the gates. She had been in communication with her friends back home and Batu Khan's village. It was her intervention that resulted in my rescue. During my escape she stayed in Persia Emirates to monitor the Kumari's activity until I was safe.

As customary I did not inquire her name but she did show her lapis birth stone carved with intricate letters. In addition her face's tribal tattoos she possessed five symbols indicating she was a spiritual initiate of high standing. She had light brown eyes, waist length black and graying hair hinting to her timeless beauty. She lacked two fingers on her right hand. A dark blue sash gathered the loose dress about her thin waist. Rose energy radiated from her calm demeanor and I sensed she was well known among the Seers. I was shocked to see Radha's name embroidered within geometric designs on her black and tan vest. When she explained her family gifted Taleju's book to the Aqaba tribe, I realized she was connected far more than she revealed. Her energy field was guarded so even if I showed bad manners by prying into it, I would fail. She observed all with far away eyes as did Taleju with that same, quiet assurance.

As per Seer customs, unless giving permission they address each other by their spiritual rank. Since she wears a blue sash of a high initiate, I address her as Blue. An elder said she is but half a dozen such esteemed persons, a very high Initiate called Aiftalah.

Day 17. I spent the day with Blue and Badu Khan at a small meeting chamber decorated with wall paintings and rugs. With daylight streaming through a window that bathed the room in gold light, we discussed Taleju's book, sipped tea and enjoyed dried pears while outside birds sang and flittered between rain storms. Blue was very interested in my translations and impressions of Taleju. She demonstrated how Seers mind connected and how to travel not only the physical but far deeper into spiritual realms. Until now I had a rudimentary understanding of Far Travel and limited in our world. Compared to her, my Far Sight was akin to an infant learning to walk. She and Batu Khan communicated via telepathy then Blue explained she would train me to achieve the goal Taleju wanted.

When I asked her to explain this further, she just smiled.

Blue is what they call a Celestial Dweller: people who accessed the inner realms or guide others. She explained each realm, like the earth, had unique sound and light roots; by focusing on these spirit are able to transcend time and space and enter. Until now my understanding of these places has been very limited and my access were sometimes haphazard and uncontrolled.

Blue 'locked' my awareness and gently guided me into these realms. Although this was but an introduction, I was frightened because my body felt like it was pulled apart.

The journey began by clearing my mind and peered through my third eye. I was here before, however, Blue kept me in this space instead of letting me to move out as I did previously. For awhile we waited, her soft voice encouraging calming myself and just waiting. Then gradually light and sound wrapped us I heard a far off sound. Then I immerse myself in this; a sensation of falling followed. Moments later I was at a strange world. Blue was beside me. We communicated via impressions about these worlds and how they were described by Taleju's Dream and Echoes. This was the first time I consciously controlled my visits beyond the physical. When finished, I was very exhausted and my head throbbed with a buzzing echo.

Applying the books deeper knowledge gave me profound understanding, a mixture of wonder and dread. I asked Blue about the book but she was not forthcoming with its history. She replied it is what is, and does not need stories to distract its importance.

Day 19. *To understand the Shadow Realm we must journey like gypsies with the enthusiasm of a new born. This is Spirit's quest: that thirst which drives our dreams, our curiosity, setting us upon the karma wheel of tears and joy. It is a difficult journey fraught with misgivings, doubt and loss and yet here is our ultimate expression: Compassion.*

Our species has for too long been enamored within its self imposed prison. The real work begins when we step from our darkened cell and see the sun for the first time.
   ----Taleju-Dream and Echoes-

   This morning Blue and the council discussed my future. The Seers have watched me since leaving Sofia and, despite my faults, conclude I am distained for a pivot role uniting us with the Normals---although to how or when no one knows. My translation of Dream and Echoes demonstrated my growing awareness and dedication to Taleju. They knew things about my past I do not, although I cannot think of something as damning being the cause for the Purge. They did not share these when I inquired. It is knowledge I must discover for myself (sigh).
   They were concerned that, every though I have translated the book, I am still in my infancy in my understanding and awareness of Taleju's practices. They hinted I do not have more incarnations to work on this. I have suspected this but until now I could not find answers. I felt like an uneducated child expected to master a complex musical instrument.
   Thus the Council and agreed to `show me the celestial path'. Blue explained it is a forced spiritual Awakening and came with all kinds of dangers, including madness or death.
   Oh, that is great! If it is anything like the previous session I dreaded this. I needed the day to think about this. I was turn between the pilgrimage and opening myself to all kinds of forces— forces I may not be able to control.
   But, by the time the sun set I gathered my courage. Perhaps my curiosity won or perhaps it was Taleju's words. So, here I go!
   Therefore this is perhaps the last evening of my old self. Tomorrow I will undertake the Seers intense journey into Taleju's mysteries.
   I asked Sarah, Yusuf and Sami to watch over me, tend to our needs and conduct the evening dedicational when I cannot.
   I am ready to face my fear and step into the abyss.

Day 25. I am unable to write due to my state so I dictated to Sarah after six days passed since my last entry. I lay upon bolsters at night. This room was but a dream; everything was transparent and vibrated with a multitude of melodies. Sarah sat at the table, her face impressions of gold and rose; I cannot tell if it was the lamp or her inner light.
   Sarah reported that a crowd waited my return from the hall. I have spent four days in the Hall, hovering between awareness and madness under the watch of Blue. Time meant nothing. I

was suspended in Infinity as Blue and Badu Khan cared for me. I shook, muttered incoherently and sat rocking back and forth, arm folded tightly across me while strange melodies swam through me being. I slipped in and out of consciousness.

They returned me to my room and I woke in a groggy state where Sarah offered meal and comforting hand and smile.

Ali, these sessions tortured my body and mind. I sometimes thought I partook in some grand experiment whose future is uncertain. I was forced into things I do not understand; yet bits of Taleju's information trickled through. Knowledge that cannot be explained, only comprehended directly. I was taken to the apex of Life by those who did not know what I do. I chuckled when recalling my childhood teacher saying 'the blind leading the blind.'

It is strange that I can enter these places where others cannot. Even Blue, who has journeyed with me to the deepest places within stayed behind while I proceeded, waiting patiently for my return and navigating the realms to bring me back.

I suffered continuous headaches, nausea, general ache and my head spun in drunken delight. I felt as though I ran a million kilometers for weeks without nourishment. I cannot sleep because wonderful images, melodies, color and sound relentlessly drowned me. I was too weak to speak. It is like I have died in this body and as spirit I am free. I do not see this realm but many overlaid upon each other like a kaleidoscope snapshot. It was so frightening and fascinating.

I joined Taleju when she died in that life long ago and Rawdha wept for days in that windswept, lonely place. I journeyed with the Kumari Mother to the Emotional, Psychic, Mental and even the Causative realms. I felt her tears, desires, loss and rewards having lived a trillion incarnations. She wandered the Halls of Incarnation where we go to select another life. She selected another and . . .

She who brought the Purge and the Awakenings is now she who walks here. The circle is complete. . .

Day 29. Sarah's note. Our beloved Taleju's representative is comatose for four days. She cannot be moved from her bed and so Blue joins me here to conduct the journey. She sits for hours on the floor, eyes closed and utterly quiet. I am compelled to think her asleep except for her occasional chant. Noora mumbles and several times I have seen her actually rise off the floor by invisible hands. A man comes by and sits in the corner, creating wonderful melodies with a large, metal bowl covered in writing. The entire room seems to shake and dance.

I thought I saw Noora stand beside me, surrounded by gold light but I am not sure if I was awake or had dozed off.

These people with their music and mystical ways scare me. They are like Djinn: shadowy and mysterious.   I will be glad when we leave.

Month 10 Day 1.   I cannot put into words what I have seen nor done these past days because I am very weak and disoriented. This afternoon I woke with Blue and Sarah seated nearby. My arms were unresponsive thus I dictated my words to Sarah while Blue listened.

I have taken that journey through the celestial gates; to that moment when I as spirit dreamt the desire that began my long journey upon this Incarnation wheel; wheels within wheels, forever and ever, a trillion orbs with a trillion different faces within this Shadow Realm. I was the first humans: a frightened creature taking that step outside my domain and walked beyond the distant hills where trees and grass no longer were the same. I was that which moved restlessly from place to place; afraid, alone and anxious. I saw threats in shadows, in streams, in meadows and in those companions around me. I feared myself and my own shadow cast by the hot sun. I traveled afar in quest of curiosity; yet I was still frightened from all which I walked through. I was a stranger to this world I explored; I felt apart, alone and different. Although this world brought comfort, the rocks, trees and rivers mocked me; I struggled against their insistence to isolate me from who I am.

Although I am spirit, I inhabited a foreign body prone to unsettling feelings, pain and harm. I am removed and lost within my reality.

I journeyed far to the ends of this world and bent nature to my way because I feared its invisible wisdom. That anxiety which I left long ago still haunts and walked beside me. I run as fast and never rest but it was here, always.   I cannot trust these things which I cannot see or understand, Most of all I cannot trust myself or others because I might lose this temporary body which I cling to so desperately.

Time moved and as far as I journeyed my eyes no longer saw wonderment or recalled who I am. Now I have only fear, dread and distrust in my heart. I am lonely and apart to this world of form.   I bent all to my will, hoping to forget pain and apprehensions. Yet no matter how much I tried, it was always with me.

This is the reality of mind and emotions' shadow which I am walking. It has no substance but what I gave them. However, this too, is but transparent dreams.

I woke after travelling this tormented path, spewed with billions of tears and stormy rage. Now I am that sun and this is my world in which I walk. I feel the ground beneath my feet, smell the fragrance flowers, I hear the waterfall and know these are reflection of who I am. The incarnation which I choose is but an extension of all that I AM; not isolated or alone.

I am humanity: Living in the impermanent and permanent realms simultaneously.

Day 2. Again, Sarah transcribed my words. I was confined to bed and raked by chills. I shivered from strange emptiness and waves of pain. M head throbbed and vision spun, forcing my eyes shut. Blue tended me and applied more tattoos to my forehead and face: Taleju's symbols of enlightenment. Sarah assisted turning me onto my stomach where Blue added more tattoos to my shoulders. These, she explained represent the realms I mastered their secrets. I have six, Blue five. Later a purple crystal speckled with gold was secured by leather around my neck. This was my birth crystal; I am now officially a Seer. Blue calls me by my new title: She who has Mastered All. I do not feel worthy of such praise for I am confused by this distinction because only Taleju held this title.

Later Batu Khan and others came by and performed ceremonies admitting me into their tribe. My clothes were taken away and were replaced by a blue, ankle length dress slit up the sides; white and purple long vest; black, baggy pants and cloth boots. The gold sash and embroider indicated my status. However I insisted I wanted to keep my yellow turban.

Tomorrow I hope to be strong enough to meet the pilgrims.

Day 3. My body still hummed and vibrates as my etheric energies were   integrated with my Being. I imagined I am a musical instrument receiving tunes from the inner realms.

Our physical eyes are invisible to the energy currents surrounding us which resemble waves of wonderful, translucent lights and patterns. Perhaps this is best because they can be distracting.

When Sarah set my tea on the table I was still in bed and reached up for it. Instead, I observed the cup not as a physical object, but its energetic makeup. My intent created disturbance in the energies surrounding it and as they solidified it caused the cup to move towards me via invisible hands. Startled, I quickly ceased. I never have performed Psychogenesis.

Intrigued, I observed how energies interact when Intent is triggered. It is like being in the ocean and every thought displaces currents that affect their surroundings. Concentric rings echo from the energy displacement, triggering some physical object response, weather movement or manifestation.

Having visited realms where movement is accomplished by intent I did not expect this here. Although tempting and infinitely slower in effect it can displace the natural flow of the physical realm and cause unwanted consequences, such as unintentional echo disturbances. I must be careful. Sarah's frightened expression reinforced this.

After and with great effort, I cleared these energies underlying physical manifestations from my head and focused on my physical surroundings. I was still very weak and unsteady on my feet. Dressing proved challenging; navigating the long passages and climbing the stone steps to outside take all my energy. Sarah accompanied and she assisted me onto a sunny rock and we watched the valley in the afternoon sun. This is such a beautiful and remote place.

The sun felt good and great age permeated here in the form of many colored energies overlaid upon each object. Everything was solid beneath my feet and I saw reality with startling clarity. Wherever I looked each rock, grain of sand, clouds, shadowy peaks and all reality noises: bray of cattle, children's laughter, bird fluttering in the azure sky, the snake slithering in the crags—here was life in all its splendor; a vast dream within a dream—solid, yet transparent and forever transient.

To observe Life suspended upon the Great Nothingness and know this _is_ energies of Infinity is unlike anything I imagined. Nothing in the Awakenings spoke or prepared me for this. Even Taleju's rainbow book only hints to Its greatness. We are blind to that in which we live, sleepwalking in this Grand Dream.

This evening I lead the dedicational. Many participated; it was a big crowd and the night grew long as I sat upon my rock answering questions. In the full night their faces vanished. Instead, I watched swirling energies and wonderful pulsating, music. Their beauty never ceased to amaze or astonish me.

Day 5. Throughout Dream and Echoes, Taleju said 'May your mirror be the Mirror of All Things,' of which I started using today at the conclusion of our Dedicational ceremony. I explained that we, as spirit, are reflections of the Infinite Consciousness. 'Ko eei tah ku,' is how Seer says this, and sounds like sparkling crystals reminding me of wind chimes. This saying reminded us of our goal and the path we walk. With changing this it refocused our attention away from the Kumargi to Taleju and her teachings. Thus began our transformation to self awareness outside religion.

On the first week of this month the Seers celebrate a three day event called The Butterfly. According to tradition, it was on the tenth month when Taleju and her companions, stranded in the White Desert, discovered her true identity as a Seer and Kumari Mother. This later led to friction among her companions and the division between Normals and Seers.

Each year Seer villages meet and select a person to represent the First Seer. My visit has stirred up much interest and thus I was chosen for this honored task. Beginning this morning my diet, which honored Taleju, was water and dates for two days. Other duties I will expect to do: make an effigy of the Purge Dubai building, collect hundreds of silk prayers in special containers, perform all night ceremonies honoring our long connection to humanity and perform the role as Alimajh at the sunrise dedicational. I fear it will leave me utterly exhausted and sleep deprived. I certainly hope I do not play a fool and botch this!

Day 6. The villagers continued preparing for the big festive tomorrow. Fresh paint was added to doorways, we replaced faded prayer streams on trees and dwellings, preparing the feasts, distributed ceremonial white tunics and crates of colorful dyes. As the First Seer---which is one of many titles I am known as--- I helped with assembling the huge thangka brought out each year for the ceremony which will be unveiled at the climax. Additionally I will preside over rituals and recite important passages. Sarah assisted in the community kitchen, making flat bread spiced with cinnamon and raisins. Pavlo and his family composed and practiced songs, Sami and Yusif tended camels and wagons and oversaw the running of our camp. Blue was constantly by my side, training me in the complex ceremonies. Everywhere there were singing, laughter and smiles.

This evening Batu Khan and the council called an emergency meeting after a rider delivered a sealed letter. I sense foreboding.

I worked through the night to finish copying passages from Taleju's rainbow book. When taking a break I discovered it was twilight! I franticly searched Dream and Echoes for a passage to share in our sunrise dedicational.

The mirror of our transient identity may shatter, but our reflection never dims. . .

As I spoke a meteor shower lit up the northern heavens. We watched, transfixed.

Day 7. Ceremony of The Butterfly. Late night. I huddled over lamp to write about this wild day, exhausted and covered in sweat and paint.

This busy day began before the sunrise dedicational when I shared a meal of bread, cheese, hummus and tea with Batu Khan and the village elders, marking the end of my two day diet. After having just water and dates this meal was especially tasty and wholesome! But I had stomach cramps the rest of the morning.

Afterwards we transformed into Purge Children. We carefully applied black, red, white, or red paint to our hands, face, feet and hair to resemble skeletons. We wore simple white tunics as a sign of death. Families covered their tunics with names of deceased friends, relatives or important events from the previous year. I, being the First Seer, lacked any writing because I represented our world before the Purge. Instead I had a black and gold lettering waist sash representing the world's karma.

Just as the western sky started waking, we gathered at a special cliff beyond our village where upright rocks have been painted with red, blue, green and purple symbols. I sat beneath a massive tree thick with budding waxy leaves, surrounded by crates and distributed red dates to each, solemn person. When first light illuminates the distant hills, I reminded the crowd that today we began our journey into Rebirth by eating the same dates as our Kumari Mother. Then, I held up my copy of Echoes and Dreams and announced Taleju's gift was ready for the Children of the Purge to share her vision. What was silenced for millennium is now spoken.

I was so nervous I feared I might forget the message, but Blue sat with me and gently coaxed these words from my mouth.

We are spiritual beings sharing the common awareness of who we are; this gift is not exclusive to anyone, nor owned by anyone but accessible to all without condition or promise. Herein lays a path to our Infinite journey which only we can undertake and only we alone can face our hardship, triumphs and tribulations. This is our personal experience into Enlightened Beings as Taleju's spoke.

Sarah and Blue distributed copies we had slaved over for so long to bring. I did not hide my feeling of accomplishment. I was giddy with the excitement that Taleju's word was finally accessible.

Silk prayer flags stuffed in ceramic jars were loaded onto carts and transported to the place where the wood and paper effigy of the Dubai tower stood in the middle of clearing. After placing the jars around the effigy, I led the group to a cliff where waited the huge thangka. Standing on either side, Blue and I lifted the blue and gold coverings. The thangka was an intricate work showing Taleju's journey from birth to death. These events revolved a central geometric pattern representing the Wheel of Life. For each year this thangka was in this ceremony a mirrored glass was added to its border. There were five rows, showing this thangka was over a thousand years old.

Pavlo played a sacred melody on his flute while I tapped finger bells and sung.

Kumari Mother who brought the Light. Kumari Mother who gave us Music and Flight from the Illusions we created. We honor you; we sing Infinity's praise and set our feet upon the path of awareness; beyond space, time or action. To the infinite moment, that place of calm understanding where all manifestations are but suspended patterns in Nothingness. All are transient except us. We see where blindness reigns.

Finishing, Blue set ceramic pots filled with powder dye before me and I smeared purple dye on my face. Then the crowd line up in front of ceramic pots filled with powder dye. This represented our new Seer human: colorful in our vision, aware of the energetic melodies permeating life. Everyone took hand fill of dye and flung them at the crowd, uttering prayers and blessings. At first they were reserved and timid but the music and dance worked their magic and soon give way to eager abandon. It was everybody's goal not have specks of white remain but reflect life's abundant colors. Rainbow dust clouds enveloped all as people laughed, danced, sing, and pelted one another. Even I was caught up in the mood and as I went among the crowd, joining the merrymaking. I was soon transformed into a colorful expression!

Food was abundant and the special sweet bread complimented the heady wine fueling this occasion. When my senses whirled and exhaustion set in I sat upon a rock and, covered like an artist palette, watched the festivities late into the afternoon. I hardly recognized Sarah and the others, for they are so disheveled and covered with dye. After the afternoon dedicational we dispersed to partake feasting and merriment with relatives and friends. I joined the pilgrims and Seers and shared special sweet bread with them. With prodding from Blue, who constantly kept watch over me to make sure I did my tasks correctly, I reminded them that when taking nourishment from our physical labor and gifts, so too, should we immerse ourselves in Infinity's Music and Light, as our guide.

At evening the rainbow masses assembled for the evening dedications. We were reflective and quiet as I led the ceremony. We watched stars slowly replace the day and when the silver moon appeared I led the crowd to the effigy, shaking small bells, rattles and clacking hollow sticks. From the gathered crowd Batu Khan and I approached the tower and lit it. In a few minutes roaring flames danced into the sky and covered all with soft amber illumination. As sparks floated up and joined the stars in the heavens,

I announced that we were now Butterflies and never again will we allow the Purge consciousness to poison us. We are spiritual beings now, raised from the ashes.

Then, everyone strips off their drenched clothes and tosses them onto the fire. Naked we watched the flames take away the memories, each lost within our thoughts. I remembered you, Bishma and Ali, and the events that brought me here. So much pain, loss and hopes dashed. My heart ached for your comforting touch; I was so alone and tears wetted my cheeks.

Then, when the flames transformed into glowing coals, we quietly dispersed. People greeted me with our new saying. I sensed a new beginning on this night.

Day 8. Today the village rested while I continued my duties as First Seer. I was up before first light and having washed and in fresh clothes, I felt renewed. I led the Council and Batu Khan to the pyre where we took the burnt jars to the craftsmen where they transformed these into new glass ornaments.

In the afternoon we handed these 'Butterfly medallions' to each family who exchanged last year's medallion. These we will take to the White Desert to complete the ceremony. The thangka was disassembled and stored for another year. I visited each residence, handing our sweet cakes, offering blessings and inspiration. Naturally I had to share this offerings and by evening I was tired and sick from overeating, hiding my exhaustion behind feigned smile and enthusiasm.

I confess that after all I've been though I am still uncomfortable around people, their accolades and their expectations. Ali, you know how I prefer to be alone with my thoughts. This notoriety goes against my character.   At times it is a struggle to listen and offer words because I feel awkward and unworthy of their attention. Taleju said she experienced these and I will have to accept this. Ugh! Not what I'm looking forward to.

Day 9. Today I was supposed to prepare a select group for the trip into the White Desert and complete the Butterfly ceremony. However, an unforeseen development dashed this plan.

This morning Blue brought a poster of me distributed by the Central Kumari throughout Persia. It was given to the Zhayyd

Council who did not tell me until after the festivities. I was so enraged. In part it reads:

Be it proclaimed that Noora Al-Monte of the Sophia Commonwealth, who joined the Transformation ceremony on 1262 AP, is hereby convicted of these crimes: heresy, <u>blasphemy</u>, falsifying testimony, inciting disobedience, refusing to cooperate with the Western Kumari Daughter, claiming to be a Kumari Deputy, threatening Kumargi integrity, their pilgrims and spreading false doctrines.

Our Central Kumari Daughter, beloved representative of our Kumari Mother Taleju, hereby sentence Noora Al-Monte to death and summon all Kumargi to eradicate this heathen threat. As reward for fulfilling this edict Kumargi and their families will receive special honor as 'Taleju's warriors' and granted permanent Kathmandu residence as Mokti. Her body may be delivered to any Kumari temple for identification.

Signed: Central Kumari Daughter

Included was information about my height, weight, appearance and distinguishing marks. Blue mentioned the Kumari was pressuring the Persian Emirates and businesses to cooperate or be punished. I knew it was but a matter of time before the Kumargi showed its true self.

I left the meeting under silent rage. Later I dismissed Sarah and Blue and spent the day drowned in my dark anger.

Our religion created from the Purge ashes threatens to divide us, a religion which originally intended to unite us as spiritual Beings.

At first I ignored it, then I tried running away but I as fated to assume the role and heal this divide. After journeying into the Realms I understand I incarnated here to fulfill my destiny. Same stage, different set pieces.

I am depressed, lonely and confused. The whole world's weight is upon my shoulders. How shall I approach this?

Day 10. Today I visited Batu Khan's family, sharing their chores and preparing for the trip. Their white stone house was modest, with a central courtyard and inside two fruit trees reputed to be several hundred years old. In keeping with Seer tradition their house was built into a hillside, connected by many tunnels and has a predominant purple dome, the spiritual level of his initiation. With the exception of the courtyard, most rooms were dug out of native rock and decorated with Life Rugs or wonderful murals. From the courtyard gate I sighted the distant gray peaks of the Hindustan Corridor shrouded in heavy clouds.

Batu Khan knew my troubles and promised support. However he cautioned my response will not only affect us, but Normals who currently are suspicious of other. He warned we cannot gamble humanity's' future by returning to the past. I agree. However my methods may not be what he intends when I decide to act.

Yet, conversing with his daughters and sons, sharing their family pride, their role in the village and dreams of a world where travel and trade offer far off opportunities, smoothed my moodiness.

Batu Khan was the son of a merchant who extensively traveled beyond the Levant and Anatolia. He spent childhood visiting the known world, mostly staying within the Seer commonwealth but occasionally ventured into Purge nations long turned into dust. He suffered the indignity of fear, resentment and mistrust—all those subconscious emotions that plagued humanity. As a teen he took over his dad's business until settling here after being elected onto the Council. He dedicates him life to his people—always striving to incorporate Taleju's wisdom in everyday life.

His wife, Ameen, from a mountain settlement far to the north, is an expert in healing medicine; using herbs and energetic to balance illness. They had four children, ages 8-15 and seemed very happy. Like many villagers, they believe I am the next evolutionary bridge between our two species.

And Taleju's messenger.

At the evening Dedicational I spoke of the gathering storm and courage we must face. We will resume our pilgrimage as promised and meet the Kumarisattva in Nepal. To encourage them, I read from Taleju's Awakenings:

The journey is hard, long, filled with doubt and self discovery. We are huddled here, in this desolation; little food, no water, far from our homes and blind to what lies ahead. Our spirits are low; our bodies wracked by exposure and little rest; yet the passion burns in our hearts. We are determined to visit those places scarred by the Purge and bring hope to the suffering and stories of our adventures to those back home. We live not for us but our Purge Children.

Day 11. Far sight showed Deva and her followers camped in a valley about a month's trip away, their progress halted and forced to wait until the monsoon flooding season ended. The soldiers numbered a hundred, consisting of the Persia Commonwealth and Kumari. The pilgrims harbor resentment and dissention runs deep. I sensed Deva's anxiety over her responsibilities.

When I touched Altus's mind he was momentarily startled and seemed aware. I quickly withdraw, not wanting to reveal myself.

Oh, how I miss them!

At the big hall I and Blue sat on prayer rugs and met with the Council. We discussed the threats and my intentions. Although they were reluctant, they agreed Seers had to move against the Kumargi and begin humanity's healing. I could no longer live in the shadows. They believed once I left Khorasan Wedjh then eminent threat to their homelands would stop. I doubted this and warned Normals may decide Seers are too influential to coexist.

Despite our reluctance, and how distasteful the reasons are, we had to use Normal's fear about us to create the dialogue to heal things between us. Superstition has, thus far, has kept us apart and fearful.

When it came to religious affairs, eventually their ancient fear will no longer protect us. Again it was emphasized the outcome must not jeopardize our future. Batu Khan volunteered his warriors to accompany to ensure our safety.

Blue kept quiet through the meeting until we were alone. She remarked I would have to overcome my demons and karmic past if we are to survive. I assured her I will.

This evening at the Dedicational I outlined our plan to leave in two days. Excitements run through the group. They were restless and wanted to resume pilgrimage to Nepal.

Day 12. Thunder, lightning and rain torrents cloaked our world. Sarah and I packed our belongings. During those brief moments between storms I wandered outside and watched the waterfalls, pools and inhale fresh, damp air. It was invigorating; like washing away the old dust before a journey. I shall miss this place and its innocence; it has been my home. In some ways I felt that I was born here and will hold it close to my heart.

Day 14. We camped twelve kilometers from Zhayyd after a grueling day of travel. It was still raining and I huddled warm and dry beneath our black, goat's hair tent. We departed this morning with about four hundred eager devotees who had the distinction of being the first Seers making the pilgrimage. We will visit the White Desert to perform the last Butterfly ceremony before heading into Hindustan Corridor and intercept the pilgrims. It promises to be a fast paced trip; for we have to cover nearly a thousand kilometers in less than three weeks. By the next new moon, the Pilgrimage will resume. Batu Khan explained this is the summer and the passes will then open.

To travel fast we carried minimal provisions and expected to procure supplies in villages once we enter the Hindustan region. I will have to be extra diligent because we cannot attract attention that might warn the main group of our approach. I do not yet know what will happen when we find them. I am frightened and eager for our encounter.

The rain created hundreds of waterfalls along the plateau traversing the valley, promising greenery and abundance for another year. In Taleju's time there was nothing but desolation and disease. She spoke of passing dead cities heaped with bones and covered by rats. Now time has healed this land; I occasionally glimpsed concrete walls through sand and dirt; we followed a flat stretch covering an ancient road. We rode or walked hunkered down in our thick robes against the rain and breeze. Sometimes we detoured when torrents blocked our trail. At times it was slippery trekking through canyons heaped with smooth boulders. We were ever watchful for slides and flash floods. Whenever we could, we travelled above the bottom of ravines. I used my Far Sight to study conditions and made abrupt changes, saving our group from perilous ordeals.

Sarah served tea. In the waning light I read Dream and Echoes, trying to gleam answers for my upcoming role.

Day 18. We broke camp early and for days travelled before sunrise to long pass sunset; allowing the moon to illuminate our path until Batu Khan halted us. With minimal rest, the long hours blended painfully slow into one another. My muscles ached and I was numb from riding. When I walked my hips reminded me of my old wounds.

We made good time and sometimes the rain stopped, giving hours of sunlight and fog rising from drenched soil. We crossed a plain of red sand which left black tracks in passing. Batu Khan said we were on a buried field of dried tar, a product from the Purge. Taleju called this the Black shell and was like glittering glass when she passed through here.

At the base of lava cliffs we found a stream and let the camels drink while we filled our containers. Mosquitoes, bugs and snakes were thick, making this their temporary home before it dried up. The mosquitoes liked Duce and when we left he was covered with itchy welts. Blue applied herbs to alleviate his misery.

Later, while I rested in the shade, an emerald snake with red and black stripes bathed on a sunny rock next to me. It watched me. I was warned it is very poisonous and one bite is fatal. I did not feel threatened, only admiration for this creature and its desolate world.

My inner vision saw this valley hummed with green and blue energy. The sound it created attracted the life we observed. And as I close my eyes I distinguished the energetic melodies of bugs, snakes and other unseen creatures. It was a peaceful island in this desolation.

We paused only briefly for the evening Dedicational and then travelled another five hours. Our pace was so frantic, I had but minutes to write and capture some sleep.

Day 22. For the past week we traveled between violent storms and violent winds, forcing us to delay as we sought shelter. Time seemed to crawl, we covered kilometers yet the terrain did not change. We hurried, resting but a few hours. Our travel seemed like a dream, my memory blurred.

Yesterday the storms which constantly harassed us vanished, replaced by a stark cloudless sky where the sun burned unprotected skin. I had to realize at this higher altitude the air was thinner, therefore the sun's light is more intense than Sofia. We rode in drenched clothes as our body heat dried them out. I itched and my joints irritated by sand. At places our tracks break through the hard, packed sand, revealing pools which quickly filled. In some ways we were lucky because in the high summer this valley was covered with white dust that clogged breathing and acted like sand paper on flesh. In the Awakenings Taleju wrote:

Kilometer and kilometer of powdery dust; it lingers like a fog to the horizon. In places visibility is reduced to a few meters. Even with cloth about our faces and goggles tight each breath brings irritation and dries out the lungs so my throat is raw from coughing. Sometimes I glimpse strange objects lying like corpses in the middle of nowhere. When we draw closer I realize they are wood and steel ships.

Batu Khan remarked before the Purge this was a huge lake with many cities.

Bone chilling damp and cold sucked our body's heat after sunset. At night this was a frightful place with moaning winds and the bodies of ships playing tricks with our vision. We hurried and continue far into the night.

Day 23. I copied this account of Taleju's journey not found in the Awakenings but her original manuscript attached in a separate section of her rainbow book. There are about 5 pages. This passage hints that she is a Seer and the reason for the Butterfly celebration.

Iran, White Desert

Here, beneath the only tree in this desolation, a scrawny specimen about two meters high with large, waxy leaves and a bottle shaped truck I take refuge from the sun. It is hot, dusty and frightfully still. Nothing moves in the afternoon light.

Yet I hear music. These delicate melodies surround me: sometimes whispers, sometimes like flute, string or drum. It pulsates, dance and beckon. Each note I feel moving through every cell in my body. Accompanying these melodies colors swirl in, around and through me as if this music is me. They become patterns: spirals, streamers, twinkling, grids, geometric and circles within circles all connected, mingle and move through each other; this dance of life. Then my mind opens and I am suspended upon infinitely. I understand these patterns of color which exist beyond my physical eyes. This is the world in which we all walk and are blind to its beauty. So many patterns suspended in Nothingness; a great, cosmic wheel ever turning throughout Infinity.

I realize all things. We are this: Spirit dancing through Infinity.

The White Desert is part of the dry lake's eastern area, composed of kilometers of blinding, sparkling gypsum. At times we were forced to turn our gaze away or kept heads lowered and faces covered. The ground crunched with each step, sending up fine dust and coating everything. The flat terrain was undisturbed except distant, black rocks. In this nothingness, on a small rise we came upon the biggest tree I've ever seen; a lone sentinel offering shade and shelter. Its massive roots stretched for kilometers; at places they rose like walls and we had to cautiously navigate this maze.

We reached this tree midday where legend said Taleju discovered she was a Seer. Its broad trunk was more than thirty meters across and covered with sacred carvings. The main branches measured nearly ten meters thick and twisted about each other like vines. I guessed this tree was more than a hundred meters tall. The Seers call it 'The Dream Tree' and dangling from its branches were thousands of glass ornaments from each Butterfly ceremony since more than a thousand years. From our camp we had a continuous view of the flat plain to the horizon.

The massive tree was home for large black and red birds, snakes and iridescent green beetles. Bird activity and melodies broke the deafening silence since leaving Zhayyd. The beetles created a cascade of low and high pitch thumps as they scurried over branches. It was early summer so the giant tree was covered with purple blossoms the size of grapefruit. They gave off sweet perfume. The breeze conducted a light show to tinkling music from ornaments that seem to have a life of their own. Someone said the tree was dancing a greeting.

We had but a few hours to perform the ceremony. A large, sealed ceramic container covered with symbols and dated 1263 were unloaded and stuffed with prayer flags and last year's ornaments. I tied blue and gold streamers round its thick side and lead the group carrying it to the bottom of the rise. There, peering through sand and dirt were many more such jars; heaped up through centuries and forming a huge base around the black rocks surrounding the tree. A hole was dug and I place it inside and then I recited the blessing. Using red wax sealed the symbolic dreams for the coming year. I wondered about the thousands of other jars and the hopes and dreams they carried.

Batu Khans handed me an elaborate, silver necklace of bells, chimes and blue glass. A harness was tied around my waist and shoulders. I watched in apprehension as an assistant stood atop his camel and tossed a thick rope over the nearest branch as thick as a man's torso. Then, securing one end of the rope to the camel saddle he gently guided it forward, pulling me into the sky. Dismayed I watched my world spin until grabbing onto the branch and with much effort pulled myself up. I was twenty meters above our group, clinging desperately to this tree limb. After crawling to the outermost area I hung the necklace but lost my grip. I fall off, screaming and suddenly felt a hard tug breaking my fall. For a few minutes I dangled in the air, swinging and twirling until the rope was lowered and I was freed.

Ugh! I never want to go through that again.

Batu Khan slipped an identical necklace around my neck and proclaimed that I will always be referred to the First Seer. It would take an entire paragraph to write all the titles I've accumulated, none of which really suit me.

But, I was shocked and angry when Blue called me Taleju. It was one thing pilgrims using her name, but not my close companion! I do not know if it was deliberate or a slip. I was not silent reprimanding her.

It was now sunset and I led the Dedicational. Standing upon that rise, watching as the light faded beneath the purple horizon I realized tomorrow will mark more than a year since leaving home. I am sad and anxious when I recalled all that has happened.

Day 26. So much has changed since taking that naive step outside my home. I was filled with hope, dreams and wishes;

wanting to prove my dedication and complete the promise I made to you, Ali and Bishma. I sought the Kumari's approval and wanted to wear the Mokti title proudly.

Oh how that innocence is gone! As Joseppi promised, the journey will change me in ways never imagined. That optimistic, shy woman is forever gone. Her innocence shattered like a virgin after her wedding night. I sometimes wonder if our village is but a dream and that I have spent my life in this harsh desert with my family of Seers.

Ali, there are many times I shiver with doubt. This task I have taken is so great, so vast that I fear I will be crushed by its weight. If you met me on the street you would not recognize your beloved wife and Bishma would think I am a stranger. I have changed so much that I do not know who I really am. It is only those small, ceramic bottles with your ashes that keep me connected to myself and the past we shared.

Today we passed the Khorasan Wedjh border after climbing out of a gravel plain and steep canyon. We camped in a lava field filled with massive boulders and black pumice. Ahead lay a range of hills and beyond the Hindustan Mountains bordering western Nepal. Dark, storm clouds roamed their peaks, reminding of that I am rushing toward my fate. What it holds for the Kumargi? I only see darkness as I stare into my heart.

The Hindustan Corridor

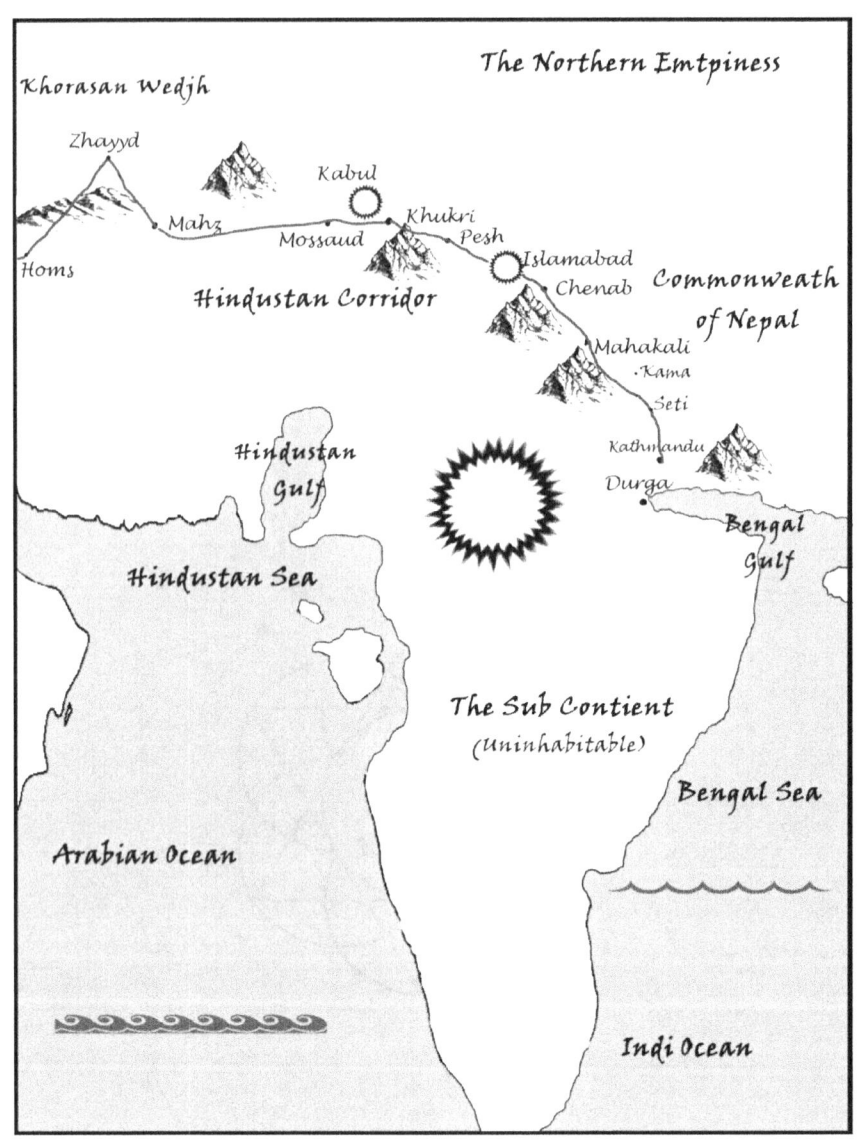

Month 10, Day 30.   Mahz, Hindustan Corridor. We travelled four days and reached Mahz, main trade center. Routes north to the Caspian Sea, south to the Hindustan Gulf and east beyond the Hindustan mountains met. This is the final stop before venturing into the great ranges separating us from Nepal.

Mehz is a collection of mud and tiled, domed buildings interspersed by rings of communal gardens and orchards. It overlooks a long, arid valley where at the far end red and speckled brown cliffs mark the borders to a salt lake which they harvest. Not much grow here due to lack of moisture but the city created intricate cisterns, supporting goods they export: salt, yogurt, spices, some variety of fruits, salt, carpets and baskets. Because of its location it does brisk business from all over the known world. Batu Khan remarked it is the only city of size in the Hindustan Corridor. Beyond Mehz, we will only find isolated villages.

Mehz is also important to the Kumari. Supposedly Taleju's footprints are embedded in a river rock. A building encases this and for a fee devotees can see it. My curiosity compelled me to visit, although we won't be staying long.

The world ahead is void of any living creature as I stand on a rise and gaze west into a hazy, steely horizon. On a flat plain populated by sand, gravel and black boulders we found a wadi with pools of sour water and camped in the protection of the bank from harsh, cold winds sweeping down from the north. Our party is sick and weak from our ordeal across the mountains and constant exposure to the elements. Dark, menacing clouds cover the southern sky, reminding me that the subcontinent pestilence carried on raging storms may reach us.

A strange sight greets me. Across from where we camp is a red and black flower in the rocky bank. Its petals are texture of crape and its center is faded red but grow more intense towards the tips. In the flower's center is a black ring with yellow tipped pistils. It is the first color I had seen in months. I brave the pool and ankle deep water to see it. I nearly trip in the slippery pool and smooth rocks but I reach it. The flower is sweet and I spent an hour admiring it there until the cold wind overcame me.

---Taleju's account at Mahz-

This flower is called `Taleju's Eye' and is the town's symbol displayed on banners, buildings and clothes.  The city's name is `Flower' in the Hindustan dialect.

We encountered Seer travelers but the inhabitants did not give them unwanted attention. While the main party camped kilometers away in a canyon our small group went for supplies.

We posed as book merchants while Batu Khan tended to business. Seers are famous for offering old books and manuscripts to an eager public thirsting for material from far off places. With our distinct camels identifying us we set up portable stalls near the main gate. Soon a crowd gathered. They did not recognize me because I kept my face covered with scarf and goggles. Members of the Kumari, in their distinct red and yellow robes came by, pretending to shun us but interested in our books. They bourse and purchased some old manuscripts. Later towards evening when Batu Khan returned with camel and provisions, I and Blue visited the city.

Oh, how I loved the din of activity and the smell of spices and wonderful food! This city was rich in sensual delights. Despite people in drab brown or gray robes and tunics, their kufi and vests were decorated with bright, colored mirrors, making them sparkle. Likewise, their flat roofed dwellings had colored mirror accents around windows and doors.

There are many religions here echoing from the Pre Purge; a belief in a sky warrior god whose son visited earth long ago, another honors a messenger or another worshipping the Eternal Flame. But the predominant belief is Taleju. We went to the temple having Taleju's footprint but our entrance was blocked by Kumari officials whom I recognized visited us earlier. It was then I noticed the poster about me tacked to the door. I was angry but do not make a scene. Rather, Blue and I sat near the entrance, listening to the Dedicational call and watched devotees shuffle into the temple. With far gaze I roamed the room, admiring lush carpets and delicate, colorful wall murals depicting Taleju. In the middle of the chamber and atop an ornate pedestal was a smooth rock. On it were what appeared to be three, vague footprints but could be whatever people believed.

In the darkness Blue, I and the others returned to camp.

It was late. A storm threatens and we leave in three hours.

Month 11, Day 3. *I come to prove to humanity that we can break the chains of spiritual slavery and be free from our self imposed prisons. The Old Ways have not served us well because they enslaved and destroyed our world though dogma and self serving idolatry. It is time we realize we are spirits connected to all things throughout Infinity and no one holds us hostage from our destiny. This unity is available to All.*

We are not separate tribes. We are a planetary community of spiritual expression.---Taleju, Echoes and Dreams-

Although we are fragmented and still cling to tribal mentality, we are further along in our spiritual understanding than before the Purge. However, the Kumargi insists on discouraging outsiders from questioning its role. It is this spirituality control Taleju warned against and the reason I must act. I loathe conflict and spent my life avoiding it. However, I now see I have incarnated to ensure her original teachings are available as she intended. I must brush aside my doubts, trust my vision, and have the courage to face the Kumargi nightmare as well as mine.

During these long hours of wake and sleep I wrestle with my desires. I fear I shall bring disaster upon this world if I am not careful challenging a powerful, spiritual ideology. Yet, if I do not act then we chance slipping back into the Old Ways where selfish greed and fear ruled.

My closest friends sensed my struggle but they cannot help. This is a journey I must take alone, to bring balance and come full circle to that which began so long ago. I accept what karmic echoes I create, although reluctantly.

We travelled day and night and slept little. The mountains gradually closed in. The terrain was varied: gravel or lava fields, rocky valleys and steep slopes so massive our progress was but a few kilometers on narrow switchbacks. Since leaving Mahz we have not seen a village or met anyone on the trail. At night the air was brisk while travelling in the day were hot, dry and hazy. At times my breath was irritated by the sandy air. I developed a persistent cough.

The ride was tough. We pushed ourselves until exhaustion. Every muscle ached; my nerves tingled and at the end of each day I suffered a stupor where thoughts came slow to my painful body. At times I was too uncomfortable to ride thus walked, other times I could not stand after being hours in the saddle. I ate little. Nothing was appetizing and everything had that same, grainy, sandy taste. Yet, by my calculations, we were gaining. The main group was but a few days ahead.

A particularly stiff breeze blew down from the mountains this afternoon. Blue wanted to fly a special kite she brought to break our misery and cheer us up. We camped early while she and others assembles the large silk kite resembling a phoenix. It even had articulated wings. Oh, it's red, blue and yellows shone brightly and enriched our gray and brown world! When its wings flapped, beautiful melodies played and reminded me of the swans back home! It did not take long for Duce and his family to add music, nor Batu Khan passing around a heady wine. Our silence was replaced by laughter and dance. For awhile we forgot our purpose and lived in this joyous moment.

Day 5. *The journey through the Hindustan is so rough I wonder if chancing the Sub continent's plague, desolation and sickness was a better idea. Although we are far from the Subcontinent's gray ash, their Black Clouds reach us and we are exposed to their horror as it falls in torrents, sometime appearing so quickly we have no warning. We are covered in black, stinky and sticky droplets, getting through our clothes and into our months and eyes. We hide in whatever shelters we find or, unlucky, have to endure this pestilence in the open. Sometimes we wait days for the storm to pass. It leaves us sick and weak; we are delayed in our journey which now stretches seven months instead of three as planned.*
----Taleju's trip into the Hindustan region-

Yesterday morning we passed a stone column painted brown with white symbols. Batu Khan explained we have entered the Six Tribe's territory. The pilgrim camp was only three days away. He guided us to another trail far removed from the main road.

The valleys closed in with tall mountains on either side. The roar of waterfalls echoed through the valley and cascaded through ravines, at times obscuring the trail with dense, cool mist.

Later I saw distance stone dwellings and the few trees marking a settlement. The structures were decorated by multicolored pebbles embedded in their walls and window and door frames painted bright blue or yellow. Some roofs had long poles holding metal cans to catch water and produced low hums in the constant breeze. These sounds filled the valley with mournful, disturbing wails, adding to gloominess which permeated everything.

I was curious about these people and used Far Sight to observe them.

The women wore blue dresses, dark green coats, felt boots and pointed, felt hats. They adorned themselves with heavy, silver necklaces, bracelets and rings. Their black hair was braided, hung over their back or coiled down to their slender neck. The men's clothing was brown, baggy pants tucked in felt boots, and long gray or black tunics. Over these they wore decorated blue, green or yellow vest and a pointy, felt hat with dyed fur band. Unlike the women, they did not have jewelry but carried silver daggers in wide, waist sash. They shaved their heads and had hawkish faces, bushy beards or thick moustaches.

We kept to the narrow trail for another day then around midnight we climbed out of the valley. We rested, about a day from our goal. We forego fires Everyone was tense, tired and quiet.

Day 7. Taleju wrote. *We came upon a wide valley after spending weeks descending a broken road. The valley is littered with rusting steel and ruins buried in rock and dirt. Patches of black road peer between the wastes that once carried people to a pre Purge place called Herat. Wild dogs and rats inhabit this place, constantly threatening us. The dogs' mournful cries echo across the valley, leaving us uneasy.*

Yet, there is beauty. Towards evening at the base of a waterfall we find a brackish pool. Yet when I placed my hand in to test its quality the pool sparkled like a blanket of stars. The illumination lasts but a short time but reappears when agitated. We spent hours here amusing ourselves with this soft, glittering pale blue glow. Parvati calls this the Valley of Light.

Since Taleju travelled through here over a thousand years ago the Valley of the Light has remained the pilgrimage resting point preparing the last leg of their journey. In times past they waited for the snows to clear from higher elevations but since then global warming has rendered the passes mostly free of snow. Now they waited for the spring monsoon, brought from the Subcontinent, to subside. These floods have claimed many foolish travelers. Even the Hindustan avoid these trails during this time. Generally our pilgrims would have reached Nepal prior to the monsoon but our setbacks had finally caught up with us.

Tonight our group reached the entrance into the Valley of Light and, although we were exhausted, we were restless about our meeting tomorrow. We observed the valley bathed in full moon from our elevated perch in the hills and rocks. A river, covered on each bank by heavy trees, meandered between steep hills. The river was swollen, but by late summer it will shrank to but a shadow of its former self. The river vanished behind steep, tooth like rocks to a dimly lit village called Six Tribes. Here was the neutral zone overseen by the dominating tribes.

No violence is permitted and all disputes are handled through the council. Even travelers are warned to be cautious in their dealings. Although it is suppose to be peaceful, transgressors are severely dealt with. Batu Khan warned all dealing with the tribes is delicate and we must consider many factors so no tribe is offended. The old, tribal ways of the pre Purge still reside here.

Over these past few nights I could not sleep as I wrestle with my plan. Despite Batu Khan's fervent warning to control my feelings, my anger has dominated my journey since leaving Khorasan Wedjh. I sensed mounting tension between my pilgrims. Some want me to return, others not. I am torn between how to proceed.

Day 8. The events of this day lay upon me, wrapping me in shocked despair, leaving me despondent over my foolishness.

I hoped our meeting would usher new dawn of peace where we could continue our pilgrimage as united devotees. But instead I violated the Seer's most sacred oath and brought shame upon myself and others.

Where to begin?

Shortly before sunrise we broke camp and reached the valley at midmorning. They were expecting us. Via Far Sight I saw their camel riders drawn behind a line of shields and spear in front the main camp. When they spotted us they sent the alarm via a horn that echoed though the valley.

We slowed and Batu Khan ordered no escorts were to raise shield or swords, lest they would mistake us for aggression. Drawing a breath of courage I and Batu Khan led our group. They fanned out in single row behind me and we quietly proceeded in a line, our banners held high, fluttering in the cold breeze.

I hoped our behavior would be peaceful but the sharp echo of swords being drawn told me otherwise. From soldiers red angry lights swirled like the hiss of hundreds of snake, betraying their emotions. This energetic force overwhelmed me with nausea, momentarily paralyzing my thoughts. I quickly cleared this vision.

Hundreds of hostile eyes watched us as we stopped before their battle line. Tense moments passed after I demanded to speak with Deva. Before Bramaputra replied, Deva and Altus barked orders. The line of defenders parted and escorts followed them. Deva ordered them to stay and they approached us alone. She looked gaunt and distressed, Altus anxious.

I dismounted and joined them. I foolishly thought this would be a joyous reunion. I quickly learned it was not.

Deva showed the Central Kumari letter. She and Altus pleaded we should leave because our presence would bring trouble. I said I was aware but we could reach a compromise and reach Nepal together. I explained I was just trying to bring Normal and Seer together and share Dream and Echoes.

I added, even if we left I will be hunted because the Kumargi considers me a threat and because of this I will not run.

Altus was disappointed and Deva looked at our riders. She shook her head and commented please forgive her for what happened. I echoed the same and we parted.

With no order from either, Bramaputra signaled and archers fired arrows. Some landed in front of our camels. Batu Khan raised his shield and blocked several arrows. His riders did the same. One ripped through the shoulder of my blouse but the only damage it did was to my pride. My anger swelled and, trying to control my rage, I turned and walked back to my camel, arrows striking the ground around me. But instead of mounting, I faced them defiantly as my hatred.

Bramaputra shouted and his soldiers charged, their yelling and clattering of armor shattered the tension.

I stood, watching as arrows fell around me. My heart was consumed by fire.

Then, the rage I carried since this pilgrimage drowned me in red a fiery storm tore through my inner restraints. I pulled energies around me like a person dying of thirst and focused it through my hands. The surrounding energies blinded me, its heat searing my mind; I was all consumed with power and realized I could crush these bugs with hardly an effort.

I waited, like an archer drawing the bow.

Then I released my hatred. A sickening, ruby flash smashed the group and through the chaos I saw physical energies dim as riders scattered in this explosion of violence. Horrible screams followed.

The field was momentarily stunned but the soldiers quickly regrouped and charged again.

This time I did not fear and walked at them, cursing and shouting.

This was a fight to the death. All this power! I felt invincible and caught in the moment. Unable to control myself I became a focus of energies, taunting my enemies with shouts and curses. All around me I saw only red and the shadowy flicker of spirits torn from their limp bodies.

Horrified, Batu Khan waved for the party to retreat while he and my red sash guards surrounded me. Batu Khan shouted a phrase and my energies suddenly vanished like a fire extinguished. I was paralyzed, stunned. As I collapsed, Duce grabbed me and set me on his camel, quickly retreating. At a safe distance he pulled me from the saddle where I laid in the sand.

By now Bramputra's attack seemed to hit a brick wall and quickly retreated in chaos and terror.

Blue pulled an arrow from her saddle and watched me in disappointment and pity. Batu Khan's angry shouts echoed in my ears. As for the others they watched me in fear. I looked past them and saw the carnage I left on the field.

The realization of my emotional reaction crashed upon me. I stared in disbelief as tears swelled. I buried my face in the sand and wept.

Although we live, my acts have doomed us. What to do?

I fear the ramifications of what this karma will bring us. I am nauseated and my heart wrestles to understand. Yet my determination and anger looms like a restless beast, a beast whose thirst is not quenched.

Taleju what I have done?

Those who opposed me lay mingled in heaps on the dusty valley floor. This is the first violence I brought upon us and sickens me.

In a rash moment I brought the Purge curse upon us.

Day 9. *It is our nature to be violent but we do not have to be enslaved by this. We are given choices.*

Our history is journey into this madness. Yet, we can transcend this by compassion and understanding. Dwell within the egos' selfishness and we continue walking this path of shallow contempt which separates us from Infinity. But, seek to comprehend and see who we are beyond this illusionary façade, and Infinity is at our command.

The transition from ego to Awareness is not easy and many incarnations will become dust in the process. However, this painful transformation is necessary for the benefit of All to balance our karmic tides and embrace the future as Enlightened spirits belonging to the Single One.---Taleju- Dream and Echoes.

Since the conflict we, like Bramaputra's soldiers, were too stunned to resume. We rested and tried to make sense of what happed. In the predawn, with tortured heart, I walked the battlefield where my violence lingered over the area like a thick, nauseating cloud. It left me exhausted, bitter and with painful headaches. I sat alone with the dead until mid morning. Bramaputra and our soldiers watched me silently as I wept and cursed myself what I had done.

Looking across that field I swear there would be no more killing—no matter how much rage I carried. The images of those I killed—their bodies crumpled like broken dolls—burned deep in my heart and mind. I cannot close my eyes without seeing their pale faces, or their spirits shifting beyond. Are they looking at me with question or pity?

I am shocked and depressed by my actions. It was so easy to s succumb to this madness, but this was a mere taste of the Purge and what the spiritual sickness humanity harbored.

Taleju's warning blazed in my mind and heart. Each victim's face, twisted corpse, the stench and the emotional illness gripping me reminded me.

The Kumargi camp was active preparing for another battle. I noticed this evening they did not hold the Dedicational. I sense pilgrims fear directed me and my Seers.

Today, although our groups were separated by meters, it seemed like thousands of centuries. The new and the old separated by time because we are fundamentally different people.

I sought council in Batu Khan and Blue but they were at a loss of words. I was so plagued by bouts of self misery I cannot stem my tears. This karmic web I created entangles us all. It is up to me to restore trust and compassion for that which I so heedlessly destroyed. I have never felt so alone. Despite my boasting, I never wanted to bring pain to the Kumargi. I am just a simple soul seeking pilgrimage to Nepal.

In the morning I shall ride into their camp.

But before then I must rid this hatred festering within my heart.

Day 10. *I learnt that thoughts and emotions possess energetic matrix that influence all they touch—both consciously and subconsciously. They are seeds we gather and grow to encompass whole nations and nourish behaviors for thousands of years without ever knowing why. They are breathing, living entities we grant power over ourselves and they have marched us into destruction untold times—even against our most noble intent.---- Taleju-*

My hand is swollen and I cannot write so Sarah does. After sunrise Batu Khan and Blue joined I and we set out for the Kumari's camp. I wanted to go alone but after what happened Batu Khan did not trust my emotions. His comment hurt me. Before setting out, Batu Khan and Blues minds blended with me and remained in the shadows in case I needed `coaxing.' With my responsibilities and self loathing any vengeance was furthest from my thoughts. No matter how many tears I cried, it could not erase my regrets.

I was instructed to remain aloof, beyond word or action; be just a sprit passing by like a gentle breeze. I was not speak or interact unless he instructed. Btu Khan would speak for us. Blue carried a white flag.

The soldiers quickly formed a defensive line and watched frightened from behind shields. As we got closer Bramaputra, seated on his camel, signaled and arrows landed at our feet. We did not stop. Then spears sailed though the air and came right for my heart. I struggled with my own fears and kept my feelings cold, indifferent while Batu Khan and Blue repelled it with invisible fists. Bramaputra signaled and men drew swords and took a step at us before they suddenly froze, dropping their swords. Their eyes were filled with terror. Other soldiers looked at each other and whispered. They let us pass. Bramaputra unsheathed his sword and laid it across on the saddle in front and followed us

We came to the main camp at the river. When I saw Altus's tent my heart sung. People either gathered under the trees or hid in their tents.

At Deva's tent eight sentries surrounded it. Bramaputra moved his camel in front. He released a string of curses and profanity at me then signaled. The guards raised their spears at us. Yet, my challenging stare did not waver from Bramaputra.

Blue's eyes flashed red and sentries convulsed and dropped to the ground. The others panicked and dropped their weapons or fell to their knees, bowing their heads. Since yesterday they knew what we Seers are capable of.

Bramaputra was not affected by our show of force and did not move. He continued watching us with hostile, threatening eyes. I studied his energy matrix, seeing it radiated red and brown hues of hatred and contempt. I kept my hands hidden, not wanting anyone to see them shake or the blood drawn when digging my nails deep into palms.

Batu Khan called.

When Altus and Deva emerged for the tent, their energies betrayed fear and apprehension. They looked around at their sentries and Deva cried out briefly, her expression etched in terror.

Bramaputra cautioned them. Deva turned to go back inside but Altus placed a gentle hand on her shoulder. They faced us, tense and mute.

Batu Khan introduced me and I removed my goggles and scarf. Our eyes met and I explained our intention.

They recognized me, but after what happened yesterday both were very afraid. Deva shrunk back, saying I must leave. My heart sunk. I looked at Batu Khan and when he nodded I slid off my camel and reached into the saddle pouch. As he explained I had a gift for them I took a copy of Dream and Echoes and approached them. They watched me curiously and I failed to see did not see Bramaputra's camel come up behind me. When I prepared to hand the book to Deva it was painfully knocked from my hand. It fell to the sand, along with my small finger.

The shock, the pain, the blood. I quickly grasped my hand, fighting back tears and anger. Batu Khan read my rage and Bramaputra, sword in hand, suddenly went lump and collapsed from his saddle before I could react.

Altus quickly took me in his arms as I became light headed. Deva retrieved the book. My hand was quickly wrapped. Altus escorted me to a bench in the front of the tent and water was pressed to my lips. The anger swelled and I struggled with my feelings. I closed my eyes, allowing painful tears to wet my cheeks. Batu Khan quickly spoke and Blue dismounted me and joined me.

Thus, I sacrificed a finger to rejoin my people.

Deva shouted orders and I was brought into the tent. As Blue tended my hand we shared tea and a meal. I felt joy and accomplishment having contacted my friends.

Per Batu Khan's instruction I said very little during that meeting. When we left, Deva and Altus lost their apprehension and were genuinely glad to see me.

Later Blue dictated my letter to the Kumarisattva, explaining who am, my wishes to continue as the Kumari Deputy, the pilgrimage and give her Taleju's book.

Later, Batu Khan released Bramaputra from his paralysis and he was appointed to deliver this letter to the Kumarisattva. In exchange, Deva will not charge him with harming a guest, thereby avoided a serious punishment. Bramaputra reluctantly agreed and with a few soldiers set out for Nepal.

Day 11. We have agreed we will travel as two separate groups until we can comfortably integrate as one: Normals and Seers. During rituals those who what to join us can; otherwise two separate Conformations, one offered by Deva, the other by me, will continue. Deva will be the pilgrims' official leader, I assistant but when it comes to Seer affairs, I am in charge.

I insisted I retain the title Kumari's Deputy to show I am still tied to the pilgrimage and, perhaps this will protect me from that horrible edict. Until hearing back from the Kumarisattva, Deva is the Kumargi representative and has issued her own edict cancelling the Central Kumari's and instructed me to be addressed by my restored title. Altus is an expert on Kumargi laws and explained when conflicting orders arise only the

Kumarisattva has the final decision. I don't understand or want to get involved with their politics.

After being gone for months it was difficult integrating us. Not only had I changed so much, the pilgrims believed ruinous stories about me and my display earlier only helped to reinforced them. In their eyes I am no longer the timid, shy woman but a real threat. To them I am a Seer roaming among them, posing as a pilgrim, but intent on more. It will take major convincing them on my part to show I am not.

Wandering through camp I sensed sometimes a mixture of feelings: relief, uncertainty and apprehension. I felt both at home and in a foreign world. These emotions are unsettling after my time with my Seers

Some who fled before the fight returned and the camp and prepared for the journey to Nepal---a three month trip if we are fortunate. Deva and Altus met with the Council of Six Tribes to make arrangements for our trip. However our Seer pilgrims complicated things. They knew of our coming, our purpose, edict and the fight. The meeting lasted all day and the outcome looked grim. Hindustan has a long history of hostilities towards Seers and the Council was adamant about excluding Seers because we disgraced the tribes. The Normal pilgrimage was welcomed to continue. Thus stand our challenges we have to overcome tomorrow.

Ugh. My left hand throbbed with sharp pain. The wound cut a long gash from the small finger stump to my thumb. Sarah tended to it several times; cleaning, applying herbs and wrapping it. In my insistent to appear normal in public, I hid my baggage hand under my sleeve.

Altus and Deva studied Dream and Echoes in private. Already there was an attempt by a Satori to confiscate it, claiming this was heresy. Deva warned anyone caught will be banished. It is a gift for the Kumarisattva who will decide its importance, but just in case Sarah and Blue hid copies.

I was exhausted from our ordeal and spend much of the day sleeping while Batu Khan, Blue, Altus and Deva tended to duties.

It felts good sitting in the evening, sipping tea and seeing the tents filled with pilgrims whom I so terribly missed.

Day 13. Had a most disturbing dream last night which left me preoccupied with my own doubt and apprehension. In the dream I met Bishma atop our home and we sat before a weather vane and watched them spin in the cool breeze. This was one resembling Batu Khan and as it danced it created sparkling lights and melodies. Bishma hummed and repeated a phrase: two is one, one is two.   Then the vane stilled and when it resumed in the opposite direction the image and music changed.   Now I watched Curtis.

Startled, I woke up.

A Six Council member came by and informed us whatever agreement we had for supplies and safe passage was cancelled because we violated the terms.   By bringing violence into the valley we dishonored and forfeiting our status.   The Council will not sanction the pilgrimage and refuses passage through Hindustan, thereby risking possible death from the tribal territory we encounter.   Hindustan is very tribal and without their permission we will be considered hostiles.

We are told to find another route.   This basically voids our pilgrimage because we will not follow Taleju's route.

Through me rash act I have condemned us as outcasts. I am devastated.

I cannot concentrate on other plans.   It looks, for all purposes, our journey is over.

Day 16. These past days have been very depressing as I struggled with my emotions and self worth. My days were filled with heated discussions, bout of irritability, frustration and anger at those I met to find solutions.

For two days Deva, Altus Batu Khan, Blue and I engaged in heated debates our options.   I searched in vain for other solutions, but no luck.   I was physically ill from having to face the problems my vanity brought upon everyone—especially Batu Khan who trusted and accepted me into his tribe. I cannot look him in the eye lest I weep.

Batu Khan said there was a solution, but it required great sacrifice. He made me promise to support and not question his decision. Fearing the worse, I reluctantly agreed.

This morning we again met the Council and I sat quietly per Batu Kahn instructions, biting my lip and digging finger nails into my palm to force myself to appear calm and cooperate. I made several attempts to object but Bat Khan's pleading eyes prevented me.

Batu Khan confessed he channeled his powers through me when attacking.   I asked him not to attack but he went against my wishes. I did not want to come here, but due to my popularity he held me hostage, planning to use me as proxy leader. He explained he wanted to be the first Seer to lead the pilgrimage. He stated I should be absolved of my action and he takes full responsibility and punishment.

Afterwards he asked the Council to grant all pilgrims 'Sky Honor.' This is an ancient tradition whereby a guest or group, regardless of their character, past deeds or religion, would be protected from their enemies. Additionally, Batu Khan would pay the price for his violation, thereby dismissing the charges leveled against our group and restore Hindustan honor.

Oh, how I wanted to jump up and shout this is not true! I felt helpless and Batu Kahn's' expression told me this was for the best. I closed my eyes and prayed to Taleju as the tears streamed down my cheeks.

After much discussion the Council agreed. I my horror Batu Khan was arrested and taken away.

I was so upset. I wept for hours. I felt helpless, like I was in a sea storm pulling me under, and no matter how I struggled it pulled me deeper. Everywhere I looked I only saw darkness in my heart, my spirit and my world. I have cursed this world, I cursed myself and most of all I cursed my dear friend!

Day 17. Sunset. The golden light slowly faded into azure and stars. On this day our camp was quiet, reflective; some folks talked around solar lights, others prepared meals, some meditated on the day's event. A crowd gathered before my tent, Carlos' family sung sad tunes about loss, remorse and loneliness. I sensed they knew this is in my heart. I sat before my tent, fighting tears, self loathing and attempting to appear strong. I held the Batu Khan's spirit medallion in my trembling hands. Inside, Blue and other Seers prepared his body for the morning cremation.

Batu Khan took his life to redeem me and wipe away the dishonor I have brought upon my people and these Hindustan tribes. He sacrificed himself so that I may continue leading while maintain my image of She Who Mastered All. History will remember him as the one who nearly destroyed our people.

I know otherwise

Batu Khan, wise and brave spirit, far more enlightened than me. I will sing your name throughout Infinity. Know that your karmic wheel has finally balanced.

Koo eei tah ku, dear friend and brother.

Day 20. We included Batu Khan's ashes, his spirit medallion and a personal letter to his family with a group returning home. They left on the morning after his cremation. Prior to his cremation the Council came to see his body then issued the Sky Honor, assuring our travel protection and commanding all tribes to provide hospitality such as shelter, feed and provisions .

Additionally they brought their tribal banners we are to display in travel and camp so the Hindustan knows we are sanctioned. We spent two days loading supplies for the trip to Massoud.

I resolved not to forget the sacrifices others made and to remind myself I am reborn into another being I meditated most of the day. The result was the birth of a new mandala I called Shakya's Mandala. This is based on the Seer material. Sarah and Seer families created the colorful flag and a banner that will be used in our Dedicational.

Deva was gloomy about what happened, my presence and the responsibility she faced. The event greatly troubled her and despite my encouragement, she will not trust me.

Ghazni, the Council's Representative, will be our guide until reaching the border of Nepal. He will be our guide and interact with all tribes on our behalf. He briefed us what to expect and empathized it is important to observe each tribal traditions while in their territory because breaching honor is a serious offense.

Ghazni stressed Deva is the only Kumargi representative recognized by tribes. Tribes will appoint their own official to join us as we travel through their lands. For this privilege, they will expect tribute.

Day 22. This morning we left the valley. Deva and Altus led the main group, I, with my flags fluttering for the first time in months, followed as a separate group behind and followed up the supply train. Our group stretched several kilometers. Some sang, babies cried, but mostly a sad quiet lingered over us.

With the summer rain and flooding the `Fall Road' is submerged, meaning we will take the `Summer Road'. If we came here in the fall, villages would provide supplies and make sure we are cared for. But, we are month away from harvest thus we made arrangements for provisions at Massoud, a remote way station.

It is six weeks to Massoud and near the ruins of a Purge city called Kabul. From there Kathmandu is another two months away. If we are lucky, we may celebrate the Kulwali festive which marked when Taleju returned home. Our party was originally schedule to reach Kathmandu before the spring vernal equinox and partake in the Ceremony of Awakenings.

By evening we camped at the base of the hilly plain where the City of Six Tribes stood like a lone sentinel against the distant, rocky peaks.

The evening dedicational was led by Deva. I was bothered by having two dedicational because it reminded me of the times in

Arabia, However, I am hopeful this will change and we can celebrate as a single group.

In my own group I spoke briefly on karma and how it comes full circle when you least expect it. Afterwards I led a guided meditation using Shakya's Mandala. Then Carlos and his family led us in song and praise honoring Batu Khan and his sacrifice.

Dark clouds covered the southern sky and my heart.

Day 23. We left Valley of Lights and passed through a long canyon still scared by the Purge. A local tells us that until after the Purge they only knew war and foreign occupation for hundreds of years. The survivors see the Purge as liberation.

We followed a Purge road partly obscured by gravel and sand at the base of towering peaks. A swollen, angry river, called Herat Rum forced us to cautiously skirt its bank. Rain was our constant companion. After months of aridness the rain was both soothing and a curse. It got into everything, pushed there by heavy winds and forced us to seek cover until it passed. The ground turned muddy and gritty sand. It chafed the skin, irritated eyes, hair and mouths. I coughed to clear my throat but it was no use. Even the scarf covering my mouth becomes thick with mud.

This weather was cold and damp, accenting our misery. We cannot use our solar catchers to light fires, therefore our nourishment consisted of dried fruit and brackish water. Our bread and cheese quickly dampened and covered by mold. Everything tasted horrible, aiding to my lack of appetite.

However, Taleju's experience was completely different.

It is hot. Have not seen a living creature in days. Our companion, the narrow river, dried up a week ago, transformed into sand and gullies. We camp in a place at one time was an orchard but now has transformed into blackened sticks, cracked ground. A stone fence hints to its previous life. It is utterly quiet. Even the breeze abandons us. Nearby is an empty village where only bones and garbage occupy rooms one decorated by faded wall paint. Parvati finds a doll missing an eye and an arm. This frightens my companions who insist we do not camp in this village. They still believe evil Djinns inhabit the world and their whisper can drive a person mad.

Judging by the terrain, this valley had not seen rain in years. The Subcontinent poisonous clouds sucked all life from here, making this land sterile. I fear we are walking into Rad sickness.

Day 24. We traveled near the river for three days under constant rain. Today scattered clouds and bits of sun broke the monotonous weather. Yet, gray clouds still obscured the higher cliffs.

Came to a painted rock surrounded by piles of stones, indicating the boundary of a different tribe, the Pushtian. We waited for our representative while Ghazi went to the nearest village to see him. Later he returned with a hawk nose man with droopy moustache addressed as `Surkh,' the title for a tribal representative. What distinguished him from other village elders was his green sash and gold vest. As per their customs he only conversed with Ghazi who oversaw his interactions with us. We give him a gray camel and, since he never ridden a camel, after amusing incidents trying to mount he was apprehensive about riding so far off the ground.

It was rare when we met people in this emptiness. We have only seen two villages since leaving the valley. Since huge mountains towered over the valleys and because of the flooding, towns are perched atop hills some distance from towering cliffs. This was to prevent destructive waterfalls from above from washing away the settlements. The inhabitance constructed intricate channels to direct rain away to the river below and fill cistern. Additionally, village orchards were terraced to protect soil erosions.

To make up for the drab surroundings, each building was painted bright colors, telling travelers their tribal affiliation. The Pushtian used green and purple, which was also reflected in their clothing.

Stone walls surrounded each structure, acting as corrals for goats and cows and kept them from blossoming trees or tilled fields. People paused by the doorway or paused in their chores, watching us. Bearded men wore tunics, baggy pants and a short vest. Their embroidered wool hats, flat atop and round on the sides, had bits of mirrors which sparkled in the sun. Every man had a dagger tucked in his sash. The sheath was decorated with silver and a deep blue stone called `lapis.' This stone was even famous before the Purge and traded throughout the world. I remembered seeing one at my parent's house when I was a child.

Woman clothing comprised intricate designs on their long sleeve dresses. Beneath this they had baggy pants and felt boots. They braided black hair and wear a similar, mirrored kufi.

When we entered through a gate in a stone wall surrounding the village, barefoot children run up to us, offering food. We exchanged them with dried fruit. In the center was a dominant, domed tower dedicated to their Sun god, Ahura Mazda. Young men gathered and inspected our papers and spent long time talking with his Surkh and Ghazni while we waited in the pouring rain. Surkh applied his seal to their documents then waved them away. They were quiet and sullen as we passed.

We camped below the village. A soulful melancholy sound permeated the air, echoing at times and left me unsettled. These were produced by colorful, upright poles capped by crescent moons surrounded the settlement. This disturbing moan was made by the wind blowing through slits and holes. Some had shiny and colorful glass attached to strings which dance in the breeze. They called them `Voice Poles' to ward off Djinn inhabiting this ancient land. I sensed heavy Purge presence to this place

Day 27. The rain fell in torrents, carving deep channels in the hills and sweeping huge boulders or blocking our way. Below, the gushing river overflowed its banks, gouging the terrain and carried boulders and dirt away. Due to landslides we had to pause and find another an alternate route on the steep slopes. Luckily, no one was harmed.

Much of Hindustan was made sterile long ago by the Dark Years and Rad sickness. Unlike most places these lasted for centuries. A combination of altitude and proximity to Subcontinent's seasonal storms hindered the Hindustan Corridor's recovery. People found little land to sustain them. Despite the millennium, this is still a gloomy place. Before then conflict raged for centuries, it tragic history had plagued inhabitants beyond memory. I used my inner sight to study the planetary energies and saw many discordant colors and twisted patterns: some natural but all affected by the overlying scars left by the Purge and earlier.

Ghazni remarked at one time these mountains were covered snow year round. Now it was seasonal and by late summer all peaks, including those in Nepal, will be bare.

The stress by the storms and altitude affected us. My stamina prevents me from traveling the distance I'd like. Only those born here were immune. We were forced to rest often, slowing progress and may pilgrims suffered headaches and nausea. Ghazni promised our bodies will adopt in about a week.

Some Normals resented Seers and do not accept my leadership if tasked with responsibilities include them, but only sought Deva's council. This created resentment among us and I reminded we must be patience and not allow this behavior to poison our group. As pilgrims our common goal is completing our journey in the spirit of Taleju. I've already experienced rejection, persecution, and threats because pilgrims fear me. We have to conduct ourselves and not give them reasons to be afraid.

I remind us that Normals' spiritual imprint is fear, whereas Seers is awareness.

Day 30. Our route weaved along steep cliffs far above the river. Our dirt and stone path was narrow and sections places hastily repaired last year or had recent wash out. We navigated around new gullies or cautiously cleared huge boulders blocking our way. The constant rain and avalanches were constant hazards. We lost four and injured six in an incident. Our nerves were frayed and everyone exhausted from the rain and challenges.

Rumors claiming pilgrims following Seers angered Taleju and are doomed to failure. This lie Bramaputra started after we escaped from Homs to undermine my efforts and now has returned because of our mishaps. Despite my efforts many pilgrims despise me. How quickly they forgot who kept us out of troubles and brought them here!

Altus and Deva are regarded as Seer puppets. A great rift is growing. Although the Sultan's soldiers returned home after the incident, some the Central Kumari continued, spreading rumors which disrupt our fragile harmony. They do not obey me and even though they consider Deva as a traitor, they reluctantly do what she wants, but with protest and threats. They promised to hold Deva and Altus accountable when we reach Nepal.

I cannot move freely through our camp but without my Red Sash guard. I tried, but they insisted, fearing that if I am harmed, it will reflect badly on everyone and stain this pilgrimage. I consented, although I can spot trouble by reading the energies of people. This is possible because intent is clearly projected in one's psychic field before happening.

This awareness was tested today. A man threw a rock and hit me in the shoulder. It left me pained for several hours and I could not move it. The camp blamed another man. Me, Blue, my guards, Altus and Deva assembled for the morning Majlis. Previously I discovered his identity by spotting his energetic patterns, and, to clear this deception asked both men to join us. While the group waited, I inquired. The guilty had opportunity to confess but instead denied it and blamed the innocent man. I signaled Sami who went for his sword and reminded the guilty that as Taleju's representative I knew the truth. To convince him, I recounted the events, even where he got the stone and which arm threw it because his other arm was injured. Horrified, he fell to his knees and wept, begging for mercy. I asked Deva what I should do. After a few minute I signaled to Sami stand down. Weeping with shame he was released, knowing he will tell others.

In some ways I regretted using my skills for it could lead to misuse, but I felt it was necessary to bring order and rein this poison seeping into our group. Some whispered I am craftier than Djinn with a thousand eyes. And those I passed afterwards looked at me with fright and respect.

Month 12, Day 3. *I am like the whispering wind. Sometimes I speak into your left ear, sometime it is the right ear. Do not be concerned from which ear you hear me, but listen to what I say. It is the same, no matter which ear.---Taleju –Dream and Echoes-*

Am I a heretic as some claim, or a person with a new vision? Is Taleju really a Seer with a new message? Am I her representative? Did Taleju taught spirituality or mysticism? If so, then the Kumargi supports falseness. Much confusion lay in the root which bind and divide us.

I am frustrated by some peoples insistence our teachings are this or that. It's like arguing where I should bite the pear: front, side or back. Yet, I have to show patience and understanding, for Normals is creatures that see our universe from the Mind, which is black or white. To them, the Awakenings is complete and the only word by our Kumari Mother. They are used to category reality in boxes because it eases that fear which is in their spiritual imprint.

Whereas Seer integrates both Awakenings and Dream and Echoes as one because they understand they are two faces of the same coin.

I reminded them not to concern themselves with Taleju's identity or whether she taught or that, but remembered the Awakenings was written for a people during a particular time and place, where as Dream and Echoes is for us in the present.

This Dedicational meeting was particularity hard for my exhausted mind and emotions. Afterwards I retreated to a quiet place where I watched the clouds and stars. Sarah, Blue, Altus and Deva joined me and commented how different the stars looked than from home. My awareness expanded and all at once I saw the intricate honeycomb mesh suspended the heavens, the great energies holding this universe together and the array of colors and patterns making up the other realms. Here I glimpsed our great Shadow Realm in its entirety and my place upon this karmic wheel at this remote place, this moment in Infinity. It is humbling and frightening.

Day 6. *We came to a cave used for storage prior to the Purge. There was a great, metal beast near the entrance. The cave interior was damp and water seeped through the roof and dripped on crumbling concrete. The sound of drops made tapping sounds as though dead spirits serenaded us with their melancholy song. Near the back, we found huge metal doors that were rusted closed. We searched the rags, boxes, and metal crates littering the place but did not food. We spent several days waiting out the storm before continuing.---Taleju-*

As a child I heard about the Beast's Cave of Pushtian Valley and the dominant role it played for tribes during harvest season. We reached it today under an umbrella of dark clouds, mist shrouded hills and the swollen river. This was a foreboding place and seemed forgotten, a remote spot waiting to wake from a nightmare.

At times a damp fog obscured the road clinging to the steep slopes. Our path was wet, slippery and at times our feet slipped, threatening to send over the cliff those pilgrims failed to navigate this narrow path.

With our supplies low and the need to reach Massoud to replenish them, we were still required to visit the Cave and pay homage to the Pushtian. We can but spare but a few hours. With Surkh, Ghazni, Deva and small group we left the main group near a deserted way station and hiked the kilometer to our destination. As we neared the Cave we encountered brightly painted columns covered with prayer flags. I sensed great violence had visited these hills.

We came to a huge tree with twisted branches and pink blooms obscuring the entrance into a domed building built into the cliff. The red door was no longer on hinges, letting moisture inside. It was dark, cold, and damp inside. Ghazni held the lamp and led us inside. The lamp soft glow illuminated the huge walls painted with religious themes stained by centuries of incense. In the center was a stone altar.

As Ghazni and Surkh knelt before the alter and offered a silk carpet and a silver plate, Deva performed the ceremony honoring our host. She recited a passage from Awakenings, her voice strangely muffled. Afterwards Surkh lead us deeper into the room and passed into the Beast's Cave entrance.

At one time there were two massive, steel doors but only one remained. Our solar lamps were swallowed by this damp darkness. Surkh moved into the darkness and we heard his sandals echo on the hard floor. His deep voice sang a hymn, reminding me of soothsayers summoning Djinn. As he chanted, he lit candles along the walls.

A few minutes' later candles chased away the darkness. Within the yellow, flickering glow an arch ceiling revealed rusting beams and crumbling concert. Drips of ceiling water created an eerie tapping sound as it struck the Beast and the floor. Like the temple, religious text covered the wall but interspersed with these were thangka, paintings of Taleju, village life and people dancing. In many niche candles created long wax trails on the walls. The chamber was heavy with damp musty and incense.

Dominating the center of the chamber was the `beast;' a massive steel box resting on wheels. Upon this was a smaller, rectangular box with a long pipe affixed to its side. The Beast was steel, with thick hatches and covered with multicolored paint. Ghazni explained these were applied by the devotees and caretakers. In some places mirrored, glass chips added brilliant accents. In the candle light they reflect like hundreds of stars. This gave the Beast a carnival appearance.

Despite its benign appearance, I sensed great darkness about this ancient object. I walked around and studied it.

On that protruding pipe someone scrawled a passage from the Awakenings: crumbling monuments to our collective selfishness.

Curious, I climbed the wood steps and peered into the rectangular box. In the flickering illumination I notice the cramped compartment filled with pipes, cables and dials.

Deva inquired its purpose and Ghazni answered it as a Purge machine to generate lights, or control floods.

I placed my hand near the pipe where someone had placed a candle and dried flowers in a niche. Instantly my mind clicked, flooding me with dread. I freeze and felt weak, I leaned against the Beast. Impressions, emotions and images rushed in. I was back in the Purge. I watched the Beast tear through streets and left death and destruction in its path. The dust, violence and victim screams filled my head. The terror took away my strength. I was rooted to that spot! I am lost in this nightmare holocaust.

I struggled for words.

I scream and screamed in an attempt to speak   A million voices seemed to burst from my mouth.   I wailed, wept. I pulled at my hair. I collapsed.   The Beast was not a carnival ride, nor did it have anything to do with controlling the water and lights.

This was a Corporate Nation States death machines whose only purpose was to impose their will.

This was a war machines!

Altus and Deva rushed to my side. I screamed and thrashed as they lifted me off and assisted me to the floor. In panic I ran until I was outside and collapsed beneath the tree. In the pouring rain I sat and brought my knees to my chin. Wrapping my arms around them I rocked back and forth, whispering it was a death machine.

Devi saw the horror in my eyes. Altus quickly got Ghazni. He took a leaf from his pouch and placed it on my tongue. I became drowsy. I did not recall them carrying me back to our group.

Day 11. I am still deeply disturbed by my experience at the Beast Cave. I had to isolate myself from everyone in order to spend time exploring my reaction. I accidently discovered I have the ability to extract impressions and history stored in objects. Meanwhile Sarah and Blue acted on my behalf. It has taken nearly a week to come in grip with my ability and find ways to be a `indifferent observer' and settle my nerves. Meanwhile we pressed on while I rode my camel, watching my surroundings mutely and avoided interaction with the pilgrims.

Today our trip brought us to a circular, stone tower located on the swollen river banks. Taleju mentioned this marked ruins of an ancient city when the trade routes passed through here long before the Purge.

Pilgrims paused to add their names on the walls. Now, at thirty nine, Altus has returned and showed where, at eighteen, he added his name. It was a reflective moment and we spend in the afternoon discussing his dreams and the wisdom he developed over time. It forced me to reflect on my own change and how I lost my naïve innocence.

Nearby a painted boulder marked the bordering to another tribe. This completed Surkh's obligation and after respectful good bye he and two camels loaded with tribute of spices, rugs and pottery returned to his village.

Our new Surkh from the Kunjhur tribe met us. She was a girl of eleven and wore a large silver necklace. Her cousin and escort, a big man carrying a wide sword, presented Ghazni with documents. When she spoke it was articulated, thoughtful and carried an attitude far beyond her years. She name is Mahsa, a chieftain's daughter and because of her status, she is addressed by name. Besides being our representative through her territory she will be the first of her clan to visit Nepal.

Her cousin, Farzad, stressed this is the ultimate honor bestowed by her tribe. She has waited five years to join us to make the journey. Even Ghazni has not even hearing of this and if Deva should refuse her it would bring dishonor, risking our passage through Kunjhur tribe land. At first Deva was reluctant because her tribe was an Eternal Flame Worshipper and the Conformation did not include `outside' religion.

Because Seers are `outsiders' I suggested she travelled under my care, thereby won't violate their laws. During the meeting Mahsa was very attentive. I had the impressions this was a test of our character and group cohesiveness.

In the evening I showed her and her cousin the tents they were assigned to. Her tribal banner was set outside her tent. Sarah made Mahsa comfortable before she retired. Additionally I instruct Sami to share sentry duties with Farzad as a show of solidarity and hospitality. At first he refused, but after assuring him I will be safe, saw this wisdom.

Day 15. For three days the weather cleared, offering relief from the muddy trails.

During this reprieve we covered more kilometers each day, but this brought urgency to our plight. Because of the weather, travel demands and accidents our supplies are nearly exhausted. Many were sick from exhaustion and lack of food. Deva sent riders and pack camels to Massoud, where they will return with supplies.

Mahsa wandered through our camp and attended our daily Conformations. She was intrigued by our Majlis because her father met citizens only on rare occasions. Devi explained the Kumarisattva started this many centuries ago as a way to address concerns and support communities.

She rarely rode and confessed camels frightened her. Instead she wandered up and down our procession, sometime talking, mostly silent and observant. I had given up walking long ago due to exhaustion and leg pain. Sometimes she walked besides me and we shared our customs.

Farzad and Sami developed a brotherly bond. Sometimes they sat by the fires and swapped stories. Being a Wadi Hanifa Arab he could not grasp Mahsa's independent streak and inquired about her vulnerability with strangers. Farzad replied she can take of herself and the tribe encouraged this trait in any chieftain's daughter.

Everyone in the caravan knew Mahsa's location because a sweet melody always accompanied her. She carried a carved stick topped with prayer streamers that produced sounds in the breeze. These changed notes and pitch with the breeze intensity. She explained her `musical stick' kept Djinn away while streamers offered spiritual strength. I found this far more pleasant than the Voice Pole of earlier.

Lucinda and Pavlo were fascinated and spend much time discussing her musical creation with Mahsa. They are planning to replicate one. Farzad cautioned them that each tribe had their own melody and, to avoid insult, create songs distinctly foreign.

Day 19. This morning we reached a Purge bridge foundation. It was originally made of concrete but mostly collapsed. Prior travelers attempted repair using stones and timber, but recent flooding and avalanches torn away their efforts. The torrent, churning current was but a few meters below.

It looked frightfully hazardous.

Altus led the repair party using logs and ropes. While we waited, Mahsa and Farzad lead our group to a nearby village seeking food and to petition her local deity for safe travel.

The village was small, fields bare and the fruit trees covered with blossoms. The stone buildings needed repair and it looked run down. Most inhabitance has not returned from Mehz where they migrated during this season. We met with the few inhabitances and Deva discussed our plight. They explained Bramaputra and his soldiers took everything and threatened punishment if they helped us. Mahsa reminded them that her tribe was the only authority in Kunjhur domain. She cautioned tribal honor would be questioned and it was their responsibility to uphold it. After arguing, they grudgingly donated a cart of grain and dried fruit. I and Deva discussed returning a portion to them as a good faith gesture. She authorized it.

For their support Mahsa, an important priestess because she was the king's daughter, visited the village shrine and offered blessings.

The breezy air was cold and damp as a villager led us the only yellow building at one side of the village. Its entrance was guarded by a winged, robe figure holding a flame, carved over the entry. The colors had long ago faded from the stone artwork. The room small, floor covered rugs and walls painted to represent the heavens and sky.

A raised circular altar covered with different size brass casings Farzad explained came from the Purge. Mahsa first polished the brass until it sparkled and then prepared while we watched quietly. She poured a blue powder into a brass bowl and then reached beneath the altar and added oil from a silver container. She poured water into a similar bowl.

She took a crystal and gold disc from her robe and set it upon the altar, making sure the crystal lay atop the disc. Moments later bright yellow flames rose from the disc, illuminating the room. Reciting a prayer she dipped her right hand into the bowl until it was coated in blue powder then quickly passed it over the flame. The material flashed and produced a blue flame. A sweet scent similar to frankincense filled the shrine. She continued until the flame turned red then stopped and dipped her hand in the other bowl.

Completed her ritual she remarked that the sparkling pattern, lights and music thrilled her. Everyone looked confused. I caught Mahsa's knowing smile as our eyes meet. As a Seer I had too witnessed this brilliant spectacle. I inquired how long she noticed this. She answered since birth.

Day 21. Exhausting and tense two days trying to cross the river. We had originally planned to attempt in the morning and before dawn we sent a group to the bridge. However, we discovered the night rains swelled the river, partly submerging it. The repair crews worked to reinforced it and after a long meeting led by Deva it was decided to attempt a crossing.

We made several tries, however, the current sweeping over the bridge made it impossible. After several children and parents were swept into the rapids, we halted. Luckily all but one child was recovered further downstream. Altus performed a ceremonial for him. Our moral is low, defeated. I tried offering encouragement, but in my heart failed. The rain, lack of food, the journey wore and darkened our spirit.

This evening Blue and I discussed Mahsa. After Blue performed an energetic scan, she explained she had Seer potential. We debated whether to tell her but it would be best for her to discover this rather herself and seek our advice, if she wanted. Besides, I had reservations about how her tribe would react. Blue said this was the first time a Normal showed latent quality. This indicated our evolution was happening beyond the Seer domain. I had my suspicion for a long time but until now never shared them.

Day 25. By the next afternoon the river dropped enough we got across the river without incident. In order to make up for lost time and the weather abated for now, we travelled into the late night. The mountains gradually closed in into steep and narrow gorges. The echoing river vanished below in fog while immense cliffs blocked the sky.

No inhabitants or greenery, just gray rock and brown slopes. This land was so barren it reminded me of the journey from Riyadh to the coast. Our trail wound before us as a gray ribbon, vanishing in rocky cliffs. We encountered Purge tunnels and find most had not weathered the centuries well. Some were open but littered with rocks and consistent rain drips made for uneasy passage. Others collapsed and our party was forced to traverse paths barely wide enough for a child's foot.

My exhausted body suffered bouts of cramps, headaches and nausea. But, I was not alone. Since climbing into the mountains this sickness was widespread through our camp. The acclimated Ghazi promised has taken longer than he expected.

Great disturbances plagued this land. Although outwardly it seemed normal, inner vision revealed a different story. The earth's energy grid is twisted and chaotic; affecting not only the weather but giving rise to terrible storms of which we suffered constantly. I felt I was walking against an energy vortex determined to push me over. Only through trying to unravel its matrix I learned to neutralize it. It affected all in our party by tapping our strength. It was as though shadowy shapes clung to us and tried pulling us into the ground. Sometimes we are forced to halt for hours due our exhausting, having made only a few kilometers progress.

Mahsa called this the Hall of the Djinn and we will soon enter the Valley of Ghosts. Pilgrims knew it as simply the Kabul valley. This evening in camp I read what Taleju written.

We are outside a Purge place called Kabul. The Rad sickness prevents us from travelling a more direct path and so must leave the road we follow. The land is dotted with many craters and the evidence of a massive city stretches even many kilometers. It covers the valley and I cannot imagine its vastness. I guess several million lived here. A number I cannot grasp. I doubt even our entire world has that many.

I sense many inhabitants met violent ends; there is sadness and anger here. Black clouds cover the sky and deathly silence permeates everything. The constant wind bring stink of decay and desolation. Near a hill are marble ruins where we camp. Everyone is so afraid that we do not light cooking fires.

This is the first huge Purge city we've seen. The scale of death and violence overwhelm our hearts. We perform a cleansing ceremony to neutralize the energetic violence lingering here.

I have bad feelings about this place.

Day 27. The riders returned with distressing news. Massoud was deserted, our badly need food missing. The riders searched all day and found our cache empty. They conclude Bramaputra's group had moved them elsewhere. Both Altus and Deva was deeply stressed and felt betrayed by her Kumari. This feeling was shared by many. Others blamed their plight on us Seers, thus raising our camp tension.

This evening I spoke at the evening confirmation and shared a small bag of dried fruit. I cut very small pieces and Mahsa handed this gift to each pilgrim. When we run out she donated some of her food. Everyone shared our meager bounty. Some fights broke out when some pilgrims attempted to take more than they were allotted. This evening I read a passage from the Awakenings.

Our physical material goods are not owned, but merely rented, like an actor borrowing costume for performing on stage. By keeping this truth in our heart we do not allow greed, which brought the Purge, no place in our consciousness. By sharing all, equally, without conditions we as Spirit rise above these attachments and the fear they breed.

I remind us we are One on a journey of many; sharing the same dream, challenges, hopes, sorrow and pain. Our strength is our salvation, our determination, our inspiration. By staying true to ourselves we will not be defeated by small, bitter minds. The more hardship and challenges we face, the stronger our bond become.

Afterwards Deva, Altus, Blue and I discussed solutions. Our situation has become desperate. I turned to our Seers for help.

Day 28 . I am exhausted by my ordeal, therefore Sarah records my words. This afternoon I summoned the strongest Seers at my tent and performed a `Psychic Link'. It was never tried because it can be very dangerous. However, this was the only course if we are to survive.

The Psychic Link is conducted by one person, called a Guide, who leads the group psychic connection and then directs their energy. This boosts the Guide's ability for Far Sight. But if not performed correctly it can leave the Guide with chronic headache and in extreme cases, death. This risk for misaligned or trapping chaotic energies is fraught with dangers. I appointed Blue as my guard and instructed her to break my link if energy disturbance were detected.

In the afternoon I and Blue sat in the center of the group. First the group connected their minds while I read their energetic make up and then I balanced the group energies before merging them. Once this was accomplished I `entered' their mind matrix and took control. Although this boosted link greatly increased my awareness, controlling it was extremely difficult, like a tight rope walker in a storm. Despite this I was exhilarating and frightened. Having enhanced Far Sight tempted me to soar far into the heavens, which I struggled to keep on task.

I soared above our world and impressions came quickly as blurred images flooded into my awareness. I heard and saw wonderful, complex melodies, radiating from our group and the earth; layers and layers of multicolor energetic grids covered the earth and sky. I saw twisted and disrupted patterns upon the planet's lay lines. Behind the energy grids I was aware of structures and anything underground since their signatures were different than the surrounding land.

Eventually I came to Massoud village. It was empty. Nearby I found a building where our cache was stored, the door missing and empty crates scattered about. Tracks lead further into the hills. My headache intensified but I pushed through the pain. I told myself to hold on for just a few more seconds. I sensed some in the group weakening and my Sight failing.

Then, just before Blue broke the link, I found our objective.

The abrupt delink struck me in the stomach like a brutal stab. My head exploded in burning light and I was gripped by horrible convulsions. Blue and Sarah assisted me onto my bed. Blue placed a hand on my forehead, and felt rose energies washing over me. The convulsions subsided. Just before consciousness slipped away I whispered its location.

Year 1264 New Year. Month 1, Day 1. Massoud, Hindustan Corridor.

We travelled two days without food to Massoud and spent today clearing the rocks and trees from a Purge era bunker where Bramaputra hid our supplies. So many of us were exhausted and suffered illusions of food we nearly went insane from want. Now we have enough supplies to last us a month.

To our pilgrims this was a miraculous event. Many say it could only have happened because Taleju spoke to me. Again, I have proven myself in their eyes and cast doubt on the Kumargi accusations. My status was helped when Deva claimed I am Taleju's messenger.

But, those who really deserved credit were our Seers. They suffered nausea and headaches for two days, and some experienced temporarily vision loss.

This bunker served as a burial chamber. The room was crowded with centuries of the dead accumulated clothes and personal artifacts. As per Hindustan custom when someone died their belongings were not reused but disposed because they believed djinn may inhabit them.

Bramaputra deliberately hid our supplies, knowing we would not risk dishonoring Hindustan custom by disrespecting the dead. It is a grave offense for travelers to deliberately violate tribal custom and the guilty are severely punished.

But, he did not count on our Kunjhur clan representatives. Massoud is part of her tribe. When Mahsa gave permission to visit the cave she accepted responsibility. This set up complex rituals required to maintain tribal honor and hold violators blameless.

First she wrote a letter to the Six Tribes explaining her reasons. She then supervised the construction of an altar where at midnight she held a ceremony honoring the moon.

She circled it nine times, recited prayers for the spirits and then cut her forehead to offer blood. She pledged to punish Bramaputra group. Until then, her tribal honor is tainted. She tied a white sash around his arm to declare her intent. Then she painted her tribe's symbol on the door before securing it.

Month 1, day 2. Last New Years I was in Aqaba. Now I am in a remote place far away of civilization. I cannot believe a year has passed. Back then I could not image the physical distance I covered or my profound spiritual awakening. It seems my experience is a jumbled collection of seemingly unconnected events yet when I peer deeper it is not, but a complex meeting of many incarnations.

This afternoon stragglers arrived who we left due to their pitiful state. Twenty people died from weakness and expose. We will cremate them tomorrow. Our group is very weak. We will rest three days before entering the Valley of Ghosts.

It was impossible to celebrate the New Year on the grand style we wanted, so we perform the Festive of Lights as best we could. As the wind and dark clouds shrouded our morning in heavy rain, we huddled around our solar lights and talked, sang and fasted on dates and olives. We built a large, paper lantern and Blue and Deva visited the camp so pilgrim could add their name. It took all day and by evening the rain ceased and stars shone through wispy clouds. Later, gathering in a clearing, Deva read from The Awakening. I spoke about our dedication, our journey and our transformation since beginning. Then Marcus's family led a song they composed for this occasion. I and Deva set the lantern in a pit and lit it. Pilgrims passed the fire, reciting blessings or tossed in prayers written on paper for the coming year.

Nature seemed to approve, for it entertained us with a meteor shower far into the night.

Day 3. The weather improved, taking away the clouds and heavy rains. Mahsa explain the rivers will soon recede and we can travel the summer route.

Today we held a solemn ceremony for the dead. The bodies were wrapped in linen, covered with sacred symbols and piled together. Pilgrims surrounded them with solar crystals and in a few minutes the concentrated light cremated the bodies. While they were consumed by flames we said prayers to Mahsa's Sun god and praise to Taleju. They had come long away from home to die on this trail in a foreign land. For them Nepal for was an unobtainable task. We are tired, frustrated and to many pilgrims the goal of Nepal is but a distant dream. l recited from Echoes and Dreams.

A man journeys to a mountain which he think is close. He walks and walks for what seems years. But no matter so far he travels, the mountain remains forever elusive.

Infinity is not stationary, or a fixed place and size as some think. It expands and no spirit will ever reach Its 'boundaries'. The journey of spirit is never ending, because Infinity expands based on our collective and incarnated experience. This is what Infinity means--goes on forever, for all time and beyond it.

I finish by stating although our pilgrimage will eventually finish, our spiritual journey will never end.

Day 6. Three days from Massoud the river led through a gap in the wall of mountains, dropping us onto a wide valley. The Herat rum still swelled its banks but it was receding, revealing a hidden trail nearby, abandoned farms, huge boulders and fresh slides. The weather deposited huge boulders and brown sediment in nearly formed gullies and slides, forcing us to deviate from the road.

Something very violent happened here and as we get closer to the Valley of Ghosts, that feeling intensified. My uneasiness was felt by Blue and the other Seers.

Mahsa instructed us to 'show reverence and respect' for the ghosts by building musical sticks and setting them on our path until reaching Khukri, the next city on the edge of the Valley of Ghosts. From there the Khukri Surkh will give us musical sticks to ward evil spirits until we leave the valley. She warned travelers could go insane without their help.

Altus added during his first pilgrimage his party got lost for two days. The desolation and the horrid sounds plagued them with frightening visions and by the time they escaped half the party went mad or vanished in the night. He describe sandstorm sudden appeared and vanished; turning day to night and affecting their compasses.

We did not need any further warning and stopped. Under Mahsa's guidance we made more musical sticks. She painted sacred symbols and we distributed them. As we travelled, these sticks were placed upon our route so the wind could catch them. Soon our path replaced the moaning, sad wind with bright musical melodies.

I am resolving to uncover the mystery to this gloomy place. I suspect it is related to energy displacement and violent residue from the Purge.

Day 9. We camped near the Kunjhur border and Mahsa showed Blue, Sarah, Deva, Altus and my escorts a place not generally known: a Purge Drawings. It was about two kilometers from the main trail in a gulley where a group of stone ruins were tucked into the hillside. Tribal painted stones were the only indication. Mahsa leads us through the maze of stones to a cliff and foundations of a small village.

Mahsa took a wood ladder hidden in rocks and set it place. She climbed it and pushed a rock aside, revealing an opening. We followed and soon we entered a dark, ancient room. Mahsa held a solar lantern and we gazed upon dark pictures and writing in fainted paint on the walls and ceiling. At first I thought I was looking at birds and insects in a field of mushrooms. Then I peered closer.

The birds I recognized as Purge flying machines. The mushrooms were explosions and the insect war machines like the Beast. This field below was covered with boxes, rectangular, flames, smoke and holes which I assumed representing buildings. Near the buildings ghostly images of people covered with flames and what appeared spirits rising into the sky and many skeletons scattered on the ground. This event was carefully rendered and the valley showed predominate hills as if marking locations.

Mahsa traced a finger over written symbols and said it is `Kabul.'

I was overwhelmed by sadness. Their fate and sorrow were impressed like a broken heart on these walls even after all these centuries. I was so disturbed I did not speak a word even at our Dedicational. I sat in solemn repose while Deva, speaking in a shaky voice, reminded of our reverence for these spirits who perished in Kabul.

Day 11. We are two days from Khukri, having entered the Valley of Ghosts shortly after visiting the cave. The valley was wide with empty plains and bare mountains far to the horizon. Even before entering we heard eerie sound made by hundreds of music sticks competing with the mournful wind cursing this place. The louder the wind got, the musical sticks tried their best to obscure its soul chilling eeriness with minimal success.

Underlying all this I sensed an overwhelming foreboding and gloom. This is not the visible desolation I worry about, but glimpsing fleeting mirages in my inner vision. The land's energetic grid was twisted, at times broken. When we passed through these disturbances some fell sick, felt nausea, vertigo and blacked out. This greatly disturbed our group and I visited them reassuring it will pass.

Since our precautions did not stop these frightful feelings, I and Blue explored notes that will neutralize and heal this disturbance. When we found the combination, we create our own.

As planned, Mahsa and Farzad waited at a round, painted rock and a fluttering banner until late evening for the Soro Surkh. He never arrived. They returned, both concerned and troubled. The Soro were sticklers for appointments.

Day 12. By midmorning we grew tired of waiting and continued to Khukri, hoping a representative would show up enroute. Towards night we came within sight of it glittering on a hill. Both sides of the road were lined with musical sticks and Soro tribal banners. Still nothing from them.

Day 13. In the shimmering morning air I saw countless mounds and foundation indicating a vast city. The Haret rum, which we followed, turned and vanished in the ruins. I recognized some predominant hills from the drawing and know this was Kabul. A shadow lingered over everything and unease settled over me. I was aware of millions ghosts observing us and I glimpsed the city before and after its demise, like two photographs superimposed over each other. These impressions are locked in a `time loop' caused by energies released, lingering emotions and violence marring this valley. This time loop will play out for centuries before this energy dissipates.

But to realign the Kabul valley will take more than physical musical sticks. This goes much deeper where its root disruption is stored. To do this I will have to access their imprints from the Causative Plane. I have only travelled here once and to do so I will need Blue and maybe our Seers but I am hesitant. This calls for something I have never done and am very unsure of my skills.

Our Rad sickness meters indicate we are safe along the valley perimeter but venturing deeper we risk our health.

Day 15. Yesterday an intense sandstorm lasted all day and forced us to seek shelter in the rocks and canyons. The wind chafed exposed skin and our clothes and the sand became so thick it nearly suffocated us. Supplies not secured tightly were carried away, scattering them or burying them under suddenly appearing sand mounds.

Afterwards we searched for our missing camels and supplies. I bled from cuts and wind whipped skin. We lost five travelers when the sand buried them so fast they had no time to dig themselves out. My precious porcelain bottles with my husband and daughter ashes got lost in the storm. I had to use my inner vision to see below the sand. They were buried in a gulley a hundred meters away. I confess I was distraught until finding them.

This morning a group on camels arrived from Khukri. Mahsa asked why did not meet us until now. They did not reply but I got the impressions her status did not matter because the Soro and Kunjhur tribe has bad blood going back centuries.

Their aloof manners bordered on hostility. They escorted us to the city which we reached in the afternoon. It is a round, fortified city overlooking the Kabul valley. It is surrounded by hundreds of musical sticks, resulting in sometimes conflicting and discordance melodies. These and the massive stone wall painted with prayers and Kumargi quotes are supposed to keep Kabul ghosts away.

We were instructed to camp at the gate while they took Deva and her group to see the ruler. We were to wait for their return. As evening fall, all along the rampart solar lanterns cast light and reminded me of star clusters. The huge, iron gates were shut and locked. They offered nothing to extend hospitality even though many pilgrims were injured by our ordeal. After getting months of respect this was an insulting slap.

In night an unsettling wind blew off this empty plain. The musical sticks and the constant clack of wood gourds tied to the pole was very upsetting. The ghosts pressed deeper into our subconscious. The past violence was palpable. During meditation I saw several layers of events: all horrible, all showing death raining onto fleeing people. Its intensity was so disturbing I could not mediate and feared sleep. Rather, I huddled by my lamp and read until the morning I was never so glad to see the sun rise in the brisk and dusty air.

Day 17. After two days we have not moved. Deva sent word they were treated well and our delay was the result of the Chieftain had not made up his mind about my role. Seers were not welcomed in Soro territory and having us with the pilgrims left him confused. I don't mind waiting, but I am angry they ignore our pilgrims' needs.

Last night we lost several pilgrims after hearing ghosts calling them. We located them but it caused great anxiety because pilgrims believed evil Djinn were trying to steal their souls. Sarah, Blue and I went through camp, tending medical problems as best we could. They were grateful for our visits but their face reflected their lingering fear.

Later Deva's group returns led by a Soro official called Satori Beyet. He was a thin, tall and shaved head. His wore his red and yellow robes with dignity and carried himself with assurance. We met in Deva's tent and Beyet explained Khukri was a holy site and our presence placed the Chieftain in an awkward situation. About a month ago Kumari soldiers delivered explicit orders not to lend assistance to Confirmation Pilgrims because a Seer posed as Taleju's messenger and took control of the devotees. If this order was not obeyed, the city risked losing its important status as a religious site. The Soro tribe was dependent on visitors, commerce and the Kumarisattvas grace. Therefore the Chieftain did not recognize us and requested we leave immediately.

We were outraged. Deva replied within the Hindustan Corridor the Six council supersedes the Central Kumari's authority. The Council recognized Deva as the pilgrim leader and she would not leave her post. Beyet warned we would be stopped at Nepal's border and prevented from continuing. Since Deva has not prevented me from continuing as ordered, the Central Kumari has disavowed this Conformation and instructed pilgrims to return home. Deva has never heard of this edict and demanded to see documents. Beyet waved her off, angering her more.

Then Ghazni reminded him that the Six Council expected the host tribe to cater to the Conformation travelers. Otherwise the Soro tribe was guilty of dishonoring all tribes. He produced the permission letter and set it on the table.

Mahsa remarked her tribe was aware of Soro deceit and habit of dishonoring other tribes. She had hoped this had changed. She demanded to see the Chieftain and, because of her status, the Chieftain could not refuse.

Awkward minutes pass. Beyet answered he will relay our message to the Chieftain. He promised a reply tomorrow.

Day 18. Beyet returned. The Chieftain would only see Mahsa. She refused, saying we would accompany her or the meeting was off. Rather than wait for Beyet to return with an answer, Mahsa, using her political powers, assembled our group.   Under her insistence Beyet escorted Mahsa I, Ghazni, Blue, Deva and Altus to the city.

Khukri is a modest settlement. All structures are circular because inhabitance believes ghosts hide in corners and the city layout also reflects this. Behind the walls orchards and tilled fields make the outer parameter with gradually smaller rings for people, craft shops and souks. Each section is separated by trees and ornate gateways. On a natural rise at the center is the chief resident and the Kumari's gold and red temple. Solemn people watched us and we passed quietly. Mahsa rode proudly on her camel, her harness bells jingled softly. The scent of perfume and spices carried on the warm breeze. Musical sticks echoed from the high walls.

The temple steps were worn smooth by centuries of worshipers. At the entrance guards met us. I noticed they do not carry swords but musical sticks. We waited quietly while Mahsa placed smoky incense sticks in huge, brass pots and paid homage to her god and Taleju.

In a spacious room the chieftain waited a purple cushion, surrounded by Kumari officials in red and yellow robes. We took cushions facing him. Hundreds of thangka dangled from rafters and the air with thick with sandal wood. A gentle breeze passed through open windows, touching many bells.

Beyet introduced him as Syed, Chieftain of the Soro tribe. Ghazni introduced Mahsa who presented him with a gift.   We were served tea and Syed spoke with a weak, but commanding voice. He was from a small town on the coast of the Great Sahara Desert.   He settled in Khukri after completing his second Conformation at age nineteen. He travelled to the Levant and the Bengal. His was an Awakenings scholar and taught at a madrasa in Shaidajad. He has heard about Seers but had never met one because they avoided thc Hindustan Corridor by traveling further north. He seemed curious by my mannerism and asked about me.

I explained my role, our tribulations, translating Taleju's book and getting guidance from her. Our goal was completing the pilgrimage on her behalf.

He asked about the book and I explained its spiritual contents was written before the Awakenings and went far beyond its contents. He then asked our group if they believed Taleju spoke to me. Everyone agreed, citing some examples.

He explained Khukri is a famous pilgrimage spot because Taleju camped here when passing through. It received this classification more than four hundred years ago and did active trade which brought great wealth into the community. Before then, it was a remote settlement shunned because of the ghosts. It was Khukri's status which my presence threatened.

To emphasize his point he led us to a small chamber housing a wall covered with faded, blue writing. In front were hundreds of waxy candles and prayer wheels crowded with petitions left by devotees.

He asked if I had seen relics from Taleju's Awakenings. I replied I had. He invited me to inspect this relic and give my opinion.

Curious, I inspected the faded writing and its energetic signature which would reveal its age. It took me several minutes to form a well constructed answer. It and the wall were only several hundred years old and written attempting to appear as ancient Nepalese. The letters and sentences were inaccurate, but to pilgrims hungry to believe it appeared authentic enough. I stated that the person who `discovered' this was the same who created it. Our eyes met and he clearly knew. It was a sham perpetuated on believers.

In contained anger he called me a liar. Syed reminded me I was a dissent and false prophet if I truly believed Taleju communicated through me. Only the Kumarisattva was her true Voice and I, a self serving pilgrim was untrained in religious doctrine. My accusation about this relic was heresy. Then he waved, indicating our meeting was over. We were insulted. Mahsa spoke privately with him then we were ushered from the room.

But proving I was not a simple pilgrim with visions of grandeur, I offered to find her real camp location. He ignored me.

We were escorted into the night and the gate locked behind us. We were once again on this haunted plain. This disregard of tribal etiquette left Mahsa and Ghazni the angriest I had seen them.

Day 19. A very busy day. After the noon Conformation I met Deva, Altus, Mahsa and Ghanzi when Beyet shared documents his chieftain sent to the Kumarisattva. They included his reply to the Central Kumari edict. Beyet stressed the consequences if Syed failed and the loss of Khukri's livelihood if he did not obey. Syed promised to extend Soro hostility and escort our pilgrims under his banners to the borders, however, the Seers were not allowed to join them and would have to return home. In exchange, Deva would immediate hand me over to Bramaputra waiting at Nepal where he would deliver me to the Kumarisattva. I was nauseated, sensing my world crashing around me.

Deva reminded him that I was the Daughter's Deputy and immune to all persecutions until my case could be reviewed by the Kumarisattva. She refused to exclude Seers, saying they are out guests.

Shocked, Beyet realized where her loyalty laid. He left the meeting and spoke briefly with the messenger waiting outside. He returned with another offer. The Chieftain was willing to give me five days to locate Taleju's real camp. If successful he would drop the charges and I was free to leave. If failed, I would surrender peacefully and be held until a Kumargi escort could take me to Kathmandu.

Deva and Altus protested but, even though I harbored doubt, I agreed

While Beyet returned to the city I spent the rest of the day preparing for the biggest journey I will take into the Inner Realms. I meditated and reviewed Taleju's rainbow book. I confided my reluctance and personal fears with Blue who would act as my assistant. She was instructed to pull me back if any potential problem arose.

An important prerequisite is I had to still my mind and empty all emotions in order to allow the Causative Realm sounds and color matrix to guide me. Once undertaken, any break of concentration risked getting stranded in the Shadow Realm or ending up insane.

It took all my inner strength to steady myself as this stormy energetic ocean swirled around me. Then when I reached that point between breath and stillness, energetic sound and lights washed over me, filling me with warmth and serenity. It settled into my Third Eye and I soared towards my destination, following its gold light and wonderful melodies like a moth to the light.

I passed though the Shadow Realm. Millions of transparent images some familiar, others not, layered on top of each other, danced to ethereal music and brilliant colors. It reminded me of viewing a kaleidoscope. For an instant I was suspended in Infinity, seeing myself as I really am and connected to all things. Then I reached the Causative Realm and my previous incarnations opened before me.

A grim world showed itself. During a sand storm Taleju's group took refuge in a marble building. They were exhausted and three members recently died. They huddled with their supplies and camels beneath travel robes, coughing, choking and trying catching their breath while sand whipped around them. The storm lasted two days and blocked out the sun, leaving them very weak, sick and briefly disorientated. When it subsided they marked their location near a window looking at a distinct peak.

At the end of my session I shook violently and curled into a ball. Blue drew out the residual energies until I calmed.

Day 20. Before daylight Beyet returned with our escorts, supply camels and another Satori.

Our party included Blue, Mahsa, and my personnel guards while Deva and Altus stayed behind to oversee our pilgrims. We left after a hasty meal and struck for the heart of the valley. The wind was strong and the valley filled with musical sticks trying to ward off evil spirits. Despite my confidence I felt dread and shared our groups apprehension. This was a gloomy, oppressive place. We rode in uneasy silence. The Rad meters warned us we had just three days to complete our task.

Deep craters, hundreds of mounds, scattered concrete and steel walls stretched to the hazy horizon made up this Valley of the Ghosts. In some places we encountered black roads exposed by the wind. The Haret rum river, blue and swift eventually vanished beneath the ground, leaving just a sick appearing, brown ribbon flowing through weeds and boulders. Around noon we passed what had been a bridge. Sometimes the steady winds subsided revealing a horrible silence only broken by camel harness, other times the moan of musical sticks played on our nerves. I was aware of faded images overlaying this desolation; haunted faces twisted by terror and pain. My heart was sick and heavy. The suffering spirits permeates every millimeter of this place like a thick, brown slug.

We camped beneath a rocky hill marred by hundreds of craters. We waited for the terror of night.

Day 21. Today everyone was exhausted by our frantic journey into Kabul's great tomb. Throughout the night some complained ghosts' voices, cold hands or Djinn watching them. As we eat breakfast I stood on a rise and, hand to shield the morning glare, searched the ruins. I got the impression we had to change course. This upset Beyet's group who thought they were risking their lives for a mad woman. I assured them I will protect them but it did not ease their apprehension.

Our travel was tense and our riders, apprehensive. The presence of ghosts was strong here and when the breeze lay quietly it magnified our uneasiness. I watched this world and although most saw only ruins, I occasionally glimpsed Kabul before the Purge.

By evening a sand storm rolled across the valley. We were about ten kilometers from our destination and found protection in cluster of ruins near a gully. We huddled for protection; Mahsa clung to me, burying her fright on my shoulder. The sand stung and the howl, deafening. By night it covered us in sand and left us exhausted.

Day 22. A very exhausting and tense day. At first light I woke ill and dizzy. During night an escort wandered away, claiming djinns possessed him. After searching we found him, incoherent and muttering. I scanned his energy field and neutralize a dark shadow attached to his psychic body. This was the first time I attempted energetic healing and glad Blue was here to assist me. After calming him we resumed our journey.

We spent the day travelling though ruins dotting the hills. By afternoon we reached our goal: a mass of craters, piles of rock, and bits of concrete walls. Unlike others I was too exhausted to leave my camel so while others shared a meal I closed my eyes and my vision shifted. In future time my camel stood in a courtyard while Taleju's party took shelter in a room with many windows.

Beyet suddenly cried out and stood, pointing. The others dropped their food and stared at the direction in disbelief. They called Taleju's name and franticly rushed a knoll where her transparent image had been there moments before. They fall to their knees, offering supplication and prayers. They frantically removed debris and excitement followed. Beyet motioned for me.

I rode to the spot and painfully dismounted, Blue and Duce escorted me. Everyone's eyes held us as I hobbled to the area where I found a message nearly buried by debris. Blue, Mahsa and Duce removed centuries of rock and sand, exposing marble wall. The others quietly stood back, waiting for my reaction.

On the exact spot in my vision we found Taleju's faded handwritten below a window sill, done nearly twelve centuries ago.

Month Ashadh, year 32 AP. 92 days out. Kabul valley. Taleju Shakya Tian Nawari

Beneath were star coordinates, crescent moon, and blue hand impressions from Radha, Sanjari and Pravati.

Day 25. Since my last entry we returned to Khukri with the news and spent the next day recuperating. Despite having avoided the

Rad sickness, we were affected and for a day had no energy and threatened with bouts of nausea.

That evening I felt strong enough to meet with Syed and after his men confirmed my discovery, he held a feast the next day in our honor. The town's generosity even amazed Mahsa. I ate too much, danced too much and paid of it the next day. I suppose I should feel guilty because I am setting an example as a devout pilgrim but, I am only human and it is unhealthy to dwell in stoic life for too long. Like all people, I love to enjoy myself!

Having been outfitted for the next leg of our pilgrimage, at sunrise yesterday and escorted by Bayet and Soro banners, we left Khukri under cheers and song.

Our lonely road was serenaded by hundreds of music sticks marching to the distance, casting their sad melodies in the chilled air. Far to the horizon bare mountains shimmered in the chill air, calling us.

We are all glad to leave this place. I came through here more than thirteen centuries later and it is still the most disturbing place I've visited. During Taleju's time it must have be unbearable. The Valley of the Ghost will forever haunt me.

Deva carried letters from Satori Beyet and Chieftain Syed to the Kumarisattva describing the miracle and disavowing the older correspondence. It did not mention the location but said the 'Taleju's vision' occurred near the Khukri temple. I was given credit translation and praise for my dedication. Naturally we were sworn to secrecy.

No doubt by the end of summer the Soro will have copied the 'found' writing and will replace the fake. This will continue attract pilgrims but, despite this is a copy, it is a more true representation of the real artifact. I really doubt anyone, would be willing to venture into the ruins to glimpse the real history.

Day 26. Today we reached a stone column marking the end of the Valley of the Ghosts and connected with a mountain trail skirting the valley. We gradually left the floor and the ruins vanished behind haze.

Then something I heard absent for months returned: singing and laughter. Our spirits lifted; smiles replaced pilgrims' gloominess and devotees dreamed reaching Kathmandu and meeting the Kumarisattva. Some abandoned their sticks along the roads for others to take, other kept them for their soothing melodies.

Towards afternoon a dozen riders wearing red and yellow robes and carrying the Kumarisattva banners met us. Deva halted the group and rode ahead to talk with them. She offered tea which they politely refused then they exchanged documents. After brief conversation they turned and vanished up the road.

Apprehension filled my heart. Deva returned, wiped the dust from her face then handed me the letter.

I trembled as I broke the seal and read its contents. The Kumarisattva's delicate handwriting leaped from the pages and I scanned the content. In disbelief I reread it.

The Kumarisattva had received reports on our pilgrimage. She concluded by these conflicting reports that something extraordinary was taking place and wanted to meet me. Meanwhile she instructed I am to retain my Daughter's Deputy and, if need be, assume leadership if Deva could not continue. All Normals and Seers are to share the pilgrimage and all towns are to treat us with respect. She reminded that Deva and I acted on her behalf and show the same reverence if she was here.

Deva instructed I should wear the Kumari's necklace I had packed. She instructed I will ride with her and my banners, absent since the tragedy at the Valley of Light, will join her banners.

I felt at least we were at last integrated as a real pilgrimage, welcoming all people. My heart sung as we rode beneath my banners.

Towards evening I noticed purple and gold flowers and new grass on the slopes. Their colors were shocking after traveling months in a gray and brown world.

At the point where our party reached an old tree marking the boundary of Soro land, Beyet's group said good bye. We shared a meal, give him gifts and watched quietly as they turned towards home. Ghazni said from here we did not require a Surkh because they are near the Nepal border which all travelers are to move freely. Ghazni would continue the tribal representative until reaching the border.

Day 27. We met our first traveler from Nepal bringing tea and spices to the Persian Emirates. They were very curious and spent a long time conversing with Deva; they heard much about our pilgrims and assumed we were a militant group. They were pleased this was not so. As our long pilgrimage train occupied the trail travelers paused by the side, reciting prayers as we passed. Our Seer camels were a curiously and children come to touch them. After months of isolation it was good to see travelers again.

We stopped at a village bordering the Shinwari territory. While their representative inspected our caravan, we went to the village to buy fresh bread, fruit and vegetables. I cannot describe my utter ecstasy tasting fresh flat bread and oranges again! The village was brightly painted and covered with thousand of prayer flags. Box kites with long streamers flew from roof tops. The citizens went about their tasks in bright and colorful fabrics. Men and women wore variations of baggy pantaloon, long shirt, vest, and turban and kufi catching sunlight from bits of mirror sown in fabric. Some women draped ornate cloth around bare shoulders. All displayed heavy necklaces and multiple bangles dedicated to their ancestors. Both men and women applied a dot their between their brows, signifying all knowing Eye of Life or noteworthy accomplishments such as parenthood or death of a family. Colors meant different meanings. They were intrigued by my gold and blue clothing and face tattoos. Altus said the clothing reflected Nepal culture.

After Deva conducted a Kumargi ceremony with the locals, we presented the tribal leader with a bronze medallion. Mahsa shared private tea session with him and explained their tribes are related.

This evening we camp at a roadside inn. It was modest and crowded with travelers. Its spacious courtyard was surrounded by camel stalls. Above this were our rooms. I don't remember when I last had a warm dinner by the soft glow of lamps! It was comforting and serene. This evening I lead the dedicational and afterwards thanked everyone for their patience and hard work. Then Deva performed the ceremony honoring pilgrims perished since entering Hindustan: 150.

I returned my room where Sarah made my bed ready, Blue meditated. I read Taleju's accounts of this place before retiring.

This was called Khyber Pass and was an ancient gateway into the West. After the Purge this highway is but a shadow of itself. We follow the Purge road but are forced to take many detours because of slides and damage. We pass many rusting hulks of carriages and death machines. Somewhere we enter small villages; bones and rats are its only occupant. A warm breeze blows constantly, bringing the smell of sand and decay. This land is empty except for us. A mountain glitters brilliantly like glass, we are forced to look away. After five days travel through this mountainous region we camp on a sheltered bluff overlooking the Kabul valley. It is hazy and fills me with dread.

Day 28. Around noon we reached the Khyber summit. On a bluff we saw a fort with commanding of the view of the trail. The stone dwelling was covered with names of travelers. From a gold dome roof hung hundreds of fluttering, prayer flags. White steps surrounded the building and busy travelers lit incense and prayed. On one side of the enclosed courtyard ancient trees sheltered the caretaker residence. This was a main pilgrimage spot after leaving Nepal

The old, toothless man in faded red robe and his descendants have been here for centuries. They warmly greeted us. They served tea and invited us, for a fee, to look upon an ancient thangka their ancestors brought from Nepal. The old thangka hung in the shadow and covered by clothe. When he removed it, weather had damaged and faded the colors almost beyond recognition. In gratitude I lit candles, placed coin in the bowl and recited puja.

Travelers I met were intrigued by my tattoos, our camels and the fact Seers were with pilgrims. When they asked about me I said I'm Taleju's messenger from the West and this was my first trip. Someone asked if Mahsa was my daughter, she replied no, but related by spirit.

Deva and Altus performed the noon Confirmation session then we distributed spices, food and supplies to the crowd.

Our trail followed Kabul River. It began as in a nearby gully and swelled to torrent meandering through steep, rocky canyons. Its noise echoed pleasantly. Far up cliffs I noticed remnants of the original Purge road and caves; a twisting ribbon scarring the land even after all these centuries. It was so remote rendered it inaccessible. Travels enshrined it as a symbol of our violent past and many stone markers covered with prayer flags dotting the road.

The afternoon sun was warm and a brisk, comforting breeze led us as our road gradually descended. By evening we camped beneath the ruin of a concrete bridge. Previous traveler had left their names. Some enterprising individuals built small courtyards or stone shelters. From the cliff fruit trees heavy with unripe fruit offered shelter and comfort. I set up my camp beneath the shade. It was a good day.

Day 29. In the morning we turned onto another Purge road and followed a river through the mountains. In some places old stone embankment had washed out and crude replacements of brick and wood keep the trail open. We were the only travelers on this road until we come to a tunnel then met others eager for news about our progress. The tunnel was dark and long and feeble illumination was provided by candles in niches. As we passed, our solar lamps cast flickering, distorted shadows on the dark rock.

Through centuries visitors added wall paintings. The tunnel was damp, cool and dripping water. In some places the floor cracked and in places the original tunnel walls collapsed. We cautiously navigated a path worth smooth by centuries of travelers. At the tunnel's end we paused near an altar piled high with prayer tablet and waxy candles. Altus and Deva offered incense and prayers on behalf of our group.

The air was noticeably warmer now and a gentle breeze hung with rich scent of earth. It was as though the tunnel dropped us into another world. Ahead the valley opened into an emerald blanket. We rested near the river and road leading further into a valley.

This evening our camp filled with music, song and dance. Mahsa and Farzad attempted to teach tribal dances to honor the Sun god and Earth Spirits. Mahsa used her musical stick and Farzad his sword, waving them with almost hypnotic precision. Rather, our group was stricken by laughter while we fumbled through the moves. I know the deities appreciated our humor!

Day 30. Stressful day. I nearly lost my urns and life. I thought I was above 'attachment' but I discovered quickly no matter how we try to fool ourselves, we really are not and, giving the right event, fear sweeps away our common sense.

Our eagerness showed in our haste to reach Pesh before evening. The Peshawar Valley is a concentration of flora and fauna richness I had not seen since leaving Sofia. Until now surrounded by lush life that was absent for more than a year, I didn't realize how much I missed home.

With each step I sensed pulsating energies permeate the land, sky and the sunlight, filling me with melodies like gentle breeze. We followed the raging river into a canyon blocked at the end by a Purge era concrete wall. It had collapsed in the middle and centuries of floods carved deep gouges and deposited huge boulders onto the road. Some stones were covered with statues, colorful paintings, quotes from the Awakenings. Small shrines showed evidence of melted candles and brightly gifts for nature spirits. The path wound and narrowed, at times huge boulders were tunneled though. After few kilometers we left the boulder field and came to a spot shaded by trees. We paused. The river seemed peaceful, gently cascading over smooth, moss covered boulders. We allowed the camels to drink for a stone trough near the bank.

Tired, dirty, I looked forward to bathing and, I confessed, impatient. Thus when Deva led the ceremony honoring the river spirits, I fidgeted and thoughts wandered to the river.

The bathing pools were among mossy rocks and marked by colorful banners, statues and a dense grove of very ancient trees.

I ran to them. Blue, Mahsa and Sarah joined me.

The sounds of the rapids and overhead birds distracted me as I fumbled with my waist sash. It loosened. My foot became entangled and I tripped onto the slippery, wet rocks. I struck my shoulder and tumbled in the river, and swept by the strong current. As I struggled for air, I realized my robe came loose and my urns missing! Anxious, I fought the current and struggled to search the area, groping, desperately clawing at the sand, trying to resist the force slamming me into boulders. I became orientation and in panic I thrashed, looking for a handhold to keep me from being taken away. I sensed my consciousness dimming as I was pulled under, tumbling and losing my orientation. My hands gripped something in the sand just as Blue and Sarah pulled me from the water. Dropping to my knees and hands I coughed and gasped. I struggled for air. I hurt all over and covered with bleeding gashes.

Mahsa, soaked, ran to me with my jars. I eagerly hugged her. Deva and Altus joined us. As my strength returned Blue assisted me up. Shaking, I glanced at my hand and saw I held a smooth lapis. Deva and Altus faces went ashen and they looked to each other in shock. Sami joined us and assisted me to the trees.

Deva lit incense and asked the River Spirit to forgive me and then performed a cleansing ceremony. Feeling embarrassed and angry with myself I raised my hoarse voice and choked a thank you. Afterwards they both seemed preoccupied.

Sarah tended my gash. My muscles throbbed and riding was uncomfortable. I placed the stone in my sash. Later we passed a lake where hundreds of trimmed trees rose up from the surface like fingers. They grow into long arches in rows. Boats inspected branches heavy with fruits. In the evening we reached Peshawar and camped in a caravanserai. But Deva's reaction I cannot forget. After the evening ceremony I asked. She was hesitant but later we spoke in private. Her voice was almost a whisper and made sure no one could hear.

In the Reincarnate Karma Decree it was prophesied a thousand years ago that Taleju would return when she found a blue stone in a river.

Month 2, Day 2. From The Awakenings: *We pass empty villages and steel carriages crowded the black road. With them are strange objects we conclude as war machines. They have many different marks and I conclude they represent their Nation States. This valley does not seem to be have suffered damage as others we been in. Our Rad meter shows this place was sheltered. In some I notice large craters and land turned up violently as though a giant* *tried to plow over this destruction. The hundreds of buildings we pass are a maze of pile of stone, concrete and steel. The land is dry and nothing grows here. Evidence of prior abundance is seen in tilled fields and roads. We come to a large city, spreading across the valley floor like blight. Some buildings still retain paint, signs and windows. A great sea of bones lay in the street, partly covered by sand brought by the constant wind. We follow a dried river though the city. Its stone channels have collapsed; a wide bridge blocks the river. Near noon we come to a spacious building at the edge of the city. Its former life seems to be a gathering place. The entire building is made of marble and exquisite tile still retain blue, green, red and yellow of flowers. I am amazed that Purge people had such talents. Beneath a dome Radha finds a small carpet showing what this place looked like. Even though it faded and soiled it has fountains, two gold roofs and minarets. In another room someone had written `Pesh'. Since we do not have a name for I will call it Pesh: frontier town. This is the first Purge metropolis we've seen.*

I dreamt again of Bishma reminding me pilgrims are waiting for me to speak. I stared past the crowd and their numbers vanished to the horizon. I think I spoke with Batu Khan but the dream was interrupted when the call to the morning dedicational call echoed from the city. It left me momentarily disoriented because it has been months since I have heard it.

We were visited by the Pesh Satori. He was a middle age man, squat, swarthy and with sparking eyes and face etched by laughing lines. His bald head was covered by tantric tattoos. Over his red and yellow robes he wore huge mala of bodhi seeds, which is sacred to the Kumari because they believe Taleju's garden had one. I learned he is a Nepalese and worked in the Central Temple for the Kumarisattva before being transferred here. His energetic presence shone bright gold of wisdom and rose of compassion. Besides Altus and Deva he was the only Kumari official who was not threatening, fearful or vindictive.

He has followed reports and the controversies surrounded me since I left my home and if these stories were true then I must be a remarkable woman, or greatly misunderstood. How could the Kumari be so bothered by a devotee was beyond his comprehension. With Deva's latest report about the river incident my mysteries only deepened.

After Deva showed the Kumarisattva's letter, he returned the letter I originally sent with Bramaputra. He suggested I keep it until meeting the Kumarisattva. I reflected when I wrote it, my experiences since then and decide it was a wise request.

After the Dedicational he visited pilgrims, bestowing blessings. He met our Seers then him and Deva discussed my relationship with them. I confessed the Seers were startled by his respectful manners.

Then he asked about the book and I showed him my translation. He was intrigued, but confused he could not read the colored text. I explained their meaning. He remarked Taleju was many things to all people and she never failed to surprise us.

Then he discussed miracles and if I could read past incarnations as some clamed. I replied I do not perform these and reports are exaggerated. Pilgrims attached supernatural meaning because they do not understand what is natural and may seem as miracles. But my abilities come though by understanding the Shadow Realms taught by Taleju. The only miracle is our incarnation in this moment.

He returned after noon Dedicational and took us on a tour of the city.

Pesh is a vibrant city and lacked outer defense walls. It is surrounded by tilled fields and orchards, two rivers and located on a lake. Prayer flags, bells and crystals, filled the air with brilliant colors and wonderful melodies. All buildings are painted in bold, bright colors with intricate patterns continuing for several blocks. Every dwelling has balconies and terraces. The clean roads are covered with stone and plenty trees offer shade from the heat. Most roadside trees are covered with prayer flags. The citizens dress in bright colors and adorned themselves with silver or crystal necklaces, rings, bracelets. Like Seers they wear crystals which possessed healing properties. I was stopped several times and asked about my necklace.

Pesh is at the intersection between Nepal and the southern route to the Hindustan Sea at the Peshawar valley near the ancient city. Here, goods travel through the Hindustan Corridor to the north Persian Emirates, Khorasan Wejdh, Caspian Sea and to the mysterious Land of Fog. Trade extend to places I've never heard of, such as Bengal Chen Union and South Asian States.

We visited a large chamber off the main religious hall. It was filled with a collection of curious artifacts and instruments. As I wandered, I absorbed impressions from these artifacts. After all these centuries layers of energetic residue of their identity and who had handled them waited me like an open book.

The Satori explained he has been collecting religious artifacts and scientific instruments from all the world with plan to create a library so future generations can learn without having to travel great distances. His goal is to understand how the Purge people lived and thought, thereby giving insight to avoid mistakes. As an example he handed me a device and explained it belonged to a special instrument guiding Purge era mechanical birds. I shook my head and corrected him, saying this was used at a factory to extract the Black Blood. The Satori wondered how I knew. I smiled and did not reply. I felt embarrassed and uncomfortable explaining my abilities.

We followed him to a cliff overlooking a field where workers cleared a site. Through the poles of stone and soil revealed stone wall, mosaic floor and columns. The Satori explained it was a temple and believed it was the place Taleju mentioned. He asked if I would identify it. He's been looking for years with plans to locate the new library on this temple. I peered into the Causative realm, seeing Taleju's group here when it was dead. Finally I suggested checking the north section for the word `Pesh'. It will be buried beneath green tile.

After sharing a meal with him we returned to camp. My visit left me disturbed by the impression he thought I was more than Taleju's messenger, that I was endowed with exclusive knowledge. I experienced this from many pilgrims and it is a dangerous view; it went against what Taleju taught. The Purge history was filled with stories about these enlightened spirits who devotees gave them mystical abilities, and the tragedy that followed.

Perhaps these religious men meant well, but their descendants morphed their words into something entirely different.

That evening I included a passage from Echoes and Dreams.

See me a teacher and you are my students. I am here to give the key to Enlightenment and awareness we share. There is nothing supernatural about them; these Universal and Spiritual guidelines belong to everyone, and not exclusive to a single being, or group.

It is a grave mistake to associate personality for Enlightenment. Do not be concerned with what I look like, or my habits, or manner of dress. Do not imitate me, hoping to thereby understand my teachings because you will fall into the trap from Emotion and Mind. These will only confuse my teachings. My gift of knowledge is important---not my personality.

I am not a deity, special chosen, or representative of a greater power. I am none of these. I am but a humble teacher of Spirit. And in this incarnation I am called Taleju.

Day 4. Yesterday evening Pesh townsfolk prepared a feast honoring us and we basked in their warmth until the early morning. .

Prior to leaving this morning the Satori and his attendants inspected our massive thangka, made necessary repairs and added their portion, thereby completing our portion of the 1262 AP pilgrimage thangka. When we started our thangka was ten meters, now it doubled with contributions from all countries we visited. Altus explained when we reach Kathmandu the other half will be added. It would be displayed for three days then replaced the 1252 AP pilgrimage's carpet in the main temple. Like the one it replaced, the carpet will be cut into pieces and distributed to the populace.

Refitted and with our morals high we left Pesh. This was the first time in months we felt the Kumari officials treated us with respect. Some people followed us for several kilometers, singing praises and showering us with adulations. We passed the lake, tilled field and orchards then turned on the east road heading into the mountains while the main road continues south through the valley.

It was hot and humid beneath an azure sky and steely sun. I checked the solar meter and the ultraviolet ray was nearly twice as intense as home. I made sure I was covered and my goggles proper fitting.

Outside Pesh this trail lacked settlement or travelers. We saw deer, goats, wild cows and elusive large, yellow cat with brown stripes. Some wildlife observed us from the distance. Overhead in the heavy scented trees birds serenaded with cries, growl and hoots. Someone suggested they were announcing our arrival.

At evening we camped on a hilly field. As the night closed I glimpsed the towering peaks of Nepal. This was our first time to saw our destination. It stirred our heart.

Day 5. We were hoping our next stop would be the Purge city Islamabad because Taleju briefly mentioned it. We were lucky with Jerusalem and hopeful to repeat this, but it was very remote with no direct trail. Instead we followed a Purge road that was blocked by avalanches, forcing us to find alternate route. We crossed Purge era bridges having fallen to disarray and passed though treacherous tunnel in which our riders crouched low to pass safely. Our group was alone on this remote trail and wild life seen earlier was conspicuously absent.

Around noon when we rested our scouts returned reporting the Rad Sickness was too `hot.' We abandoned our goal of Islamabad. Disappointed, we found an animal trail that eventually reconnected with the main highway.

We camped twenty kilometers from Islamabad in a place called Pothohar Plateau. It was scarred with many craters. Through the looking glass I noticed mounds where the great city was.

Since the river incident rumors spread that I am the reincarnated Kumari Mother. Despite the secrecy surrounding the Incarnation Karma Decrees someone shared it and its prediction travelled through the pilgrims. I suspected it is the Pesh Satori accompanying us to Kathmandu.

I did not berate him since the damage was already done. Our pilgrimage was plagued by such trivialities since the beginning. However, it placed more stress and expectations on my role, which I find already overwhelming. All I can do is deny and play down this absurd claim.

I cannot be angry with them for their innocence. Rather I found it humorous how a lonely mother from Sofia, just wanting to experience my pilgrimage, is now elevated to our Teacher! I've always been a humble spirit, dedicated to Taleju's teachings. Throughout my life I've seen myself only as a candle's dim light in the sea of bright lanterns. Yet Ali you saw through my inner doubt and said my ` light' attracted those hungry for illumination. I really did not know what you meant---until now.

I suppose this is why Bishma called me her `Sunbird.'

Day 6. Today we continued through Pothohar Plateau. It was pleasant.

After setting camp Mahsa was very excited and showed me a star chart. Surya, her sun god, would reveal his crown, thereby renewing his promise to always wear the Flame of Enlightenment. According to her religion during the Purge he was so overcome by grief he removed his crown, resulting in chaos and darkness. He wore it only after hearing his followers' prayers.

She said it would happen on the morning sixteen days hence. As the representing official, she would to lead the ceremony.

Later I checked our calendar and found it occurred during the Kumari's Light, which we celebrate our religion's birth.

Day 7. *Tonight we reach a barren summit having spent days following a Purge road in a desert valley. The valley is jumbled of rocks, dry, cracked earth, and concrete bridges span dry river beds. In whole places the signs of civilization are everywhere, covering the valley as far the horizon with scattered bones and rusting vehicles.*

Sand storms force us to cover our months and constantly adjust our goggles but the invasive sand finds way through our clothes, rubbing skin raw. We constantly stop because howling winds threaten to blow us from our camels. We are covered in sweat, encrusted sand and at times our visibility reduced to a meter. The sky is overcast with brown and gray clouds. I have not seen the sun since leaving Nepal. When the wind stops this valley is deathly quiet. We march like spirits stuck between time and worlds.

I cannot imagine anyone living here for a thousand generations. This depressing place hints to what await the further we penetrate the Hindustan Corridor.---Taleju-

The transformation would astonish Taleju. We watched sunset from the edge of a huge plateau. Far to the horizon rows of bare peak; their rugged magnificent stretched to the heavens to dizzying height. Here is Nepal. Below the valley was shrouded in mist. The map called this place ` Valley of many rivers.'

What accounted for this remarkable healing was the intersection between planetary energy grids and magnetic Lay Lines. Additionally, green energy, the primordial color of this planet, is abundant. The world was healing from the inside out. Primordial Music rose from the earth, trees and hills that delighted my inner senses. I could not resist dancing to their beat while it washed over me like cleansing water! How it is so freeing to my spirit!

I suspected Nepal and Kathmandu lay along this grid, suggesting why their recovery was better than most. I sense pilgrims' calmness after being absent for months. Was it because we were near our destination or shared consciousness with this land?

This evening we rested in a grove where Taleju supposed camped. There were many ancient trees covered with glittering crystals in the branches. The breeze created ebb and flow of tinkling glass melodies. This reminded me of the Psychic Planes' primordial sound.

In the grove was a huge temple with hundreds of prayer cylinders in the walls and covered with carvings representing Taleju's trip. Deva called this the Memory Grove. We performed dedicational for the dead by circling the temple, spinning prayer cylinders and recited text. As I walked, their faces flashed in my memories and I realized how many lives and dreams were sacrificed. Afterwards we gathered dangling crystals and each pilgrim was assigned a name to write their name. Since it was getting late, we will resume tomorrow.

The evening breeze brought the sweet scent of oranges and rich earthy smells. The peaceful, warm night and stars arched across Infinity's mantel like sparkling jewels. They beckoned me and so took my blanket to sleep under the stars.

Day 8. Today I revisited my sorrow, a sorrow I had thought I had buried and locked away. Since this event, I was so overwhelmed by my responsibilities I forget it---until now. Blue and I were given two names: one was a Satori and Batu Khan. Without saying who they were, Blue placed the name on the table and asked me to choose. Without looking I selected the ribbon with Batu Khan's name. I gasped and tried to paint his name on the crystal but my hands shook uncontrollably. My struggle left me breathless and a flood tears blinded me. All my pent emotions and memories about this gentle spirit gushed out. I sobbed and could not finish. Distraught I took refuge underneath the crystal tree, searching unsuccessfully for comfort from the distant mountains. I want to the huge prayer wheel and spun it for a long time, hoping to find an answer. At that instant I felt I carried the karma and suffering for the entire Purge survivors. How was I to heal myself and accept my past? I have no idea. It is a burden so large I am frightfully alone in this vast universe.

In my grief I was too paralyzed so Blue finished my task. Rather than include it with others I kept it. For now I felt I had to keep him near. Maybe this will heal my sorrow.

We traveled until evening then after making camp a group of Seers came by and expressed their dismay having disturbing visions. They heard energetic music, and saw lights coming from the land. It interrupted their sleep and chores. A few had shared our far Sight experience, but most did not. Until now I did not share my visions.

This was because I had been reluctant to share my knowledge except for a few, fearing it may reinforce the claim I am Taleju. Blue cautioned untrained powers were more dangerous because Seers do not how to control them. It appeared Seers were spontaneously waking into their latency. She suggested it was time to include Taleju's teaching from Dream and Echoes. I had a duty to pass this to the next step of humankind evolution. I was given the gift and it is not for me to determine who receive the blessing, but Taleju.

To avoid complications I discussed my plan with Deva. She gave it her blessing.

This evening I conducted the first training from Dream and Echoes. Blue and Sarah distributed copies. Altus and Deva and forty seven Seers and Normals attended. It was much larger audience than I expected. Blue assisted me. We gathered in a Memory Grove. The evening air was cool.

I cautioned Dream and Echoes was not a substitute to replace Taleju's Awakenings. Rather, it was supplemental to help us understand the deeper meaning of Taleju's wisdom. I explained our place in Infinity, Consciousness, our karmic laws and the energetic sound and light making up our worlds. They were eager to understand, hanging on my every word. I concluded with these words.

Our dilemma in understanding life is we are spiritual Beings encased in physical clothes.

I sensed this evening was a major turning point in our relationship.

Day 9. We travelled all day but we were still on the Pothohar Plateau. The path was narrow and filled with switchbacks. Because our trail followed Purge roads, we encountered avalanche and hastily repairs. The neglected condition of this remote trail hindered our progress as we were forced to pause and repair many sections. This took most of the day and by darkness we camped in a wide spot on the trail. Tomorrow we'll need to attend a damaged bridge before continuing. Everyone was exhausted and I did not eat my meal, retiring early.

Day 11 . Yesterday our group left Pothohar Plateau and dropped into a valley. Today around noon we completed the thousand meters descent into the valley and the humidity and heat noticeably greater. Near an orange grove there was a shrine with a life size, painted statue of Taleju and a hundred butter lamps at her feet. Her hands made the madra of compassion and forgiveness and her eyes sparkle with knowingness. It was strange to see her without her tattoos, giving her a `just a pretty woman look.' The alcove was heavy with scent of sandalwood scent sending blue smoke from a bronze holder. One either side gold guilt prayer cylinder pilgrims turned while reciting prayers. In my Inner vision their activities created bell like music and produced hundreds of gold flecks shoot into the sky. They were so beautiful I was briefly disoriented to my surroundings.

Behind this a small, square building with gold dome radiated hundreds of prayer flags. Others attached to the surrounding trees created canopies of colorful, fluttering cloths. Next to a blue door were symbols and musical sticks, marking the Kashmir, the last tribe boundaries in the Hindustan Corridor. As we rested we spotted orchard workers preparing huge vats of fresh tea. They encouraged us to join them beneath fruit trees and served steamy, full body tea and spiced biscuits. They were small stature and wear extensive, intricate pattern colorful robes, vests and stiff caps accented with reflective, multicolored mirror chips. Their dark eyes were lined with kohl and had tribal tattoo on their cheek. They were intrigued by Blue and my tattoos and Blue explained their meanings. The leader, the only man with blue and yellow vest, asked to see the blue stone I found in the river. When I showed him it created excitement. Another man inquired about my necklaces and when I told him I am a Seer he said he thought we were but legends. He pointed towards Nepal and added there were rumors of ruins of a Seer Community.

Then he asked if I was Taleju. I answered I was a messenger. But, judging by his expression he was not convinced.

This evening we presented the Six Council's permission letter to several men. The man with the blue and yellow vest was introduced as the Kashmir Surkh. After exchanging gifts, he signed the document granting permission through his territory.

At our evening Dedicational Pavlo's family plays a song based a melody Mahsa heard when meditating. It rich, haunting, melody reminded me of songs from the Purge. It also sent healing energy, which brought the group to tears.

There is a home from which we journey.
To many distant lands
Forever lost by time
I see my home with a thousand eyes.
Beyond the mountains and valley I cross.
No promises or restraints will prevent me
From crossing the stars
And again I will dwell in that place called Home.
I'm going home.

I am tearing and must retreat to my tent. I think of my life, past lives, my loved ones and the horrors I brought to our world. Karma is a harsh, unforgiving judge.

Day 14. This colorful land was absent of people until linking up with the main road in the afternoon. Then we met travelers offering food and news. We heard about the monsoons and great floods postponing most travels for months. Rad sickness still prevented exploration into the Indian subcontinent. Durga port, Nepal's only city on the Bengal Gulf, was closed until last month due to weather.

We rested under pleasant, warm nights in fields. Tonight I saw dancing lights which Altus said a bug created this curious, illuminating glow. They created excitement and giggling children raced around our camp trying to catch them.

As we travelled east the Nepal Mountains grow in size. For the first time, I noticed emerald foot hills at the feet of those imposing wall of brown and black, craggy peaks and deep, blue sky.

In the quiet of the evening I spent hours conversing with my students. I confessed it was difficult to concentrate with my head filled with anticipation reaching Kathmandu.

Day 17. We made good time, covering more than a hundred kilometers in four days. I attributed this to our road and level ground. We camped on a huge river near a city called Chenab. Residents painted their squat houses with array of rainbow colors and each were interspersed with gardens. Colored walls surrounded each dwelling and at each entrance was polished a copper door. Kites and musical sticks added a host of melodies. At the north end we encountered a Purge bridge decorated with colored mirrors and solar lights. It spanned a fast moving river.

Our train of more than five hundred camels and over two thousand pilgrims proved a logistic nightmare for this small town. It will take more than a day to cross just using the bridge so they offered to split our group. Half will cross by the bridge the other by ferry.

I plan to visit Chenab in the morning and oversee our supplies the city donated before going shopping. I promised Mahsa we would visit the souk where she hopes to find a `spinning ball' which this town is famous for. In the evening I am schedule to dine with the Chenab's Sultan.

Day 18. I wish I could remove this day from my experience. However, I feel it is my duty for future generations to understand my difficulty and challenges when someone goes against the Kumargi dogma. Taleju's new message is a struggle between the old Consciousness and our evolving Consciousness.

But I am assuming others will read my words. Is this vain? Only history will tell.

Our day begun with great hope shopping and immerse myself again in exploring local goods while Mahsa searched for a spinning ball. On this day I threw caution to the wind and dismissed Blue, Yusuf and Sami from their duties, allowing them to explore the town at their leisure. Farzad could not forsake his promise as protector and so watched Mahsa from the distance. The busy and noisy souks were near the river bridge. Spices and alluring smells carried on blue smoke from crowded stalls.

We paused at a stall serving bread, dhal soup and tea. I thought about not stopping, but the awning offered needed relief from the heat and dust. Mahsa and I sat at a small table, my back to the shop owner and as we enjoyed the meal we chatted with friendly customers. It felt good just relaxing and living as a `normal' traveler.

Then, as we prepared to leave, I and Mahsa got sick. When I stood my world spun and I collapsed to my knees, vomiting. Shadows closed in and hands lifted me up. Then I lost consciousness.

When I woke I was blindfolded. Someone was dragging me by my bound hands across the ground while someone beat me with a cane. They struck my ears, face and arms. The blows send painful, electric pain through me. I screamed and nearly swallowed the rag stuffed in my mouth, I gagged and cough.

Someone talked in hushed tones. They dropped me onto the ground with my back against a post and secured my hands behind. My body throbbed, my headache felt as though my head will split. I lurched forward, spit out the cloth and vomiting onto myself. Mahsa screamed for me but then a thump silenced her. Rough hand tore off my clothes and instantly the sun's burned my skin. Panic gripped me, I moved around trying to stop from the heat from burning my skin, I struggled to force myself to remain calm enough to access my situation. Shifting my awareness I was a pair of eyes looking down at a naked, bleeding woman strapped to a stake in the center of a circle of solar collector. I was being watched by four men, one of them is Bramaputra. He commented the only way to kill a heathen was to burn me while is assistants focused the solar collectors on me. He added the sun will ensure there would be no trace for others to make me a martyr. A bound and knelt Mahsa sat behind the solar collector, her eyes and faces twisted in anger. A large welt bruised her cheek. A man held a rope around her waist and occasional yanked, taunting her. She tried kicking him and he pulled tight until she cried. In desperation our minds connected and I felt her rage

Two more lamps trained on me, burning my skin and I screamed. Now pain gave to emotions, and this turned into fear, finally rage. I recalled Batu Khan's warning about using my skill to harm, but I abandoned my reservation. Mahsa and my minds blended and simultaneously we became Far See soaring over the hill, noting our location. I sight Farzad leading the group. Blue was among them. I connected with her mind, showing where we were. She corrected our course, taking charge and hurried into the hills.

Bramaputra, shouted this was the Kumari justice for heretics and liars. Then he positioned the last collector on me. The heat burn, my skin blistered. My desperation, the heat and the pain condensed into rage. It exploded. I was bathed in stormy, crimson light and the deafening roar fermenting from my heart and gathering like a coiled snake in my eyes. I squirmed until the blind fold fell away enough for me to see my surroundings. My inner vision scanned Bramaputra's energy field, seeing chaotic and anger spewing from his heart and emotion body. I know what I must do.

My world momentarily flashed red as I directed and released my anger. It struck Bramaputra in the chest with an energy fist sounding like angry, hissing snakes, followed by thunderclap. The crimson light disrupted his heart chakra and, gasping, he collapsed, falling on a solar collector. One assistant drew his sword and, screaming, changed me. I dropped him with another energy blow in the stomach and his life's energy faded. Another grabbed a bow and notched it but before he brought it up my blast paralyzed him. He collapsed, dead. The last man produced a dagger on set it on Mahsa's throat. Suddenly he gasped and dropped his dagger as a wide blade broke through his chest. I watched indifferent as his body dimmed and his spirit vanished like a mist. Farzad cuts Mahsa's binds. Sami knocked down the solar collectors. Blue and Yusuf rushed to my side. Yusuf undid my bounds. The red light of rage passed. Blue retrieve my robe and covered me. Shaken and whimpering they led me from the area.

Looking back Sami checked Bramaputra then thrust his spear into his heart. I quickly turned way.

Blue talked calmly to me, washing my energies with her rose calming color. This gradually dissipated my anxiety and trauma. I sobbed, hugging her tightly while she dried my tear. She passed her hands over me, her palm chakras glowing. I felt her energies cooling the violent energies like cool water. Mahsa ran to me and hugged me, weeping. She commented during my attack my eyes glowed like an angry Djinn.

Sami, Farzad and Yusuf buried the bodies.

My storm passed. My body was burned but will heal. However, this event will never heal. I made everyone swear this event will never be spoken about. I feared what it will do to Normals if they found out. I explained I only got ill after taking a walk and Blue found me.

I was upset and saddened by this. I cannot get Bramaputra's from my memory. In the afternoon, after I recovered, I performed a cleaning Spirit ceremony for my assailants. I reminded those involved they were on their own karma journey and we must honor this and not judge them by their action. When I said this, peace settled over my heart. I felt sadness for their actions, but understood the greater picture. Like Batu Khan they played their roles.

We got back after dark. Because of my burns I had to avoid the sun. Sarah gives me a healing salve to apply.

These blisters, made writing painful and the ghost of my violence lingered in the recesses of my mind. The solar radiation makes me feel cold inside and hot outside. I trembled uncontrollably at times.

I hope I will never visit my anger again.

Day 19. However, bits of the story circulated. Blue visited the vendor and 'reinforced' the imaginary memory. I stayed in my tent, being nursed by Sarah. Mahsa and Farzad came by. While Blue 'cleaned' the energies still imprinted in Farzad from the violence, Mahsa either sat by the bed and held my hand or used the spinning ball. It spun produced brilliant colors and delicate melodies, calming us both. We discussed why people like Bramaputra existed since so much about the Purge is known and we shunned their behaviors. I commented we tend to cling to the past traditions because we are afraid of change.

My camel was being modified with a palanquin. It was still very painful to recline on pillows. My skin was red, blistered and covered in shiny healing suave.

That evening Blue and Sarah assisted me to the ceremony and I addressed an eager crowd. I thought of the events, my dilemma and discussion with Mahsa.

Taleju reminds us.

The many spirits are parts of the whole Consciousness that is life. Everything we see is part of this greater wholeness, although we see it as unconnected pieces.

This too, pertains to all within the Universe. We do not know the challenge or lesson our fellow spirits are learning, or their karmic disharmonies they have chosen to balance. We see them for only a single incarnation, yet we judge people on external sight and never see their past echoes. As spirit we have an obligation to hold our words and be wise not to curse or hold ill will. We should bless them because our deeds will have ramifications in their future life. What you say now may be the spark they need to break their Karmic Wheel.

From no prompting of me, the pilgrims began our evening Dedicational with songs performed by Pavlo's family. It has been our 'Evening Dedicational song for more than a month. It had become a ritual. Mahsa flute accompanied Yusuf playing the mandolin. I saw this was good; their melodies created healing light and the pilgrims expectation was reflected on their smiling faces.

 Day 20   This morning we resumed our journey. I rode in my comfortable palanquin among rugs and bolsters, shifting to find a place where the pain was bearable during the constant swaying. Throughout the day I dozed or read Echoes and Dream. Sometimes I rechecked my precious urns and stilled my mind. The palanquin was stuffy and hot. The rhythmic camel bells and musical sticks soothe my frayed nerves.

We paused in the shade and Altus pulled aside the curtains. He placed a ceramic platter heaped with green and brown circular objects in front of me. I looked out at a forest of strange trees with overhanging branches that shadowed the road.   They were unlike I had ever seen. They were massive with wide leafs and thick branches composed of hundreds of vertical trunks bound as one.   They reminded me of melted wax dripping.   Altus called them Banyan trees and their fruit were figs. Legend state Taleju had a Banyan tree at her house.   When I bit into the firm fruit my mouth exploded with sweet graininess and juice ran down my chin. The scent of earthy sweet lingered in my palanquin.

Towards evening we stopped in a clearing in the Banyan forest. Since the Kumari's Light celebration and the eclipse will happen tomorrow we decided to rest. I attended the evening ceremony and Deva led because my throat was swollen.   I could hardly whisper because of the pain. Sitting before the pilgrims I was weak and could not concentrate. I shivered and Blue covered me with a blanket.

A spot was made beneath a Banyan tree. It was warm and the air sweet. Mahsa curled against me and soon slept. Utterly exhausted, this was how I spent the eve before this auspicious ellipse in a land so far from home and my Ali and Bishma.

Nepal Commonwealth

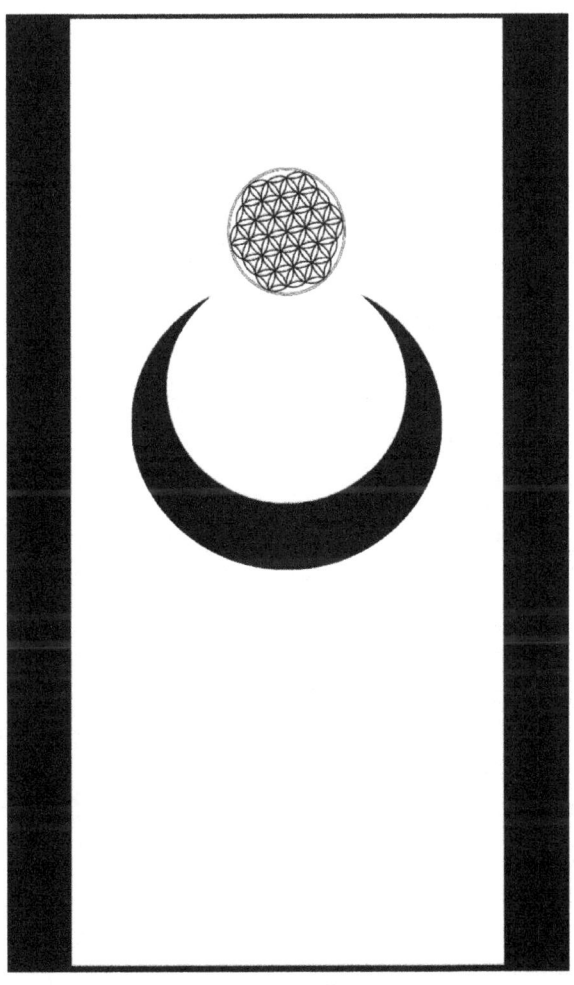

Noora's flag

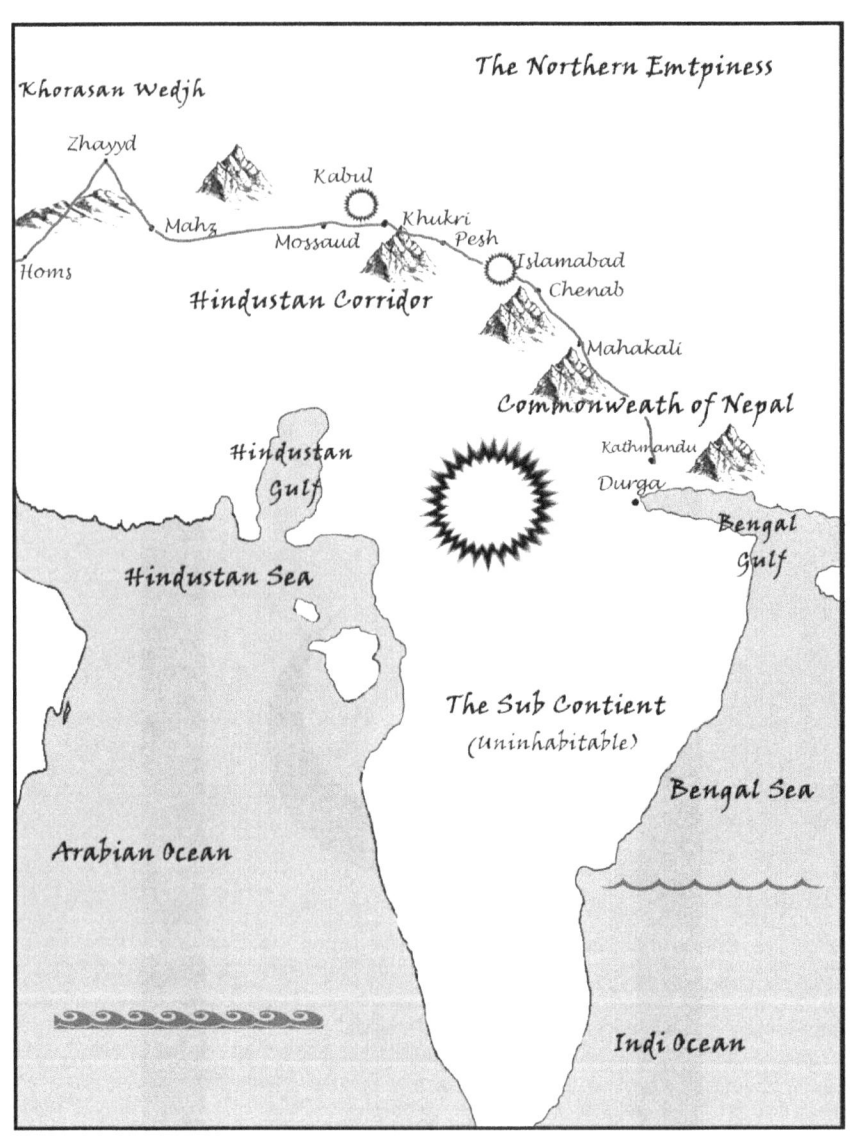

Year 1264. Month 2, day 21. This has been a most wonderful day. Up before dawn Mahsa and Farzad prepared a circular altar in a nearby clearing that served as both the Eternal Flame and Kumari's Light ceremonies.

Mahsa shared breakfast tea then stayed inside her tent, preparing for her ceremony. A meditative quiet descended upon our camp as we reflected on our struggles and searched our hearts for meaning in our pilgrimage.

Around noon Farzad escorted Mahsa to the altar. Mahsa covered her face with sacred writing and had sewn glass bits of mirror into her ceremonial blue and white dress and baggy pants. When she walked, she shimmered in the sun.

Farzad set a sliver bowl out and lit incense. As its sweet, blue smoke wafted in the breeze, Mahsa faced the sun and, raising her arms, sang.

Ahura Mazda, your people wait to see your crown.

I sensed shift in the energies. Gradually as the eclipse dimmed daylight Mahsa's sweet voice recited prayers. She stated this eclipse hailed a new dawn as it did during the Purge. Her sun god promised darkness affecting spirit will not happen again. His gift for all beings is his crown of the Eternal Flame to light their way through this life. Mahsa placed a crystal on the altar and a blue flame sprung up. She and Farzad circled the altar three times, repeating Ahura Mazda's words. The heavens grew darker, the air cooler. When the strange twilight descended full upon us calmness settles over everything, Mahsa proclaimed her god covered his face to show his crown of Eternal Flame.

The earth hovered between breathes and I felt a deep connection between the Shadow Realm, my past, future and present moment.

Mahsa recited prayers and lifted her arms towards the heavens again. She placed metal and glass objects in the altar, which represents the four elements of creation, and asked him to accept these offerings. Then Farzad took the silver bowl and they circled the altar, Mahsa waving incense at the crowd. She chanted this smoke is his promise to purify our life and walks beside us on our pilgrimage.

Slowly daylight returned. The birds woke and filled the air with their song, the world warmed and we were filled with a profound sense of peace. The sweet incense lingered long after the eclipse was finished.

This event left us profoundly moved and your stunned silence lasted far into the afternoon.

Afterwards we prepared for the evening ceremony. I sat in the shade, my back against a trunk, assisting with musical sticks. Mahsa, beside me, hummed tune and positioned sticks around the shrine. The breeze carried their calming melodies across our camp.

I reflected on how I changed since taking that first step from my beloved Sofia. For the longest time I was alone, outcasts from my pilgrims. Now, a thousand Normal and Seers pilgrims made up our collective consciousness, each possessed by a single purpose: we share the same connection to Taleju's teachings

Later Sarah assisted me into the same blue and silver dress I wore at my initiation in Zhayyd. At sunset we gathered at the shrine and shared a sparse meal of cucumber, bread and olive

Deva planned to carry the Kumari Light but the pilgrims insisted I do this. I apologized because I was still too weak. Therefore, Mahsa had the honor taking the Kumari's lantern and, with Sarah's assistance, I meet each pilgrim. They touched the lantern or placed a finger between my brows. Their delicate touch generated hundreds of sparkling lights on my energy field. Calmness washed over me.

Returning to the shrine I was assisted onto the ground. Mahsa handed me the lantern.

I told the crowd we honor all spirits past, future and in the present who share our incarnations in this world. This included Normals and Seers. Now Taleju's wisdom is truly universal, speaking to all level of spiritual awareness. Today we are truly reborn, our light grows brighter each day.

We then raised our voice, singing.
Although our Light nearly vanished in the past
We keep this Light alive so it forever shines.
We sing its blessing and walk in Unity by
Banishing greed and selfishness from our heart.
We are the Children of the Purge.
Reborn from our ancestors' ashes.
And today walk in Taleju's wisdom.

Afterwards I placed the lantern on the ground and, creating mudra of enlightenment and compassion, I closed my eyes. I focused on my Third Eye and softly recited passages from Dream and Echoes. My heart chakra energies, gold and green, connected with the crowd. I watched my healing energies touch their heart chakra. Wonderful melodies danced us: brilliant rose, white and green lights swirled into the sky as our energies mix. Some gasped, others touched their forehead to the ground, others wept, a few shivered uncontrollably. Our melodies became layers of songs, spanning eons and realms; reaching into our past and echoing into our futures. This morphed into our collective Consciousness symphony.

Afterwards I blessed them.

Ko eei tah ku. May your mirror be the Mirror of All Things.

Day 23. No matter how I discourage them, pilgrims insist on call me Taleju or the Kumari Mother. I suppose they think this is a title. I have plenty of these accolades and I do not like these! But their insistence lends toward grave misunderstandings and that ancient trap religions fell into: attribute the messenger as the son or daughter of a greater being.

I have already be attacked and accused of heresy and false messenger. I wish they would leave me alone. I am just a pilgrim, nothing more.

Taleju constantly struggled against this and was never successful to bring an end to it. Even her most devoted followers were smitten by this spell. This is why today, after more than thirteen hundreds years, I struggle to undo this mistake. It is bad for Taleju and me. Most of all it is bad for the pilgrims. By creating this pedestal it excludes them from the equity all spirits share. I suppose it is human nature to look upon those with great insight as special or attribute them to super beings.

On a more cheery note our classes are establishing foundations for Seer knowledge and human insight. My students are eager to explore the Shadow Realms. My voice is improving so I talk softly without breaking into fits of cough and gasps. At first I was reluctant to introduce the next step in training because I doubted my own understanding about Taleju's writing and feared I would misrepresent them.

However, with Blue's encouragement, this evening I introduced a new method of meditation that places the user in direct contact with the primordial forces, thereby using their own energies to explore the worlds and open awareness.

Blue and Mahsa assisted. Mahsa's progress was swift and had completely embraced her Seer identity. She is proud and never hesitates reminding our students. We use Echoes and Dream as guide and refer to Awakenings when needed. This gives the Awakenings a deeper meaning and the students conclude its basic teaching caters to mind and emotions. They realize Awakenings was written for a different culture and time. Now, we are taking the next step in a new consciousness. My students drew this conclusion by themselves for I have never claimed this.

Mahsa best explained this. Awakenings were like a person studying shadows to understand the sun, rather Dream and Echoes study the sun.

To distinguish themselves for others they wore an orange turban with a symbol of the Flower of Life. It generated questions and in some cases admirers but I was quick to caution about self importance. This was a trap we had to be cautious. I know I cannot forbid this, for they feel this is a badge of accomplishment. However, I reminded them that living in Universal Awareness will keep spirit pure.

Day 26. I am well enough to walk today. It first it was painful but gradually subsided. It felt good spending time outside my stuffy palanquin and in the fresh air, admiring our surrounding. I was greeted by pilgrims inquiring about my health or about subjects covered in our class.

We left the flat valley and trekked into gentle hills dense with foliage and banyan, orange trees and nut trees. The intense green attracted a host of birds and wildlife watching us in passing curiosity. The humid air was heavy with rich earthy scents. This seemed like another planet from where we travelled from.

This morning our guide, Ghazni and Kashmir Surkh parted ways and returned to their homes. It was a bittersweet occasion. Ghazni shared so much our hardship I considered him one of us. I wrote a letter of appreciation and invited him to see us in Nepal.

In the afternoon we reached the Nepal border! It was marked by a huge stone with carvings of Taleju and writing. I was never so happy seeing these words!

The Commonwealth of Nepal, home of our beloved Kumari Mother Taleju.

Hundreds of candle crowded the stone marker. A maze of prayer flags crisscrossed the massive trees lining our trail. Musical sticks announced us and flags fluttered in the gentle breeze. Many were overcame by emotions and collapsed at the rock; prayed, wept and thanking Taleju. Our many months, our thousands of kilometer and our struggle brought us here.

Beyond the forest bare mountains marched into the roof of the world. I was awed by the magnitude these brown and gray craggy barrier stretched. I recalled childhood legends telling us in the past Nepali peaks were covered by snow year round. Their brilliance must have lit the sky for thousands of kilometers.

There was no reason to continue today. We basked in the land of our Kumari Mother. Tents went up and celebration soon followed. At our evening Confirmation I reminded our pilgrims why Taleju left her beloved Nepal for her arduous journey. But instead of reading from Awakenings, I referred to Dream and Echoes because it hinted another, perhaps a deeper purpose.

Why do I leave my home a second time, you ask? Like a bird released from her cage I see the wonders around me; the play of wondrous sound and lights permeate everything; a cosmic of symphony which I dance in joyous occasion. I cannot explain or show these to my friends because they cannot see them. They feel connected to the earth through faith and physical sights, but I do not. I seek a deeper awareness. These flashes of color, those haunting melodies call my restless spirit.

I was worshiped as the Kumari when I was a child but do not know why. They said I had wisdom beyond my years but I didn't: I was but a scared child fearing to disappoint my keepers and visitors dependant on my guidance. I had so many unanswered questions, so many desires to understand myself and my role in life. But I had to forsake them for my public.

Now I have travelled beyond our mountains and witnessed the Purge madness when we allowed greedy, heartless spirits to rule our lives.

Now I will return to teach our Children this new Consciousness we are awakening to, this next step in human evolution. From our ashes we will be born into a new connection to all things, without mind or emotions dictating our viewpoints. Pure spiritual awareness based on who we are in Infinity's House.

A profound silence permeated the pilgrims. Eventfully they stirred from their shock and some asked if Taleju was a Seer. I replied each person has to judge for themselves.

Day 27. This morning the Hill of Pilgrims above the village Mahakali sparkled like a field of glass. As the sun rose it changed colors and the energetic music sounded like delicate chimes. All those who heard this were transfixed.

Mahakali is surrounded by terraced fields and orchards. Prayer flags and bright kites flutter from flat roof are coordinated with the blues, purple, orange, red and yellow of their dwellings. A river meander below the village, its banks covered with shrines and alcoves spewing rich, pungent and sweet incense. A brightly painted arch bridge is crowded with travelers rotating prayer cylinders in passing. The bridge drops travelers to the center of town.

We were met by curious crowds wanting to touch our tattooed camels. Children danced and giggled, running their hands along our camels and then checking their hands to see if they were discolored. The officials from the Kumari temple greeted us with smiles, passing oranges and hot tea to our weary travelers. They took interest in me and regarded me as someone of great importance. To my dismay some addressed me as Kumari Mother. I was quick to correct them.

Pilgrims waited in the temple courtyard and fed while the local Satori took Altus, Deva, Blue, Sarah and me to the main hall. It was spacious and through large windows illuminated a world map painted on the floor, showing dates and locations of Taleju's journey. Many thangka hung from open beams while rows of flickering butter lamps covered the altar. Breeze played with wind chimes and heavy incense created a soothing, meditative world. The Satori invited Deva to perform a dedicational honoring the Kumari Daughter. Surprisingly, Deva deferred this honor to me, explaining I was the Daughter's Deputy. I was shocked and placed me in an awkward situation. The Satori apology made me uncomfortable.

Per the ritual, I removed my turban, goggles and stood in the full sun near the window. I expected him to react in disgust when he saw a Seer's facial tattoos but instead he enthusiastic complimented on my accomplishments. Blue and I exchanged excited, mental comments before I ended our telepathic conversation so I can concentrate on my task.

Positioning myself before the niche displaying the Flower of Life, I led our group in a recital honoring the Kumari Daughter. When I called her name the Satori rang a bell. I removed the silver necklace of Authority and set it on the niche. Pressing my palms together I concluded with a prayer, bowing to the announcement of the bell. Then they gathered around me while I entered the Kumari Daughter in a ledger, its browned pages crowded with officials who perished during the Confirmation pilgrimage.

1262 AP Indrakeel age 42, West Kumari Daughter, Neostella, Italia Commonwealth.

I paused and stared, filled with loss and choked with regret and sorrow. I was moved to tears. I did not harbor anger, only respect and sadness for this lonely and reluctant leader.

Towards afternoon the Satori led us on a narrow path into to the Hill of Pilgrims and its enclosure. Here I found a sea of crystals attached to upright rocks with pilgrimage dates. They spanned centuries. We went to the place designated for our pilgrimage and spent the afternoon adding the crystals we carried from the Memory Ceremony to metal pegs. When I removed Batu Khan's crystal my hands shook and dropped it. After my feelings subsided I hung it on the hook and quietly sat for a long time, praying. When I said good bye a profound peace settled over me.

We spent the remaining daylight rebuilding the stone wall, removed weeds, cleared rocks, washed crystals and repaired the site. It was near dark when we finished. The Satori activated a dozen solar lamps throughout the yard, their soft yellow glow were like miniature universes in a sea of sparkling crystals. In the warm, evening breeze our host guided us back to the temple for hot meal and celebration. We danced and sang into the late night.

Day 28. We rested today. Pilgrims visited Mahakali while my duties included: preparing for our next leg, procure supplies, hold Majlis and assisted Deva with rituals. We unrolled the great thangka and inspected for damages. It required minor repairs and cleaning off stains accumulated over these past months. By evening I was utterly spend and Blue conducted the spiritual class. A subject discussed was Consciousness versus Individual awareness.

Blue read from Echoes and Dream.

The natural order of our Universes is collective. Our galaxy is composed of billions of stars, contributing to the cosmic music our sun dances to. All cosmic movement is based on the collective whole interacting with individual stars.

So too is the same with us: we dwell as individual spirits but are small parts of Consciousness making up the Shadow Realm.

However, our individual behavior within this realm is antithesis to natural order. This is because our mind cannot grasp our role within our collective community. In essence no individual acts alone or is immune. What we create we sew and our community shares its consequence.

Blue reminded students the Seers cultural foundation assures collective balance. As we wake into our potential it becomes most important we understand this.

Day 30. Yesterday the temple sent two messenger pigeons to Kathmandu, announcing our arrival. It will take a week to reach Kathmandu. Our ultimate destination is still about a month's trip through some very rough terrain. We are making final preparations and will leave in the morning.

Blue and I visited the artist quarters on the temple grounds and met artists making tiles, banners, doors and thangka. While walking past the line of artists working on tiles we were stopped by an old man in red and orange robes and whose wrinkled faces reminded me of raisins. He was instantly drawn to our facial tattoos. When I replied we were Seers from the west he mentioned seeing similar marks on a Taleju's thangka in childhood when his family made a pilgrimage to Navikaraṇa. Apparently Nepalese made trips to remote Himalayan region as a show of religious dedications but this practice ceased due to dangers.

His family undertook such a journey but got lost in the wasteland. Only he survived and after wandering for weeks later reached Mahakali. He was near death and for several months a Satori nursed him to heath then the boy became an artists. He claimed Navikaraṇa had tombs and paintings showing Taleju with tattoos. He told this Satori parent about this but was accused of being driven mad by Djinn. It frightened him enough he kept quiet about it. I asked him the city's location and he thought it was between wide canyons in a desert.

Later we told the Satori about of our conversation. He replied he was a boy then and was profoundly affected by his experience. To this day he cannot distinguish reality from fantasy. This is why they call him `storyteller'.

Yet per my insistence he explained Navikaraṇa is a persistent legend about a lost village. It was guarded by Djinn who condemned anyone searching for it. The locals are very afraid and believe anyone journeying there goes mad with fright. This village is rumored to be the first post Purge settlement outside of Kathmandu.

Then the Satori took a map and drew a circle on a blank area, saying it was supposedly in the Himalayan Desert, a week's journey. He cautioned us about placing much faith on the old man's story.

We discussed our idea with Deva and Altus. They were curious about the village and saw it an opportunity to get more history about this region. We decided to look for the village while the main group continued to Kathmandu. We calculated the trip will take two weeks and planned to regroup at Seti, the halfway point.

Day 31. After the morning dedicational we said goodbye. My group, Mahsa and several Seers from our class joined us. Our camels, burdened with two weeks of supplies, reached the dense hills just as the main group moved from the temple compound onto the main road. I glanced back and felt pride in my heart. Here was our group. Altus and Deva rode ahead of the column, surrounded by purple and white flags and silver gilt Kumari standards leading the group, long procession of people, the baggage train and colorful banners and streamers like a long carried dream.

By evening we camped in a hilly grove of trees. Beyond the hills receded like steps until meeting the rugged rocky pillars of the sky, the Himalayas. Here they seemed as though I could touch them, yet they were still hundreds of kilometers away.

This evening we conducted classes and introduced the new members to enhanced Far sight. Our attempt left participates with throbbing headaches and me exhausted.

Month 3, Day 3. These four days we traveled more than a hundred kilometers in our exhaustive search.

There were no trails so we headed north east, passing through land untouched by people. Our companions, birds and creatures, watched from brush and trees. A dry wind came up from the desert, proving relief from the hot and stifling weather. The only sound was our camels harness bells, swaying leather, cloths or footsteps. We travelled on the edge of the world. We followed valleys and distant landmarks and used stars as guides from an old chart giving us by the Satori. By noon we came to edge of a high plateau called The Himalayan Desert.

Our altimeters showed we gained more than one kilometer altitude since starting.

This morning I held an in depth lesson on the Far Sight. Unlike before, I found my ability to adjust participate energy fields easier and better control our headaches. In addition I also comprehended differences in interactions between our subtle body energies and our individual melodies.

This had greatly improved our connectivity and my ability to not only link, but more effectively directs our energies. Today I expanded my Sight to fifty kilometers and unlike earlier attempts I was able to share what I saw. We now are many eyes seeing at once.

Far Sight is not done by the Mind as I originally thought but through the Psychic Realm corridor, our Third Eye. This is also the place where Purge rulers controlled people emotions and thoughts for their own, selfish gain. I taught my students what and how Psychic energies rulers used and how to distinguish them to avoid their deception. I used Bramaputra and the West Kumari Daughter as examples.

All this is important because Far Sight also use the Psychic energies.

Dark, gray tint purple is bad; bright, pure light like the sun shining through a prism is good. Later, when we have time, I will train them on how to `neutralize' these destructive energetic properties either by altering their colors or root sound. For now, it is beyond them.

Towards evening we sighted a dim light by an unknown source on the hazy horizon. It lasted about ten minutes before vanishing. We calculated it was still several days away.

Per her wish, Mahsa led the Dedication ceremony and I was very impressed by her Awakenings scholarship. Later Farzad found a yellow root and after a ceremony honoring the valley spirits he ground it into a fine paste and baked cakes for us.

Day 5. Our Far Sight group continued improving under our practice. The headaches and struggle are absent and we grow into a stronger and more unified group. We travel further and time is instant, rather than minutes.

Our sessions proved priceless. We charted our travel by what we saw from Far Sight, getting excited when we came upon landmarks. Our Sight now range over a hundred kilometers. I think this is the limit I can achieve until my students master deeper understandings. Like me, they are very proud of their accomplishment.

For two days we followed barren hills and rugged valleys in a northeast direction. This place was flanked by empty mountains; dried rivers, bits of Purge roads, avalanches, ancient, terraced hills and ruins. We were all that moved in this desolation.

A great of sea of sand dunes stretched west. In the afternoon the wind picked up, filling the hot air with low morning cries and at times echoed through the area. It played with our imagination. Some pilgrims claimed these were the Desert Djinns. It was challenging at times to calm our suspicious travelers and maintain clarity when emotions stormed the mind.

I confess though, this place disturbed me with the magnitude of the Kabul valley

As we travelled deeper, gradually colors drained from the land until everything became the same brown tones. Inside this unending terrain of canyons and sand dunes the wind reduced our visibility to several hundred meters.

We lost our direction. We relied on our instruments and our Far Sight to navigate and they failed. Despite trying to see using the energetic grids for navigation, the weather prevented us. It was as though the Himalaya Desert wanted to remain hidden. I now understood the dilemma pilgrims faced and their fate getting stranded here.

Exhaustion settled over us after making camp and despite our attempts, we could not shut out the wind or sand.

Day 6. This evening we camped in a wadi covered by canyon and mountain shadows. Since morning we travelled though gravelly fields populated black rocks ranging size from hen's egg to a house. Like previous days, our travel was tedious and I imagined crossing into a realm where time did not exist and our distance illusionary. My throat, despite keeping my mouth and nose covered on this journey, was sore because of the sandy air. My eyes itched, sullen and my vision blurred. The sand got into everything: clothes, food, tents and saddles. The camels made their disapproval by frequent and belligerent growls and grew more temperamental than usual. This is a hostile, harsh world. I am beginning to doubt a village existed except for what was in the pilgrim minds.

When we performed Far Sight the wind covered the land as far as we saw. The energetic grids, which I hoped would assist with our location, were badly distorted and it was impossible to distinguish them. We gave up, disappointed.

Using calculations based on charts we are still a day's journey.

Day 7. Early in the morning the weather cleared enough I performed Far Sight. We discovered we were heading in the wrong direction and but closer than I thought. We changed course and after following the wadi we spotted piles of stones. Nearby we found trail markers covered in ancient Nepalese. By the generous use of color, I suspected they were meant for Seers.

When we ascended a steep dusty trail strewn with large boulders and scarred by floods we reached a plateau. At the summit we saw a long valley and ancient wadi. In the shimmering distance we glimpsed cliffs dotted with foundations, caves and ancient fields.

We found Navikaraṇa!

We took reading, entered coordinates on our map and descended in the valley as the sun raised full into the sky. The village seemed to shift. One time it appeared close, sometimes vanished and only to reappear much further.

Time seemed to freeze. We were still some kilometers away when the sun touched the distant peaks. Quickly this place was cast in purple shadows, the sky grew very dark. The same brilliant lights we saw at evening suddenly appeared from the ruins. Delicate sounds like hundreds of glass chimes echoed across the valley, causing us to pause in wonderment.

We retired early, filled with excitement about visiting the village in the morning.

Day 8. Today we journeyed into the past and placed Navikarana on the map in the middle of a blank spot. The altimeter showed we gained more than two kilometers since starting. We spent all day exploring the village. After examining sky cave writings and preserved documents buried by sand, I estimated Navikaraṇa was settled about a hundred years after Taleju's trip in this valley. It was one of a few areas not affected by the drought and Rad sickness. At one time two rivers converged here and this was where about a hundred settlers made this their home.

Surviving temple paintings showed the Himalayas still covered by snow and fed rivers all year. This nourished this valley, settlers farmed terraced fields and orchards.

The layout echoed Zhayyad and by accounts was known as City of the Golden Light--a reference to a Psychic Plane city thought to be heaven by many religions. Near the city and carved from predominant cliffs, twin hundred meter niche sheltered Taleju statues. In their time they must have been imposing figures. Paint and colored mirrors once covered them. Whole sections of white and blue glass remained in their niches, hinting to their former glory.

In the afternoons sunlight reflected the glass, creating the spectacular lights we'd seen on our journey. Additionally, at one time crystal and brass wind chimes sung throughout this valley. Records claim travelers heard these great wind chimes fifty kilometers away and the statues shown like a beacon which travelers followed.

The original settlers lived in dwellings carved from the rock with a network of large halls, passages, dwellings and storage areas. As the settlement expanded structures were added to the outside. These building were blues, gold, red and white, depending on their function. Back then there weren't solar lamps so rooms had soot stains from candle and hearth fires.

We had no problem exploring the outbuildings near the river but access into the sky caves, being high up on the cliff, proved treacherous. The rock cliff dwellings had cracked and weakened through the centuries. Rock crumbled under foot, making our climb nearly impossible as rock broke off. More than once I nearly fell off onto the rocks below.

Disappointed, we were forced to explore sky caves by Far Sight. Sitting beneath the giant stature of Taleju we linked and I directed us to the ruins. Like a bird we hovered over the opening and floated through the ruins.

Many caves had crumbled into sand and rocks. In a few faded, wall painting piqued our interests. We found four large chambers we concluded were community rooms. One had murals depicting an after Purge scene Nepalese people leaving ruin cities and coming here. In another chamber with floor fire pits it chronicled everyday life; harvesting, processing, prepare, distribute bounty, sharing meals. In the third room we studied murals representing artists, musicians and festive dance. The fourth was the largest and by its layout we reasoned it functioned as a provision warehouse. The walls showed tattooed camels, laden with supplies, heading towards a prominent peak to the west.

When we explored murals in the outlining buildings we saw their style changed. The inhabitants were Nepalese but had different shape and eyes colors. Although their clothing styles varied they were distinctly Seers. Mural text was written in original Nepalese and an early form of Seer script.

But the most astonishing find lay partly buried in rock and sand in a depression near the massive statues: a domed structure. After clearing sand Sami crawled through a narrow opening and found a remarkably well preserved chamber. In the illumination cast by our solar lamps we gazed with amazement on a representation of Taleju unlike any we had seen. She had facial tattoos, tunic, pants and jewelry exactly as I described in Dream and Echoes. She stood on a dais of a crescent sun and a flower with three layers of pedals. Above her head were six crescent circles which I concluded represented her Six Etheric bodies. In the background red, blue and yellow spheres of creation's primordial colors surrounded her. In her right hand she held the tetrahedron: the basic spiritual building block for manifestation. In her left hand was Flower of Life, the seed for all manifestations throughout Infinity.

It mural brought us to tears.

In was the afternoon when we finished exploring Navikarana. I was drawn to a high plateau opposite the city and we climbed the summit, finding a sky burial site and the stump of a huge tree that vanished long ago. Scattered on the ground were hundreds of rectangular clay urns embedded with names and dates. The deaths ranged from 210 AP and to 340 AP.

From here we had a splendid view of the valley; I saw evidence of worked orchards along the wide rivers and surrounding foothills.

As I turned, my foot caught something. Curiously, I cleared the sand and found a stone tablet showing the identical Taleju painting in the domed building. It was heavy and Sami and Farzad carried it to back our camp in the gathering dusk.

That evening we discussed what we discovered: an early Seer community. Towards evening Sarah showed me a blue Flower of Life on a piece of white pottery.

Meanwhile, I could not sleep, for so I was filled with excitement. Rather, I recalled the painting and I was compelled to recreate the mandala. Maybe I will finish it by the time we meet the main group.

Day 9. We planned to continue exploring City of the Golden Light but the wind picked up, bringing threatening, dark clouds. Recalling the old man's warning and our own experience with weather here, we reluctantly abandoned our desire.

We hastily gathered our things and we barely reached the hill when a blinding violent sand storm descended upon us, bringing stinging wall of choking, brown sand. We sought shelter in rocks and cliffs. A few minutes later visibility was reduced by gathering darkness brought by black clouds. Day became night. I could not see my hand. My goggles filled with sand, forcing me to clear them and exposing my face to elements and blistering sand. Then the full force of the storm struck. It rained so hard it felt like I was constantly hit by rocks. It lasted until afternoon. When it lifted cascading water threatened to sweep us away. We were buried in wet, gritty mush and it took until night to dig ourselves out. We only had one meal this day and it was dried fruit laced with sand.

Day 11. After the storm yesterday the village vanished. The storm buried it. We can't even guess where we traveled since everything has changed. The sky was threatening and, between storms, we were forced to move on in attempt to outrun the storm. Travelling on the plateau we were caught in the wind and sand long after sunset. We found rock shelters to camp.

Today we followed the dunes and reached barren hills bordering the desert. Briefly the sun came out and the brown and rocky hills were covered with purple and white flowers and sweet scent carried on the hot air. Enchanted by the sudden burst of life we paused and gathered the flowers. Sami called the flowers 'Rain Honey' because they came after rain and were sweet. They made a wonderful snack we ate while riding.

The rains also removed sand, revealed buried roads which we followed through canyons and gravel plains. Within hours the winds covered them again. I was amazed by the transient nature to this place.

The hot wind subsided this evening. Lush earthy scent filled the air. It was a hard ride, leaving us exhausted. After our evening Dedicational I did not eat but spent time with my journal and the mandala while the others slept.

Day 14. Two days ago we reached the main road connecting Kathmandu. To alert the pilgrimage of our progress, we released a message pigeon.

The road wound through steep hillsides, thick forests or meadow covered with brilliant flowers left by the passing storms.

We met travelers and camel caravans heaped with goods for trade bound for distant lands. They were curious about us and sometimes rode with us or exchanged pleasantries and gifted us food. When they heard we were part of the pilgrimage, they reported they camped at Seti.

We came to our first caravanserai today. It was modest by the Persian Emirates standards and not crowded, we had the place to ourselves. The family running this inn gave us robust tea and fresh oranges and sweet cakes.

At sunset firebugs hovered in the darkness like fairy lights. Unlike like the deathly quiet of the Himalayan Desert this world was alive with the sounds of life: crickets, owls and cicadas. Mahsa caught a firebug and we admired it. It had iridescent green, hard shell, transparent wings and red eyes. The light is generated by flapping its wings.

I finished the mandala yesterday and at our class I used it in meditation. The Seers remembered seeing the original and were very excited. Because of its complexity, we felt this was made exclusively for Seers. We felt strong connections to our past. We felt at last we could walk proudly as Taleju's children after so many centuries of isolation.

Since leaving the desert I am restlessness and cannot sleep.

I sense tension and anxiety grew as the night wore on. I thought it was just me but Blue shared her feelings. She said she had a dream the group traveled on the road leading to Mount kaili sha,, a mountain on the Causative realm. Altus and Deva led them, Everyone was singing and wore broad smiles.

I sat beneath the quiet night sky and stared at the stars, mind wrestling with its meaning.

Day 15. Today, I was consumed by dread. The journey was peaceful, but I was not. Then around noon the birds suddenly went quiet and the air stilled. Abruptly we were surrounded by energetic tension that suddenly released with the sound of a crack, throwing our world in violent shaking. Our camels stumbled and went berserk and we were hard pressed to control them as rocks and dirt tumbled onto the road. I checked to make sure of everyone was safe. My dread intensified because I did not want to face with I suspected.

After regrouping we performed Far Sight. Sitting in the middle of the broken road with debris around us our minds soared above the trees and travel east to Seti. To our horror, we saw the road and village buried beneath kilometers of rock and earth. The mountain above them has collapsed.

I cried and fought tears. Nauseated overcame me. I retched. Blue came to me and I wept, trying to force words out. I could not. I was shocked, mute.

We were still more than a day out. Fighting panic we quickly resumed. Duce's cane coaxed his camel and quickly became lost in the woods, praying that his parents safety.

I cleared my mind. I did what I can to reassure us but their expression was heart breaking. Like me, many knew what would wait us.

Day 17. Since my last entry we have not paused. I led our group in the darkness, aided by the moon and my inner vision. I studied the energetic patterns in the ground and it showed the road as clearly as day. Our ride was grueling, hard; we hardly stopped, driving by our desperation.

We covered nearly a hundred kilometers in less than two days before exhaustion forced us to rest.

I write as evening descends. We rested in an ancient fruit orchard. After repairing a collapsed well we found good water. We are eager to continue but our bodies refuse. We are quiet, each wrapped in our own thoughts of what awaits. We do not take time for the Conformation ceremonies, preferring to mediate privately or perform ceremonies for loved one, asking Taleju to protect families. I offered support but I inside felt helpless. Everyone's faces wore apprehension and fear. I am lost for words.

Day 18. This is the hardest entry I've ever did. My hand shook and I was consumed by grief. My spirit is cloaked in sadness and grief. Oh, Ali and Bishma I wish I did not have to do this and seek comfort in your arms!

We are here. The road had collapsed, leaving   massive cracks blocking our path. We spent most of the morning finding a way around. We reached Seti by mid afternoon. The horror we found was unimaginable. The city that had been located midway up a hillside that collapsed from above. The slide buried Seti and covered the valley with mud and huge boulders stretching many kilometers.

When we arrived survivors were still in a state of shock but attempting to dig those buried or searched for pilgrims. Later we did a count: one hundred and three people survived: sixty Normals, rest Seers. Among the living was Duce. Pavlo suffered a leg wound and Lucinda perished. Among those unaccounted for were Altus, Deva, all Kumari representatives and guides.

I am distraught with sorrow but refrain from showing emotions for the benefit of our group. As the leader I am expected to be strong---no matter how much it is tearing up me inside.

Mahsa suggested I should locate survivors by viewing the ground energy. But I was so overwhelmed Blue took charge. I moved through the horror in a daze, visiting, saying words of encouragement. My voice sounded hollow, absent, lacking the determination and instead echoing the words of a defeated soul. Their tears and wails surrounded me, melting my heart until I descended into helpless. I was forced to retreat and clear my energy fields and emotions to continue.

The pilgrims were helpless, angry and lost. A few were so shocked all they could do was sit and stare. I struggled to shield myself and tried neutralize this emotional energy, hoping to grant them some relief. After awhile I grew numb and constant nausea hung like knot in my stomach.

The spirits of those departed, the emotions hung over this valley like an oppressive blanket. I saw many faces, watching me eagerly for something to say. But what could I say?

I, as their leader, was consumed by my grief. Blue sensed my distraught and took charge, organizing work parities to treat the wounded, feed hungry and to recover victims. Bodies were gathered and their names added to a list. Toward evening we found the bloodstained Confirmation manifest. By solar lamps Blue updated the list. Later Blue came informed me that based on her Far Sight, Deva and Altus were covered by more than a kilometer of slide, making their recovery impossible. She held me while I cried.

In the late evening we stopped due to exhaustion. Some determined pilgrims wanted to continue but knew they did not have the strength to continue. Our helplessness turned to sorrow.

The pilgrims looked at me for help. I hardly could move, for I was so weakened. Blue and Sarah assisted me to our group. I surveyed them, searching their tired faces for words that would comfort them.

Then as my inner vision opened I noticed Ali and Bisha standing in front, her comforting, peaceful eyes giving me strength. She held out her hands towards me and commented we were waiting for Taleju to speak.

Then in the crowd I saw countless spirits stretching far into the past and into our future. Batu Khan, Altus and Deva were next to Bisha, their faces eager. I wiped tears and steadied my voice as the image of Taleju filled my heart. But she was no longer memories but here in the present, standing before these weary pilgrims who dedicated their whole lives to her. The spark of realization stuck me like a bursting star, dissipating the doubt I carried for so long.

I realize that I am Taleju returned as Noora.

As I spoke gold light radiated from me and touched the group, washing over them like loving, soothing waves. I saw Infinity, my incantations and roles I played in this Grand Journey. I had many names but I am still the same.

We are the many echoes of the Grand Echo. Like actors we enter the stage and share our dreams. But our time is brief and our role momentary. When it concludes we move to another stage, another town.

This is the transient aspect of life; the sorrow, the passion, and fulfillment we experience are but memories we carry to the next stage. In time, we may meet again at a different play and enjoy a dance with the similar melody.

Keep comfort in your hearts knowing their play ended and we are touched by their performance. Find strength in your own realizations as spirit we are walking in Dharma's footsteps. We all return to that place from which we began, only this time wiser.

Day 20. Rumors circulate Taleju spoke to us and afterwards our love ones appeared to say good bye. Some pilgrims claimed they met their Purge past life and their karmic were balanced. Whatever, the group seems calmer today and I sensed a growth of awareness of life. The pilgrims continued address me as Kumari Mother with greater reverence than before and no matter how I discourage this it does not stop. It leaves me upset and embarrassed. When I asked Blue for her opinion she replied it gives Pilgrims hope and courage which we should not interfere with. Then she inquires why I was denying this. By having entered the Causative Realm, I surely knew my past incarnations. Am I afraid or do not feel worthy?

It is none of these. Taleju was in the past, I am Noora now. By dwelling on the past it can forfeit what is needed to accomplish in the present. The pilgrims are too eager to compare the past with the now. I will never be the Taleju what they envisioned. Noora is not the same person. Therefore, I will never openly admit who I was.

Still very exhausted I went about my tasks keeping our group together and focused on our immediate tasks. Many were still gripped by emotional loss and I spend much time encouraging them. We sent search parties to find missing camels. In late afternoon we recovered our huge thangka under the rock and dirt. It was soiled and damaged. Towards evening fifty camel were retrieved.

We made litters to carry the wounded. Supplies, blankets, tents, food, utensils and lamps we divide among survivors. Blue led the evening Dedicational because I retreated and sat where the town of Seti was buried. I surveyed the destructions and contemplating my life before this journey and what brought me to my current role.

I am a small player in this larger play; I had seen births and deaths; hopes dashed, then reborn. I shared dreams and then these vanished like dust until I was emptied like a broken vase. I felt the weight of my journey and many pilgrims I affected. I saw the faces of those who I loved pass though my thoughts.

Right then I felt I cannot go further; this pain was too to bear. My sorrow wrapped in these past lives flooded into my heart. My heart broke and I cried torrents of tears. I do not when I slept. I woke in the morning, found a blanket around me when the call for Dedicational echoed through the valley.

Today we dedicated time to put the past behind us. The bodies were cremated after I led the pilgrims in a emotional ceremonial. We placed stone markers and painted them red and gold on the spot where Seti stood. We scattered prayer flags, light incense and said our goodbyes.

In the late afternoon we departed this valley.

Day 22. Today we lost Pavlo. He never recovered from the loss of Lucinda, his wife. Despite Duce's care he died in the early hours. Mahsa, I and Duce were by his side to say goodbye. This added more sorrow to my heart. Afterwards Duce, Sami and Mahsa played music, hoping it would lighten my mood, but nothing could break the dark cave of sadness I found myself in.

Farewell dear friend, we will miss your music and laughter.

Day 25. Travel was difficult. My leg protested when walking the inclining trail. I had come to rely on my musical stick for support. My camel carried a wounded man. Sometime I double with Sami but his camel was weak and by carrying two riders tired quickly. When he had enough he sat and did not move unless we spent an hour prodding him. Since it was more bother than I had patient for I walked. Sometimes Sami and I switched places but his foot injury limited his time. Mahsa rode with Farzad. With so few camels left we used our camels for provision while we are forced to walk or ride atop heaps of supplies, furthering exhausting them. This slowed our progress.

The trail left the river and followed steep hills. It was narrow and sometimes treacherous. The quake weakened the trail and in some place the path collapsed. The quake left signs everyplace we passed through. Great landslide or fissures scarred the pristine landscape. Our trip seemed to drag on forever. We descend into a valley and reached a lake a day later than planned.

On the afternoon on the third day since my last entry we are met by a party from the Kumarisattva. Kumari representatives were sent with her Invitation and standards: gold crescent sun and an eight point star which we included with ours. Their appearance was met with much enthusiasm. They could see we were weary and exhausted. They brought food and more camels.

They were surprised to discover I was their leader and as the Daughter's Deputy pledged their cooperation. When they inspected the pilgrim ledger sorrow etched their faces.

They found me gracious and they refrained from asking too many questions. My mannerism startled them. I suppose I was not what they imagined. The stories of my exploits reached the Kumarisattva who was eager to meet me. They said the quake did minor damage in Kathmandu and she had to attend her citizens, thereby delaying her response. Kathmandu was less than a week away.

While talking with our pilgrims I was surprised they were not shocked when they addressed me as the Kumari Mother. In the evening, when I led the Dedication the visitors listened eagerly.

On this night there was much signing and music in our camp, the first time I heard this in many days. It was peaceful and filled my heart with joy. Our weary travelers, having walked though the Purge world for thousand of kilometers, were thankful for being here.

When the moon rose above the mountains, two messenger pigeons were released with their reports.

Day 29. It has taken four more days to reach our goal, the Kathmandu Valley. And so we returned to the beginning of our journey.

We camped on the edge of the Kathmandu valley. Our exhaustion had dampened any enthusiasm. It was warm and the damp air rich with earthy scents. The valley's location was marked by small, white, square shrine with blue dome at atop a single hill. Some of us visited this temple. Around its base were hundreds of bronze prayer wheels, burnt candles, incense and offerings. There was a niche in the west corner for Taleju. From its crescent, gold sun and eight pointed star hundreds of prayer flags hung from cords tied to surrounding trees. At the summit of the blue dome glass chimes struck delicate melodies. Sandalwood incense permeated the temple.

We passed minimum traffic who reverently watched us pass. They pressed palms together and bow low in respect. Some whispered reverently my mane and pointed at me.

Day 30. Last night we camped at a roadside in damaged in the earthquake.

We were met by three red and orange robed officials called the Satori Council. They were very attentive, friendly and we sat in a circle on rugs. While we talked, a scribe sat nearby recording what we said. With Blue, Mahsa and Sarah by my side we shared tea and spent hours discussing the Kumargi, history and my understanding of Taleju's teachings. When asked about my book, I reminded them it was for the Kumarisattva.

When I recounted Bramaputra actions they were shocked and reassured it was not authorized or known. They said a few misguided spirits had taken a radical view which led to troubles in the past. They apologized for any troubles he caused.

They asked me if I was Taleju as most claimed. Their question hinted to more than just a passing interest. I did not reply but quietly sipped the tea, watching them. They laid at my feet six objects at my feet. They were: metal singing bowl, water pitcher, a wood doll missing arm and head, a child necklace, bronze door lock and a child's felt boot. Then they asked me to choose one. Both Blue and I studied them, and I was not sure what they meant. Then I saw myself as a child in a dark room with peeling, green and white paint. I was covered in dirt and holding this same doll--except it had a head. Its face was white and it had a gold crown. The other objects belong to others. I selected the doll, remarking I played with it when I was very young--but, in another life.

Then they asked doll's name. I though and replied `mama' because like my mom, she only has one arm. They quickly prostrated themselves on the floor, muttering Taleju's name. I was suddenly felt embarrassed and said they must stop. Then I inquired what these objects meant.

They have been searching for the incarnated Kumarisattva to replace the current one. Then when they saw me they knew who I am: Taleju. Then he showed me the list called Reincarnate Karma Decree from which Deva referred to after my river experience.

Taleju will incarnate with these life experiences.

She come the west.

She will not be born in humanity's house.
She wears facial mystical symbols
Her left hand is missing a finger
She limps on her right leg
She will find a blue stone in a river
She will appear after an earthquake.
She rides a camel with blue markings.
Her two companions are a desert woman and a young girl.

When I read this I was stunned and speechless. Blue and Mahsa looked at me for a long time. I shook my head. It was not that they knew my past identity, but this list, written centuries before my present incarnation had been a roadmap for my journey all along.

I asked that I am still Noora and only the Kumarisattva needs to know my past.

Day 31. Bishma, you would love The Kathmandu valley. It is like an emerald blanket filled with beautiful creatures and inhabitants. I wish you were here to share it with me.

With our banners and flags held high our pilgrims followed the narrow dirt road, leading us through valleys heavy with dense trees overshadowed by mammoth gray peaks reaching into the stark, blue sky. Here, we encountered villages with tended fields and orchards about 30 kilometers apart. Buildings were one or two story, red brick or stones painted in multi colors. Each village had shrines and ceremonial flags and each building flew streamers and caught breeze with sparkling glass chimes. Sandalwood incense hung in the sweet air and with soothing wind chime melodies settled our nerves and dispelled our fatigue. I noted each settlement was aligned to the energetic lines of the earth and they were very careful to live in harmony with their surroundings. Residence wearing colorful robes greeted us in passing. We are given fresh bread and pomegranates and oranges. I am called the Kumari Mother by many and wondered how this news got out.

At one village we encountered a crowd requesting I give a blessing. Leaving my camel I limped into the crowd and spoke. This led to the crowd enthusiastic chanting `Taleju.' I immediately wanted to correct them, but Blue stayed my tongue with a gentle hand on my shoulder. She reminded me this they waited for years for the pilgrims to arrive and after the loss of the earthquake the Nepalese needed my understanding. Seeing all the joy filled faces I agree with her. She reminded me that even though I was Taleju, I would always I would be Noora to her. As I left, people touched my robes and later joined us for the final walk to the palace.

Month 4, Day 2.   This is our city, Ali and Bishma. I promised I would take us to Kathmandu city and today we reached it.   The squat, sparkling buildings are huddled in many forested hills near a full, sparkling river. It is smaller than I thought; about six thousand inhabitants. There are white buildings, courtyard and streets interspersed in trees. Dominating the hill's summit and surrounded by orange orchard is the red and gold House of the Kumarisattva. It is flanked by steps lined with statues of Taleju and sacred symbols. Hundreds of banners flew from courtyards and sparkled like a million stars in the morning sunlight. Music, the product of hundreds of musical sticks, echoed across the valley.   Their melody is underlying note is c sharp, the root sound of the earth. I sensed rich, green, healing energy wash over us, immediately melting any anxiety or frustrations that have lingered.   From my inner vision I watched gold patterns radiate form the Kumarisattva's House, a great spoke wheel across the earth and connect with the universe.

Our group stood in awe as we came upon this. Joyful weeps and tear overcame our group.   We have been on the road for more than seventeen months. Here were we desires, dreams and our purpose to our horrible struggle. Pilgrims collapsed onto their knees, prostrating and offering blessings. Some stared, numb, unable to grasp our journey was over. Many wailed and lifted their hands to the heavens, their faces wet with tears.

A crowd carrying banners and standards of the Kumarisattva House met us. Music accompanied them.   In the crowd I saw a woman in red and gold robes and wearing a gold hat decorated with streamers and sacred symbols. Her presence radiated the gold and white energy of enlightenment. Her heart glowed the rose illumination of compassion. In her right hand she carried a crystal, in the left a silver mirror.   For a moment I think I see Radha.   Then as she got closer she transformed into a thin, Nepalese in her thirties. With her were a man and young boy whom I sensed was her family.

I, Blue, Sarah, Mahsa and my escorts dismounted and formed a group. I was so weak I used my singing sick to lean against. As the woman stopped and regarded me I saw her eyes were heavily outlines and her forehead decorated with a crescent sun in yellow paint. She wiped tears and she dropped to her knees, placing the crystal and mirror at my feet.   She looked up and in a shaky voice she welcomes Taleju, her pilgrims. Then she asked for forgiveness.

And so, we entered Kathmandu.

Year 1264, Month 4, Day 3. This is my last entry. Today we held the ceremony of the Returning Pilgrims. We joined the two sections of the huge Thangka to the Kumari Daughter and hung it on a hillside. It was a splendid sight: twenty by fifty meters and sparking in the sun. There was much ceremony, dance and singing. I spoke on the importance of the Kumargi and looked ahead as we integrated all of Taleju's teachings. I pledged our spiritual freedom, the need for healing by integrating Normals and Seers, and our understanding of who we are.

As part of the ceremony she returned a short time later having shed her Kumari outfit for in plain clothing of a commoner. Then the former Kumarisattva handed me the mirror and crystal. When I accept these I felt not only great accomplishment, but profound heaviness with my new role. The transition was complete. She was ending, I was beginning mine. With solemn ceremony we planted the Sultan of Persian Emirates trees in the Kumarisattva's House courtyard. Despite all they had been though, they spouted fruit.

When I was alone later this evening I took your bottles and buried beneath an ancient, orange tree whose girth was larger than ten meters. Rumor claimed Taleju planted it before leaving on her quest. I released your spirits and wept for my loss.

Ali and Bishma, it was a long trip but I fulfilled my pledge. Welcome home.

I leave this record of my journey for those seeking inspiration. You are not alone in your struggle to understand.

Noora Al Monte, Kumari Mother-
Kathmandu, Nepal Commonwealth

Noora paused, holding the pen over the page. She raised tired eyes and looked through the room's window at the courtyard. Gold light bathed her in this first sunset of her new home. She sighed and closed her journal. Reflective, she strolled to the chipped dresser and opened the drawer, reverently placing her writing on top of her clothes.

Later, dressed in her indigo tunic, baggy pants, and purple and white vest Noora slid open the door from her private quarters. She looked at the new thangka hanging on the opposite wall. It was her yet a blend of Taleju. Her dark, tattooed face and gold fleck black eyes shined all knowing. She wore this same Kumari's robes and her Seer necklace. In the right hand she held her new book and in left her musical stick. She sat cross legged on a river's bank which began as brown and turned to blue. The background showed clouds, snow peaked mountains and the Flower of life.

"Not bad," Noora commented, taking the final steps through the threshold into the narrow passage.

As she headed down the green painted hall her limping gait fell on wood flooring, reminding her of a nervous crow tapping windows. Sami waited at the hall's end and opened a narrow door. She quickly sat in a wood chair. Blue, Sarah and Mahsa, each in matching purple and white tunics, descended upon her. Noora waited patiently as they coiled her long black hair and secured with the silver pin. A jewel was temporary attached between her brows then her eyes carefully outlined in kohl. Then her orange turban was secured.

She held a mirror and checked the reflection. A thin woman with wide eyes and blue tattoos stared back. She hardly recognizes her. Then when her eyes flashed gold she smiled

"Has the morning lessons been distributed to the students?"

"Yes, they have been informed it will follow the Dedicational, Kumari Mother," Sarah replied.

"Please call me Noora. We need to set an example of our people. I am just like you, Sarah, just a spirit in a play."

"Yes, Kum . ..ah, Noora."

Blue did a final inspection. Mahsa gave her the musical stick and copy of Dream and Echoes.

She looked around the small chamber with its ancient wood shelves, thangka and lamps. She thought of her childhood in a previous life. Back then she never liked this windowless room with its musty smells and gloomy memories of spending days cooped up here while the world was dying. Commotion from above. Noora glimpsed a bird that had slipped into the room. It fluttered on the rafters, chirping.

"He welcomes the day," she said fondly.

She stood and whispered what she did every morning. "I go in memory of those who came before me."

Blue, Sarah and Mahsa watched quietly as she paused by another red wood door opposite from where she came in. Taking a deep, calming breath Noora nodded. Blue slid the door back and Noora stepped into a white and purple room with many windows and waiting crowd illuminated by steely sunlight. The former Kumarisattva and her family joined the audience.

Noora sat on the raised divan and greeted them.

"Koo eei tah ku."

Glossary

After Purge. The yearly AP designation denotes separation from the old calendar counting system before the Purge.

Aiftalah: A Seer word for High spiritual Initiate.

Alimajh: (They are learned). A Kumargi selected from a group to lead the Conformational ceremony. Sometimes they read from Awakening and lead discussions after the ceremony.

Antyesti: Ceremonial Cremation honoring a Kumari Daughter.

Ascension: Where, according to legend, Taleju died in 137 AP.

Black Blood: The earth's life force. Black, viscous fluid the Purge rulers fought to control.

Black Monsoons: These originated in the Sub Continent and travelled to north, bringing ash, radiation and acid rains.

Cave of Marceilla: Earliest known post Purge drawings by survivors of the cataclysmic event. Attributed to 15 AP.

Celestial Dweller: a person who accesses the inner realms or guides students. It refers to spirit knowledge and experiences of the deep mysteries the Realms.

Central Region: The Daughter's House in Homs, Persian Emirates.

Ceremony of the Butterfly: Occurs the first week in the tenth month. Taleju discovered she is a Seer and Kumari Mother. Celebrated by Seers.

Companions: three childhood friends who accompanied Taleju's second journey. Sanjari, Parvati and Radha.

 Sanjari established the Kumari religion based the `Awakenings' Talejus and her spiritual insight. Additionally, Sanjari was a Taleju's childhood friend when she lived in the Durge House as the Living Goddess. Many customs and ritual based on this goddess practices were incorporated into Awakenings, forming the core of the new religion.

Parvati was a neighbor and, when their parents died when they were fourteen, they combined families into Taleju's home to share resources and protect each another. When she and Sanjari returned to Nepal Parvati was appointed as the first Kumari Daughter to assist her with her new religion.

Radha. One of the first Taleju's devotee after she left the Durga House. Radha shared much spiritual information and it was Radha's curiosity to compelled Taleju to leave Nepal and see the world. Radha never returned to Nepal and joined Taleju's trip to the Bay of Biscay.

The Confirmation pilgrimage: Every ten years devotee retrace Taleju's route mentioned in the Awakening from Neostella, Italia Commonwealth back to Kathmandu, Nepal Commonwealth. Every devotee is required to make the trip onetime in their life time. They gather from around the world to meet at Neostella, where the West Kumari resides and begin the journey. The West or Central Daughter alternates leading the group and is sponsored by cities they visit. The pilgrimage takes roughly eighteen months to complete and they see places mentioned in the Awakenings. It is very difficult and generally only 20 percent survive. If towns are beyond the Italia Commonwealth Kumari representative visit cites about a year before the trip in the Spring vernal Equinox. Officials are given a list of those given permission by the West and Central Daughters for those who wish to partake, prepare and travel to the meeting point. Children less than five and older than sixty are excluded.

Referring to The Awakening the travelers walk the same path and see the cities mentioned in her writing. It is a both journey into the past and present by reading Taleju's account while visiting these places in the present. This way it reinforces the Purge destruction and healing.

Daughter's Deputy: a proxy leader if the Daughter cannot fulfill her duty, such as severe illness or death. Generally elected from the Kumari Companions.

Dedicational Ceremony: A ritual of prayer honoring Taleju performed three times a day: sunrise, noon and sunset. It is done in groups if possible since it is a social occasion. Devotees face Dubai (Where the Purge supposedly began) and repeat three set of rituals and sayings. If a Satori is not availability someone is selected from the group to lead the ceremony (Alimajh).

Dharma: the eternal and reality's inherent nature underlying incarnation, manifestation, right behavior and social order.

Djinn: Spirits existing in the physical world. They live in remote places or abandoned buildings. They can sometimes appear in human form. They can be kind, mischievous, or indifferent, depending how the human interacts with them.

Eastern Region: The Sister's House in Kathmandu, Nepal.

Dream and Echoes: Taleju and Radha's book completed shortly before their deaths. The book was kept in safe keeping and passed through the centuries to trusted caretakers until reaching Noora.

It is an in depth study and guide to Consciousness, spiritual Realms, karma, incarnation and Esoteric energies of light and sound. Its knowledge shows how spirits can ravel beyond this life and dwell within the ever Moment. It is a guide to `how to' access the light and sound of Infinity to understanding reality.  It was not written for the general masses but only for Seers, who could comprehend this.    It was written in a `future language' later developed by Seers for those who, may some day, find and translate it.

The 8 pointed star of Life: This is Taleju's guide for becoming aware of ourselves as spirit and the conditions upon which incarnate.

Far Sight: Ability to leave the body and see beyond physical confines. It generally refers to see within our physical world. One of many skills of an evolved spirit.

Flag of the Kumari: Crescent sun in eclipse (legend said a solar eclipse occurred during the Purge) and an eight pointed star. The sun indicate a new era and the star the Eight Flames of Life. The yellow background means compassion and red for passion.

Flag of Noora: The crescent sun with the flower of Life. The sun represents a new era, the Flower of Life means spiritual wisdom. Has a wide band on the vertical border edge.   This indicates Human and Seers.   White background signifies spiritual enlightenment; purple art signify the narrow path because purple is made of red (hot color) and blue (cool color)   Too much of either color creates disharmonies.

Flower of Life: Spirit and energy DNA from which all life is created.

Initiate: Different levels of spiritual mastery within Seer community. Green, red, white, purple, blue, gold.

Karma: Spirit's inherent energies created through the act of manifestation which set up cause and effect. Spirit's current actions influence future incarnations.   Karma has thee binding principles: Karma, Causality and Rebirth.

Kathmandu, Nepal Commonwealth: Birthplace and location of the Kumari religion.   It is the seat for the Kumarisattva, the Kumari Eastern Region.

Koo eei tah ku: Noora's greeting based on Seer language and the Dreram and Echoes. `May your mirror be the Mirror of All Things'.

Kumari: Originally it was title of the child representative of the Living Goddess, Taleju, in outer form. A child was selected near age 6 and held this title until her first menstruation when she was replaced by another Kumari.

Later it evolved into a religion based on the writing of a former Kumari called Shakya Tian Nawari. At the core of its teaching is all spirits hold the key to their own enlightenment, destiny and can balance their karma wheel through right living, thought, action and balance with our surroundings. By practicing devotees are born into Enlightenment. They believe in a universal Consciousness of which all spirits are part of and the notion of a Supreme Being is foreign. There is no afterlife rewards or punishment but spirits are bond in the Glass Wheel—what they call karma. Their actions in this life dictate their fate in future lives. They see current Incarnation holding conditions for their unrealized lives. Therefore, they do not believe deliverance from karma, but each is responsible for their Incarnations. They are masters of their lives. Through understanding and balance within all existence leads spirit to enlightenment.

Kumari Companions: twelve Satori who assist the Kumari Daughter with responsibilities for the pilgrimage.

Kumari Daughter: Special representatives appointed by the Kumarisattva from within the Satori initiates. They are selected for their compassion, understanding of Taleju's teachers and living a life of an Enlightenment Being. They represent the Kumarisattva and her religion. There are two regions: West in Neostella, Italian Commonwealth and Central in Homs, Persian Emirates.

Kumari Ghar (palace): Residence of West, Central and Eastern Taleju's representatives. They include temple, Satori living quarters, their families, administrators, visitors, working shops and schools.

Kumargi: a follower of the Kumari religion.

Kumari Mother: Taleju Shakya Tian Nawari, the author of The Awakenings and Dreram and Echoes.

Kumarisattva: Leader of the Kumari religion and selected by the Satori Council. She a scholar and practitioner of the spiritual path set up by Taleju. She embodies the Sattva wisdom and life devotees aspire to. She is believed that is reincarnation of one of the Three Companions: Sanjari, Parvati or Radha.

Roughly her reign is 32 years and then replaced by another Daughter. The child is selected between 4-6 years and trained by the Satori Council and the Kumarisattva until she is ready to assume duties, roughly when she is mid teens. Afterwards the Sattva assume advisory role until she retires when the new leader reaches 21 years.

Lights of Awakening: marks the beginning of the New Year which occurs on the summer solstice. Legend says the Purge started then. Devotees celebrate for three days. It is a time of refection, mediation and eliminates the negatives and inviting the positive. Customs dictates those negativity impacting someone's life is forgiving and everyone starts new.

Madrasa: Libraries and educational centers dedicated to preserve Purge books and manuscripts.

Majlis: Rulers or leader hold daily meeting or `open court' open to the public. Visitors bring their complaints and petitions where judgment is rendered. It's an opportunity for rulers to judge the state of the subjects or problems needing attended to.

Mandira: A Taleju temple for place for prayer, worship, rituals and social gatherings. Each temple conforms to specific layout based on the Kumari's Mandala. There are four `corners' that open to the four directions. The main entrance faces west representing where Taleju vanished. Inner circles of air, fire and ethers, the niche of Dedicational facing Dubai, six pillars representing the primary windows to see beyond death, a central dome for Infinity, stained glass around the domes' base meaning the creative energies, an arched entrance duplicates the Third Eye, Flower of Life pattern on rugs or cast by ceiling illumination. In the corner facing Dubai is the niche of the Purge Mirror and Purge symbol, which worshippers' face when performing prayer rituals.

An enclosed courtyard facing Dubai representing rebirth, eight fruit trees for the Eight Spiritual Laws, washing basin to clean and `purify' before entrance and three steps into the temple resenting the Kumari Mother, Sister and Daughter.

Atop the dome is a crescent sun depicting a partial solar eclipse and eight pointed star. This means the Purge darkness is temperately and the sun is Taleju's light. The eight pointed star stands for Taleju's Eight Flames of Life. These temples are tended by at Satori (Pujari) and their helpers.

Mandala: A spiritual symbol representing the Universes used in mediation. The Kumari Mandala is creation, chaos and enlightenment. Shakya's Mandala came later and was introduced by Noora. It is Consciousness, Secondary Echo and Shadow Realm.

Minbar: a three step platform and covered with gold cloth from which the (pujari) address worshippers.

Mokti: a pilgrim who completed the Confirmation Pilgrimage starting from the Western Region and reaches Kathmandu, the eastern Region.

Mudra: hand gesture empowering participate in spiritual connection.

Normals: Humans. They are limited in their psychic skills.

RAD meter: Instrument measures radiation levels

RAD Sickness: Invisible sickness caused by high concentration of radiation.

Reincarnate Karma Decree: When Taleju reincarnates she will experience fixed conditions in her life.

Puja: A devotee performing the Confirmation pilgrimage. ` Those Who Seek Taleju's Divinity.'

Pujari: (Taleju's Voice) A Satori leading religious gatherings, teach, hold community services and spiritual guidance.

Purge. The worldwide catastrophic event which nearly destroyed all life and later accelerated global warming. According to tradition a solar eclipse occurred during the event. The Purge lasted two weeks and was followed by ten years of darkness. The human population was reduced to less than 10%. Many legends existed why it happened: greed, exploitation, and fear dominated the global consciousness.

Pustakalaya: Educational centers associated with Taleju's House, or temple. They can be secular or religious institutions.

Sacred Tirade: As per the Kumari Religion: reincarnation, karma, compassion. As per Dreram and Echoes: red, yellow, blue creative energies.

Satori: A religious scholar who works closely with the Kumari and Kumarisattva and has been initiated by completing the Conformation Pilgrimage.

Satori Council: Three specially selected Satori to conduct tests to locate the Kumarisattva's replacement and training her.

Surkh: a tribal representative who joins the pilgrimage when traveling through the Hindustan Corridor.

Supreme Satori: Highest rank within the Satori group. The Supreme represents the Kumari Daughter of her region. She is her proxy for visits and ceremonies and holds the same authority.

Seers: Humans more evolved using psychic skills with abilities to see into the invisible realms and connect with these energies. They are far more aware as spirits. They are the next evolutionary process for our species.

Shakya: the birth name of the Kumari Mother. Shakya Tian Nawari was responsible for authoring the spiritual text which the Kumari religion is based.

She who has Master All: Complete mastery and understanding of all six spiritual Realms. The highest Seer Initiate.

Spirit: Consciousness in its primordial, non-form state.

Solar Collector: brass, glass and mirrored instrument for collecting sun energy to use for cooking or lights. It uses clear crystals placed in the box.

Taleju: the inner spirit of the Living Goddess which cannot manifest except for through her representative. It is believed the Kumari is the `outward' incarnated Taleju.

Taleju Shakya Tian Nawari. She was called Shakya until returning to Nepal from her first trip. Many people claimed she was the living goddess having chosen a woman's body instead of child. `Taleju' is the goddess's title.

Shakya was born a century after the Purge (100 BP) in Baktupor, Nepal, of the Nawari tribe. From age 6-12 she lived in the Duga House as the Living Goddess (Taleju). When she was replaced by another Kumari people sensed her importance and they continued visiting her, seeking wisdom and guidance.

At 19 she left Nepal and travelled west, visiting places affected by the Purge. About age 27 she returned to her home and shared her experience with her people. Her stories and spiritual insight became legendary. They were so profound she developed a loyal following and because people were so hungry for reasons for the global destruction. Eventually she became a religious figure. People traveled to Nepal to sit at her feet.

Three years later she heeds her calling to spread her wisdom beyond Nepal and left with her three Companions: Sanjari, Radha and Parvati. During this second trip she wrote 'The Awakening.'

Sanjari and Parvati claimed Taleju supposedly died in Italy. She was 43. However, Shakya had a disagreement with two of her Companions as to what direction her teaching should go. Radha and thirty devotees remained with Shakya who continued to the Bay of Biscay. There, Shakya and Radha wrote `Dreram and Echoes'. Shakya died age 47 (147 AP). Radha died a few months later.

Thangka: Religious painting of Taleju, Kumari or other important religious themes either displayed in temples or carried by pilgrims. They are believed to carry great powers.

The Awakening. The journal of Taleju's travels though the Purge lands and spiritual guidance. The core of its teaching is spiritual awareness leads to enlightenment and understanding our role as spirit Beings. Material covered is precepts, behavior, karma, self responsibilities, caring for others, deeds, thoughts and awareness of inner realms we simultaneously exist in.

Tika: a blue tattoo dot on Third Eye in the center of the forehead. It is earned when a devotee obtains Mokti.

Time of Cloud and Darkness: The nuclear winter following the purge. It lasted 10 years.

Twin Sisters: Name for the Mental and Emotional Realms which are interdependent and coexists together. They cannot be influenced without the other.

West Region: The Daughter's House in Neostella, Italia Commonwealth.

Year: Year: 366 days, divided into 12 months. Month1-6: 31 days, 7-12: 30 days. Months and days are only numbered. New Year starts on summer solstice (the Purge date June 21 on Gregorian calendar).
Noora's journal record the year, month and day.

Important religious days:

1. New Years (called the Lantern of Lights). Last 3 days.

2. Butterfly. 3 days. Celebration performed by only by Seers. It occurs on the first week in the 10th month and celebrates when Taleju discovered she was a Seer.

3. Ceremony of Dead. Held on the 3rd month, day 21. Remembrance who died during the Purge.

4. The Mother's birthday. Month 3, day 18

5. Kumari's Light (when the religion was established) Month 2, day 21

6. The Ascension (Taleju's death established by the Kumari). Month 10, day 14

7. The Enlightenment (when Taleju left on her second journey) month 9, day 21

8. Kulwali : Taleju returns to Nepal, Month 4, day 1

OM symbol with Taleju's 8 point star

Creation's primary colors

Karma wheel

Purge Solar eclipse

Taleju's star

Kumari Mandala

Noora's Mandala

The Kumargi flag

Noora's flag

The Purge Mirror

The Purge

Creation

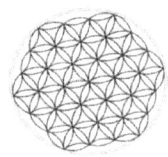

Flower of Life

Made in the USA
Middletown, DE
31 December 2019